Labors of an Epic Punk

A Novel

Mark and Sheri Dursin

Enjoy the adventure!

S6 £ Dn

TEEN
DUR
c. 1

Published by Twin Wizards Press
ISBN: 978-0-9988336-0-6
Library of Congress Control Number: 2017914376
Labors of an Epic Punk/Mark and Sheri Dursin
Digital distribution | *Twin Wizards Press,* 2017
Paperback | *Twin Wizards Press,* 2017

DEDICATION

For Charlie and Alex,
our heroes and our inspiration

Demetrius,

Even heroes need to survive adolescence.

That's my profound insight for today, and what better demigod to prove my point than Phaethon. Here's the story we learned in school: Phaethon, a teenager brimming with youthful exuberance, learns that his father is Helios, god of the sun, and travels the long journey to meet him. Awed by his father's power, he asks him for a favor. Helios, happy to meet his son at last, agrees without even knowing what the boy will ask and even swears by the River Styx, of all things, that he will grant him whatever he wants. Naturally, Phaethon wants to take the Sun-chariot out for a little spin (what teenager wouldn't, right?), and Helios, knowing it's a terrible idea, has no choice but to keep his promise and grant the favor. Lacking in experience, Phaethon quickly loses control of the powerful steeds and starts scorching up the earth—until Zeus zaps him with a thunderbolt, sending his flaming body into the Eridanus River. Shortest father-son reunion ever!

I know what you're going to say. That Phaeton deserved it. For acting too rashly. For presuming that a mortal could play with a god's toys. And there was a time I would have agreed with you. But now I see the story another way. How about Helios's role in the whole mess? After all, Phaethon went a long time without even knowing who his father was. Of course, he was going to be overly excited to meet him! Of course, he was going to be dazzled by his divine father's power! If Helios had made any attempt to know his son, he could have seen this whole thing coming.

Before you die of shock over my criticizing the gods, you know I'd never, ever, ever do that. It's just that for years, I believed what teachers told me about Phaethon—about his lack of humility, his youthful pride, all that. Then I met Mac, who helped me realize a few things. That maybe having a famous father doesn't mean squat if you've never actually met him. That maybe Phaethon had another side to him, other than his "reckless punk" reputation. That maybe this kid had something to prove—to his father, to the world, to himself.

Yeah, Mac helped me see that whole story differently, all right. Then again, he helped me see a lot of things differently.

—Homer
*(Excerpted from a letter to his
scroll-buddy, Demetrius)*

PART ONE

CHAPTER ONE
Attack of the Temesian Hoopoe Birds

No one on the field that morning had any idea that all Hades was about to break loose.

Well, *one* person did.

The stands were over-crammed with students, all chirping away about their summer travels, each one trying to out-fabulous the other. But Mac wasn't talking to any of them. (No surprise there.) Instead, he just stared at the empty stage in fist-clenching anticipation. For the entire morning, the entire summer, the entire two years he'd wasted at this gods-forsaken school, he'd been waiting for this moment. His moment of glory, of genius. The moment when he'd finally and irretrievably cross The Line—that hard-to-define boundary between tolerable and intolerable. Between a week of detention and *expulsion*. All he needed was for Head-master Gurgus to blow on that shell.

Come on, come on.

Just when he thought he couldn't wait any longer without throwing up, Mac heard the band play the opening notes to "Yielding Never," Pieridian Academy's absurdly overblown fight song. The Opening Ceremonies were officially underway.

From his seat high up in the stands, Mac watched intently as the members of the so-called Grand Procession marched onto Garthymedes Field: the entire faculty and staff, wearing shiny red gowns and smiles full of phony reverence; followed by the honored students, also in ritualistic red, condescendingly waving at the crowd; followed by a grotesque, nine-headed Hydra. (Not an actual hydra, of course, but the school's mascot—basically, a wooden frame draped with snot-green cloth and garishly bedecked with multicolored streamers and jewels.)

Lastly, waddling ten paces behind the Hydra, in all his roly-poly, four-hundred pound glory, was Headmaster Gurgus.

Make that four-hundred-and-four pounds; as always, the headmaster was accompanied by his freakishly tiny dog, Iota. But what she lacked in stature, she compensated with the frequency and volume of her *yipping*. Every waking moment (and most non-waking ones), from every corner of the campus, you could hear her yip, yip, yip. Mac was way up in the stands that day, and he could still hear her yipping, even with the school band playing.

Mac watched Gurgus and his pet lumber down the aisle, and for a moment, the absurdity of the visual—an elephant of a man being led around by a rat of a dog—made him smile. Then he got serious. With total focus, he studied Gurgus as the headmaster slowly, painstakingly ascended the stairs to the main stage; as he placed his beloved Iota onto a red pillow; as he straightened the laurel wreath encircling his round, bald head; and finally, as he produced, from the folds of his shimmering indigo robe, a massive kochlos shell.

It was time for the headmaster's solo.

With both hands, Gurgus hoisted the shell over his head. At that moment, everything stopped: the band members laid down their instruments; the crowd silenced itself; even Iota the dog somehow knew to stop yipping. Satisfied he had everyone's attention, Gurgus brought the shell to his bulbous lips, puffed his already bloated cheeks to extraordinary proportions…and paused. He really stretched out the moment, to underscore the majesty of it all. Then he blew into his instrument…and let fly a sound resembling that of all ten Titans breaking their immortal wind at the same time. And on that horrific, robustly atonal note, the ceremony would officially begin.

At least, that was the plan.

For the two Opening Ceremonies Mac had personally endured, Gurgus followed the same formula—same stupid Hydra mascot, same stupid little dog, same stupid and ridiculously pretentious pause, same stupid, flatulent kochlos solo. And right up to the moment when Gurgus brought the dreaded shell to his lips, this year's Opening Ceremony seemed no different. But Mac, and Mac alone, knew otherwise. For only he knew the preparations he had made over the month leading up to the big day…

Dawn is just breaking. A shadowy figure, feeling the early morning dew on his bare feet, makes his way to the very center of Garthymedes Field. He paces, trying to approximate where the stage will be set up for the Opening Ceremonies, before he finally settles on a spot. He takes one last look around, even though he knows he's alone; most students have gone home for the Intercession, and any who may have stayed are definitely still asleep.

He hears the squawk. He looks up and sees, high in the sky, three black forms cutting across the early morning clouds. Just as he had hoped.

From under his tunic, he takes out a kochlos, recently swiped from the band room. He blows into the shell several times, trying to mimic Gurgus's patented farting noise. He takes out a handful of seed and scatters it all over the field. He waits. And waits. Eventually, the three Temesian hoopoe birds swoop down.

He backs up nervously as the gangly birds start pecking around the grass. Up close, the birds are larger than he had expected—almost as big as his arm—and uglier, too: black, except for scattered patches of white and pink, with a crown of erect feathers on their heads. From a safe distance, he watches them eat the seed, squawk at each other, then clumsily fly away. All in all, a successful first morning.

Next morning brings the same routine: the lone figure emerges from the mist, walks to the same spot on the field, blows into the kochlos, scatters the seed. Birds swoop down. Eat. Squawk. Leave. Next morning, same. And the morning after that. And after that, for four weeks.

Finally, on the morning before the Opening Ceremonies, the mysterious figure doesn't have to scatter any seeds at all; as soon as he blows into the shell, the birds arrive—as many as twenty this time. As they swarm in circles above his head, the lone figure stands on the nearly assembled stage, leans on the podium, and smiles. This is going to work.

As he watched from way up in the stands, Mac almost felt a

flickering of pity for Gurgus. The poor fool—how could he have known? How could he have possibly predicted, when he brought the kochlos to his fleshy lips, the glorious chaos he was about to unleash?

Almost instantaneously, as soon as the horrible blast flew from the kochlos shell, a flock of Temesian hoopoe birds—twenty-five, at least—descended on the stage, seemingly from out of nowhere. They squawked and flapped their giant, gangly wings, searching for the food that wasn't there. From the stands, Mac could barely see Gurgus through the black swarm, but he could definitely hear him, shrieking like a dying Harpy as he flailed his fat arms all over the place. Through the squawking and the shrieking, Mac heard a familiar sound: Iota's yipping. Oh, that dog was yipping and yipping like she had never yipped before, only shutting up when one of the much-larger birds accidentally bumped her off her little red pillow and onto the stage floor.

Within moments, pandemonium engulfed Garthymedes Field, as anyone on or near the stage, convinced the world was coming to an end, started screaming and scurrying for the exits. The mass exodus resulted, naturally, in mass destruction; the grass got torn up; the abandoned instruments got trampled upon; even the grotesquely bejeweled Hydra mascot was ripped in two. (The six unlucky students operating the thing had all darted off in different directions, resulting in two half-Hydras, one with five necks, one with four.)

Meanwhile, the parents in the stands were also screaming and beating hasty retreats. Not the students, though; many of them stayed put, laughing and cheering uproariously and slapping high-fives.

Through it all, only one student remained seated and silent. Expressionless save for the wispiest grin, Mac looked around and marveled at the bedlam unfolding before him. He breathed it all in— the screeching, the stomping, the raucous laughing. A frenzied, jubilant noise that *he* had created. In that moment, Mac felt power. But he felt something else, too: a fleeting *connection* with all the other students, a sense of belonging that he had never felt before.

Then something happened, something Mac hadn't foreseen: the

general commotion actually *startled* the very birds that caused it. And apparently, Temesian hoopoes, when startled, instinctively release their waste. And twenty-five startled hoopoes can generate a *lot* of waste.

They crapped on Headmaster Gurgus. On the fleeing teachers and students. On the two half-Hydras. They crapped all over the stage, the banners, the abandoned instruments. They crapped over *everything and everyone* on or near the field.

Yes, even Iota the dog got covered in disgusting, milky, sticky Temesian hoopoe crap.

Half the students started hightailing it off the stands, while the rest stayed to revel in the madness. Some young man had the bright idea of ripping off one of the wooden railings—for no reason, just because some teens enjoy dismantling things. Soon, a bunch of others joined in; within minutes, the entire seating area was pulled to crap-coated pieces.

The student body considered it the most memorable Opening Ceremonies of all time. The administration, however, had a decidedly different opinion and immediately sprang into action. The next day, all students were corralled to an emergency assembly; there, Headmaster Gurgus, stern and stone-faced, began with a status report. Garthymedes Field, he informed them, was ruined, as were the stands. As were all the instruments (including his very own kochlos). As was the treasured Hydra costume—a gift from a former student named Polyphites, and one that could never be replaced. But the damage to property and material, he assured them, was nothing compared to the damage done to the reputation of the Finest! Academic Institution! in the World!

Eyes blazing now, his round face getting redder and redder the longer he spoke, Gurgus roared that he did not regard the bird swarm to be an omen from the gods, as some had theorized. No, he had an anonymous tip that a *student*—yes, one of Pieridian's own—had perpetrated this vicious attack. School security, he announced, had launched a full-scale investigation into this travesty. The culprit, naturally, would face the severest of consequences.

Mac figured as much; in fact, he had counted on it. He had finally done it. He had played pranks before: stashing a crate of rotting fish in the auditorium, giving the statue of Aphrodite a butt enhancement thanks to some strategically placed clay. But these acts of mischief only edged him up to The Line. This time, he didn't just cross The Line. He didn't even gleefully breeze right past The Line. He did to The Line what those hoopoe birds did to the field: he *took a massive dump* on The Line—on the entire school, really, and everything it stood for. Mac knew this was the end of the road for him. It had to be.

But for seven straight days, no one came to question him. He almost thought, with grave disappointment, he had gotten away with it. Then, on the eighth morning, a messenger showed up at his door—woke him out of a sound sleep, in fact—to escort him to the Main Disciplinary Chambers.

Soon, Mac found himself sitting in a cavernous room used for handing down sentences for all manner of crimes against the school. Before him, on a raised platform, sat nine members of the Disciplinary Committee—nine wrinkly, self-important men in their wrinkly, self-important cloaks—and in the middle stewed Headmaster Gurgus himself, leveling Mac with a furious glare. To the headmaster's right sulked a freshly cleaned but muted Iota; apparently, the bird attack had so traumatized her that she hadn't made a yip since.

If the large, echoing Main Disciplinary Chambers was meant to intimidate students, it didn't work on Mac, who remained—on the surface, at least—as unflappable as ever. At first, he said nothing, just studied the unsightly globules of spittle collecting in the corners of Gurgus's mouth and legitimately wondered if he should point them out. When the committee questioned him about the Opening Ceremonies debacle, Mac kept all his answers clipped and vague, making sure not to *deny* sabotaging the proceedings but not exactly owning up to it either. Why make it easy on them, after all? He expected his school advisor, Asirites, sitting to his left, to fill in the gaps with some impassioned plea for mercy, as he had always done for Mac in the past. Only this time Asirites, like Iota, was uncharacteristically silent.

Finally, after what seemed like hours of questions and evasions, the committee ordered Mac to go into the hall and await its decision. Giving them a mocking smile and an exaggerated wave, he strutted out of the room and into the hallway, plopping himself down on a wooden bench next to the Chamber's big, black marble door. And for a long time, he sat on that bench next to that door, in that long hallway filled with benches and doors.

He tried to listen to what they were saying, but he couldn't decipher much. Every once in a while, though, one of the administrators would bellow out something loud enough for him to hear, some insult naturally directed at him. Mac began rating these insults, in terms of both creativity and venom.

"Delinquent!" (Eh…not great…)

"Godless punk!" (Getting better…)

"Arrogant, unworthy barbarian!" (*Now* we're talking!)

Of all the terms emanating from the other side of the door, only one legitimately got him angry: "that boy" — as in "That boy is lost!" or "That boy has gone too far!" It seemed dismissive to him, belittling. First of all, he wasn't a boy; he was sixteen. Second of all, could a "boy" have had the resourcefulness to pull off a stunt like that? Don't think so. Third and fourth of all, he was still a prince, not to mention the son of their most famous graduates. So…sure, he'd ruined their Grand Procession and made a total mockery of the school's most time-honored ceremony…but that didn't mean they couldn't show him some respect.

"Mac?"

He looked up from his slumped position on the hard wooden bench to see a girl who seemingly materialized in front of him. He blinked a few times, struggling to place her, until it clicked: that girl, from last spring. What was her name again? And what could she possibly be doing here?

"I heard," the girl began, as she nervously pulled at the ends of her long, dark hair. "It's going around that they caught you and you might get expelled. Well…I just wanted to say…I know we don't know each other very well, and we haven't talked since…well, you know…" She trailed off and looked at the ground before continuing.

"Anyway, I just wanted you to know, in case I never see you again, that I…well, I'm never going to forget you."

Mac wished he could disappear. What could he say to that? That she absolutely should forget him? That he wasn't worth one moment of her time, let alone a life-long memory? Or he could be even more brutally honest. Tell her he was thoughtless and did stupid things sometimes. Being with her felt good at the time…but it didn't change anything. It never did.

"Uh…this isn't the best time to talk," Mac gestured at the big, black door behind him.

"I could wait with you?" she suggested, hope evident in her eyes.

"No—" he said immediately. He never really enjoyed any kind of company, but he especially didn't want any now. "Just leave me alone," he snapped. Then he looked down at the stone floor, unable to meet whatever he'd see in her gaze: disappointment, anger, disgust. He kept looking down, listening to her scurry away, and only when he heard the last click of footsteps did he remember. "Gia…right…" he mumbled, as he finally summoned the name.

He almost wished he didn't remember her name, because it reminded him that this nervous, awkward girl was an actual person, with actual feelings. On the other hand, he figured he was doing her a favor. Why should she waste her time on someone who was already gone?

After the girl left, it occurred to Mac that he had been out in that hallway much longer than necessary. What could they possibly be debating behind that door? *He trained a bunch of birds to defecate on them!* Shouldn't that be enough? In an attempt to calm his nerves, Mac began pacing down the long hallway. As he walked along, he glanced at the marble statues lining the walls—tributes to gods and former instructors. Eventually, he found himself among some newer, shinier monuments, marble busts depicting the heroes of the Trojan War. Menelaus. Achilles. Agamemnon. Odysseus.

Mac paused at the last one and looked into the bust's cold, marble eyes, eyes that seared into him with penetrating disappointment. More than ashamed, Mac lowered his head, to the plaque at the statue's base. Its inscription read, *"Son of Ithaca. Hero of Greece.*

Bravery, Courage, and Cunning. From a noble horse comes a mighty victory." Mac had heard descriptions like that before, for his entire life, in fact.

But who are you really? he wondered, risking one final glance into the marble eyes.

And then it hit him: they were right, those nine guys behind the big, black marble door. Everything they said about him that morning was absolutely correct: he really was a punkish, unworthy *boy*. He didn't deserve their respect, and he didn't belong at this school — not now, not ever. Maybe he didn't belong anywhere.

"Mac!"

He turned around to see a bushy-bearded man in a rumpled robe standing in the corridor: his advisor, Asirites. He was leaning heavily on his cane, beaten down by the Disciplinary Committee's outrage.

"Right here," Mac sighed, as he walked back down the hall. As was routine, he stood to the left of Asirites, offering his arm.

"Let's go," Asirites ordered, pointing with his cane. "My office."

At first, Mac led their way through the ornate halls in silence, each one — student and counselor — waiting for the other to speak first. "So," Mac finally began, "did you help them see the humor in the situation?"

"Not yet," Asirites deadpanned. "I think Tartarus will freeze over before that happens."

"You gotta admit — as far as pranks go, it was pretty resourceful," Mac quipped.

"Actually, I don't have to admit that. Conditioning a flock of birds to destroy Garthymedes Field and defecate all over the headmaster? I don't think I'd call that resourceful. Reckless, maybe. Pointless. An act of willful self-sabotage. But 'resourceful?' Not quite."

"Well, I didn't anticipate the crapping on him part," Mac shrugged. "That was a bonus."

"You don't get it. They've had enough. The pranks, the poor attendance, the lousy grades, the whole world-weary act you've been putting on for the past two years. Unfortunately, up until now, you've been smart enough, 'resourceful' enough, to know exactly how little you need to do in order to squeak by. But they've finally had enough."

Mac buried the attitude and put his head down. "So what did he say?"

"Gurgus? He said a lot of things, most of which I don't feel comfortable repeating in front of a child," said Asirites, keeping his pale blue eyes locked on the nothingness before him. "Bottom line: he said you're not worthy to be a Pieridian student. He said you're nothing like your father." At the mere mention of his father Mac winced, as if punched in the gut. Then Asirites stopped, forcing Mac to stop as well, before adding, "He said you have to go, Mac."

They had reached a small bridge overlooking the quad. Not wanting to look at Asirites (who had an uncanny ability, though blind, to peer into his soul), Mac stepped to the railing and watched the students milling about down below, on their way to class or their residence halls or wherever. As always, they traveled in groups—two, three, four. Rarely did a kid walk alone. "Well," he sighed, gazing over the edge. "I guess that's that, then."

Suddenly, Asirites appeared at his side. "No, that's not *that*," he said, accenting the second "that" by thumping Mac, with remarkable precision, in the head with his cane.

"Ow..." Mac whined, as Asirites seized his arm once more and started walking.

"I didn't spend the last two hours getting screamed at so you can throw everything away with a 'That's that,'" Asirites continued. "I made a bargain with the Disciplinary Committee."

"Oh, not this again," Mac balked. "What, I have to maintain certain grades and—?"

"It has nothing to do with grades. Everyone knows you're a genius. It's your character that stinks. So this is what we've decided: you have until the next Intercession—three months—to prove that you deserve to be here, that you're *worthy* to be here."

"And exactly how am I supposed to do that?"

"You have to prove that you are your father's son."

"My...father's son?" Mac floundered. "Father's son? What does that even—?"

"Do something your father would do. Something to honor his

legacy. If you can't do that at the end of three months, you'll be expelled."

"Well, that's easy: I don't need three months," Mac said. "I'll just leave now."

"Don't you know what you're saying? When you were devising your brilliant scheme to ruin the Opening Ceremonies, did you even once think about the consequences? You are the prince of a kingdom without a king. And someday, those people—your people—are going to look to you to lead them. Do you think they're going to accept as their king a kid *who was kicked out of high school*?"

"You honestly think I care what any of them think of me?"

"Maybe you don't, but they'll be depending on you," Asirites said with a growing sense of urgency. "The only thing worse than a lost king is a weak king. Your enemies will be watching and waiting. If they don't respect you, then Ithaca will always be vulnerable. You can't afford to fail." Asirites pointed his cane at Mac. "You have three months. Three months to prove you are your father's son. That's the deal. No more chances."

"What makes you think I want any more chances? What makes you think I want *this* chance?" Mac said, more defiantly.

"Don't do this," Asirites said. "I fought for you. Not just in there. Not just this week. For two years, I've been fighting for you."

"Well, who asked you to?"

"Oh, I forgot. You're Telemachus. Prince of Ithaca. Son of the great King Odysseus. And the most aggressively lonely person I've ever met. You don't bother anyone, no one bothers you. I've watched you systematically shut yourself away from anyone who might've become a friend, an ally—insisting instead on doing everything on your own, without help from anyone. Somehow, you think that makes you brave, but even I can see how scared you are."

At this point, they were standing outside the closed door to Asirites's office. "You think this prank shows how little you care," Asirites said. "But I know better. I know you're desperate to care about *something*."

Mac didn't respond, just looked down at his own sandals. When he finally looked up, he noticed the gray hairs that had sprouted in

Asirites's beard and wondered how many he had put there. "You're wrong," Mac finally answered. "I'm sorry, but you're wrong. I don't care. And you shouldn't either." His voice fell to a whisper. "Just let me go, will you?"

"Go?" Asirites asked. "And just where do you plan on going, exactly?"

Mac fell silent. Truth is, home was the last place he wanted to go. "I don't know," Mac finally said. "Anywhere but here. A place where no one knows me…or the great King Odysseus."

Again, Asirites stared at him — *through* him — before finally giving in. "OK. If that's what you want, then…OK. Just one thing: who's going to break the news — me or you?"

"Break the news to who?"

Asirites nudged open the door with his cane. Across the pristine expanse of the office, Mac saw a woman, gazing out the window, her back to the door. He couldn't see her face, but he immediately recognized her slender frame and her long, raven-black hair tied back in a series of brass coils.

Suddenly, it dawned on Mac why it took eight days for the Disciplinary Committee to call him in. Obviously, they didn't need that long to identify him as the culprit; it just took a little bit of time to send word to Ithaca.

Immobile, Mac fixed his eyes on the woman across the way. "That's so…cheap," Mac muttered to Asirites, who smiled slyly.

Over a year had passed since Mac had last seen his mother, and he could tell, from her slumping shoulders, things had changed. She used to be such a defiant queen — weakened by circumstances, but strong in will. Now, she looked like a sad, defeated, disappointed *mother*. His chest tightened as he realized, for the millionth time in his young life, that *he* was the one to make her feel that way.

"Go on in," Asirites said. "She's been waiting for you."

CHAPTER TWO

Penelope and the Pomegranates

For several uncomfortably long minutes, neither one spoke.

Instead, mother and son remained at opposite ends of Asirites's spacious office—Penelope, standing at the window, gazing blankly at the courtyard below; Mac, sitting in a chair, looking at all the elaborate tapestries on the wall, not out of genuine interest, but to avoid eye contact with the distant figure across from him. Between them was Asirites's well-organized desk—and all the history, all the emotion, all the things unsaid that fed the uncomfortable silence.

Penelope, mercifully, spoke first. "So, I have to know..." she began, still keeping her back to her son, who braced himself for what was sure to come.

"Why does a blind man need such an impeccably decorated office?" She finally turned around, revealing the slightest smile.

If she intended for her comment to diffuse the tension just a little, it worked. "I...I don't know," Mac mumbled, returning her smile. "I've wondered that, too."

Penelope inched forward, still keeping the desk between them. "Your hair's gotten long..."

"Yeah?" Mac responded, shuffling in his seat, running his hand through the thick brown hair, hanging raggedly just above his shoulders. "I guess so. I haven't cut it in a few months."

Penelope smiled, a sadder smile this time, and said quietly, "I haven't seen you in such a long time."

"I said I'd come home over break," he countered. "You told me not to."

Mac's defensiveness sent Penelope's eyes back to the window. "The palace is no place for a child," she said absently.

No kidding, Mac thought. Silence invaded the office again, until

Mac finally asked, "Well, has anything changed?"

"No, not really…" Penelope sighed. "The suitors are still there, still acting like they own the place. But I did come up with a new idea," she brightened, glancing over to her son. "I told them I was going to weave a shroud for Grandpa. 'When I'm done,' I said, 'I'll decide which one of you I'll marry.' So every day, I'm at the loom, weaving away. And every night, I secretly undo it all. They have no clue."

Mac grinned. At that moment, he felt close to his mom again, bonded by their mutual love of pranking. "They're so stupid…" he marveled.

"Speaking of stupid…" Penelope segued indelicately. "You really did it this time, Mac."

"Oh, Mom, do we have to—?"

"Just tell me," she pressed, more forcefully now. "Did they kick you out?"

It occurred to Mac he could have kept Asirites's bargain a secret. He could have told her they'd expelled him, that he'd finally spent all their good will. Quite possibly, she never would have found out the truth. But he looked at her—this exhausted, faraway woman on the other side of the room—and he couldn't do it. He couldn't lie, but mostly, he couldn't disappoint her again.

"No, they didn't," he admitted. "They're giving me one last chance, which is—what?—my thirty-fifth last chance? It's a joke, Mom. Anybody else would have been given the boot a long time ago. They're only keeping me here because of Dad."

"You don't know that. Maybe they see something in you that—"

"They don't 'see' anything in me, Mom. They don't want me here. No one does. I don't *matter* here, Mom. I could leave today, and no one would even notice."

"Well, whose fault is that?"

He ignored her question and went on the offensive, hoping if he could convince her to let him leave or, if she finally told him he *had* to leave, then he wouldn't technically be disappointing her. "Let me come home, Mom. At home, I can help you. Protect you." He knew that last part was a lie, of course; he *wouldn't* go home. Not while *they* were still there. If he got kicked out of school, he would go as far away from Ithaca as he could get. It didn't make a difference if he went home, anyway. He knew he could never protect his mother. Not after what happened.

He had already failed that test. She just didn't know it.

"I don't need your help, thank you, and I don't need your 'protection,'" Penelope said, with a firmness that surprised Mac. "I know how all this must look to you—that I live in chaos, that I've forfeited control of my life to a gang of vultures. Maybe your father would be horrified if he could see what was happening to his kingdom. Don't you think I'm horrified too? Believe me, if I didn't think it would invite the wrath of Zeus himself, I would have sent the suitors away a long time ago. I didn't exactly have a choice, did I? Except to get you out of that palace and send you here," she said gesturing to the air around her. "Before he left for the war, your father and I promised each other that we would send you to Pieridian Academy. To give you your best chance in life. That's a choice I'm proud of. Your father would be proud too."

"Well, how will he ever know?" Mac interjected. "It's not like he's ever coming home."

"Your father is *not* dead," Penelope shot back sternly.

"I didn't say he was dead," Mac responded. "I just said he wasn't ever coming home."

As soon as he said it, he knew he shouldn't have. Everyone—Mac, his mom, everyone—entertained the possibility that Odysseus had never returned to Ithaca because he found some other woman, built some other life. But no one ever voiced it, and the brute force of the comment yanked the freezing silence back into the room.

Penelope's quivering lip told her son that she wanted to lash out at him but was holding back. Finally, she answered, with pathetic resignation, "You know what? You're right. You have to choose your own fate. Don't stay here because of your father. And don't stay here because of me. But…don't leave because of us either."

Another thick pause. Finally, Penelope announced, "I have to get back. Who knows what they've been doing while I've been gone? Oh, here," she said, picking up a sack next to Asirites's desk and walking toward her son. "I brought you some of these."

Mac stayed in his chair while Penelope placed the sack on his lap. As she did, she leaned in and gave him the quickest kiss on his cheek. "Share these with your friends…if you…" A crack in her voice swallowed up the end of her sentence. As she hurried out of the room, Mac knew she was trying—and failing—to hold back tears.

Mac didn't follow her out. Slowly, he opened up the sack, even though he already knew what was inside: pomegranates, at least a dozen of them. He took one out, held it in his hand, and got lost in a tempest of memory.

It was the last time he was in Ithaca, the break between his first and second year at Pieridian. Mac had just turned fifteen, and like many fifteen-year-old boys he kept to himself. But unlike many fifteen-year-old boys, he found himself evading a houseful of his mom's suitors.

Dealing with one unwanted guest in the house for just a day or two can be a challenge. Dealing more than a hundred, for over a decade? That's a nightmare, especially since these slobs did more than just get in the way; they spent all their time eating, drinking, and generally making a mess of things. In their minds, they were simply biding their time; seeing the absence of King Odysseus as an invitation, they all asked Penelope for her hand in marriage. When Penelope graciously declined, they decided—every single one—to stick around until she changed her mind, knowing she couldn't turn them away. Penelope wasn't budging…but neither were the suitors.

In addition to running roughshod all over the palace, the suitors had another favorite sport: making Mac's life miserable. When he was younger, the suitors would amuse themselves by chasing Mac around the palace or coming up with the most creative insults to hurl at him. Sometimes, they even got physical, but not in ways that could be seen by anyone else. Like Mac himself, the suitors were experts at going right up to The Line.

Over the years, Mac learned how to keep his distance from the suitors, but it was tough to ignore them completely. On this particular night, the last time he was home on break, he was sneaking a crate of pomegranates up to his bedroom. (The suitors would eat anything in sight, so Mac had taken to hoarding food.) As he walked along the open corridor, he heard some ruckus in the courtyard below. He looked down and saw four of his mother's suitors, sitting around a fire, flirting with a group of noble ladies who hung on their every word. They were all drinking; more accurately, they were drunk, joking and hollering and having a grand old time, as usual. After all, why let the simple fact that they were all competing for his mother's hand in marriage stop them from enjoying each other's company?

Mac had almost reached the end of the corridor when the booming voice of Antinoös stopped him in his tracks. Out of all the suitors, Mac detested this one most of all. A sober Antinoös was merely loud and crude and impossible; a drunken Antinoös was dangerous — and he was drunk a lot. A drunken Antinoös tended to break things — furniture, rules of decorum, the jaws of his fellow suitors. (In the morning, though, all would be forgiven in the suitor camp. Apparently, there's honor among monsters.)

As he peered down to the courtyard below, Mac saw Antinoös waving a torch and yelling to his drinking buddies, "I have an announcement! I have an announcement! Just a little while ago, the Queen made her decision. And to no one's surprise, she has chosen me. Because she knew, because she's always *known, that I am the only one who can save this joke of a kingdom!"*

As his cohorts laughed, this man Antinoös stood up on a chair and raised his goblet.

"She told me last night: 'You're the only one who can be king. The only one who can satisfy *me!'" (As he said this, he thrust his hips forward and took a giant swig from his goblet.) "'And the only one who can turn that lazy, pathetic, punk-ass son of mine into something resembling a man!'" His cronies roared.*

Above them all, Mac was standing in the shadows, having to listen to all this. Instinctively, he took one of the pomegranates from his crate and hurled it down at the posturing suitor. He missed, but he hit one of Antinoös's cohorts in the forehead — a direct hit which unleashed a fury of objections: "Something hit me!" "What is this?" "Who did this?"

Mac didn't say anything. Instead, he crouched behind one of the tapestries draped over the balustrade. Shaking and ashamed, Mac listened as the voice of Antinoös filled the darkness: "You throw fruit? Is that what you do? Show your face, you coward!"

Mac was disgusted — at Antinoös, but mostly at himself, because he knew Antinoös was right. He was a coward — hiding behind a tapestry, saying nothing, doing nothing. He grabbed another pomegranate and, darting out from behind the tapestries, fired it at the suitors below. Then he threw another. And another. And another.

The suitors down below were covering their heads and shouting at their mystery attacker, but Mac wouldn't relent. Like a boy possessed, he kept pelting them with fruit, letting years of pent-up rage and shame crash out of him.

Finally, he was doing something. Something he should have done years ago.

Just as he leaned back to hurl another, a harsh whisper stopped him: "Telemachus!" He turned around; from the shadows emerged his mother.

As the suitors down below continued their bellowing, mother and son looked at each other in silence. All the righteous indignation from a moment before drained out of Mac's face; now he just felt foolish. What was he really doing – hiding in the dark like a little boy, attacking grown men with fruit? Hanging his head, Mac dropped the last pomegranate, which landed on the stone floor and rolled toward his mother's feet.

Without a word, Penelope picked it up.

Mac watched as his mother weighed the red fruit in her hand. She looked at it intently; it seemed to Mac she was contemplating throwing it. For a frozen moment, he actually thought she might do it. A feeling like hope flared inside him. Maybe she really would understand. Maybe she might forgive him – for this, for before, for everything.

Then the moment passed, as suddenly as it arose. Penelope let the pomegranate fall to the floor. "Go to your room," she said simply. Mac sighed deeply as he trudged away, leaving his near-empty crate of fruit behind.

"Let me guess: pomegranates. Right?"

Mac hadn't even noticed Asirites had entered his office and was sitting in the chair next to him. Returning to reality, Mac looked down at the crate, full of fruit and memories, and mumbled, "How'd you know?"

"I know things," Asirites said. "The loss of sight brings an increased awareness of things other people miss: the aroma, the slightest squish of the fruit as you shift it around in your hand. Plus…your mom just told me she gave you some. Care to split one?"

"Sure," Mac replied mindlessly, as he walked over to Asirites's desk. He placed a pomegranate onto the desk and took a small blade from his belt.

"So...just pomegranates?" Asirites asked. "Nothing else in there?"

"Yeah, well...they were always my favorite, as a kid," Mac replied, as he cut the fruit and then split it in two with his hands. "Whenever I was hurt or bummed out about something, my mom would always give me pomegranate seeds."

Asirites leveled his unseeing gaze at Mac. "Were you hurt often?" he asked quietly.

Mac slowly put the blade back in his belt. He knew what was behind those words; in the past, Mac had dropped hints about his life with the suitors, and Asirites wanted him to reveal more. As usual, Mac side-stepped the issue. Dangerous territory.

"Whatever. I was a kid. Kids get hurt," Mac shrugged, as he walked around the desk, took Asirites's hand, and put a pomegranate half in his open palm. Then he sat down in the chair next to Asirites and kept talking. "Anyway, I got to love pomegranates. Even my favorite bedtime story, the one about Hades and Demeter, involved pomegranates."

"Hades and Demeter?" Asirites asked, arching his left eyebrow.

"Yeah, you know the one: Hades kidnaps her daughter, Persephone, so Demeter goes to the Underworld to get her back. But Persephone has already eaten six pomegranate seeds...so she has to spend six months in Hades and six months on earth."

"I know the story," Asirites smiled, placing a seed in his mouth. "It just seems like a curious story to tell a kid before he goes to bed."

"You never heard my mom tell it," Mac said, becoming more animated. "She *sold* it. She'd sit on the edge of my bed and change her voice for all the characters. Build to that moment when Persephone is going to eat the seeds. And I'd be there shouting, "No! No! Don't do it!' And every time—I remember this, so clearly—she'd lean over, and kind of playfully pin my arms to the bed, and say, 'She ate the seeds! She's *locked in!*'"

Mac laughed a little, despite himself, then slunk back into the chair, staring at the pomegranate in his hand.

"Locked in, huh?" a smiling Asirites repeated. "I guess that *is* a good story."

"Yeah, until I realized how unfair it all is," Mac said, his small smile slipping away. "Persephone didn't know the rules, that you couldn't eat from a tree in Hades. Just so…wrong."

Asirites nodded knowingly, as if appreciating the grave truth of the story for the first time. "True," he said finally. "On the other hand, at least she gets to spend six months on earth, with her mother. That's better than no months, right?"

"Yeah, that's what my mom always said," Mac sighed, staring at the walls again.

For a long moment, both silently popped seeds into their mouths. "Your mother's in an impossible situation, Mac," Asirites finally said, with obvious care in his voice. "There's a code. Rules about how to treat guests. If she breaks those rules, she risks everything. Losing the respect of the city-states. Alienating Ithaca's allies. Even tempting divine punishment. The suitors know this. They have her backed into a corner."

"Yeah, I get it," Mac interrupted.

"You know, everything she's ever done, she's done for you."

"I *get* it," he repeated forcefully. Deep down, though, he wondered if he really did "get" it, if he understood his mother at all. "So what am I supposed to do?"

"What do you mean?"

"To stay here. What do I have to do?"

"What I said before: prove you are your father's son."

Mac rolled his eyes. "That's what they came up with?"

"Not just 'them.' I had a little something to do with it as well."

"Well, do you mind telling me what that means, then?" Mac huffed as he stood up and moved to the open window.

"I told you: do something to honor your father's legacy."

"Which is…what? Build a giant wooden goat in the quad? My father's been gone for sixteen years. I've never even talked to him. How do I know what it means to be his son?"

"Telemachus," Asirites began, as Mac cringed. Asirites only called him by his full name when he was scolding him or readying for a heart-to-heart talk, and he already did the scolding. "You may not know your father, but I do. I first met him when he was your age — younger, even. And I can tell you: you're close, Mac. Closer than you think. The greatness I saw in your father, way back then, I see in you now."

As Mac looked out the window, he could see the small figure of his mother darting across the quad, heading off campus for the ship that would take her back to the chaos of Ithaca. "I can't give you the answer you want," Asirites continued from his chair across the room. "I can't tell you what it means to be your father's son. You need to figure it out for yourself. And you *can*. You can do this, Mac. The only question is: do you want to?"

"Well, do I even have a choice?"

Asirites shrugged. "Not much, no."

As he watched his mother finally disappear into the glare of the late-morning sun, Mac popped a final pomegranate seed into his mouth. There was a chance — every chance in the world — that he would fail his mother, just like he did so many times before. But for the first time in a long time, he wanted to try. He *had* to try. He was locked in.

CHAPTER THREE
Introduction to Orations

A few days after he saw his mom, Mac found himself wearing a goofy battle helmet, leaning against a giant magpie statue—and wondering why he ever decided to stay at this stupid school.

He was in class—a required course called "Introductions to Orations." Now, normally, he would hate a class like that on principle alone; after all, Mac had nothing to say and no desire to hear what anyone else had to say, so what use would he have for orations? But the teacher—this scatter-brained, crazy-haired guy named Grimbar—had a driving passion for the subject matter, and he always tried to do something a little different in class. This particular week, he had been taking the class outside, to a small courtyard on the edge of campus. Each student would then have to deliver an original inspirational speech they had prepared—the kind of impassioned address a general might make when "rallying the troops," as Grimbar said. So, to help establish the mood, Grimbar handed out some costume battle gear—helmets, cloth breastplates, shields, and assorted junk lifted from the Drama Club's storage room.

Of course, Mac hated the helmet. In fact, he only agreed to wear it once he realized it shadowed his face, which meant he could shut his eyes without being detected. But he respected the fact that Grimbar was at least *trying* to make the class sort of interesting, especially since most teachers seem to go out of their way to make their classes completely *un*interesting. But no fancy costume or change in venue could make up for the simple fact that the speeches just *sucked*. Then again, Grimbar let the students choose their own topics, so how could they *not* suck?

Already that week, the class had to suffer through the original works of a parade of rhetorical geniuses, like the girl who rewrote the lyrics to the school fight song ("We'll grind our rivals into dust/ They'll wish they were in Tartarus"), or the boy who monotonously rattled off an interminably long list of the ships who went off to fight in the Trojan War, or the kid who proposed offering teachers as human sacrifices as a way to cut down on homework. (Mac suspected that last one was a lame attempt at satire.) Just painful stuff.

Mac opened his eyes to see a girl delivering her speech to the class, and he realized that he actually knew her. Or knew her name, at least—Calliope—and he only knew that because she was the twin sister of his latest roommate, Theo. Even though she and Mac had never exchanged more than a few pleasantries, Mac got the sense she was nice enough. A little weird, maybe—a "Drama Club freak," according to her brother—but overall nice. That was pretty much all he knew about her, but that was still a lot more than he knew about most other girls at school.

Mac didn't exactly hang out with any girls, but he did know a few over the past two years. Girls that were determined to flirt their way into his life, hoping for any scrap of attention he might give them. Maybe it was being the son of a great war-hero, or it could be his "brooding loner" persona. He didn't know and rarely questioned it, sometimes giving them what they wanted for the moment. But for Mac, it never lasted beyond that moment. He wasn't looking for a girlfriend. His policy of isolation didn't allow for one.

As Calliope delivered her speech, Mac was surprised to find himself actually *listening* to her. No, not because she was Aphrodite or anything (even though she was definitely not bad to look at with her gentle smile, long legs, and silvery blonde hair, which fell sleek and shiny all the way down her back). And not because she was saying anything particularly interesting to him: instead of delivering a speech, she was reciting an original poem, about Eros and Psyche. No, he was listening to her because of her *voice*. She had one of those voices that could command attention, not because she talked loudly—just the opposite, in fact. Her voice had a soft, musical quality that drew him in and momentarily distracted him from his current mess.

Mac didn't even care that her poem was about something as corny as love and the ordeals that Psyche had to go through to prove her devotion to Eros. Nor was he particularly bothered by the fact that she sanitized the actual story by removing all the fun, dirty parts (like how Eros would visit Psyche under the cover of darkness and sleep with her, without ever revealing his identity). He was just entranced by her voice. Clearly, the rest of the class was, too, as all side conversations died away.

Finally, with her hands folded in front of her stomach, Calliope recited the final stanza:

The desperate quest, the impossible test,
The journey to the very ends of the earth
Psyche endured all for her Eros.
Just what is your love worth?

Then: applause. And not just polite, required clapping, but genuine applause. Calliope responded with a shy smile and then calmly sat back down on the grass. Mac wondered how this girl could possibly be related to his roommate Theo. They seemed to have nothing in common: Calliope was the picture of poise and serenity; Theo was a slovenly, boisterous good ol' boy, who said "dude" a lot, who laughed at his own deliberately corny jokes and somehow got everyone else to laugh too. Granted, Mac didn't know Theo that well (in fact, he hadn't known him at all before the administration threw them together as roommates), but it seemed to Mac that Theo was too goofy, too *shallow* to pull off a performance like the one his sister had just given.

"Very good, Calliope," Grimbar said, when the applause died down. "I think we have time for one more. Who's next?"

Mac felt sorry for the poor fool who had to follow Calliope's act. He felt even sorrier when he realized who it was.

Mac never remembered his name. He only knew him as the short kid with the bad foot and the big mouth who had the distinction of being, almost without peer, the least "cool" kid in school. Not because of his height, exactly (he barely reached Mac's shoulders), or any other aspect of his physical appearance—his floppy black hair, say, or his ill-fitting school-issued tunic. And not even because of his pronounced limp, caused by a twisted, misshapen left foot. Those things didn't help, certainly, but he could have been better looking than Adonis himself, and none of that would have mattered. He was just *different*.

And today, the kid was definitely different. While everyone else had on these goofy battle accessories, this guy was decked out in an obviously homemade furry cape with a hood, a circular mane-kind-of-thing tied around his chin.

"What are you supposed to be?" Mac heard someone ask, as the pitiable sap limped to the front of the group, wearing his weird get-up and clutching a large sack and a bunch of scrolls.

"For your information," the kid said, disdainfully, "this is an original Nemean lion costume." Met with silence, he clarified. "Uh, Nemean lion? Heracles had to kill it as one of his labors? You people honestly don't know the Nemean lion?"

"Why do you have it?" another person asked.

"My mom made this for me when I was in the fifth grade."

"You can fit into something from the fifth grade?" an anonymous voice asked.

The kid didn't respond. Instead, he straightened his mane, then reached into his sack and pulled out a small figurine, which he held out to the class. "Perseus," he announced sternly. "Slayer of Medusa. Tamer of Pegasus. Founder of Mycenae." He set the figurine down on a stone bench and took out another: "Agamemnon. Leader of men. Great commander who took to the battlefield of Troy to fight alongside his warriors." And another figurine: "Heracles. Killer of lions and Hydras and boars."

Dramatic pause. "These men are *heroes*. Men of principle, purpose, conviction. Men of valor, who understood courage, who went beyond what was expected, who left behind unforgettable legacies."

He scowled at the students sitting in the grass. "You people are *nothing* like these men. With your money and your personal trainers and summer palaces in Crete, can't conceive of true heroism. Do you even remember the Trojan War? Of course not. It ended, after all, a whole *six* years ago. You don't understand sacrifice, honor, nobility. But if you listen, and let my words seep into your teeny-tiny minds, you may be able to change." He took out one of his scrolls. "What I have here is a list of thirteen things you all need to do in order to better yourselves."

At that, Grimbar spoke up. "You know what? Looks like we didn't have as much time as I thought. Maybe we can pick this up again tomorrow?"

Obviously, Grimbar was trying to save the kid from getting pummeled by his classmates. But the fact is, his intended audience—the jocks and snobs—didn't even notice him. He was so beneath them, they hadn't paid a drop of attention to what he was saying. One member of the class, however, did hear what he had to say, loud and clear.

While listening to this kid's venomous attack, Mac remembered what made him so different: he was a hero-nerd. Everything that came out of his mouth, in every class they ever had together, involved heroes, monsters, wars, missions. He wasn't just a fan; he had an obsession, an obsession that made him such a social outcast, even the other hero-nerds at the school kept their distance. But on this particular day, this bizarre fetish of his, which drove everyone away, drew Mac over to him.

As the other students shuffled down the hill, Mac sidled hesitantly up to the boy, who was busily putting away his figurines. "Hey," Mac began, as he tossed his helmet in a pile with the other battle gear. "Hooper…right?"

"*Homer*," the boy grunted in reply, not even looking up.

"Homer, yes…" Mac half-smiled pathetically. "I guess we've never been introduced."

"Guess not," Homer muttered as he scooped up his scrolls and began hobbling away.

"Hey, hold up," Mac called out, following down the hill. "I was hoping I could talk to you about something."

"You never talked to me before."

"Well, don't take it personally. I never talk to anyone."

"Of course not. Because you're Telemachus, Prince of Ithaca," he said, not looking over at him but keeping his eyes straight ahead as he limped onto a stone pathway. "Your father is Odysseus, whom you've never met but whose oppressively famous shadow hangs over everything you do. Your mom is Penelope, the beautiful but beleaguered queen besieged by suitors who clearly have trouble picking up on subtle social cues. You deal with all this by aspiring to become the biggest, most reclusive slacker this side of Parnassus — figuring, I suppose, no one will notice what a sad, embittered disappointment you've become if they don't actually *notice* you. Oh, and you're right: we *haven't* been introduced."

Mac paused, more than a little freaked at the biographical sketch this complete stranger just provided. "OK, that's creepy," he said. "You know more about me than *I* know about me."

"You don't say," Homer sneered. "Because you always struck me as a guy who's really into self-reflection, who spends a lot of time pondering his wasted potential, his tarnished legacy. Yeah, you're all about that — that is, when you're not sulking, brooding, scheming about the best ways to rain shame and embarrassment onto the school."

Homer glanced over at a bewildered Mac as he breathlessly continued. "And I can tell by the look in your eyes right now that you're thinking, 'What's up with this guy? What's it to him?' Well, I'll tell you what's it to me. First of all, I was one of the six kids in the Hydra mascot the day of Opening Ceremonies. In fact, I was the butt of the Hydra. And that's not waxing poetic or anything: I was actually the one responsible for controlling the tail of the Hydra. And when those hoopoe birds swarmed around, and everyone in the Hydra costume ran in separate directions, I was left in the middle of that field, wide open to attack. And I got coated with hoopoe bird crap, which — I can assure you — is not particularly pleasant.

"But secondly, and much more importantly," he continued, "Odysseus is my *idol*. I would do anything to have him as a father. And it kills me to see you take his good name and drag it through the dirt like Hector around the city of Troy!" Homer stopped and let out an exaggerated "phew," as he finally looked at Mac square in the face. "Man, that felt good," he exclaimed, before turning on his good heel and limping away through the crowded courtyard.

Once again, Mac stood there stunned, more confused than hurt by the verbal thrashing he had just received. When he realized he had taken all this abuse without even getting the information he needed, he hurried after him. Thanks to the kid's limp, Mac caught up to him instantly.

"You know," Mac said, "just seeing you in class, I always thought you were a little weird, but I have to say, you're at least ten times weirder face-to-face."

"Then stop following me."

"I need your help with something."

"You? Telemachus? The Great Lone Wolf? You'll lower yourself to—?"

"Oh, shut up, will you? For the love of Zeus, will you just shut up for one second? Yes, I need help. I'm in a jam, OK? A huge jam. They're going to kick me out, and for real this time, if I don't big-time shape up. All they've said is that I have to prove that I'm my 'father's son,' but I have no idea what that means, and no one wants to tell me. Then I see you, babbling on about heroes and wars and all your other crap, and I think, 'Hey, maybe this kid can help.' So, yes, I'm asking you, as a *favor*, can you give me the slightest clue what I'm supposed to do?"

"Oh, as a favor, I see. And I'd do this 'favor' for you—why? Because we're such good *friends*? Because we have such a great track record of helping each other out?"

"No, because..." Mac tried to conjure up a reason why this stranger should help, before he ultimately appealed to his obsession. "Because...helping someone is the heroic thing to do!"

"Well, that's an excellent point," Homer replied snidely, hugging the scrolls in his arms close to his body. "Such an excellent point, in fact, that it doesn't seem like you need me at all. Seems like you got this hero thing pretty well figured out on your own."

"Look, could you just give me one—?" Mac began.

"I best be going," Homer cut him off, walking backwards as he spoke. "Sorry I couldn't be more help with the whole 'getting kicked out of school' thing, but I'm sure, with that brilliant, criminal mind of yours, you'll come up with something. Been great catching up. Talk to you soon…moron." Then he whisked around abruptly—too abruptly, as it turned out. He ended up crashing right into another student, a hulking muscle-head, who happened to be walking across the quad with two other hulking muscle-heads.

From a few steps away, Mac witnessed the whole thing: Homer dropped to the ground, as if he had run into a stonewall; in the process, he spilled his scrolls and the contents of his bag all over the ground; with abject terror etched onto his face, he looked up at the muscle-head…who just kept walking, with his muscle-head friends, as if he hadn't noticed anything had happened at all. In fact, if the brute looked down at all, it was in the manner of someone trying to see if a pesky gnat had landed on his calf.

Meanwhile, from a few steps away, Mac broke into a satisfied grin, observing how the kid who had just bitched out a class full of jocks was now cowering on the ground after confronting one of them in person. As he watched Homer scramble around, crab-like, in his goofy Nemean lion costume, gathering up his scrolls and figurines, Mac couldn't decide whether to laugh loudly and then walk away, or just walk away.

Only he didn't do either. Instead, before he knew it, almost without realizing it, he found himself crouching down, picking up a figurine. He read the name carved in its base: Odysseus. Of course.

As Mac handed over the figurine, Homer whispered, "Can I meet him?"

"Meet who?" Mac asked, still in his crouch.

"Your dad," Homer said, pointing to the icon in his hand. "If I help you out, could I meet him?"

Mac paused for a long moment. "Tell you what, if I ever meet him, you can meet him."

"OK…" Homer said, before looking off, lost in thought. "So tell me again: you have to prove you are—?"

Mac finished his sentence. "My father's son."

"Father's son, father's son…" Homer repeated, closing his eyes.

"Do you have any idea how I can do that?"

"Yes, I do," Homer opened his eyes, his mouth curling into a grin. "You need labors."

Suddenly, he bolted up and started limping away, more of a bounce this time. "Yes, labors! Like Heracles skinning the lion or fetching the golden apples. Every hero needs labors. Yes! Oh, this couldn't be more perfect!" As he babbled on, he looked back, to see Mac still in his crouch, looking completely confused.

"Yo, slacker-boy!" Homer said. "You coming or what?"

Demetrius—

No, I wasn't super-receptive when Mac first asked for my help. But then a few realizations hit me, sort of all at once, like when the contents of a high, cluttered shelf fall on your head, as you attempt to retrieve your prized Bellorophon-astride-Pegasus figure, which your mom put away during one of her cleaning frenzies. (Does this ever happen to you? Because it happens to me all the time. I feel like I'm always dumping stuff on my head, because of my height. To me, everything seems out of reach.)

So, why did I decide to help this stranger, this shady and utterly unsavory character? First reason is obvious: He's the son of Odysseus, for Hera's sake! You and I have always wanted to meet a real-life hero. Maybe this would be our way in.

Next: We're always plotting and dreaming of doing something heroic, and maybe you will actually do it someday, Demetrius, but as for me...let's face it: I'm a short kid, born with a club foot. That pretty much sealed my fate as far as being a hero goes. So I figured, even if I can't do anything heroic myself, at least I could hitch my chariot to someone else who can.

Finally...well, I think I wanted to help him because no one here ever asks me to do anything. That's why I jumped at the chance to be in the Hydra costume for Opening Ceremonies. Yeah, the whole ritual is stupid and self-important and full of pompous pomp. And yeah, they stuck me in the Hydra's butt, which meant I had to walk backwards, and pretty much in darkness, the whole time. And yeah, I found out later they only recruited me because some student's little sister was supposed to do the tail, but the costume made her claustrophobic, and she bailed in a huff at the last minute—which means, in a pinch, I can substitute for an eleven-year-old girl. (No, that's not a blow to the ego at all.) And lest we forget: the whole ordeal ended with me getting coated by a shower of Temesian hoopoe crap.

But despite all that, I was thrilled when they asked me to wear the Hydra costume—because at least I was a part of something. The fact is, I don't think many people at Pieridian even know I exist. I mean, no one exactly teases me, for playing with hero figurines or liking boys or anything like that. But then, how can they tease me, when they don't even notice me?

So, I guess you could ask, "Who are you really trying to help here—this Mac kid or yourself?" And I guess the answer is both. I am trying to help me—and I know there's nothing at all heroic about that. But if I don't help myself, who else at this gods-forsaken school will?

-Homer

Chapter Four
Andromeda

When Mac had first approached Homer, he'd dismissed him as a knowledgeable but bizarre little runt. Once he really started listening to him, however, he felt reassured by the confidence in Homer's voice. When it came to heroes, the kid knew his stuff. Plus, Homer had such enthusiasm for helping his new friend out of his predicament, Mac couldn't help but think this alliance might actually work.

Over an hour later, deep into the woods, Mac realized he was right the first time: Homer *was* a bizarre little runt.

After a quick stop in Homer's dorm room, to drop off his scrolls, figurines, and lion costume, Homer led Mac off campus and into the woods, through a maze of trees that led them farther and farther away from school. Mac traipsed along, but Homer, driven by his idea of "labors," flew ahead, his twisted foot dragging behind but not slowing him down. All the while, Mac could hear his guide chattering to himself as he glanced through the trees at the sun and clumsily waved his arms in an arc, as if measuring something. Finally, Homer stopped in front of a cypress and studied it, a befuddled look creeping across his face.

"Let me guess," Mac sighed. "You're lost."

"Not lost," Homer mumbled, his eyes moving from the oak to the paths on the ground. "Just…in the process of finding." Then, he nodded and announced, "This way."

Mac hadn't done a good job of hiding his frustration with this mystery trip, so Homer attempted to cut the tension with some conversation. "I have to say…" he began. "I'm surprised they didn't kick you out after the stunt you pulled at Opening Ceremonies. Actually, I'm surprised they didn't kick you out long before this. I thought you'd be somebody's 'one' a while ago."

"Somebody's 'one'?" Mac asked.

"Yeah. You remember our very first day of school, two years ago, when Gurgus addressed the new students from the podium? He said to look to your left, look to the right. Then he said, 'One of those two students won't be here when you graduate.' Remember that?"

"Not really…" Mac mumbled.

"Well, I did, mostly because I thought it was a pretentious and vaguely threatening thing to say. But I remember I looked at the two kids sitting next to me. The guy on my left had this very fuzzy unibrow and the girl on my right had eyes that were really, really far apart, almost like they were on the sides of her head, like a fish, like a carp or a yellowfin tuna or —"

"You know what?" Mac interrupted. "Maybe we could walk and not talk for a while?"

"Oh, OK," Homer said, clearly embarrassed. "We'll have companionable silence, then."

"Whatever…"

Eventually, Homer began to tire and Mac pulled ahead, just as the darkened, wooded path turned sharply and opened to a scene popping with color — crystal blue water, rippling white sand, green bushes, pink-fuzzy flowers, all glistening in the brilliant light of the midday sun.

The Pieridian campus — located on a small island, Iarmithia, one of nine islands off the coast of Cape Malea — had plenty of beaches in walking distance, and Mac thought he had explored all of them; he would often end up on a beach whenever he skipped class — and he skipped a lot. But he had never made his way to this small and secluded stretch of shoreline, and as he took it all in, he regretted he had never ventured out this far. This beach — high cliffs curving around a small cove — was amazing.

Still, he wasn't sure why Homer had led him here. "So let me get this straight," Mac said, as he emerged, hot and sweaty, from the shade of the trees, "we go to school on an *island*, which means I can basically roll out of bed and land on any one of nine different beaches, and you decide to take us on an hour-long hike…to see sand and water? That's great…"

Homer shoved past him. "Yeah, well, do those other beaches have these?" he walked to his right, to an area Mac hadn't seen yet, a sight that seemed out of place amidst this peaceful scene: a broken circle comprised of deteriorated stone pillars, collapsed ramparts, and smashed and craggy rocks.

"OK, but what are they?" Mac asked, as he started walking toward the remains.

"Well…ruins, obviously."

Mac rolled his eyes. "Yeah, I get that…ruins of what? What got ruined?"

"Oh, I have no idea…" Homer shrugged, as he glanced around the decayed courtyard. "Impressive, aren't they?" he said, surveying the crumbled stone pillars. "Still standing here, like forgotten warriors, waiting for their king to return, not realizing that the king had been duped into wearing a coat dipped in poison, which ate away at his flesh."

"Huh?" Mac asked.

"It's a…sorry, it's a simile…" Homer muttered.

"Yeah, I know what a simile is," Mac said. "It's just so weirdly *specific*."

"OK, OK," Homer said, obviously embarrassed. "I was just trying it out."

"A 'flesh-eating coat'? Really?" Mac critiqued.

"It needs some work…I got it," Homer grumbled, obviously trying to shut the conversation down. Then they both just stood there in silence, in the center of the ruins, until Mac spoke. "So…what are we doing here?"

Still scanning the decimated pillars, Homer replied, "I'm looking for someone."

"Someone you know?

Homer smiled. "You could say that."

At that moment, Mac felt a prickling sensation as the hairs on the back of his neck suddenly stood on end. Instinctively, he shouted, "Get down!" as he threw himself and Homer into the sand. He looked up to see a single arrow buzz over their heads.

"Homer!" A voice—gruff, but unmistakably female—boomed through the courtyard. "How many times do I have to tell you? *Stop following me!*"

Mac looked in disbelief down at Homer, pinned underneath him. "I said I knew her," Homer shrugged. "I didn't say we were best friends or anything." As they both stood up, Homer called out to their secret attacker, in a lame attempt to sound chummy, "Hey, Andie! What's up?"

"How did you find me? Did you follow me? Did my roommate tell you? She told you, didn't she? I'm gonna kill her!"

Homer glanced nervously at Mac before calling out, "So, what are you doing way out here?"

"Why should I tell you?" the mystery girl shouted back. Meanwhile, Mac's eyes flew around, trying to determine the source of this shouting. As he squinted, he could make out someone, silhouetted against the sun, half-hiding at the top of one of the stone towers. "Now, get out of here," the voice called out. "This is my beach!"

"Well, OK, but first, how 'bout you come on down?" Homer continued. "My friend and I want to ask you something."

"You don't have any friends, you freak!"

"As a matter of fact, I just made one. Come on down, I'll introduce you."

"And what if I don't? Will your 'friend' train some birds to crap on me?"

"Well, the crapping part was a *bonus*," Mac muttered.

"Great! So you've heard of Mac," Homer shouted back to the pillars. "Well, he's got himself in a bit of a bind. See, after his deplorable behavior at the Opening Ceremonies, the powers-that-be have decided he's got to prove himself a hero in order to stay here. And I said, what better way to show off your heroism than to undertake some labors, am I right?"

No response from above, which Homer must have taken as a good sign, because he kept going. "So, I'm thinking about a possible labor—a mission, even—and I hit on something, something only *you* can help us with. So, what do you say, Andie? You wanna help us out, answer a few questions?"

Mac could see that Homer was trying, in his pitiable way, to be charming: he smiled broadly, spoke with passion, and even held out his arms in the pantomime of an embrace. And, within moments, Mac could also see none of those tactics had worked, as another arrow zipped over their heads, sending them once again into the sand.

"Go away!" their mystery assailant screeched. "Or next time, I won't miss!"

Homer, scared but also frustrated, had enough. He shot up and yelled, in a voice tinged with desperation, "That's it! Tell me where the Minotaur is!"

"Stop asking me that!" Her scream bounced off the stone towers. "For the last time, leave me alone!"

Homer brazenly took a step forward. "I *know* you know where it is! Just tell us, and I promise I won't ever bother you again."

"The Minotaur is dead!" The girl hollered from above as she finally leaped out from behind a crumbling rampart. Aiming her bow right at them, she shouted, "Just like you'll be if you—" But she never finished her threat, because at that moment, a loose chunk of rock gave way under her foot. Her leg shot out from underneath her, and she fell away from the rock wall, hurtling nearly two stories down.

Instinctively, Mac jumped forward and put out his arms. The girl slammed into him with a thud that sent them both sprawling onto the soft, white sand. For a few stunned seconds, the two of them lay in a tangle of arms and legs—Mac flat on his back, the girl sprawled out on top of him. He held her, tightly. After a frozen moment of looking right into Mac's eyes, the girl jumped off him so quickly she stumbled a few steps backward, muttering, "Get away from me." Mac wanted to fire off a sarcastic "You're welcome," but for some reason, the words wouldn't come.

Mac wouldn't have remembered her name if Homer hadn't said it, but he definitely recognized her. At least, he recognized the top of her head, considering she was usually slumped over her desk in their Olympian History class. He never really got a good look at her up close. But now, as she stood a few feet away from him, Mac's eyes swept over her, which didn't take long. She was tiny. Not quite as short as Homer, but just small all over. Unlike most girls at school who wore their hair long and tied back in elaborate styles, her dark brown hair was cut short, curling just below her chin and tucked messily behind her ears. Her face was pink from the sun, with sand freckling her cheek and a patch of skin peeling on her nose. Instead of the traditional school uniform of deep scarlet lamb's-wool edged in gold cording, she wore a faded, pale green tunic tied over one shoulder with a thin strip of leather.

But it was the way she held herself that really caught Mac's attention. Ramrod straight with her chin raised up a little…like she was trying to make herself look taller than she really was.

Homer had called her Andie, but Mac remembered teachers calling her by her full name: Andromeda. Mac watched as she silently fetched her bow and the scattered arrows she had dropped during her fall. As he watched her shoulders slump, Mac could tell she wasn't the same brash girl from the tower; the ungraceful fall, maybe, had shaken her. Still, she had to get the last word—as she picked up an arrow near Homer's feet, she muttered, "The Minotaur's dead."

"You don't know that," Homer countered. "No one has proof Theseus actually killed it." Homer turned to Mac as he continued. "In fact, there's a popular theory that Theseus only *captured* the Minotaur, and kept it caged up in a labyrinth—a second labyrinth, a secret one—that no one could ever find or find their way through."

"It's not a *popular* theory," Andie said, still facing away from them. She spoke in a controlled, even voice, but Mac could see her hands clenching into fists around her bow and arrows.

"Well," Homer said forcefully, "it was popular enough for your father."

That did it. Within a split-second, Andie spun around and aimed one of her arrows right at the center of Homer's skull. In response, Homer let out a shout before hurling himself into the sand and curling himself into a ball.

"Don't you ever mention my father again," she hissed in an

unsteady whisper as she pulled back on the string of the bow.

Initially, Mac just stood off to the side, immobilized not by fear but by confusion. He first looked at Homer, trying to bury himself in the sand, then at Andie, who was breathing heavily and glaring at her target, her eyes wild with possessed determination. A closer look revealed that her eyes glistened, not just with hatred, but with tears that threatened to fall at any moment. The sight of those tears finally spurred Mac into action.

"I think we're done here," Mac said, stepping between them. He put his left hand on Andie's bow, just below her hand, his fingertips grazing her fisted, white knuckles. Keeping the arrow pointed at Homer, she glanced over at Mac, who could see her blinking furiously, as if trying to dam up her tears. "I'm not sure what this is about, but we obviously caught you at a bad time. So…" he continued, keeping his voice calm and quiet. "Let's forget the whole thing, OK?"

Andie maintained her position, her lip quivering but her bow perfectly still, as Mac hauled Homer out of the sand and pushed him out of the way. He smiled meekly at Andie before walking away, backwards at first. Then he turned and jabbed Homer in the ribs with his elbow. "What's the matter with you?" he lectured. "The girl is *armed*! Why are you trying to upset her?" The two had almost made it to the woods when the girl called out to them. "Wait!"

At the sound of her voice, Homer sank to his knees once again. Mac shook his head, disgusted at Homer's cowardice, before he turned around to see Andie, her weapon lowered, walking toward them. Ignoring Homer, she marched right up to Mac and stood in front of him. Without a word, she scanned his entire frame. Her tears were gone, replaced with a smirk that began inching its way across her face.

"So…what was that you said before?" she asked. "You need…a mission, is that it?"

"Well, he's calling them *labors*," Mac shrugged, gesturing at the cowering Homer.

"I'm not going to tell you what you want to know," she said, looking down at Homer. "But I might be able to help you in another way." She paused, shaking her head and breaking into a full-fledged grin. "And maybe I can get something out of it, too."

"What are we talking about here?" Mac asked, finding himself smiling right back at her.

Andie tilted her head slightly. "Have you ever ridden a wooden horse before?"

CHAPTER FIVE
War Games

It had taken Mac and Homer an hour to reach Andie's hiding spot; she got them back to school in half that. The grueling pace she set through the woods reduced both Homer and Mac to panting, doubled-over lumps; Andie, meanwhile, hardly even broke a sweat.

She led them to a dune overlooking a stretch of shoreline that was close enough to Pieridian that the students could lay claim to it, but far enough away that the school had no jurisdiction over it. Pieridian Academy boasted many impressive, pristine beaches within walking distance of campus; this was not one of them. Its sand, for example, had taken on an almost ashen color, thanks to the many student bonfires and their accompanying debris. Even the water seemed somewhat ashen.

Most of the Pieridian students could overlook these obvious flaws, but Mac—something of a beach snob, having grown up in Ithaca— couldn't. Still, after the run he had just endured, the water, polluted or not, absolutely beckoned him. In fact, he would have dashed down to the surf and plunged in, if not for all the *people*. Hundreds of students, as far as he could see, jam-packed the beach—some stretching and running, some shoveling and hammering, some chanting the Pieridian fight song. Off in the distance, a small group of students raised a large white flag with two depictions, in red, of the Pieridian seal, nine interlaced magpies encircling a three-pronged crown. And in between the seals, in big red letters, two words: "War Games."

Standing on the ridge, her bow in her hand, Andie surveyed the scene before her like a general assessing a battlefield. "Six years," she seethed, more to herself than to Mac or Homer. "Six years ago, at the height of the Trojan War, a group of Pieridian students had an idea:

'Hey, let's honor the great warriors by starting our own games. Completely student-run. Open to anyone.' Sure. And you know how many women they've let compete in those six years? That's right: Zero. As in, not one. Sexist cretins."

She turned around to her companions, still hunched over, trying to catch their breath. "So this year I called 'em on it. 'Say, why are there never any girls in the competition? This is the only school in all of Greece that admits girls, after all, so it stands to reason they should be allowed to compete, right?' Finally, after a *lot* of harassing, they said if I could find a partner, they'd let me in."

"And you never found one?" Mac wheezed.

"I *found* a partner," she said, indignantly. "I found three, as a matter of fact."

"I see," Homer interjected, "and that's why we found you sulking in a rundown tower all by yourself, with no people anywhere?"

"They all...backed out," she mumbled.

"Hard to believe," Mac said, pulling himself up, "because you're so easy to get along with."

Andie grabbed Mac's arm and yanked him closer. "See that smug, irritatingly good-looking fatneck over there, the one in the red tunic?" She pointed her bow to the beach below, in the direction of a towering young man, thick with muscles, in the middle of a crowd of students. Mac didn't know him, but he recognized him as one of the three guys who had intimidated Homer into spilling his figurines all over the ground earlier that morning. "That's Melpagon. He's an upperclassman, Fourth Year. He's also the head sexist cretin *and* the reigning War Games champ. He secretly met with all my potential partners and convinced them to back out. I'm sure of it."

"Why would he do that?" Mac asked skeptically.

"Because he knows I can beat him." She took a deep breath to ready herself. "All right, follow me," she said to Mac. "And please, try to look at least a little intimidating."

Andie bounded down the dune and pushed her way through the crowd, Mac meekly trailing behind. When she got to the registration table, she stood there, not saying a word, waiting to be noticed; Mac lingered a few paces behind her, doing everything he could *not* to be noticed. On the other side of the table, Melpagon—the irritatingly good-looking fatneck—was drinking from a goblet and laughing it up with some of his equally fatnecked friends. He loomed at least five inches taller than any of the other students near him, but he appeared even bigger due to the person right next to him: a puny, scrunched-up man, even shorter than Homer, with long, stringy hair which fell down into his squinty eyes.

The little guy, whose head barely peeked out above the registration table, noticed Andie first. "Hey," he announced, in this scary, gravelly voice, "look who's back."

Melpagon glanced over quickly. "You know the rules, Andie: you gotta have a partner."

"I have one," Andie proclaimed proudly, gesturing with her thumb to Mac, who responded with a small and decidedly unintimidating wave.

"Him?" the little guy cracked to Andie. "Man, you must really be desperate!"

"Oh, on the contrary, Mermeus," Melpagon said, smiling at Mac. "This is, after all, the son of Odysseus, a real live war hero. We're honored you crawled out of your shell to join us today, Telly," he said, his voice dripping with sarcasm as he sunk down low into an exaggerated bow. "Personally, I'm looking forward to facing some worthy competition for a change. That way, when I beat you, it will mean so much more."

Mac, not knowing what to make of either this smug giant or his pint-sized brute of a sidekick, didn't say anything. Finally, Andie responded, evenly, emotionlessly: "We'll see."

"Aw, spunky, little Andie," Melpagon jeered. "So much heart, so much spirit. I almost feel bad about crushing it all the time." He picked two yellow scarves from the registration table and threw them at her face. "Almost." With that, Melpagon strode away, his gang in tow, leaving Andie to fume silently before stomping away herself.

As he'd done several times that afternoon, Mac followed. Not even turning to him, Andie started in. "Since this is a social event, where people actually talk to each other and hang out, can I assume you've never been to War Games before?"

"That would be a safe assumption, yes…" Mac acknowledged, although he did have another reason for staying away from the Games: on principle, Mac avoided any activity that reminded him of the so-called "heroes" of the Trojan War.

"All right, here's the deal," Andie explained, weaving her way through the crowd. "There's a series of events. We each do one solo, the rest we do together. You get points if—oh, you don't need to know how the points work. Just plan on always coming in first."

Suddenly, a loud, piercing voice cracked the air: "The archery event will be commencing shortly. One competitor from each team should report to the west-side of the beach." Mac looked up and saw Melpagon's tiny associate, Mermeus, sitting above everyone on a tall bamboo chair, screeching into a speaking trumpet only slightly smaller than himself.

"You stay here," Andie instructed, handing Mac her bow as she tied the yellow scarf around her waist. "I've got this."

"Archery?" Mac asked. "You didn't even come *close* to hitting us before. You sure archery's your thing?"

"Pretty sure," she smirked, taking the bow back and tapping him on the shoulder with it.

She was just about to join the other archers, when Homer caught up with them. "Well, this has been fun," he said, "but we're leaving."

"So soon? Shucks. Well, see ya." Andie dismissed him, as she turned to leave.

"No, I said *we're* leaving," Homer said, waving his finger several times between himself and Mac. "As in both of us. As in I'm pulling him." Hooking his arm through Mac's, he attempted to yank him away from Andie but couldn't even remotely budge him.

"You're *pulling* him?" Andie said. "What, are you his mother or something? Can't he decide for himself?"

"It's better when he doesn't. So, on his behalf, I'm telling you he's not going to have anything to do with this ridiculous competition."

Andie took Homer aside, but Mac could hear the entire con-versation. "What's your problem with this, exactly?" she asked

Homer. "Aren't you a Trojan War freak?"

"The Trojan War was about honor and courage and sacrifice," Homer snorted in disgust. "This is about how many figs someone can shove into his mouth at once."

"Actually, they don't do that one anymore…"

"Telemachus has to do something *heroic*. Where's the heroism in this?"

"Where's the heroism? He's coming to the aid of a girl who needs help! A damsel in freakin' distress — what's more heroic than that? I even have the same *name* as the original Andromeda. It's perfect."

"I want the Minotaur," Homer insisted.

"Well, you're not gonna get it," she said simply. "So…if that's the way it's gonna be, then…forget it. Forget the whole thing. It's not that important anyway."

But as she spoke, Mac could see her eyes were locked on Melpagaon, who was making his way over to the archery area. Clearly, this *was* important to her. "It's fine," Mac interjected. "I'll do it. Let's just get it over with."

Andie looked at Mac for a moment. She opened her mouth as if to say something, a word of gratitude, perhaps. Instead, she turned with her bow and sprinted down the small slope toward the raucous mob that began to gather on the west end of the beach. Mac kept watching her until she disappeared into the crowd. When he finally turned around, he noticed Homer was scowling at him.

"What?" Mac shrugged. "Maybe she's right. Why can't I count this as a good deed?"

Homer shook his head. "You are so clueless. This is meaningless. It's *recess*. I only agreed to your involvement to humor her, so she'll eventually spill it about the Minotaur."

"Hold on. When you two keep saying the 'Minotaur'…you don't mean *the* Minotaur? Half-man, half-bull, ate a lot of Athenians — *that's* who you're talking about?"

"Yes. The mutant offspring of Pasiphae who lived in Daedalus's Labyrinth. Of course, *the* Minotaur. What other Minotaur is there?"

"And you think it's still alive?"

"Well, the gods made it immortal, so yeah, I think it's still alive."

Even in the few hours they had known each other, Homer had a way of seeming constantly exasperated with Mac.

"And you're saying Theseus, instead of killing it, actually captured it?"

"And trapped it in a second labyrinth, yes."

"OK, even if I believed any of that, which I'm not sure I do, how would 'Miss Sunshine' over there know where that labyrinth is?"

"Well," Homer replied with a knowing glance, "because 'Miss Sunshine' just happens to be the daughter of Hieronymos."

"Ahh," Mac arched his eyebrows in mock recognition, until he deadpanned: "Who?"

"Really? Have you done *any* studying while you've been here?" Homer sighed heavily before rattling off the man's qualifications. "Hieronymos. Renowned philosopher, teacher, explorer…probably one of the smartest mortals that ever lived. He spent most of his career at Argus University. His specialty: Greek heroes. Specifically: Theseus. I've studied all his work. Groundbreaking stuff. His research on the heroic journey was absolutely…"

But Mac was only half-listening as his eyes drifted to the archery event. From his vantage point, he could see two students arranging three clay water jugs in a straight line on top of a long, high table; from above, on his bamboo chair, Mermeus shouted instructions at them. Though he couldn't hear much, Mac quickly gathered the object of the game: to shoot an arrow through the handles of all three water jugs and into a wooden stake at the other end of the table. Even to Mac, who considered himself pretty decent at archery, it seemed impossible.

The competitors, however, didn't seem too concerned about the level of difficulty; they all stood in a huddle yukking it up and taunting their opponents. In the center of all the revelry, chortling louder than any of them, Melpagon was back-slapping a fellow titan, a blond replica of himself (whom Mac later learned was his War Games partner, another lumbering oaf named Kerrtennikos). And far away from the pack, not talking to any of them, Andie attended to her bow.

She wasn't laughing.

As Homer continued, Mac watched the first competitor position himself at the far side of the long table. He shot his three arrows in quick succession but didn't even come close to making it through any of the handles. Only one of the arrows even grazed the first jug.

Next up: Andie, who marched calmly up to her mark and drew her bow. From where Mac was standing, he could take in the entire scene: Melpagon and Kerrtennikos standing behind her, superior expressions on their faces; Mermeus, high above, using his speaking trumpet to hurl insults at her; Andie, blocking out the world, zeroing in with deadly focus on the water jug handles.

The next instant, Mac saw the arrow in the stake.

"Holy Charybdis! Did you see that? She's like an Amazon with that thing!" Mac shouted to Homer, raising his hand in a high-five gesture. Homer looked at him blankly. Realizing his high-five wouldn't be returned, Mac rolled his eyes and took back his hand.

"OK, so you were saying about her dad…except maybe skip to the point where you start to make sense."

"Hieronymos did the first serious work on Theseus. In fact, he was the first person who came up with the theory, based on ancient writings and archeological evidence, that Theseus was not, in fact, the Minotaur's slayer, but its tormentor, first by asking the gods to punish the beast by giving it immortality and then by banishing it for eternity in a secret location."

"The second labyrinth," Mac said, keeping his eyes on Andie, who was preparing to shoot her next arrow. "OK, so what happened?"

"The location, it turns out, was a little *too* secretive. Hieronymos never found it. But that doesn't mean he stopped looking. For years, he searched for it. It festered into an obsession, finding this labyrinth—to the point he didn't even notice how his reputation began to suffer. Everyone at the University—colleagues, administrators, students—thought he had lost his mind. Finally, he lost his job, along with his credibility."

Homer paused as Mac watched Andie's second arrow fly into the stake, just slightly below the first one. Mac let out his breath in a whoosh of amazement.

"But he never lost his will," Homer continued. "Wanting to prove to everyone he wasn't crazy, he doubled his efforts. Finally, he came across new information—a map, reportedly drawn by Theseus himself, pinpointing the labyrinth's exact location. So, one night, all by himself, he set out to find it."

"And?" asked Mac, eyes still locked on Andie.

"He was never heard from again."

As if to punctuate Homer's words, Andie's third and final arrow hit its mark. Without saying a word to any of the astonished onlookers, she just picked up her bow, gathered her arrows, and walked away.

Mac was awed by her performance. He could never do what she just did. Reflecting on Homer's story, he also felt a twinge of a connection with her; it looked like maybe he wasn't the only one with a less-than-ideal father.

"What happened to him?" Mac asked Homer.

"Hieronymos? No one knows."

"Did he ever find the Minotaur?"

"No one knows."

"So let me get this straight," Mac said. "This supposedly brilliant man spent his whole life looking for a creature that's already dead, tucked away in a labyrinth that doesn't exist. That doesn't strike me as particularly brilliant if you ask me."

"He *was* brilliant, the Minotaur *is* alive, and the labyrinth *does* exist," Homer insisted. "I *know* it."

"Well, even if any of that is true, why would she know anything about it?" Mac asked, motioning to Andie, who was making her way up the slope.

"If you found a map that would prove your sanity and restore your reputation, would you keep it a secret? No way. Her father must have told her something. Andromeda knows *something*. And that 'something' is your ticket. That's how you prove you're your father's son. You find the Minotaur, you can stay at Pieridian Academy."

"That's it? That's what you want me to do? Find the Minotaur—*that's* the act of heroism?"

"Well, find it. And then kill it, of course."

"Kill it?" Mac repeated. "Are you…are you out of your mind? Kill it? How do you expect me to do that?"

"Hey, one thing at a time, please…"

"All right," interrupted Andie, returning to their sides and brushing off Mac's attempts to congratulate her. "Let's get to work."

****

Considering they'd only met earlier that day, Andie and Mac made a formidable duo. They won the first team event, a relay race with some swimming thrown in. Mac had never seen a race like it, but Andie quickly explained the rules. First, he had to sprint down the beach to the water's edge; once there, he would swim out to one of a series of five baskets, tied to a rope so they were equidistant from the shore. In the basket, he'd find a dead, slimy fish, which he had to transport back to shore without dropping. (Since there were only five baskets and ten teams, the competitors who didn't reach the baskets in time to grab a fish would be automatically eliminated.) Once he swam back to the shore, Mac then had to sprint back to the starting line, where he would hand off the fish to Andie; she would then go through the same cycle, only this time returning the fish to the basket.

As he positioned himself at the starting line, Mac took a quick glance back at his partner. She appeared confident and completely focused, but Mac suspected she had her doubts about him and his abilities. How could she not? She knew nothing about him.

Right then and there, Mac decided to throw himself completely into the first team event—not because he needed to win, necessarily, and not even because he wanted to help her, but because he had a strange desire to *impress* her.

He ended up doing all three. He got a good jump off the starting line and made it out to the baskets before anyone else. He dug his fingers into the fish so it wouldn't slip out of his hands when swimming, and he even handed off the fish to Andie without bobbling it. Thanks to his strong start, Andie ended up coasting past the finish line a good five feet before Melpagon. Naturally, his team had a complaint: apparently, when his partner Kerrtennikos went to reach in for the fish, he found a bigger fish chomping on it. Snatching the fish away, he claimed, cost him precious seconds. Even the obviously biased officials had to balk at that one.

The yellow team's victory in the relay event put all the other teams on notice and set the stage for other impressive showings. The two came in a respectable second in the javelin throw and, in a major upset, won the "Stone of Sisyphus" contest. Traditionally, that particular game—which required each team to push a sixty-pound "boulder" (really, a sack filled with rocks and laundry and other assorted stuff) up a hill—favored powerhouse teams like Melpagon and Kerrtennikos. But, in this case, haste and bad luck worked against the big guys: while rushing up the hill, Kerr slipped on some pebbles and accidentally fell into Mel's leg, which caused the "boulder" to roll over them. That, plus their ensuing bickering, allowed Andie and Mac to sneak past and score the victory.

They probably would have won the long-jump match as well, if Melpagon's minuscule tag-along Mermeus hadn't intervened. Mermeus, Mac found out later, was a Pieridian graduate who never really left. He attended the school at the time of the very first War Games, and he came back every year, as both the benefactor for the Games and the honorary announcer, referee, and scorekeeper—jobs he took very seriously. He brought with him that enormous speaking trumpet, not so much to introduce the events and competitors but to taunt anyone he didn't like. He'd even had a nine-foot-tall bamboo chair made for himself, apparently to help him see the action but really to make himself feel important. Throughout the Games, he would get some unfortunate first-years to carry the chair from event to event. Then he'd inch up the ladder and sit like a king on an oversized throne, his feet just barely hanging over the edge.

Pretty much everyone found Mermeus annoying, if not entirely loathsome, but the students in charge of War Games kept bringing him back every year, mostly because he helped pay for the big post-

Games party. He also wasn't above cheating to help the people who sucked up to him—as Mac and Andie discovered.

The long jump was pretty standard—both partners jumped separately, and their distances were added together—except it took place in a giant mud pit. On a purely practical level, the mud allowed officials to see the imprints of the jumpers' feet; on a purely disgusting level, the mud made the game a lot more entertaining for the spectators. Before the event started, Andie had bragged to Mac that they would win the event handily, and they did—until Mermeus, from high atop his perch, called a foot-fault on Mac. From his vantage point, he claimed, he could clearly see that Mac jumped after the line. Andie objected, knowing her partner made a legal jump, but it didn't matter: Mac was given a five-foot penalty.

Even Homer, who had regarded the whole War Games concept with contempt up to that point, couldn't believe Mermeus's blatant favoritism: "Are you just making up the rules as you go?"

"Zip it, shorty!" Mermeus snipped from his perch. His ruling stood, and Melpagon and Kerrtennikos got the win.

Soon after, Mac found himself down at the shoreline, cleaning the mud off his legs and watching Andie do the same. She stood apart from the crowd, hunching over a bit as she rinsed out her short, dark hair in the foamy seawater. Tugging at a stubborn piece of seaweed that was wrapped around her leg, she was almost knocked over by a wave and hopped awkwardly on one foot until she regained her balance. Mac found himself smiling as he realized how pretty she was.

"Where's your sidekick?" she asked, as she wandered over and plopped down beside him.

"Oh, no. Don't ask," Mac answered. "Just enjoy the peace and quiet."

And then Andie did something he hadn't seen her do before: she *smiled*. Not a smirk, not a self-satisfied grin, but a legitimate smile; soft and genuine, it said she not only appreciated his joke but that maybe, somehow, she had even begun to appreciate *him*.

Mac smiled back before looking down into the water. "So, what's next, boss?"

Andie pointed behind them. "That's next. The wooden horse."

Mac turned to see a group of students dragging a large wooden contraption to the center of the beach. "Wooden horse?" Mac repeated.

"Can't have a Trojan War celebration without one," she quipped, as she stood up and started walking to the event, but more slowly this time, letting Mac catch up with her. As he walked with her, Mac found himself slipping back into the all-too-familiar brooding persona that he wore so well. His defenses automatically flared back up at the mere mention of the Trojan Horse. During the actual war, his dad, after all, reportedly came up with the strategy of hiding Greek troops in a giant hollowed-out wooden horse to ambush the Trojans.

As they approached, Mac could see this wooden horse bore very little resemblance to the one of legend; this Trojan Horse was a lumpy, misshapen box, covered with animal hide, sitting on top of a post, which the officials were hammering into the ground. From the four corners of the box dangled four long ropes.

"So, what's the deal?" Mac asked, even though he had a pretty good idea.

"You and your partner try to stay on the horse while your opponents try to shake you off by pulling on those ropes," Andie explained. "As soon as one guy falls off, that's game. The team that stays on the longest wins."

"Well, can you hold onto anything?"

"The guy in the front has a short rope."

"And the guy in the back? What does he hold on to?"

"He holds onto the guy in the front," Andie said, matter-of-factly.

Mac didn't hate the idea. In fact, he welcomed an excuse to pull Andie close to him. Sure, they'd only known each other for a few hours, but that hadn't stopped him in the past, with the occasional girl he'd invited back to his room. The only difference: the quiet dark of his dorm room versus a rowdy audience of cheering and jeering classmates.

When it was their turn, Mac waited for Andie to mount first and then hopped up into the empty space behind her. He wrapped his arms loosely around her, feeling both eager and awkward at the same time.

When his opponents started shaking the horse—more wildly, he felt, than they shook any of the other teams—Mac couldn't keep himself from slamming roughly into her back. He became so preoccupied with not hurting her that he could hardly concentrate on staying on the actual horse.

"What are you doing?" Andie yelled, her frustrated voice shaking with the horse.

"Just trying to be a gentleman," Mac shouted back.

Suddenly, Andie released her rope, reached down, and grabbed Mac's hands. In one swift motion, she wrapped his arms more tightly around her, ordering him to "Hold on!"—which, of course, incited a rush of whoops and whistles from their hormonally-charged opponents, who jostled the horse even more forcefully.

Mac was pretty sure she wasn't being playful or flirty or anything like that; she just didn't want to lose. She didn't want him to lose his grip on her. He didn't either and was all too happy to hang on for dear life. The few moments he took to enjoy the feel of her body pressed up against his own was all it took to break his concentration once again and lose his balance. He flopped off the horse, taking his partner with him.

Naturally, their classmates hooted uproariously at the sight: Andie, face down in the wet sand; Mac, on top of her, his face crushed up against the middle of her back, hands wedged tightly under her hips. Mac was immobilized with shock at finding himself tangled up with this girl for the second time in one day. He felt embarrassed, but not embarrassed enough to move. Andie quickly shoved him off her, squirmed to her feet, and scrubbed the wet sand from her face. Then she bent her head down low and muttered, "Way to be a gentleman." But Mac could have sworn he saw her blush as she said it.

CHAPTER SIX
Mac Versus Melpagon

I can't believe it," Homer marveled, as he rejoined the duo at the water's edge. "I was just at the official scoreboard. You two are in first place!"

"We are?" asked Mac, who had been paying no attention to the score.

"Yeah, *tied*…" shrugged Andie, who had been paying *complete* attention to the score.

"Well, that's still great, isn't it?" Mac said cheerily. "Tied for first is still first, right? So, what's say we cut the laurel wreath in half, and call it a day?"

Andie shot Mac a look that said that no mortal in the history of the world had ever said anything more stupid or insulting—and then stalked off without saying a word. As he had done for most of the afternoon, Mac followed after her.

"Cut the laurel wreath in half?" Homer repeated in dismay, as he limped behind Mac. "Where's your competitive spirit? You have to win the tie-breaker. What's the matter with you? Don't you even care?"

"What's the matter with *me*? A little while ago, you thought this whole thing was pointless. Now you're suddenly a huge fan?"

"That's before I realized the injustice of it all," Homer responded. "Melpagon and Kerrtennikos have been cheating all day. You *have* to win now."

"Just go away…" Mac said, as he caught up with his partner at a spot near the shore where a crowd had started gathering. Craning his neck, he could see that people were standing on the edge of a large circle that had been drawn in the sand. And directly across from him, Mac could see and hear Mermeus, sitting atop his bamboo perch and screeching into his speaking trumpet: "Gentle-men...and lady..." (he snickered at that last word) "...we have reached the final event of War Games. Whoever wins this event will break the tie, and he and his teammate will be declared the War Games champions!"

As the crowd roared, Mac scrutinized the circle. "Wrestling?" he asked wearily.

"One-on-one," Andie responded in a monotone. "Your goal is to push your opponent out of the circle. If you can get both of your opponent's feet outside the line, you win."

"One-on-one, huh?" Mac asked. "And I'm our 'one'?"

"Yes..." she grumbled.

"And should I take a wild guess who their 'one' might be?"

Almost on cue, Mac heard a voice behind him: "Well, Telly, looks like it's you and me."

He turned to see a shirtless Melpagon, his dark hair slicked back with his red scarf tied around his head. Accompanying him, of course, was the ever-present Kerrtennikos, who seemingly served no other purpose than to mimic his partner's every move, right down to the smug expression on his face.

"Look at this showdown," Melpagon said. "Mel vs. Tel. Nice."

He offered his hand to Mac in a mock show of sportsmanship, as Andie stepped forward. "Actually, I'm going to be fighting."

"Nice try, Andie," Melpagon grinned. "You already did your solo event, remember?"

"Fine," she pouted, as Mermeus's shrieks filled the air.

"Now, entering the ring, one-half of your reigning War Games champions..."

"Well, I just wanted to say in advance, don't feel too, too badly about coming in second," Melpagon said to Mac. "Hey, you're not your dad, after all. For a nobody, you actually haven't done a terrible job." Finally, he delivered a parting shot: "Maybe next year, Andie."

With that, Melpagon emerged from the crowd and strutted into the center of the circle. As Mel posed for his adoring fans, the full implications of this whole thing dawned on Mac.

"I'm going to get absolutely obliterated, aren't I?" Mac muttered, his eyes fixated on his enormous opponent.

"Perhaps you'd like a *girl* to fight him instead?" Homer wise-cracked.

"I would *love* Andie to fight him," Mac fired back. "She could definitely kick his ass."

Just then the applause transitioned seamlessly into boos, as Mermeus introduced Mac.

"And his opponent, wearing yellow, the color of cowards: you know him as the meddlesome kid who tried to ruin Opening Ceremonies. Now he's going to try and ruin your War Games. Ladies and gentlemen, the bad seed of the great Odysseus, Telemachus the Spoilsport!"

"All right, listen to me," Andie ordered Mac, pulling him close so he could hear her over the booing. "Don't go right at him. He's bigger and tougher. Blow for blow, he's got you. If you have any speed left, use it." Mac kept glancing into the ring, but Andie grabbed his face and turned it toward her. "Are you listening? Work on his legs. Get him off-balance. He's not bigger than you when he's on his back."

"Anything else?"

"Don't lose," she said simply, shoving him into the circle.

Amidst a commotion of boos, Mac entered the circle with his head down, in a display of something much less than complete confidence. He looked back at his team; he could see Andie but not Homer, boxed out by the taller kids who muscled in front of him. He self-consciously fixed the yellow scarf around his waist before finally picking up his head. When he did, he was standing eye-to-chin with his rival.

"You should probably know," Melpagon smirked, "I've never lost this event. Not once in three years. Hope that doesn't freak you out too much."

Mermeus's voice blared over the throng. "Gentlemen...begin!"

Melpagon crouched down slightly and took a step forward; Mac, defensively, stepped back. Again: Melpagon stepped forward, Mac retreated. Soon, the two were circling one another.

"You sure you're OK?" Mel pressed. "You look a little—nervous."

He accented that last word with a right hand swipe in the region of Mac's face. Instinctively, Mac jumped back, but he didn't really need to; Mel's swing didn't even come close to his face. Just a psychological tactic on Melpagon's part.

They continued circling each other. Melpagon held up his right hand—daring Mac to lock up with him—when suddenly, Mermeus's voice boomed over the proceedings: "Hold on! Hold on!"

A moment—that's all it took. A moment, for Mac to pause and glance up at the annoying little man in the chair; for Melpagon to ram his knee into Mac's stomach, doubling him over; for Mac to feel himself driven backwards toward the edge of the circle. A moment for Mac to realize he had been played.

"OK, my mistake," Mermeus announced snidely. "Continue."

As Melpagon slammed his shoulder into Mac's chest, pushing backwards, Mac struggled desperately to regain a foothold in the sand. Finally, he was able to stop himself, just as his heels were touching the line. In fact, Mac was so close to the edge of the circle, he could actually reach out and touch some of the spectators. So that, in effect, is what he did: with his right hand, he grabbed a goblet from a bystander and threw the liquid in Melpagon's face.

Now it was Mac's chance to take advantage of the moment. With Mel temporarily blinded, Mac slammed both of his fists down on Melpagon's upper back, forcing him to break his grip. Mac then jumped away from the edge of the circle, into safer territory. Wiping the mead out of his eyes, Melpagon turned around with a brutal grimace. Mac, not sure what to do at this point, threw up a wild punch; Melpagon easily blocked it with his left arm before responding with a right hand so thunderous that, upon contact with Mac's jaw, it actually spun him around and sent him head first into the sand.

Mac dragged himself up to his elbows and looked down to see drops of blood in the sand. But he didn't have time to register the pain in his jaw before a series of other, even more painful sensations joined in, as Melpagon dropped a knee on his lower back, then grabbed two fistfuls of his hair and mashed his face into the sand.

Mac managed to shut his eyes; in the darkness, he could hear the fans cheering uproariously, egged on by Mermeus's obnoxious chants of "Crush him! Crush him!"

Soon, Mac felt himself yanked up by the left arm. Blinking his eyes and coughing sand out of his mouth, he suddenly felt a terrible pressure on his throat, courtesy of Melpagon's massive right bicep.

"Hey!" Mac could hear Andie yelling up at Mermeus. "No choking, ref!" Somehow, no one seemed to know or particularly care about that rule. Fading fast, Mac looked over to Andie, who was now screaming at him: "Legs! Legs! Go for the legs!"

In a desperation move, Mac kicked his left foot, hard, into Melpagon's left shin. Then again. And again. Only after the fourth kick did Melpagon break the chokehold. Mac fell down and, trying to catch his breath, began crawling on his hands and knees—an ideal position, it turned out, for Melpagon to kick him in the stomach.

This attack officially moved Mac from grave discomfort to just-about-vomiting pain. He rolled over onto his back, only to leave himself wide open for Melpagon to blast him again, much to the delight of the crowd.

"Kick him again!" Mermeus cheered from above.

Drinking in the applause, Melpagon decided to showboat a little before stomping him a third time: he smiled broadly at his fans as he let his foot linger above his opponent's stomach for a few seconds—just enough time for Mac to grab Melpagon's foot with both hands and hoist him backwards, right onto his own back.

Another opening.

With Melpagon on the ground, Mac leaped to his feet, grabbed his opponent's right leg, and started kicking, just below the kneecap. Melpagon, rarely on the receiving end of punishment, screamed out and banged his fists on the sand. Mel wildly tried to kick Mac with his left foot, an attack that Mac easily sidestepped. Finally, Melpagon sat up, covered Mac's face with one massive hand, and shoved him halfway across the circle.

Melpagon struggled to get to his feet and found himself limping, not to mention completely thrown off his game; he obviously didn't expect such fury from Telemachus the slacker. And he expected what came next even less: Mac, head down, thundering across the circle, ramming his shoulder into Mel's stomach, spearing him to the circle's edge.

For a moment, Mac thought he had him, that the momentum would carry Melpagon out of the circle. And it would have, too, if Mac hadn't run smack into a blond-haired stone wall by the name of Kerrtennikos. Standing just outside the circle, he was pushing on Melpagon's back, keeping him from falling out. Melpagon ended up sandwiched between the two forces—Kerr pushing on his back, Mac pushing into his stomach with every last bit of his fading strength. Ultimately, Kerrtennikos won, shoving Melpagon into the circle and right on top of Mac.

Meanwhile, Andie had seen just about enough of the blatant cheating. Flying across the crowd of spectators, she jumped on Kerrtennikos's back and started pounding on his head. Caught completely off-guard, Kerrtennikos spun around a few times before he finally knocked off his unknown assailant. When he turned and saw who it was, he took a swing at her. Andie ducked, which inadvertently caused Kerr to hit the guy behind her, which caused that guy to hit back, which caused the two of them to start hitting each other, which naturally caused a bunch of other guys who had nothing to do with any of it to start bashing each other as well.

And thus began the long-standing tradition of the War Games riot.

In a way, Melpagon benefitted from the impromptu chaos; many fans were so distracted by the fight *outside* the circle, they momentarily forgot about the fight *inside* the circle. Good thing, too: they wouldn't have liked seeing their man get owned by this newcomer, this nobody—who just so happened to be getting his second wind, dodging all of Melpagon's reckless punches before delivering an insulting slap across his face. And if they saw how swiftly this guy took the right leg out from underneath a charging Melpagon, sending him crashing to the ground, they might have rioted—that is, if they weren't rioting already.

Someone else benefitted from the fan-fight as well: Homer, who was able to worm his way up to the front, now that so many observers were jumping into the extracurricular fray. From his vantage point, he had a great view—of Mac working over his opponent's leg, kicking the knee, wrenching the ankle; of Melpagon, screaming in pain from the ground; of Mermeus, his hands on his face in absolute shock, jumping up and down on his perch. He watched as Mac, full of frenzied confidence, dragged Melpagon, by just the one leg, through the sand.

Then, just when Mac was a few steps away from the edge of the circle, almost right underneath Mermeus's chair, Homer saw Mac stop.

"My leg! My leg!" Melpagon was yelling, waving his hands in the air, on the verge of tears. "I think it's broken! Stop! Stop!"

"What's the matter with you? He said his leg is broken!" Mermeus admonished Mac from above. "Stop! Stop!"

"Don't... Don't..." Homer said out loud to himself.

But Mac did. He did stop. He didn't let go of Mel's leg, but he relaxed his grip. Then he looked around: first, at the pathetic champion on the ground, writhing in pain and pleading for mercy, and then at the crowd. He scanned the crowd for one person, one face that would tell him what to do. He saw her on the far side of the circle; they locked eyes.

Andie's face was the last thing Mac saw before Melpagon blinded him with a handful of sand. The grains of sand stung his eyes, but that had nothing on the feeling that came next: of Melpagon's two giant feet blasting him right in the gut. The powerful kick shot Mac backwards, out of the circle and into Mermeus's bamboo chair, the legs of which shattered upon impact.

When he unclamped his eyes, Mac found himself lying amidst the debris of smashed bamboo. He looked into the circle to see Melpagon jumping around, celebrating; miraculously, it seemed his "broken" leg had already healed. Soon, his partner Kerrtennikos ran out to him, as a bunch of other sycophants swarmed the War Games champions. The only one missing from the celebration: Mermeus, who had tumbled clumsily to the ground after his perch splintered underneath him and was now lying in a whimpering heap.

As Mac sat up, forearms on his knees, watching the big celebration, it dawned on him how much every part of him *hurt* — his jaw, his stomach, his feet, everything. So when Homer finally walked up to him, Mac turned away. Given the shape he was in, Mac couldn't handle any of Homer's wisecracks. Surprisingly, Homer didn't say anything snide. He just looked at the celebrating fools in the circle and shook his head, saying, "Well, if that's what they have to do to win…I told you all along: this was stupid."

Mac had to nod in agreement as he silently looked past the celebration in the ring to the surrounding spectators.

"She's gone," Homer said, intuiting Mac's unspoken concern. "I saw her take off as soon as you fell into the chair. Who needs her? She wasn't going to help us anyway."

Mac didn't say a word, just shook his head and spit out a glob of blood that had been collecting in his mouth.

"How about you go wash off your face? It's a mess. Here let me help you up," Homer said, offering his hand.

But Mac waved him off. Instead, he got up on his feet by himself and scanned the area one last time. With a bitter smile, he grunted, "Great. Great day."

As Homer and Mac trudged away from the post-match merriment, they passed the fallen Mermeus, still wallowing in the dirt, completely abandoned by his supposed friends. "Help me up, will ya?" Mermeus whined. "I think I broke something. Ow. Ow! Help me!"

Mac kept walking; he had done enough good deeds for one day. But Homer actually paused — just long enough to say, "Zip it, shorty." Then he hurried back to the side of his new friend.

CHAPTER SEVEN
The Bonfire

Homer figured it had something to do with a girl. He wasn't interested in girls, so he could never figure out why some guys acted the way they did around them. But when he saw Mac scanning the crowd on the beach, he thought he had a pretty good idea why: to see, for one last time, if Andie was still milling about, somewhere amidst the hundreds of students now gathering around the celebratory bonfire.

And yet, as he watched Mac slump down on the ridge—the very ridge where, earlier that afternoon, Andie had railed against the oppressive, patriarchal tradition of War Games—Homer wondered if Mac had another reason for stopping. Was it possible that instead of just *watching* the students partying around a bonfire, he was actually contemplating *joining* them? Could this aloof, prank-playing loner actually want to be a *part* of something, to be included? Standing a few feet away, Homer looked at Mac, cloaked in darkness save for the faint light offered by the distant bonfire, and wondered if he might be seeing the son of Odysseus for the first time.

For a while, Homer stood there in silence, alternately watching the bonfire and Mac, but when he saw Mac take the two silver medals the War Games folks had begrudgingly given him—one for him, one for his absent partner—and toss them in disgust onto the ground, he spoke up. "Hey, don't do that," he objected, as he picked up the discarded tokens. "You earned those."

Mac grimaced as he shrugged his shoulders. "I lost, remember?"

"You came in second," Homer reminded him. "You *almost* came in first. And you got Melpagon off his feet. I bet no one has ever done *that* before. So come on," he urged, handing him the medals, "take these." Mac glared at Homer, before swiping the medals out of his hand and dropping them on the ground next to him. Then he turned his attention back to the bonfire.

After an awkward silence, Homer sat down. "Anyway," Homer continued indelicately, "you have some good moves. Where'd you learn to fight like that? Your father?"

"My father left when I was three months old," Mac answered, his eyes locked on the distant fire. "I couldn't even walk, never mind fight."

"Well, it must be in your blood, then."

"Whatever." Homer could tell Mac was in no mood to talk about his father, so he backed off. They went back to staring at the boisterous crowd, shouting and dancing around the central bonfire. One group of kids had produced some drums and began banging out a rhythm; another seemed to be competing amongst themselves over who could throw the most trash into the bonfire to create the most putrid smelling smoke. One particularly reckless student was trying to use the wooden horse apparatus as a surfboard—and failing miserably as the foamy waves knocked him down time and time again. Homer pictured Melpagon and Kerrtennikos some-where in the center of it all, their laurel wreaths on their heads, doing a jig around the bonfire as they gloated about their victory, conveniently forgetting they'd had to cheat at virtually every turn. As far as Homer was concerned, those guys knew *nothing* about heroism.

Finally, Homer spoke again—almost in a whisper, barely breaking the silence: "What you did today…I'll never be able to do anything like that."

"Like what?" Mac asked.

"Fight. Compete. Win a medal after besting someone with my strength and physical ability." Homer's voice choked a bit on those last words, as he waved a hand towards his bad foot. He hoped Mac wouldn't ask him about it, and he didn't. Homer hated the fact that he had no story associated with his foot…no battle wound from an amazing victory, no punishment from the gods for daring to challenge them. Just a disfigurement he'd had since birth. Boring and completely unremarkable.

"Well, it's not exactly all it's cracked up to be," Mac said, "In case you didn't notice, I got my ass kicked about seventeen different ways today. You should consider yourself lucky."

Homer smiled sadly. "I guess."

Just then, a bellowing voice called out Mac's name and rescued Homer from his moment of vulnerability. Squinting, he made out two figures climbing up the bluff, one of them holding a torch. When they got closer, Homer recognized Theo, Mac's roommate; the other one, a girl, looked familiar to him, though he couldn't place her.

"Mac! Dude! I've been looking all over for you!" Theo shouted on his way up the ridge, torch in one hand, goblet in the other. "You were absolutely *epic* today! I didn't get here until the end, and when I got to the beach, someone was like, 'Dude, your roommate is competing.' And I was like, 'You've *got* to be joking. I don't even think he ever goes *outside!*' But there you were in the middle of the freakin' ring, like a mini-Antaeus or something! What's up with that?"

As Theo gushed, Homer pulled up his knees and sort of scrunched his head down, in an attempt to go unnoticed. Although he had never actually spoken to him before, Theo always intimidated Homer a little. He couldn't pinpoint why, exactly, considering Theo didn't possess a single intimidating quality. And he definitely wasn't his type. A tall, lanky kid with sun-bleached blond hair and a perpetually easy smile stretched across his handsome, thin face, he certainly didn't *look* intimidating. Nor did he ever *do* anything particularly intimidating. Just the opposite, in fact; his friendly, carefree personality, good humor, and endless stream of high-fives and hyperboles combined to make him one of the more popular students on campus. Guys liked hanging out with him, and girls *really* liked hanging out with him. And yet Theo possessed some *quality*—a profound self-assurance, a breezy confidence that came from never having to fight for anything—that Homer just couldn't relate to. So maybe it wasn't really Theo himself but his aura of effortless success that Homer, whose life had never been easy, found intimidating.

"So, fill me in, dude," said Theo, who had made it just about up the slope and was now almost eye-level with the still-sitting Mac. "How'd you ever get mixed up in this crazy thing?"

"Ah, this girl asked me to—" Mac started.

"A *girl*? Nice, dude!" he crowed with sincere enthusiasm. "Who is she? Is she hot?" The second question triggered a smack on the arm and an eye-roll from his female companion.

"What? I was just asking!" Theo objected. "Hey, Mac, you know my younger sister, right?"

"His *twin* sister," the girl corrected him.

"Whatever. I'm still older. Anyway: Calliope, Mac. Mac, Calliope."

"Yeah, we have class together," Mac said, as he slowly tried to stand up. But Calliope, seeing his bruised body, gave a quick and gracious shake of the head that said, "Don't bother."

"How about this guy?" Theo asked, finally noticing Homer. "I don't think I know you, buddy." Homer smiled ruefully, not at all surprised Theo didn't recognize him.

"I do," Calliope answered. "You're Homer. You were about to give your speech this morning in Orations class about the glories of war."

So *that*'s how Homer knew her. "Oh, yeah!" he acknowledged. "And you're the girl who did that presentation on mushy love-stuff." Even as he was saying it, Homer knew it came out sounding condescending, which he didn't necessarily intend. Luckily, Calliope didn't seem fazed but just shrugged off the comment with a serene smile.

Meanwhile, Theo kept hammering Mac for information: "All right, so come on, man. Spill it. Who's this girl?"

"No, really—just forget it." Mac said curtly—or at least, it seemed that way to Homer. Or maybe he *hoped* Mac was acting dismissively toward Theo. Even though they had only known each other for a few hours, Homer felt strangely possessive of his new friend; the image of Mac and Theo being best buddies did not sit well with him.

Theo still wouldn't let Mac off the hook. "Is she here?" he pressed, turning to look back down at the crowd. "Do I know her?"

"*I* don't even really know her."

"Her name's Andie," Calliope interjected. "She's in my Modern Civ class. She keeps her head down a lot, but she seems…you know, she seems nice."

"Du-ude!" Theo leaned forward and gave Mac a playful punch in the shoulder, which caused Mac to wince in pain. "So where is she?" Theo continued. "Can I meet her?"

"She took off," Mac admitted. "I think she's pissed at me for losing."

"I doubt that. She probably just wanted to get away from Melpagon," Calliope offered. "I've seen him talk to her. He can be a little too much to handle."

"Aw, boo-hoo!" Theo said with a wave of his torch. "Screw her. You know how many girls are down there right now? Come on. I'll introduce you to some of them."

"I'm fine, thanks."

"Dude! This party is *epic*! What are you doing sitting way up here?" Theo asked.

"Well, for one thing, in case you didn't notice," Mac responded, slight resentment brewing in his voice, "they were booing me off the beach for most of the afternoon."

"Not all of them," Calliope reminded him. "Theo and I were rooting for you."

"Besides, we're teenagers," said Theo with a shrug. "Attention spans are short. All anyone cares about now is the party. If you show up with food or some juicy piece of gossip, you'd be their hero. So, let's go, dude! Let's get down there!"

"You know, I'm beat," Mac said, breathing sharply as he got to his feet. "And beat up. So I think I'll just call it a night."

Theo made a few more vain attempts to get him to join them at the bonfire before he and Calliope said their goodbyes and started back down the hill, a twin set of white-blond heads glinting in the torchlight. After only a few steps, Calliope called out, "By the way, Mac, you did great out there today."

"I lost," he reminded her.

Her brother's torch illuminated the sweet smile on her face. "So?"

Calliope answered, before skipping down the hill.

Mac sat in silence for a few moments before pushing himself up to his feet. He turned to the dark hill ahead of him, then looked back to where he was just sitting. He reached in the dirt and grabbed the two silver medals, before trudging up the hill.

Homer accompanied Mac all the way back to campus, neither of them saying much of anything. Homer *wanted* to say something to him—about how glad he was that they met and how he was going to find a great mission for him—but he didn't. In fact, the journey back to school would have lacked any significance if not for one moment. They had reached the school's main gate, when another student, arms loaded down with baskets of food and drink, passed them. Homer didn't see his face, but he heard him say something to Mac, a passing comment that actually made Mac stop right where he was standing.

Three simple words: "Good job, man."

For a few seconds, Homer watched Mac as he stood there, dead in his tracks, with a confused look on his face, as if he were trying to process not only what he had just heard from this stranger, but from what he had been hearing from people all evening. Homer, Theo, Calliope, and now this shadowy random—they all told him the same thing: that he had done something *good*.

A few more people, and Mac might even start to believe it himself.

Demetrius—

I enjoyed reading your thoughts on the relative strength of the sea gods compared to the earth gods. You make some good points. I can't wait to write back to you with my own take on the subject. Trust me, you're the only one I can talk to about these things. I've come to the conclusion that Pieridian Academy is mostly overrun with morons.

I'm not exaggerating. They are so ignorant, most of them don't even know where the name of the school comes from. Just the other day, this supposedly really smart kid in class said something about how the school was named after the Pierian Springs, and the teacher didn't even correct him. I felt like screaming, "You idiot! You don't know the school's named after the Pierides, the nine daughters of King Pierus who were later transformed into magpies by the Muses? You never looked around campus and wondered why you see magpie imagery all over the place?" (It's true, Demetrius. You would not BELIEVE how many ugly magpies are around here: magpie gargoyles on the arts building, magpie carvings over the classroom doors, magpie-shaped windows in the library. Allegedly, the school even had a magpie as its original mascot, until someone changed it to the Hydra—which is more intimidating, sure, but completely random.)

Basically, the school's overrun with magpies and morons. Part of me wonders if instead of helping Mac stay in school, I should get kicked out myself.

Speaking of Mac...did I tell you how he gave me one of the silver medals he won at War Games? Well, he did. After we walked back to campus, he kind of tossed it at me, and I took it. (Granted, it rightly belonged to Andie, but hey, she ditched us! Besides, I spent a whole day cheering them on...I deserved something!)

Anyway, I couldn't figure out why Mac gave that medal to me. Was he just being considerate? Seemed out of character for him. Was he just going to throw them out anyway, so why not give one to me? That seemed more likely. But here's the thing: a couple days later, I stopped by Mac's room, and on his desk was the other medal. He didn't throw it out after all.

I don't know why, exactly, but seeing that medal on his desk really got me thinking about who this Telemachus guy might be. And here's what I realized: maybe it wasn't "out of character" for him to give me that other medal, or to keep his own. Maybe that's part of his character. He's like a hybrid: part of him hates this school and everybody in it and every ceremony and tradition and stupid magpie statue associated with it. And another part...doesn't.

It's almost like he's a Minotaur himself: half of him is an anti-social, uncontrollable, raging-beast outsider, and the other half is just a sixteen-year-old kid. Just like you and me.

-Homer

CHAPTER EIGHT
Four Surprises

Seeing her on the dock was the third surprise.

The first surprise had occurred earlier in the week, when Mac awoke to the sight of a crinkled map shoved in his face. He blinked a few times; as the world started to come into focus, he saw Homer peeking over the map's tattered top edge.

He wasn't surprised to find Homer in his room; the two had actually hung out quite a bit in the two weeks since War Games. And somehow, Mac didn't totally hate it; in fact, he actually found Homer kind of amusing—bizarre and obsessive, sure, but still amusing. More than that, even: Mac found himself, reluctantly, *enjoying* his company.

Still, waking up to Homer kneeling on the edge of his bed and poking him repeatedly in the arm—that was a little *too much* company. "What are you doing here?" Mac grunted, re-burying his face in his pillow.

"I have another heroic deed for you," Homer beamed, as he shoved the map back in the vicinity of his face. "I think it's just what the administration's looking for."

"Who asked you?" Mac mumbled.

"You did."

Realizing he wasn't going to get rid of his intruder any time soon, Mac sat up and snatched the map from Homer's hand. Looking at the crumpled parchment with one eye as he rubbed life back into the other, he asked, "So what is this?"

"It's a map…" Homer stated.

"No kidding," Mac said, tossing it to the floor while throwing his head back into his pillow.

"…of the Maeander River," Homer continued, not missing a beat. "And here," he said, picking up the map and pointing to a certain spot, "as you can see, is the cave of a Phrygian mystic, a hermit named Kalakloptas."

"Klop-this…Got it," Mac mumbled, hoisting the pillow over his head.

"*Kalakloptas* is reputedly the keeper of the flute of Marsyas," Homer revealed dramatically, apparently assuming this would finally pique Mac's interest. When Mac didn't pull the pillow off his head, Homer said it again: "The flute of Marsyas." Still no reaction. "You do know the story of Marsyas, right?"

"If I say 'yes,' will you let me go back to sleep?"

"The satyr who gained possession of a special double flute originally owned by Athena?" Homer said to the pillow. "Who became so confident in his musical abilities, he challenged Apollo to a competition? Who was skinned alive after he lost? You know the story, right?"

When he got no response, Homer grabbed the pillow under which Mac had been hiding and asked again, "I said, you do know the—?"

"Yes, I *know* it," an exasperated Mac said, sitting up and grabbing back his pillow. "And I'd still know it *two hours* from now. So why are you on my bed, ambushing me with—?"

"That's your next labor," Homer said, with a wide, self-satisfied smile.

"What is?"

"To get the flute of Marsyas."

"Whatever happened to the Minotaur?" Mac asked.

"Well, this is Plan B."

"But *why* is it Plan B? How could finding a flute prove that I'm my father's—"

"Isn't it obvious?" Homer interrupted. "Fame! Glory! That's what all heroes are after, right? Look at Jason: *famous* for getting the Golden Fleece. This flute is *your* Golden Fleece. It's perfect: handcrafted for Athena herself, lost for a hundred years. If you bring that flute back to Pieridian Academy, you'll be the most famous guy at school...maybe in all of Greece!"

Still not sold but at least more awake, Mac took the map—yellowed and weathered, a jagged tear where one of the bottom corners should be—from Homer's hand. After giving it a cursory inspection, he flipped it over, to find a neatly printed message:

Homer, this is right up your alley. Demetrius.

"Who's Demetrius?"

"My friend."

"Your *friend*?" Mac didn't even try to stifle his laugh. "You have *friends*?"

"My scroll buddies, yes," Homer confirmed.

"Scroll buddies?"

"You know. People with similar interests as you. They tell you things, you tell them things. I belong to a hero group, so we just keep each other updated about our favorite heroes."

"And these 'scroll buddies' all go to school here?" Mac asked, a bit surprised that Homer might have other friends besides him.

"No, no. They live all over the place. All over Greece."

"Have you ever *met* any of these 'scroll buddies'?"

"Uh, no, *obviously*. That's the essence of the scroll buddy."

Mac looked back at the torn parchment. "So you guys just send old maps to each other?"

"Not just maps. We send each other all sorts of stuff, about wars, transformations, quests," Homer explained unapologetically. "You should think about getting a scroll buddy yourself."

"Yeah, I'll get right on that," Mac mumbled, checking out the map more carefully. "Why is this ripped?"

"I don't know. Maps get ripped," Homer shrugged. "It's not important. There's nothing there that concerns us."

"No? Well, I'll tell you what does concern me." He put the map up against his chest with one hand and pointed to a spot in the far upper-right quadrant. "Here's Cape Malea. And here...well, somewhere in here..." he said, as he circled his finger in the vicinity of Iarmithia, the third island off the coast of Cape Malea, "is where we are. And, as this map clearly illustrates, we are nowhere near Phrygia, which is way over here," he pointed to another part of the map. "So how would we ever get to this place?"

"Well, we'll have to take a boat," Homer said matter-of-factly.

"I see," Mac said. "And you have one, naturally?"

"No," Homer trailed off, as if that particular detail had just occurred to him.

"Well, gee, neither do I," Mac fired back. "So it looks like we'll have to go with Plan C—maybe something easier, like scaling Olympus?"

"We just have to *find* someone with a boat!"

"Oh, that's easy," Mac said. "Because people just line up to lend their boat to two teens, who have nothing to go on but a ripped map from a 'scroll buddy'! Who would do that?"

"I would," came a voice from the other side of the room.

They both looked over to see Mac's roommate Theo lying in his bed—eyes closed in apparent sleep, but with his right hand raised straight in the air.

"What?" Mac asked him.

"I have a boat," replied Theo, eyes still shut, arm still in the air. "Lots of boats, actually."

"You do?"

"OK, not me: my *dad* does," Theo clarified, opening his eyes as he lowered his hand. "But he has a lot of them. He's an exporter."

"What does he export?" Mac asked.

"Food, mostly. Livestock. Exotic pets. Sometimes rare gems. That sort of thing." Theo sat up in his bed. "Oh, yeah, it's a good gig. He's got boats going all over the place. Even here. Where d'ya think they got that pig they served for dinner last night?" He pointed both thumbs at himself and sing-songed, "My dad."

"I had no idea…" Mac said.

"Well, how would you? When do we ever talk, dude?"

Mac didn't try to deny it. The fact is, Mac hardly knew Theo. The Pieridian administrators had paired them up as roommates that year, in the desperate hope that Theo's legendary affability could somehow balance out Mac's impenetrable cynicism. But the plan wasn't working. Mac could see Theo was trying to reach out to him, but he also knew he was going through the motions. The administration, apparently, had told Theo he only had to live with him for a semester; after that, he could go live with someone he actually *liked*.

"All right! We got our transportation!" Homer beamed. "Now when should we do this?"

"Well, we have a long weekend coming up, right? Let's just hitch a ride on one of my dad's boats. We'll go as far as we can, then we'll take a raft the rest of the way."

"And how will we get back?" Homer asked.

"We just meet up with another one of his boats coming back to Iarmithia. Don't sweat the details, little man. I do this all the time." With that, Theo threw off his covers, got out of bed, and stretched. He was practically naked, not wearing anything but a very flimsy cloth around his waist. Theo was perfectly comfortable in his own skin.

"I notice you keep saying 'we'…" Mac began suspiciously.

"Oh, I'm definitely coming," Theo said as he took a few steps over to a wooden bucket of water on his desk. Taking a deep breath, he dunked his head in the water, yanked it out, and then vigorously shook his hair, splashing water all over the place. Homer cringed, but Mac didn't even react; by now, he was used to Theo's morning ritual.

"I can't just send two randoms on one of my dad's boats," Theo continued, as he ran his fingers through his wet hair. "Besides, this whole 'looking-for-a-weird-flute' thing sounds like fun. Just tell me…why are we doing this again? I wasn't really paying attention…"

Mac looked at him quizzically. He didn't seem to grasp that his roommate—who didn't want to live with him in the first place, who was essentially a stranger to him—was not only offering up his dad's boat, without a single hesitation, but wanted to tag along. And he didn't even know why Theo was doing it, except that it seemed like Mac needed it. He was just doing it…to be *nice*? People actually *did* that?

That revelation was the second surprise.

But the third—and as far as Mac was concerned, the best—surprise happened five days later, on that misty morning when Mac and Homer were going to meet Theo at Port Florios, just a little ways off campus. As they made their way to the dock, Mac noticed how distracted and fidgety Homer seemed; he didn't say much at all, just checked and re-checked his bag for the map about three hundred times.

"Everything OK?" Mac finally asked. "You're acting weird. Or weird*er*."

"Me? Yeah. I'm great. Not nervous at all, if that's what you mean," Homer responded, unconvincingly. "Well, if you must know…I guess I'm a little concerned about the trip. The last time I was on a boat, I got a little seasick. A lot seasick, actually. But I'm sure that won't be an issue. I'm more worried that we won't get back in time for your speech."

"My what?"

"Your speech! You have to give your speech in Orations next week!"

"How do you know that?"

"How do you *not* know that?" Homer countered. "Look, I'm doing my best to help you do something heroic, so you can stay here at school and rehabilitate your image. But all my work will mean zip if you end up flunking out because of bad grades. I'm doing my part, so maybe on this boat today, you can start doing *your* part and come up with an interesting speech."

"Will do. By the way, how did you know how well I respond to *incessant nagging*?"

Homer mumbled a "just saying," and then they sank back into not-talking walking, until they arrived at the large boathouse at Port Florios. "Hey, how are we going to know which boat we're looking for, anyway?" Homer asked.

"Not sure," Mac shrugged. "When I asked him, Theo just said, 'You'll know.'"

They walked around the boathouse...and they knew.

With a hull as big as his entire dorm and vast, fluttering sails that filled the sky, the *Æton* emerged from the morning mist like a massive battleship from the Trojan War. Only it didn't just look like a battleship; it actually *was* one. As Theo explained to them later, his dad—a bit of a Trojan War fanatic himself, as well as a savvy businessman—had purchased several battleships after the war ended to supplement his existing fleet. Mac had never seen a ship like this up close, and as he approached the port, the sheer immensity and majesty of the vessel amazed him. He couldn't remember ever seeing anything so breathtaking—until he saw the person waiting at the dock.

"Whoa!" Homer said, struck speechless by the *Æton*'s beauty.

"Yeah," Mac agreed. "Whoa." Except he wasn't talking about the boat.

By all rights, he should have been furious. He got pummeled for her at War Games, and instead of saying thanks, she took off, and then never spoke to him again. He wanted to yell at her, probably *needed* to. But, for some reason, he just couldn't. In fact, when he saw her sitting on that post—her arms hugging her knees to her chest, her short, windswept hair swirling around her face—he realized something. This girl mattered to him. He had no idea why, but she mattered a lot. It took everything he had to stop himself from sprinting toward her, but he managed to get control of himself. As he got closer to the dock, the ship that seemed so massive just moments before appeared to shrink in magnitude and significance, while the girl sitting in front took up his entire field of vision.

"Well, well, well," Homer commented, grinning snidely. "You actually made it."

"How about that?" Andie said, jumping off her post. Noticing the confused look on Mac's face, she asked Homer, "Give us a minute, will you?"

"What's that?" asked a clueless Homer.

"Beat it," Mac commanded.

As Homer slowly made himself scarce, the two former War Games partners stood together on the dock for a few seconds of awkward silence—Andie looking out at some distant cloud formation, Mac looking at her. Finally, she began: "Yeah, so I ran into your sidekick the other day. He said he'd concocted a new mission for you, something involving a boat. And I thought, 'Hey, I like boats.' So…" She looked over and tried to muster up a weak smile.

Mac, meanwhile, said nothing, just studied her. What was she saying, exactly?

"Look," she started again, tucking her windswept hair behind her ears. "I've been feeling bad, about not sticking around after the last event. I think…I think I owe you an apology. It wasn't your fault. Well, no…it *was* your fault. You should've thrown Melpagon out when you had the chance. But hey, rookie mistake, right? A stupid, *stupid*, naïve rookie mistake."

"Let's get back to the apology part," Mac reminded her.

"What I'm saying is you helped me out, when you probably didn't need to. And even though we lost, I thought we made a pretty good…" she paused. "I mean, I was thinking that we…that we have…" she stammered, until she looked right at him, holding her hair out of her eyes: "Don't you think?"

"I think so?" Mac responded, with a bemused smile.

"Great," Andie sighed as she looked at the giant ship behind her. "So, you have room for one more?"

"Uh, sure," Mac said, as casually as he could manage. "You might have to stay down with the chickens, but we could probably squeeze you in."

She smiled at him, that same soft, disarming smile she'd given him that afternoon by the shore, and said, "Well, this should be interesting."

"Yeah," Mac agreed, and for the first time since Homer had proposed this crackpot scheme, he actually believed this trip *would* be interesting. Not because of some lame flute—who cared about that?—but because he got to spend a whole weekend, on a boat, with this girl. He couldn't wait for the trip to get started.

"Ahoy, down there!" someone shouted. He looked up to see Theo, at the bow of the ship, peering over the railing. "What's up, Mackie? Bringing a friend?"

"Uh, Theo, this is my…" Then he stopped, not really sure how to introduce her. Finally, he just said, "This is Andromeda."

"Andie," she immediately offered.

"Coming along, Andie?" Theo asked.

"Looks that way," Andie beamed, with a hint of giddiness that Mac hadn't heard in her before.

"Great! See you onboard," Theo then gave her a corny salute as he disappeared from the railing.

Andie stood, dumbstruck, for a few seconds, before she turned to Mac: "You know him?"

"Not very well, but yeah, he's my roommate," Mac admitted uneasily.

"He's *your* roommate? And he's coming along with us?"

"Well, it's his dad's boat, so…" he mumbled, feeling the wind go out of his own sails.

And then Andie dropped on Mac the unexpected *fourth* surprise: "I've had a crush on him for a year," she gushed. "Oh, this is *definitely* going to be interesting!"

As she practically started skipping down the dock, Mac realized he was mistaken; as it turned out, he *could* wait for the trip to start.

PART TWO

Demetrius—

I'm sure you've noticed by now, I'm lousy with similes.

Based on some feedback I've received from teachers over the years, I've concluded my similes tend to fall into different categories: Unnecessarily Literal ("I limped like a person with a bad foot"); Overly Obscure ("The room fell silent, like an empty Thracian village after the citizens departed to attend a sacrifice to Batrachia, the Minor Frog-Goddess"); or Completely Random ("He was confused, like a weary traveler staying at an inn, who happened to stumble upon a room filled with all the feet that the innkeeper had chopped off the legs of his guests, only the traveler couldn't identify them as feet as such, because by this point, they're all black and shriveled up").

Try as I might, I just don't have the knack for poetry. Do you think it's because I've never been in love? See, from what people have told me, writing poetry requires access to the kind of passion that only comes with love. And my life hasn't exactly been filled with passion, you know? Sure, I've had a few crushes in the past, but when it comes to the boys at Pieridian, Eros seems to have developed decidedly poor aim.

Mac, on the other hand, has been with girls, but he's never had feelings for any of them. And now, he has the feelings, but not the girl. Quite the pickling predicament.

I know this isn't the kind of thing that we normally talk about in our scrolls (except for that epic debate we had about the best god/demi-god relationships) but Andie's been on my mind lately because something really weird happened recently and I don't know what to make of it.

The day before we left for Phrygia, I made my way down the hall of her dorm, still clinging to the hope that she'd reveal something, anything, about her father and his findings. As usual, I received exactly zero greetings from the girls loitering in their doorways. (Why am I so invisible to everyone here?) When I got to Andie's closed door, I lightly knocked. And knocked again. And again. The third knock nudged the door open, so I peeked in. Andie had her back to me, facing the side wall, which was covered with all sorts of etchings. I couldn't make out what they were, but she was clearly carving something into the wall. Isn't that weird? What exactly was she doing?

Before I could get a closer look, Andie spun around. "Get out of here!" she screamed, as she grabbed the side of a large purple curtain and flung it over the wall. Then she picked up the nearest object, an empty straw basket, and hurled it right at my head. (Thank the gods she wasn't holding her bow!) Determined to make my pitch to her about joining us on the mission, I braved her anger and walked right into her room. Here's how the conversation went:

"So, Andie..." I started. "I came up with a new labor for Mac, and I was hoping you'd come along." No response. She wasn't interested, clearly. So I suggested I thought it might be a way for her to make it up to Mac, and she said, "Make it up? Make up for what?" And I said, "Well, you asked for his help with War Games—during which he got pounded. And then instead of thanking him, you took off and never spoke to him again."

More silence. Then finally: "Oh, that..." she muttered, the whole time avoiding my gaze by turning to look out the window.

Meanwhile, I was stealing glances over at the wall with the etchings, trying to catch another look, but it was completely masked by the purple curtain. Then Andie sat down on the edge of her bed, her shoulders slumped and head bent. Her tough attitude has always kind of intimidated me, but in that moment she looked small and unsure of herself.

"Does he hate me?" she asked.

"Mac hates everyone, to a degree," I said.

I heard her sniff out a tiny laugh. "Yeah, me too..." she said softly.

"See, that's why you two were such a good team."

She turned back to me, offering that rare smile of hers. "I'm not committing to anything, but before we go any further," she said, "you have to promise me this isn't some ploy to get me to tell you about the Minotaur."

"Promise," I said.

I know, Demetrius. It was a lie, but a necessary one.

-Homer

CHAPTER NINE
Voyage of the *Æton*

I can't believe your parents named you 'Theseus.' How obnoxious is that?"

"Well, I don't know. Check out these muscles. The name totally fits."

Mac stood at the deck of the *Æton*, both hands clenching the railing. From his spot, he could have taken in all the sensations that surrounded him: above him, the sights of the massive, billowing sails, reaching into the clouds; below him, the sounds of the oarsmen, all rowing at the same speed, in the same motion; and swirling all around him, the feel, smell, taste of the salty wind driving the *Æton* through the vast blueness of the Aegean Sea.

But Mac didn't notice any of those things—not the sails, the wind, or the blue. Instead, his attention was consumed by a conversation fourteen feet away, between Andie and Theo.

"You just don't strike me as a 'Theseus' kind of guy."

"You don't think so? Here, I'll do something dashing. I'll throw you overboard and then go rescue you!" With that, Theo grabbed Andie around her waist and acted as if he were going to hoist her over the railing; Andie fought back only with shrieks and giggles.

Mac couldn't believe what he was witnessing. Granted, he didn't know her very well, but he had never seen this side of Andie before. The flirty side. The playful, blushing side. Even the *laughing* side; no matter what dumb thing came out of Theo's mouth, Andie seemed to find it absolutely hilarious.

A lot of girls fell spellbound under Theo's charm—that much Mac knew—but he never would have pegged the strong, independent Andie as one of them. The whole scene sickened Mac so much, he wanted to walk away. And yet, there he stood, fuming from fourteen feet away, eyes locked on the two of them. It was colossally unfair. Andie was different than other girls he'd been with...and he liked her. And she was hooked on his roommate.

A tug on the back of Mac's tunic drew his attention away from the flirting pair. When he turned, he saw Theo's twin sister, Calliope, standing with him at the railing, her silky curtain of pale hair woven back in a tight, intricate braid.

"Hey, there," she said, with a little wave.

"Hey," Mac smiled. "I didn't even know you were on-board...Have you been here the whole time?"

"Me? Oh, no. I just got here. Swam from school. Only took me three hours." She grinned as she flexed her barely-existent muscles.

"OK, dumb question," Mac conceded. "Sorry. I guess I didn't notice."

"Now, why's that, I wonder?" she quipped, crossing her arms across her chest as she nodded in the direction of her brother.

"Yeah..." Mac mumbled, looking down at his sandals, embarrassed at the discovery that his secret crush was not so secret. But he didn't resent her for saying it; Calliope carried herself with a sweetness that made it impossible to resent anything she said.

Eager to shift the conversation to anything else besides Andie and Theo, Mac asked, "So, what are you doing here?"

"Fulfilling my role as the original brother's keeper, I guess," Calliope sighed, closing her eyes as she leaned over the railing. "You know, I love him and all, but let's face it: Theo's not the most responsible guy you'll ever meet. I just wanted to make sure he brings home my father's raft in one piece. And besides," she continued, looking back at Mac, "I thought I'd do some field research for a drama production I'm in. I play a wild and adventurous sprite, so I figured, why not actually do something wild and adventurous, for once?"

"I saw one of your plays," Mac offered up hesitantly. "Well, we had to see it for class. I don't remember what it was called."

"Well, what was it about?" Calliope pressed.

"Yeah, I don't remember," Mac shrugged, too distracted by Andie and Theo to have this conversation. "I guess I'm not much of a theater person, to be honest."

Calliope looked at him curiously and then turned to the horizon as well. After a few moments of uncomfortable silence, she finally said, "So, where's your buddy?"

Mac shook his head. "When exactly did people start assuming Homer and I have achieved 'attached-at-the-hip' status?"

"Depends. When did you become his sidekick?"

"Hey! If anyone's the 'sidekick'..." But just as he started to correct her, he looked at her face, eyebrows up with the glint of a smile, and realized she was teasing him. "As a matter of fact, I *do* know where he is," he said. "He's down below somewhere, getting sea-sick."

"Awwww," Calliope stuck out her bottom lip. "Poor guy. Let's go find him."

Mac, welcoming any excuse to pry himself away from Andie and Theo (and sensing Calliope knew she was providing him with exactly that), followed her below deck. After wandering for a while through the *Æton*'s seemingly endless rooms, they finally found Homer, hunched over a chamber pot in a small, dark nook.

"Well, if it isn't our fearless mariner!" Mac announced from the doorway.

Homer lifted one eye out of the pot to glare at his visitors. "Go away!" he grunted.

"Don't feel embarrassed," Calliope said soothingly. "I used to get sea-sick, too."

"I've never been on a boat this big before," Homer moaned. "How can something this big float?"

"So you're nervous about the boat sinking?" Calliope asked.

"Now *that*'s embarrassing," Mac said. "Personally, I would have stuck with the 'sea-sick' excuse."

Calliope, meanwhile, knelt down next to Homer and started to speak to him in a soft, soothing voice that reminded Mac of his own mother. "You know, when I was a little girl, I got nervous a lot, about everything under the sun. So my favorite aunt gave me this." From around her neck, she produced a simple silver medallion, in the shape of a raindrop, with a purple stone in the middle. "She told me the stone had special powers of serenity. It was blessed by a sea-nymph, she said, and whoever carried it would feel calm and at peace. Now I don't know if I believe all of that, but I do know it works." She extended her hand and dangled the leather cord that held the medallion in front of Homer. "Do you want to wear this for the rest of the trip?"

Homer raised his head slightly and looked at Calliope with grateful, hang-dog eyes. "Maybe just for a little bit..." he whispered.

Mac watched the scene from the doorway—Calliope putting the raindrop medallion around Homer's neck, Homer complaining it wasn't working, Calliope telling him to give it a little time—before it all got a little too sickeningly sweet for him. Without a word, he snuck away and continued wandering through the caverns of the *Æton* by himself.

As Mac roamed the dark and deserted corridors below deck, he tried to imagine the ship in its heyday, during the Trojan War. He peered into an empty cabin and tried to picture what it used to hold. Weapons? Spoils? Prisoners? Then he looked at the damp boards under his feet and thought about who else once walked on those exact same planks—maybe a sailor rushing to a superior to report a storm out at sea, maybe a general pacing the hallway, mulling over a new strategy. Maybe his own father stood on this exact spot. Maybe this was the very ship that was supposed to bring him home. It was possible, wasn't it? And if he had been on this ship, *where was he now?*

These questions kept plaguing him as he descended a ladder to the next level of the ship, where he was hit with a cacophony of squawking, bleating, chirping, and shrieking. He didn't even have to look at the stalls lining the hallway to know he had found himself on the level that housed the live cargo, the sounds and smells of which immediately conjured up memories of Ithaca. But good memories, this time: as a child, Mac spent hours down at the stables, which he considered his favorite, safest place in the world—mostly because he knew the suitors would never go there.

Mac peeked into the stall to his right and saw a brown and white goat eating out of a trough. He reached in, petted it, and fed it from his hand before moving on down the hallway, past the horses, cows, and sheep. As he made his way down the hall, however, the stalls became cages, and the animals became more exotic: on his right, all manner of birds—cockatiels and eagles and peacocks; on his left, wildcats, a sleek wolf, even two monkeys, who pressed up against the wooden bars and chattered at Mac as he walked by.

Riveted by these new and unfamiliar creatures surrounding him, Mac didn't see the large wooden crate in his path until he nearly fell over it. Curious, he knelt down and peered through the net that covered the top of the box: inside, he saw grasshoppers, probably thousands of them.

Finally, he made his way to the last cage, which contained the most exotic animal of them all: a lion. Not a huge, grown-up lion, but not a baby, either. An in-between lion, all alone, lying listlessly on the floor of its cage. Never having seen a lion before, Mac crouched down, and as he did so, the creature raised its head. Slowly, it stood up and marched over to the front of the wooden cage, keeping its dark eyes on Mac the entire time. Calmly, the lion sat down, and the two of them—Mac and the beast—locked eyes for a long moment.

He didn't know how much time he spent there, watching the lion, but eventually, he sensed other eyes on him; as he gazed back down the hallway, he noticed two workers, looking at him suspiciously. Feeling suddenly self-conscious, Mac stood up and made his way down the ladder next to him, where he found himself in a dark room, illuminated only by two small portholes. Cautiously, he maneuvered to the door; on the other side, he could hear grunting and huffing—but all in sync, unlike the chaotic animal sounds of the floor above. He slowly opened up the door, to reveal the source of the grunting: fifty oarsmen—twenty-five on each side—who had been working this whole time to provide the propulsion for their voyage.

He was going to turn back, but instead, he started walking down the middle of the passageway—hesitantly, at first, until he realized none of these men were paying attention to him; they were too focused on the task at hand. As he walked down the hall, Mac marveled at the wall of men on each side of him, all working together seamlessly. Fifty men—different ages, different sizes, with different scars from different adventures—all hired for one purpose, performing as one unit, one team. Mac had never seen anything like it before.

When he reached the last of the oarsmen, he walked over to the exit. There, in the doorway, he saw a familiar face. "Hey, I've been looking for you," Andie said.

"Oh...Sorry..." Mac muttered inanely, looking back at the oarsmen, making sure not to appear excited to see her.

Andie stepped in from the doorway and surveyed the scene. "It's really something, huh?" When Mac didn't respond, she kept going. "Then again, this is probably no big deal for you, right? I mean, you've probably been on plenty of these in your day."

"No," Mac replied disdainfully. "Why would I have been on a battleship?"

"Well, because your dad's this famous war hero. I just figured he took you on—"

"Why does everyone assume my dad and I shared all these meaningful bonding experiences?" he snapped. "He's been gone my entire life, OK? I have no memories of him. No memories of him taking me on a battleship, no memories of him putting me to bed. None."

Ashamed he'd lost his cool, he stormed past Andie, through the open door and into a darkened cabin, identical to the one on the far side. He walked over to a small, solitary porthole and stared out at the vast sea, fully expecting Andie to walk away, back to her precious Theo.

Only she didn't. "You flinch, you know," she said, as she started walking over to him. "I was watching you that day at War Games. Any time your dad's name was mentioned, you flinched. Like you couldn't even stand to hear it."

Maybe her eyes did it, those deep, bottomless pools illuminated by the lone shaft of light that streaked across her face. Maybe the general darkness of the cabin made him braver, put him at ease. Or maybe the sounds of the oarsmen, thundering away in the other compartment, made him want to *connect* with someone. He didn't know why for sure, but instead of resorting to his traditional wise-ass retort, he simply answered her honestly.

"I just don't like constantly hearing about how much of a hero my dad was," Mac said, more quietly than before. "Everyone knows him as this amazing warrior. Practically a god among men. That's how people talk about him. They even built a statue of him back at school. But as a husband, a *father*…Well, no one's going to make him any statues for that."

"You don't think he's staying away intentionally, do you?" she questioned. "Don't you think it's more likely he…you know?"

Mac finished her sentence for her. "Died? In battle? You know, I could probably handle that, because then this whole thing would be over, and everyone could move on. But the problem is, he might not be dead. And no one can tell us one way or the other."

Mac picked a length of rope that had been hanging on a hook next to the porthole. Mindlessly, he started twirling and untwirling the rope around his palm as he spoke. "The war ended six years ago. Add the ten he was gone before that, that's *sixteen* years he's been away. My whole life. A long time to be sitting around, playing 'is he or isn't he,' hoping he'll magically show up on our doorstep so my mom and I can stop swatting away vultures."

"Vultures?" Andie cringed.

"Well, not actual vul—" he began, before stopping himself with a sigh. "The suitors, that's who I'm talking about."

"The what?"

Seeing the confusion on Andie's face reminded Mac that some people may not actually follow the day-to-day drama of the Ithacan palace. "When it became clear King Odysseus wouldn't be coming home any time soon, and would most likely be killed in battle, guys started showing up at our front door, declaring their intention to marry my mother," he explained. "You know, to help her out in her time of loneliness…and, oh, to become king of Ithaca in the process. Nice added benefit there. And when my mom politely declined their oh-so-gracious proposals, did these guys go back home? Of course not: they decided to wait her out. Stay put. Make themselves at home. All the while figuring, 'While we're here, why not eat all of their food? Drink all of their wine? Have wild parties every night?'"

He shook his head in disgust and muttered again, "Vultures."

"How many are we talking about? Five? Six?"

"Try over a hundred."

"A *hundred*?" Andie repeated. "A *hundred* unwanted guests living in your house? That's crazy. And it never occurred to your mother to kick them out? She *is* the Queen, right? Why didn't she just tell them to leave?"

"You don't know my mother. She would never do that. Where I come from, the way you treat your guests is everything. There are all these unwritten rules. If she breaks them, the gods get angry. The kingdom looks weak to our enemies."

"You really think other kingdoms would attack Ithaca because your mom was a bad hostess?" Andie asked.

"Who knows? But she won't risk it. My mother may hate every last one of them, but she won't ask them to leave." As Andie looked at him uncomprehendingly, Mac conceded, "Yeah, I don't get it either."

"Well, at least you two had each other," Andie offered. "I mean, at least she had you."

Mac chuckled pathetically. "Yeah, until I left for school. And even when I was home with her…What could I do? I'm too young to run the palace. Too *weak* to protect her from—" Realizing what he was about to say, he cut himself off. Fumbling for words, he finally just stammered, "I just couldn't stop them…from staying."

Mac kept occupying his hands with the rope as silence gathered in the darkened compartment. Eventually, Andie spoke: "I only had one parent, too, growing up. My mom died when I was three, so the only parent I ever knew was my dad. But that was enough for me. My dad was amazing. The guy that everyone says your dad was— that was my dad, to me. Larger-than-life. And then…well, I'm sure Homer filled you in on the details…"

"A few…"

"When I was growing up, my dad always had time for me. Always. And then, about four or five years ago, everything changed. Suddenly, everything was about his work and about Theseus and the stupid Minotaur. And I just felt…in the way, or something."

Mac watched her as she spoke, noticing how she acted differently around him than she had around Theo. No blushing. No hair-twisting. "And I heard what people were saying," she continued. "That he was crazy, that he was *obsessed*. Obsessed with the Minotaur. Obsessed with Theseus. And I tried to defend him, I really did. But it was hard, because I had built up so much resentment toward him. So, last year, when I was home on break I told him it had to stop. All this Minotaur stuff just had to stop. I said he was starting to embarrass himself. He didn't care what anyone else thought, he said. So I told him that he was embarrassing *me*."

She paused, to collect herself, and then resumed. "And not long after that, my uncle showed up at school with the news that my dad was gone. He left one night, to find this Minotaur. And no one ever saw him again. He just vanished."

"Well, maybe he'll come back," Mac suggested lamely, even though he hated it when people said things like that to him.

"Yeah, sure. Maybe he's hanging out somewhere with *your* dad. Maybe they're just biding their time, planning their homecoming parades," Andie cracked. "You won't mind, will you, if I don't hold my breath waiting for that to happen?"

"No…" Mac returned her smile, and at that moment, he felt it. Not just a connection, but something even deeper: an *access* to each other, as if a door—a giant iron door, locked with a key—had somehow opened up. He had never felt anything like that, with anyone, even his mom.

Just as he tried to figure out what to say next, Mac heard a commotion from the floor above them—first, a loud thump, followed by a sudden eruption of all the animals. Mac and Andie exchanged confused looks, when a voice shot out of the darkness.

"Master Theseus? Master Theseus! If you have a moment, I could use you!"

Mac looked around until he saw, through the opening at the top of the ladder behind them, a man's head peering down at them.

"Well, I'm not—" Mac started to inform him. But the owner of the head, clearly too distracted to listen, simply blurted out "Hurry!" before disappearing.

Still confused but also curious, Mac quickly climbed the ladder, with Andie right behind him, and found himself once again on the deck with the animals. Only now, the place was completely trans-formed. Feathers — mostly white, but some black and blue as well — were flying all around him; intermixed with the feathers, thousands of green grasshoppers darted frantically through the air. And then, there was the noise: all the squawking, bleating, chirping, and shrieking from before, only now whipped up into an ear-splitting frenzy.

"Whoa," Mac muttered, completely bewildered at the sight.

"I'll go get Theo," Andie yelled, to be heard above the din, before she continued climbing up the same ladder to the upper decks.

"Hello!" Mac called out as he walked down the hall, holding a hand over one ear and pushing feathers and grasshoppers out of the way with the other. He cringed as he heard a crunch under his feet.

"Master Theseus!" shouted a voice, barely audible over the roar. "In here!"

"Stop calling me that!" Mac yelled, though he doubted this man, whoever he was, could hear him. Mac made his way down the raucous hallway, peering into stalls; finally, in a stall about halfway down on the left, he found two men — the two workers he had seen earlier — one lying prone on the floor, another attending to him.

"What happened?" Mac shouted.

"I don't know! We noticed a ram's ear was bleeding, but when we tried to check it out, the stupid animal just started going crazy! It kicked my friend here right in the head."

As Mac knelt down, he could see a large bruise, the exact size and shape of a hoof, starting to purple up on the crewman's forehead. Mac gently tapped the man's face in an attempt to revive him; the man was breathing, but he remained motionless.

"Where's the ram?" Mac asked, as he looked around the stall.

Clearly embarrassed, the man responded, "It all happened so fast. We left the door open to check on it. After it kicked him in the head, it ran out and started smashing into all the other cages. The other animals got freaked."

"Where is it now?" Mac pressed. "The ram! Where is it?"

"It's collapsed, at the end of the hall," the man responded nervously. "It must have hit its head, or passed out, or something."

Mac returned his attention to the man on the ground, giving him a few more taps on the cheek. "Is there a doctor on board?"

"I-I don't think so, sir."

"Well, someone needs to go tell the captain!"

Mac started to get up, but the man tugged on his arm. "W-wait. Do we have to?"

"Of course, you have to. You have a man down and a wild ram on the loose."

"Please, sir," the man pleaded, still not releasing his arm. "This is only my second voyage, and I can already tell the captain's not pleased with me. Can't we just handle it, between ourselves?"

As he looked up at him with big, earnest eyes, clearly on the verge of a breakdown, Mac realized how young this guy was, maybe only a few years older than Mac himself.

Mac stood up and walked into the hallway, which was much less chaotic; the feathers were now coating the floor and the clamor had subsided to the general racket of bleats and cackles. The grasshoppers, however, were still darting all over the place, flashes of green glistening in the light that streamed in from the portholes.

Mac looked down the hall; he could see the body of a ram, lying on the floor in front of the lion's cage, wheezing in pain. "And you said the ram was bleeding from his ear?" Mac asked, as images began to flash through his mind, bits of memory from when he was nine years old: the stables in Ithaca; a stack of hay bales towering over him; Eumaeus, his favorite farm hand, milking one of the cows; a sudden, terrible sound; a cow, bleeding from its ear; a tenant farmer on the ground, downed by one of the kicks; finally, blood everywhere, as Eumaeus's spear punctured the crazed beast's side.

"Do you have any suggestions, sir?" the man begged.

"Yeah," Mac said. "First of all, what's your name?"

"Simpimedes, sir."

"OK, Simpimedes, stop with the 'sir' business. It's freaking me out. Now, as far as 'keeping it between ourselves,'" he continued, as he walked back into the stall, "that's not going to work. This guy needs help.'"

"I guess you're right," Simpimedes said, looking dejected. "Should we carry him upstairs, then?"

"Carry him? No way! He was kicked in the head. If anything, we have to keep him still." Mac thought for a moment and then looked over at the door to the empty stall. With a mighty shove, he rammed into the stall door, his broad shoulders straining, until it broke off. He carried the flat wooden board back over to Simpimedes and the injured crewman. "All right, I'm going to lift him a little bit, and you're going to slide this board under him, OK?"

After they got the board underneath the man's body, Mac continued giving orders. "Now we have to get some rope and tie him down. If he wakes up, we don't want him moving around too much. Then when you get to shore, he'll need to see a physician right away. Got it?"

"Uh, OK, yes, sir." Simpimedes said. "I mean, yes, Master Theseus."

Mac had actually forgotten the frantic crewman had originally sought out Theo, not him. He shook his head, about to correct him, but Simpimedes seemed so jittery, so haplessly distracted, he didn't want to add another detail on top of everything else. Instead, he let it go and walked back out into the hallway.

"That animal has an infection that's diseased its brain," Mac said, gesturing down the hallway to the fallen ram. "That's why its ear is bleeding. We need to slaughter it and throw the carcass overboard."

"S-s-slaughter it?"

"Trust me, I've seen this before. The ram will be dead in a matter of hours. And it won't be pretty. We'll show more mercy by killing it quickly."

"I-I-I've never k-killed…I don't th-think I c-can…"

Realizing that the flustered deckhand was not up to the task, Mac reached over and pulled a small dagger from Simpimedes's belt.

"I'll take care of it," Mac sighed.

Clearly relieved, Simpimedes began to calm down. "What should I do?"

"You'll need to take all the animals that were in the stalls closest to the ram and quarantine them in the back of the ship. Otherwise you may lose all the livestock to the disease. I can't promise you they're not infected already."

"OK, OK, got it," Simpimedes said, holding his hands up to the sides of his head, as if he was trying to keep everything he'd just heard from falling out. "Uh…how should I do that?"

"How about you go get some of the crew to help you?" Mac suggested slowly.

"Right!" Simpimedes exclaimed as he took off down the hallway.

"And don't forget the rope!" Mac called out. "And maybe some clean water! To clean up the gash on his head." From the end of the hallway, Simpimedes gave a thumbs-up before climbing up the ladder, leaving Mac alone with the animals.

He walked slowly down the hall, past the peacocks and the wolf and shrieking monkeys. He saw the empty crate that had once housed the grasshoppers, a hoof-sized hole in the top netting. Finally, he reached the body of the ram, collapsed in front of the lion. It had fallen on its right side, so Mac could only see the left side of its face; one eye open wide but devoid of expression. Blood was still trickling out its ear, and Mac could see feathers sticking to the crimson trail tracing its way down its neck. Except for its labored wheezing, the animal could have been dead already.

Resigned to what he had to do, Mac knelt down and stroked the ram a few times on the side of his head, making sure to avoid the bloody ear. "Look," he began hesitantly. "I'm really sorry about this, but you have to trust me. You'll be much better off if we get this over with." Then he glanced over his left shoulder: the lion had moved right up to the front of the cage, judging Mac with his stare.

"Don't look at me like that," Mac murmured, right before he quickly and neatly slit the ram's throat in a wide arc, from ear to ear.

He shuddered as he felt the life drain out of the animal, its blood staining the ground. Staying put until the ram drew its last shaky breath, Mac quickly backed away and returned to the downed man, whose eyes had started to open. It was this sight, Mac kneeling over an unconscious member of the crew, his hands red with blood, that greeted Theo and Andie as they made their way down the hallway of the cargo deck.

"What in Hades!"

In a rush, Mac reported what happened. "He was kicked in the head by a wild ram." Noticing Theo's eyes darting from the injured man to his bloodstained hands, Mac explained, "It was a mercy killing." Then he quickly added, "The ram, not the guy."

"Oh, crap," Theo moaned. "Well, what should we do?"

Mac was about to tell him he had pretty much taken care of everything, when he heard footsteps skittering across the deck. "Master Theseus!" Simpimedes panted, carrying rope and a bucket of water. "Some men are coming to help with the quarantine, just like you ordered!"

"Who are you?" Theo asked. "What's going on?"

"No need to worry, sir," Simpimedes assured him. "Master Theseus and I are taking care of everything." As if to punctuate his words, Simpimedes threw an arm around Mac's shoulder.

Theo could barely stifle a laugh. "Master Theseus? You mean *him*?" Theo questioned, pointing his thumb at a cringing Mac. "You got it wrong, dude. *I'm* Theseus. Me."

Mac looked at Theo, Andie, and Simpimedes—all of whom, it seemed, believed he was *pretending* to be someone else. "I—I didn't..." he stuttered.

"You know what? Simple mistake. Who cares?" Theo said. "Men are coming to help? Good idea. Here, show me which animals need to be quarantined."

As Theo and Simpimedes moved toward the stalls, a dejected Mac scrubbed his hands in the bucket of water Simpimedes had brought with him. He wiped his hands on the front of his tunic and then looked over at Andie, who hadn't said a word. Suddenly, all the anger and inadequacy Mac had felt earlier in the day, when he saw her flirting with Theo on the upper deck, flared up all over again.

"I don't know why you had to get *him* involved," he spat.

"His dad owns the ship," Andie answered defensively.

"You know, I had everything under control."

Andie looked at Mac as if she didn't recognize him. "Who's

saying you didn't?"

Mac looked at Andie, but all he could see was disappointment in her eyes. He may as well have been looking at his mother, Asirites, Gurgus...even the statue of his father.

"I see you're picking up right where your father left off," Mac said.

"What's that supposed to mean?"

"An obsession with *Theseus*."

Andie's face registered surprise at first, then indignation, then anger. But Mac's remained a stony mask as he flew down the hall to the dead ram. He didn't even look back at her as he climbed over the bloodied carcass, grabbed hold of the ladder behind it, and yanked himself up to the upper deck.

And that giant iron door? Slammed shut.

CHAPTER TEN

The Tale of Marsyas

Mac could tell Homer had been waiting for this moment his entire life. Everything had fallen into place. First, he had a captive audience, literally: now that the five had exchanged the vastness of the *Æton* for the close confines of a raft, what else could they really do but listen to him? Next, he had the atmosphere: the setting sun, the sounds of the muddy water slapping against the sides of the vessel, the flickering light from the six lanterns that hung from the skiff's railings. And, most importantly, he had the material: the gory tale of a half-man/half-goat getting skinned alive. All the necessary ingredients for Story-Time with Homer.

"Marsyas couldn't believe his luck," he began. "Here he is, an ordinary satyr, just strolling around the riverbank, when he sees something sticking out of the mud. So he bends down and discovers it was a flute. Except this was no ordinary flute: this flute had *two* pipes."

The group had disembarked from the *Æton* two hours earlier, when they reached the mouth of the Maeander River. At that point, they boarded a much smaller flat-bottomed boat with a pointed bow and a low railing. They planned to sail through the night, until they reached the Marsyas River, which—according to Homer's map—would take them to their final destination: the hermit who supposedly owned the flute of Marsyas.

"So Marsyas figures—hey, free flute," Homer continued. "Bonus! But when he starts playing it, he—"

"He doesn't even wash it off first?" Theo interrupted.

"What?" a clearly annoyed Homer asked.

"I'm just saying, he puts this random flute in his mouth? Pretty gross, dude."

"OK, so he washes it off in the river," he said slowly, emphatically, while glaring daggers at Theo. "And then he starts playing this absolutely beautiful music, like nothing he had ever heard before—like nothing *anyone* had ever heard before. And he realizes that, because the flute had two pipes, it could produce two melodies at the same time."

"Musical multi-tasking," Theo chirped, glancing over at Andie. "Cool!"

"Now, the satyr didn't realize it at the time, but this flute was actually invented by none other than Athena herself. She named it the aulos, and she played it all the time, filling the halls of Olympus with its beautiful music. And then one day, she noticed the other goddesses giggling whenever she came into the room. She couldn't figure out why until one day she looked down in a reflecting pool; playing the flute made her cheeks puff out, spoiling her beauty." Homer puffed up his own cheeks as a visual aid.

"In a fit of vanity, Athena threw her invention to earth, never to see it again. Of course, Marsyas didn't care how the aulos made him look; he just loved the sound of it. He loved it so much he couldn't stop playing it. In fact, he played it so often, and so well, he eventually caught the attention of the god of music himself, Apollo, who came around in search of the virtuoso creating this symphony. Unfortunately, as Marsyas's skills with the aulos increased, so did his *awareness* of those skills. He became brash, over-confident—to the point that he actually *challenged* Apollo to a contest."

To underscore the drama, Homer jumped to his left: "Marsyas and his aulos…"

Then to his right: "…against Apollo and his lyre. At stake? The winner could do whatever he wanted to the loser."

"This can't end well for our guy," Theo chimed in.

"Now, Apollo was pretty confident himself—he *is* the god of music, after all—but still, he wasn't going to allow for even the slightest chance that this satyr, this *nobody*, could upstage him. So, Apollo gets his pals the Muses to judge the contest. Well, that's the deal-breaker for poor Marsyas: he did his best, but of course, the Muses awarded the contest to Apollo. And just as Marsyas started trudging away in shame, Apollo stopped him. 'Uh-uh,' he said.

'Remember our agreement that the winner could do whatever he wanted to the loser. So, let's see, here.'"

Homer put his finger to his chin, as if pantomiming contemplation. "'What would be a suitable punishment for a brash satyr who presumed he could beat a god at his own game?'" Homer said, affecting the voice of Apollo. "'Well, I suppose I could ask Zeus to incinerate you. Or I could flay you alive. Or I could show mercy and let you go, knowing that your shame is punishment enough.'" Then he paused, looked up to the sky, and announced, "'You know what? I think I'll go with the flaying alive idea!'

"And that's what he did," Homer continued, back to his own voice. "Sliced all of Marsyas's skin right off his body and nailed it to a tree." Theo slapped his thigh and laughed ghoulishly while Calliope and Andie groaned. "And the blood that flowed from his skinless body formed the river that now bears his name, the Marsyas River."

Homer paused to catch his breath for the big finish: "Now, we'll actually be traveling on the Marsyas River in a little bit. It branches off from the Maeander way up ahead; that's how we're going to get to Kalakloptas, the hermit who owns the aulos—yes, the very aulos that caused this mess in the first place. And when we do turn onto the river, I want you to keep your ears open, because some say that, on certain nights, if you listen closely, you can hear a low moaning coming from the currents. You might think that it's some sort of weird fish or bird or something, but it's not: it's actually the voice of Marsyas himself, crying for forgiveness, for the rest of eternity"

"*Epic!*" Theo shouted, putting down his oar to applaud Homer. Calliope joined in, as did Andie. Only Mac, from the back of the boat, seemed unimpressed. "Yeah, I'm sure..." he muttered, after the applause subsided.

"What?" Homer asked him.

"So, an entire river was formed from the blood of a single goat-boy—yeah, I'm sure it happened *just* like that," Mac cracked.

"Actually, I heard another version of the story," Calliope offered. "The river was formed not by the blood of Marsyas but by the tears of the nymphs and goddesses mourning his death."

"Well, that makes *much* more sense," Mac retorted.

"Well, it just shows how something good, like a river, can come out of something bad…" Calliope explained.

"Or maybe it's just supposed to be fun, OK?" Andie glared at Mac. "What's your problem?"

"No problem," Mac sniffed. "I'm just not that big on 'stories,' I guess."

He used to be. In fact, memories of his mom telling him bedtime fables still stuck out to him as his happiest from childhood. But a lifetime of suffering through the interminable stories about his dad, not to mention the vulgar tales the suitors roared from the courtyard, had pretty much soured him on the magic of the oral tradition. "What's the point, really?"

With that, the conversation died, and for a stretch of time, a pronounced silence hijacked the raft. Mac knew his grumpiness was the cause, but he couldn't help himself. Andie hadn't spoken to him, or even looked at him, since the incident below deck with the ram, when he made that "obsession with Theseus" crack. The tension festered, and he couldn't muster up the enthusiasm that came so easily to the others. He was acting like a jerk and he knew it…and now the five of them were sitting in silence because of it.

Until their guests arrived, that is.

They heard it first—a hullabaloo of yelling and hollering from way off in the darkening distance. Only when their raft drifted closer could they identify the source of the commotion: an angry mob of about twenty people, amassed on the banks of the river—some of them wielding torches, all of them hurling fruit into the river. Their target: two men—decked out in frilly, multicolored cloaks—trying to make their escape in what appeared to be an over-sized woven basket. The garish duo were frantically trying to put some distance between themselves and the mob, while at the same time scoop water out of their makeshift vessel and avoid getting pelted by the onslaught of flying fruit—and failing miserably at all three tasks.

Mac had a bad feeling about the whole scene as soon as they

floated into view. "Just go by," he insisted. And they could have, too; the river was definitely wide enough for them to circumvent the situation completely. But the tragically absurd sight of the two costumed men, flailing around in their rapidly sinking fruit basket, shouting their desperate, heartfelt entreaties ("Help! Help! They're trying to kill us!"), obviously got to Theo.

"All right, let's go," Theo sighed, as he began paddling in the direction of the two men.

"This is a mistake," Mac warned.

Theo looked back and answered simply, "They might drown, dude." Then he shouted out to the pair, "You guys need some help?"

"Thank Olympus!" one of the two men cried, as they bobbed toward their rescuers. Meanwhile, as the raft drifted closer to the imperiled men, the folks on shore recognized the teens as a new enemy and started hurling fruit at them as well.

Mac, trying to protect his head from the onslaught of flying food, moved up behind Theo and said, "I'm telling you, this is a bad idea."

"And I'm telling you to chill out, xenophobe," Theo said. "*My* raft, OK? I'm the one calling the shots."

Mac slunk back to his seat and watched the scene unfold: the two men leaping from their just-about sunken basket onto the skiff, one of them making it, the other slamming against the railing, falling back into the muddy water, and splashing around until Theo and Andie hauled his thick, heavy body on board. Mac, meanwhile, remained seated for the whole process—making him an easy target for an incoming peach that splattered against his right temple.

"Let's go, hey!" shouted one of their new passengers as he threw himself face-down on the floor of the raft. "Hurry! Get us out of here!" Theo and Andie rushed back to their positions and started rowing fiercely away from the angry mob on the riverbank; only when the ferocious hollering faded into a dull and distant roar did it seem safe enough to slow down.

Mac was still wiping peach pulp from his face as he examined their new arrivals, hunched over and panting in the middle of the raft. One of them, the chunky one that Andie and Theo had pulled from the water, had thick shoulders, thick arms and legs, thick red hair—and a lot of it, too, covering his face, his chest, even his fingers. In fact, seemingly the only hairless place on his entire body was the top of his thick, round head—a fact that he tried to conceal with a tall, floppy hat, which he was now wringing out over the side of the skiff.

In contrast, the other gentleman was taller and more waifish, with long, skinny legs that stretched just about the entire width of the raft. He was burying his face in his bony hands, so Mac could only see his mass of chaotic brown hair at first; when he finally lifted his head, Mac saw his face—long and gaunt, with a serpentine moustache outlining his caved-in cheeks. And to complete the package: a metal patch, encrusted with five red jewels, covering his right eye.

The two men, who couldn't have looked any more different in appearance, seemed to share only one thing in common: an appreciation for outrageous clothing. Both of them wore ragged, oversized cloaks, obviously patched together with stray, multicolored pieces of cloth. From their long sleeves hung a series of tassels, also of various colors. The skinnier one wrapped his cloak around him tightly, but the thicker one wore his wide open, exposing a plump, hairy stomach which plopped over his loincloth.

"Whew!" the hairy guy finally exhaled. "I can't believe you guys came when you did! You really saved our necks back there!"

"What happened?" Theo asked. "Why were those people throwing food at you?"

"I have no idea!" Eyepatch Guy answered. "We were just doing our thing, putting on our little show for them, and next thing we know, they turned on us!"

"'Little show?'" Calliope inquired. "Are you two actors?"

"Well, not successful ones, apparently," Hairy Guy admitted. "Performing is just something we've been doing since we got home from the war."

That got Homer's attention. "Did you say—?"

"Well, look at us: you guys saved our lives, and we don't even have the decency to introduce ourselves," Eyepatch said, standing up. "My name is Basileus, and this clumsy oaf is my younger brother Blasios. And who might you fine folks be?"

They all introduced themselves—except, of course, for Mac, who had no intention of telling these two his name. Something about these men—a slickness, a corny polish—reminded him of the suitors when they first arrived. So, when it came his turn for introductions, he simply smiled and said, very politely, "Oh, I'm nobody."

Basileus peered at him inquisitively with his one eye until he finally smiled back. "OK, well...nice to meet you, Nobody."

Theo shook his head at Mac's continued rudeness, but Homer didn't even notice. "Excuse me," he squeaked. "Before, when you mentioned 'the war,' you didn't mean the *Trojan* War?"

"Sure!" Blasios roared. "What other war would we mean, by-gods?"

Basileus, seeing the starstruck look on Homer's face, sat up and grinned. "Fan of the big war, are you, son?" When Homer nodded in speechless awe, Basileus proclaimed, "Well, do we have stories for you!"

CHAPTER ELEVEN
The Tale of Bromeliss

And with that, they were off. Basileus and Blasios launched into a seemingly endless series of war stories, which inspired different reactions from their audience members: Theo was totally into it, cheering and hooting and inserting zingers of his own; Calliope listened politely; Andie was focused on rowing the raft, but showed she was still paying attention by smiling when appropriate; Mac was completely disinterested; and Homer…he just sat there, mouth half-open, hanging on the bards' every word in stunned, mesmerized silence. These were actual warriors, after all. Clearly, *this* was the greatest moment of his life.

"But, I'm confused," Andie interjected at one point. "If you're fighters, why are you dressed up like that?"

The two brothers looked at their garish costumes and then at each other. "Well, that's a whole other story," Blasios shrugged.

"A *long* whole other story," Basileus added. He paused, glanced with his non-patched eye at his brother, and then said to his audience, "What do you think? Got time?"

"Basileus…" Blasios said sternly, leaning forward and glaring. "I don't think —"

"It's all right," his brother assured him. "These are good folks. We can trust them." Basileus got up on one knee, and began: "The first thing you need to know is that Blasios and I had a younger brother named Bromeliss. Growing up, he was quite a handful. Rowdy. Mouthy. Always pulling some kind of crazy stunt. We loved him, Blasios and me, but he was a punk."

"He was a punk, but we loved him," Blasios echoed, lost in his reminiscence.

"Now, Bromeliss rubbed a lot of people the wrong way, but this one old guy in our village *really* couldn't stand him. Kraikos, his name was, but we called him Crater Face."

"Sun-burned, like a wrinkled-up grape," Blasios explained.

"Everything about him was terrible," continued Basileus, without missing a beat. "Very crabby, *very* crotchety, very...*crater-y*. He hated everyone, but he really had it out for Bromeliss, always ratting him out to our father for something or other. I tell ya, the whippings that kid endured...Well, one day, when Bromeliss was, like, twelve, Crater Face accuses our brother of...oh, I don't even remember. Letting a bunch of sheep out of a pen or something? Whatever it was, Bromeliss didn't do it. He did a lot of stupid stuff in his day, but he didn't do *this*. Unfortunately, our dad didn't believe him. So, as our old man started raining down these wicked blows on him, Bromeliss decides he's going to get his revenge on Crater Face."

Blasios suddenly stood up, rocking the raft as he took over. "Now, something to keep in mind about our brother Bromeliss—is that he loved bees. A master beekeeper, that kid—by-gods, it was almost as if he could control them or something. So, one night, Bromeliss took two small beehives, snuck into Crater Face's house, and very carefully sewed the two hives into the lining of Crater Face's tunic."

"That kid, I tell ya..." Basileus smiled reverently.

"So, the next morning," Blasios continued, "Bromeliss is hiding outside Crater Face's house, and he's waiting for him to wake up. And he's waiting. And waiting. Until, suddenly, he hears this absolutely blood-curdling scream, like nothing he ever heard in his life, as twenty to thirty bees stung Crater Face Kraikos all over—chest, legs, and..." Glancing quickly at the girls, he censored himself, "*ahem*...other places where you just don't want to be stung!"

The boys squirmed uncomfortably, sympathetic to the old man's plight, as Theo leaned over to Mac. "Now *that's* a prank," he marveled.

"Unfortunately," Basileus broke in, "right after he let out that scream, the old bastard keeled over and died, right then and there."

Calliope gasped. "He killed Crater Face?"

"He didn't mean to," answered Blasios. "Thing is, though, he didn't even feel that bad about it. He was still so angry at Crater Face for ratting him out for something he didn't do. If he felt bad about anything, it's that the old crank died before he had a chance to torment him some more."

Basileus picked up the story once again. "The crazy thing is, he didn't get punished. No one wanted to mess with someone who would go to such lengths for revenge. And from that fear came *respect*. Even our dad put away the belt after Crater Face died."

"So where's your brother now?" Theo asked.

The two paused, exchanging sad glances, until Blasios finally said, "Well, amazingly, Bromeliss eventually grew up into a fine young man. We all fought in the war—three brothers, side-by-side-by-side—until one terrible day, while rescuing some of his fellow warriors who were captured, Bromeliss was shot in the neck by an arrow." He paused and gazed up at the night sky. "This hoodlum, this punk…he got a hero's funeral. We cried so hard that day."

"I thought about him all the time," Basileus sniffed. "Wishing I could see him again. Until one night, after the war was over…." He leaned into his audience. "He came to me."

"He *came* to you?" Andie questioned.

"His shade, yes. His spirit," Basileus clarified. "He appeared to me. To us. Told us that he had been wandering the earth for the past four years, tormented by Charon."

"Charon?" Theo asked. "The creepy Underworld guy?"

"Yes, the 'creepy Underworld guy.' The ferryman who rides the River Styx, taking coins from souls and shuttling them past the gates of Hades," Blasios confirmed. "Except he wasn't going to be shuttling the soul of Bromeliss. Our brother wasn't allowed to go through."

"Why?" demanded Homer.

"Because," Basileus explained slowly, "Bromeliss didn't know when to quit. That night, the night he appeared to us, he told us something we never knew, about one last trick he had played on Crater Face, on the day of the old man's funeral. They were preparing the pyre, and Bromeliss managed to slip another beehive under Crater Face's burial robe. So when Crater Face showed up at the River Acheron with a bunch of bees swarming around him, he wasn't exactly Charon's favorite passenger. But he doesn't get mad, Charon. That's not his style. Instead, when Bromeliss himself showed up, years later, coin in hand, wanting to get on the ferry, Charon gave him a cold stare, poked him with his pole, and said, 'Not for you, son.'"

Apparently unable to stay silent for too long, Blasios jumped back in. "Because he showed so little respect for the realm of the dead, our brother's soul had to roam the earth. But worse than that, Charon cursed Bromeliss with a pursuer—a single bee, to follow him wherever he went, constantly buzzing in his ear. It darn near drove him crazy."

Basileus put his hand on Homer's shoulder and looked down on him with his one sad eye: "So here's our once-proud brother, four years after his hero's funeral, reduced to a tormented, begging, body-less mess. 'You gotta help me!' he pleaded. 'You gotta go to Charon and talk some sense into him!' It was the most frightening thing I'd ever been asked to do…but what choice did we have? He was our brother. We couldn't abandon him. So, with his guidance, we made our way to the Underworld's entrance. Instantly, piercing screams assaulted our ears—from Ixion, spinning on his wheel; from Tityos, stretched out over nine acres; from all those ordinary suffering souls. Covering our ears, we made our way down the Acheron—dark and swampy, like this river we're on right now—until we spotted him, standing on the riverbank."

Blasios barely spoke above a whisper. "Charon himself. Raggedy brown cloak, sunken cheeks, haggard beard, empty blue-grey eyes— just as we pictured him in our nightmares. Our plan was to choke him and demand he release our brother from his curse. Instead, we dropped to our knees and said, 'Please, Great Charon, let our penitent brother complete his journey!'"

"For an eternity, it seemed," continued Basileus, "Charon burned a hole into us with those haunting eyes of his until he finally agreed to let Bromeliss into Hades."

"Except it was going to cost us," said Blasios.

Basileus affected a deep voice: "'Fetch me the Coin of Aulocrene,' Charon ordered. 'Once you do, I'll let your brother pass.'"

"Coin of Aulocrene?" Blasios continued. "We had no idea what that even *was*. But we couldn't let Bromeliss down. So, for the past two years, we've searched the world for this thing. Finally got a solid lead: the Coin was owned by a farmer named Karpos who lived in a tiny village back there on the Maeander River."

"You know, we're warriors," explained Basileus. "We go into places and take what we want. But our experience with Charon taught us *respect*. So instead of storming into the village with swords-a-waving, we introduced ourselves to this man Karpos and ex-plained our situation. 'Please, sir,' we said. 'Can we have this coin? We'll gladly pay you anything you want.' And would you believe the man didn't even hesitate? Just handed it over. He was so taken by our brotherly devotion, he wanted to help us."

"You didn't have to pay him?" Calliope asked.

"We wanted to," Blasios told her. "We would have paid him anything, by-gods, but he refused. So we decided we'd put on a little performance for his village. Like we said earlier, we've been doing a little act since the war got out—telling jokes, singing. That kind of thing."

"Everything was going fine," Basileus continued, "until about half-way through the performance, when I thanked Karpos publicly for giving us the Coin. And then, all of a sudden, people started rushing the stage. Seems the villagers were interested in keeping that Coin for themselves. We had to bolt out of there as fast as we could."

"We just started booking it, with all of them right behind, screaming all sorts of filthy obscenities at us. Finally, we got to the river, and we saw some fruit baskets. So we jumped in one and tried to sail out of there. And then…well, here we are."

"So do you still have the Coin?" Calliope asked.

"Right here," Blasios said, patting the leather pouch hanging from his shoulder.

"And now you're going to take it to Charon?" Homer asked.

"Well, that's the plan," Basileus said, "and free our dear brother from his earthly prison."

For a few moments, the kids sat in expectant silence, until Blasios signaled the end of their tale with a noisy yawn. Worn out from the telling, the two brothers convinced Theo to drop anchor for a few hours of shut-eye, promising to take a turn with the oars as soon as they were rested. One by one, the kids drifted off to sleep, lulled by the rhythmic rocking of the raft. Everyone slept, but Mac, who sat vigil at the prow of the boat, his legs dangling over the side, feet swinging over the murky water. He couldn't put his finger on it, but he didn't feel comfortable falling asleep—letting his guard down—with these strangers so close by. He mulled over the details of their story, preoccupied by the parts that didn't quite add up.

Not yet able to give voice to his suspicions, his thoughts turned to Andie, and how badly he had blown it earlier that day. As if conjuring her with his thoughts, a soft whisper broke the still of the night.

"When I admitted that I liked Theo…I was telling you that as a friend."

Mac cringed as he turned toward the voice, expecting to find a furious Andie. Instead her gaze was steady but questioning as she sat down beside him.

"I know," he mumbled. "I'm sorry."

"So, are you going to tell me what pissed you off so much?"

How could he explain it to her? How could he describe how good it felt to take charge of things back on the *Æton*? How he had never done anything like that before. Never thought he could. Who would have shown him, after all?

"I guess I just felt stupid…and embarrassed," he whispered.

"Why?"

"I know how it looked. I wasn't *trying* to be Theo. The guy was just so stressed out. It seemed easier to go along with—just forget it, you wouldn't understand."

Keeping her gazed fixed on the distant riverbank, Andie shifted her weight until their shoulders were lightly touching.

"Maybe I *would* understand. Maybe I know a little bit about pretending."

"Pretending what?" Mac asked shakily, affected by her nearness.

"That my father didn't—" she choked back the words. "That things are different than…than the way they are."

Mac understood. He turned to face her, not sure what he would say, but wanting to comfort her somehow. He held his breath a little as she slowly raised her eyes to meet his.

A sudden, high-pitched yawn broke the moment. "How long have we been sleeping?" Theo asked loudly, stretching his arms high over his head. "We better get cracking if we're going to stay on schedule. Wake up, everyone! Time waits for nobody!"

One by one, the sleepy crew rose to pull up anchor and resume the journey. Mac offered to row, but Theo and Andie said they'd keep going; Mac couldn't help but notice the two brothers didn't take their turn with the oars as promised. Mac returned to the back of the raft. Frustrated that his moment with Andie was interrupted and angry at the rudeness of their new passengers, he decided it was time to find out what was really going on.

"That was an incredible story you told before," Mac began, his soft voice carrying from the back. "You really had me on the edge of my seat there."

"Well, thank you, son," Basileus smiled. "What can we say? It's all true."

"And you told it so well," Mac praised. "The way you'd help each other out, build on what the other one was saying...I guess it's like you said, that brotherly bond, right?"

"People have always said: 'two boys, one mind,'" Basileus beamed.

"I'm an only child, see," Mac shared, "so I don't have that kind of relationship with anyone. It's funny, though. You don't really *look* like brothers."

Basileus chuckled, "We get that a lot. I guess I take after our mother, and Blasios here takes after our dad...which I'm glad about, since Pop was uglier than a Thracian camel spider."

The two chortled at Basileus's zinger, like brothers do. Mac smiled, too, before asking, "Well, it's not just the looks, actually. You talk differently, too. You see, at my house, we get a lot of visitors, from all over Greece. It almost sounds like you have different accents or something. Did you two grow up together?" he asked.

"Of course!" Blasios barked, obviously offended by this interrogation. "We grew up in a loving home with our brother. Three closer brothers you could never find."

"Look, we've traveled all over the world, the two of us," Basileus reminded him. "Ten years fighting in the war. Two years looking for this crazy coin. Is it possible we picked up some different speech patterns along the way? I suppose so."

"Oh, right…" nodded Mac. He glanced over at Andie, whose eyes were telling him to knock it off, that this line of questioning was rude even by *his* standards. "Hey, I'm sorry. I hope I didn't insult you," Mac begged off. "I just wanted to say I enjoyed your story. Me, I'm not so good at storytelling, but I think I learned a few things from watching you two. You both know how to make the story come alive. For example, Basileus: you know what I noticed most about you? Your hands. You use your hands a lot when you speak."

Basileus grinned inquisitively. "I do?" he asked, scanning his hands with his one eye.

"Oh, sure," Mac confirmed, as he stood up and leaned against the railing. "I couldn't help but notice your hands as you told your story. And I was struck by how well-preserved they seem. I mean, you'd think warriors who'd been through so much would have some calloused, beat-up hands, but your hands are completely smooth, like they've never known manual labor of any kind."

Basileus's grin sank into a snarl as Mac turned to Blasios: "And you. While watching you, I was totally reminded of something they're always harping on in our Orations classes: the importance of *eye contact*. See, a lot of folks, when they speak, they just look straight ahead or focus on one thing. But you didn't do that: you let your eyes skim over the entire raft. You saw everything…including, say, that little pouch that Theo's wearing on his belt."

Theo instinctively put his right hand over the pouch. Homer, Andie, and Calliope sat as still as corpses. Mac, meanwhile, kept going: "Maybe it has money in it, that pouch, maybe it doesn't. But you definitely plan on finding out, right?"

Basileus and Blasios didn't offer up any more denials; instead, they just smiled, as if proud of this young kid for his detective work. Mac smirked right back at them: "You're not brothers, are you?" He looked right across the raft now, right into Basileus's one eye, as if they were the only two people in the entire world.

"Nope," Basileus admitted, shaking his head.

"And if you two aren't brothers," Mac deduced, "then logically, the third brother…"

"Nope," Basileus responded, still smiling.

"And that whole story, about the bees and the dead brother and the coin…that's just something you tell, right? You've probably told it a hundred times before."

"Some of it, yeah," Basileus conceded, "but the part about the one bee pursuing him was something new I added."

"Actually, I was going to tell you," Blasios said to him, "I liked that detail a lot."

"Hey, thanks, brother. Personally, if I were hearing the story for the first time, a detail like that one bee would have made me a believer. But not ol' 'Nobody' over here. He's too smart for that. And that's too bad, really. See, I would have been completely content with just tagging along for as long as we could and then splitting with all of your money as you slept or something. That would have been fine. But now—"

In that instant, he grabbed Homer with one of his bony hands. With the other, he produced a dagger, which he held to Homer's throat.

"Now," Basileus finished, shielding himself with his new hostage, "we're going to have to do things differently."

CHAPTER TWELVE
The Tale of Dynamene

Everything happened all at once—Homer froze; Blasios produced his own dagger; Theo hunched over Calliope; Mac jumped in front of Andie, but she shot up to her feet and muscled her way forward, so they were standing side-by-side.

"Now, everybody listen real good, because we're going to need a little bit more from all of you," Basileus hissed quietly. "My friend Blasios is going to open this sack, and you're going to put in everything you have. Money, jewels, weapons—everything. If you cooperate, no one gets hurt. But if you try anything funny..." He pressed the dagger to Homer's throat as he threatened, "Well, you'll put me in the regrettable position of having to remove your friend's head from his body."

Even with a dagger at his throat, Homer was the first to respond. "H-hey, you two don't have to do this," Homer stammered. "You fought in a war. You're better than this."

"Homer..." Theo groaned, shaking his head in disbelief.

"Honestly, guys, y-you don't realize who this is," Homer babbled. "It's Telemachus. The son of Odysseus, your comrade-in-arms."

Inside his head, Mac was reaching out, grabbing Homer by the throat—the very throat Basileus was threatening to slash—and throttling him. *What is wrong with you?* he was shouting. *Why are you giving these thugs that information?* But that was on the inside; on the outside, his face remained emotionless as stone.

As it turned out, he didn't need to worry. Basileus took one disbelieving look at Mac and said derisively, "This kid? Yeah, right."

Later on, after he had time to process the whole incident, Mac identified that one comment—*That kid? Yeah, right*—as the *moment,* the turning point. He couldn't say why, exactly. Why did he care if these two frauds didn't believe he was the son of Odysseus? Most of the time, he didn't even want to acknowledge it himself. And yet, as he stood on that raft, Andie right next to him, and listened to Basileus dismiss him with those four scornful words...he made a pact with himself. He would get them out of this jam. Maybe he couldn't protect his mother back in Ithaca, but he'd protect his friends, right now, on this raft.

Meanwhile, Homer kept appealing to his captors' sense of honor. "But you fought alongside Odysseus. You *fought* with him," he cried. "Don't you see the resemblance?"

"Homer, you're an idiot!" Theo snapped. "They're *lying*! They didn't fight in any stupid Trojan War!"

"Not true, actually," Blasios corrected him. "That's where we met. And we *did* fight in the war...for about fifteen days. Then we said, 'Why are we risking our lives with this crap?'"

"You're...*deserters*?" As Homer spit out the word, the confusion in his voice gave way to disgust, as if this realization somehow cut him worse than the blade at his throat ever could.

"Not deserters, kid...survivors," Basileus smiled wickedly, before turning to his partner, who had just finished collecting the valuables from the hostages. "OK, what you got so far?"

"Not much," he complained, as he fished through the confines of the pouch with his stubby fingers.

"All right, we'll take the raft. That's gotta be worth something." Then he glanced down at the medallion around Homer's neck, the one Calliope had given him on the *Æton*. "And this too." With the hand not holding the dagger, Basileus yanked the cord from his neck. When he did so, he heard a sound—a quick, almost inaudible intake of air—from the other side of the raft.

"What?" Basileus demanded, looking directly at Mac.

"What...nothing?" he answered, deliberately not meeting Basileus's gaze.

"You think you're the only one who studies human moves? Why'd you gasp when I took this medallion?"

"Why would I gasp over a stupid medallion?"

"I don't know, but you did!" He pulled Homer closer to him.

"And I wanna know why. What's so special about it?" When no one answered, he asked again, more emphatically, "I said, what's so damn special about this medallion?"

"Nothing's 'special' about it!" Calliope insisted. "It's just something I gave him to help with his sea-sickness!"

"Yeah, so if you don't want him throwing up on your feet, I suggest you give it back to him," Mac said snidely. "You're taking everything else. Can't you leave that?"

Basileus moved his eye from Homer, still frozen under the dagger in his right hand, then back to the medallion in his left. "You guys are terrible liars, you know that? I *know* lying, and you guys stink at it. So now you're going to tell me the truth," he snarled. "Why you don't want us to have this medallion?"

Obviously, no one knew what to say, since they had already told him the truth, but their silence only enraged Basileus further. "Tell me!" he screeched. "Or I swear to Hades, this kid won't have a neck to hang this on!"

From the fiery look in his one eye, Mac could tell Basileus wasn't kidding around; even Blasios seemed scared of him. It was time to set his plan into action. Putting on a defeated face, Mac blurted out, "Fine! I'll tell you! It's blessed by the gods."

"Oh, you're going to have to do better than that," Basileus growled.

"No, I don't," Mac replied simply, staring Basileus down from across the boat. At that point, Mac knew he had him: Basileus had a knife, he had a hostage, he had their possessions. But Mac still had the upper hand. He knew it, and Basileus, it seemed, knew it, too.

"Start making sense," the one-eyed thief hissed through gritted teeth, as he brought his blade even closer to Homer's neck.

Mac stepped out from the shadow, took a deep breath, and launched into his story:

Once there was a lonely fisherman named Lysandros, who was so good at his job, he could catch fish with his bare hands. One day, as he was sailing to shore, he saw a beautiful woman, the most beautiful he had ever seen, bathing in a pool. Except this wasn't a normal woman, but a sea goddess, named Dynamene.

She was a Nereid, one of the fifty daughters of Nereus, and like her father, she was a shape-shifter. So when she saw Lysandros approaching, she dove into the water and turned into a fish. But Lysandros jumped into the river after her, and as she tried to swim away, he grabbed her with his mighty hands. Dynamene kept changing her shape – from a fish to an eel to finally a red ibis. And while she was in the bird's form, Lysandros pulled out one of her tail feathers. With that, she changed from a bird into a woman.

"Please, noble fisherman," she pleaded, "return that feather, which is a part of me. I cannot return to my sea-home unless I am whole. I am a goddess; I can grant you any wish you want, if you will only return that feather."

Without even thinking, the lonely Lysandros blurted out the only thing he ever wanted: "Be my bride," he said. Dynamene begged him to reconsider – all the riches of the world, she said, could be his – but Lysandros would not be dissuaded. Realizing she had no choice, Dynamene returned with the fisherman to his village. They married that very day.

Lysandros adored his new wife and would do anything for her – except return to her the feather, which he kept locked in a strongbox. Despite his broken promise, Dynamene adjusted to life on land and even learned to love it. She learned to love her husband as well. Eventually she bore him a son...named Simpimedes.

He said that name for Andie's benefit, as a signal to her that he had a plan. When he glanced in her direction, she nodded slightly in recognition.

And then, to Andie's surprise, another voice behind her started narrating the story. It was Calliope, who picked up right where Mac left off:

The longer Dynamene stayed on land, the dimmer her memories of the sea became...until one fateful day, nine years into their marriage. Her husband was on a fishing excursion, and her son said, "Mother, I found the key to Father's strongbox. He must have left it behind."

"Give it to me," she told him. "I'll return it to him."

That night, as her son slept, Dynamene held the key in her hands, as memories of her former life came flooding back to her. She knew if she could get the feather, she could return to her parents, to her sisters, to the glorious world of the sea. But she also knew that would mean leaving her husband and son, for she could never live permanently on land ever again.

"All right, enough!" Blasios interrupted. "What does *any* of this have to do with any medallion that's blessed by the gods?"

Calliope looked over to Mac with that soft smile of hers and, just as her captors had done earlier, handed the story back to him with a wave of her hand. "I'm glad you asked," Mac said…

The next morning, the son awoke to find his mother gone. He made his way to the shore, where his mother appeared to him, emerging from the morning mist. "Forgive me, my son," she said. "This is who I am. But I will always be watching you." She held out her hand and gave him a small, smooth stone. "This will forever link me to you and your father," she told him. "If you ever need me, put the stone under the water and rub it three times. When you do, I will appear and help you any way that I can."

With that, she disappeared. The son set the magic stone into a medallion, which he wore around his neck, so he could always have his mother close to his heart.

"Hold on!" Basileus cut in. "Why do you have it? If the stone belongs to this kid, why do *you* have it?"

"Simpimedes was our friend. We went to school with him," Mac explained. "He's dead now. A ram kicked him in the head, and he was killed. But before he died, he asked Homer to take the stone and return it to his father. And that's where we're going now. So take our money, take anything you want, but please, leave us that medallion. It was a dying boy's last wish, for crying out loud—please, *please*, if there's any decency left in you, let us honor it."

Once again, a silence engulfed the raft, until Basileus finally said: "Well, that's just about the most ridiculous thing I've ever heard. You expect us to believe that?"

"I don't really care if you believe it or not," Mac shrugged. "But it's true."

Basileus scoffed. "Let me give you some advice, kid. If you're going to tell a story with magical stones, then the rest of your story better be realistic. You're telling me this goddess offers some slob anything he wants — anything at all — and he asks for a *woman*?"

"At the very least, he should have went with the money, by-gods," Blasios snorted. Then he grabbed the cord from Basileus's hand. "Tell you what, smart-guy: why don't you prove it to us? Go ahead: take it, conjure up this goddess right now and—"

"Hey! Hey!" Basileus shouted at him. "Gimme that back!" Lowering the knife at Homer's throat ever so slightly, he snatched the medallion back and started berating his partner: "Where's your brains? If we let that kid call the goddess, then he's going to use her against us."

"I thought you didn't believe it," Blasios said.

"I *don't!* But if anyone is going to call on a goddess, it's going to be *us!* That way, if it's *not* true, then we'll know for sure! But if it *is* true, then *we'll* be the ones to get anything we want," Basileus reasoned, his one eye almost sparkling in anticipation. "Get it?"

Blasios took it all in. "Ahhh! Good idea. Here, I'll do it," He took the medallion back and turned to Mac. "So what did you say, again? You gotta rub it, or something?"

"Well, you have to submerge it in the water first," Mac reminded him.

Just as Blasios started to crouch down at the side of the raft, Basileus reached out with his free hand and grabbed hold of the cord. "Wait!" he barked. "Maybe I should do it. Here, you hold him," he said, nodding towards Homer.

"Why should *you* do it?" Blasios said, looking up at him.

"Well, how do I know you'll do it right?"

"How do you do it *wrong*?"

"How do I know you're not planning to ask for something for *yourself*?" Basileus argued.

"Why would I do that?"

"How do I know you're not trying to double-cross me?"

"What, you think I'm gonna run off somewhere? We're on a *raft!*" Blasios said, grabbing the cord from his partner's grasp.

"Fine! Let's do it together, then!" Basileus suggested.

"How in Hades do it we *together!*"

"Like this. Here..." With that, Basileus pushed Homer down and threw himself next to Blasios, almost on top of him. And as Blasios plunged his chubby fist holding the stone into the river, Basileus sent his arm into the water right after him. The two struggled furiously — elbowing each other, kneeing each other, trying to get each other in headlocks. They were struggling so much they didn't even notice Theo, Andie, and Homer coming up from behind.

And they kept struggling, even as they hit the water.

Mac would have loved to linger for a bit, to watch their shocked faces as they splashed around, but there wasn't any time. Instead, he grabbed the oar at Andie's feet, and he and Theo started rowing as fast as they could.

"Dude! What *was* that?" Theo huffed. "How did you come up with that *epic* story?"

"He didn't," Calliope said. "He was summarizing the plot of *Dynamene's Lover.*"

"What's that?" Theo asked.

"A play I was in last year. Isn't that right, Mac?" she said, smiling in his direction.

Mac didn't say a word, or even look over at her, but he did let a sly smile slip across his face as he kept rowing. Only when he sensed they were far enough away from their former captors — but *just* far enough — did he put his oar down and turn around. He saw Blasios flailing around and screaming, apparently caught in some reeds. Basileus, however, who had more fight in him, swam after them.

From the floor of the boat, Mac calmly picked up one of the apricots that had been thrown by the irate villagers. He stood up. "Hey, Basileus!" he called out to him. "Tell Dynamene I said 'Hi!'"

"This isn't over!" Basileus gurgled, his head just above the water. "You'll pay for this!"

"And by the way," Mac announced, as the raft drifted down the river, "I *am* the son of Odysseus, you one-eyed son-of-a-bitch!" Then he hurled the apricot at Basileus's head, hitting him squarely in his one good eye.

Demetrius—

When I first had the idea to actually use that map you sent me—to go to the cave of Kalakloptas, to get the aulos, to do something, instead of just endlessly talking about it—I was nervous, but invigorated. What can I say? This whole "finding Mac a heroic deed" thing sparked something in me. Homebody Homer is dead. Say hello to Homer, Intrepid Adventurer.

The deeper I got into it, the more nervous I became. My stomach was jumping like a rabbit walking on sand that's so blazing, it's like the hot coals your mom uses when making a pot of her lentil soup, which no one really cares for, but hey, you're not going to be the one to tell her. (Hmmmmm...I put a simile within a simile. Sorry.)

Anyway, even though I tried to put on a strong face in front of Mac, I was on edge the whole time. And I'm not talking about how I got sick on the ship, since my sea legs are apparently just as defective as my actual leg. (You think the guys Jason recruited to sail with him on the Argo got sea-sick? No way. If they were Argonauts, I'm an Argo-not-even-close.)

I'm not even talking about how Basileus had me at knifepoint.

Before all that, before we even got on the boat, I was thinking: What's going to happen? What lies at the endpoint of this map? Who is this mystical hermit who allegedly holds the aulos, and what is he capable of? Say if he kills us, or makes us his teenage slaves, or puts a spell on us that gives us donkey ears? Or say if we go all that way and there is no aulos, which means I dragged Mac and everyone else on this foolhardy mission for nothing? That kind of humiliation is way worse than death or donkey ears.

Turns out, calling yourself an Intrepid Adventurer and actually being one are totally different.

But as we got closer and closer to our destination, all that nervousness melted away, as I realized: We're going to do this. We're going to retrieve a flute once owned by Athena. We're going to be legitimate heroes. Everyone's going to know our names, know my name. And since you, Demetrius, were the one to send me that map in the first place, I have you to thank for it.

Oh, wait...did I say "thank"? I meant "BLAME"!

-Homer

CHAPTER THIRTEEN
The Strange Cave of Kalakloptas

Homer didn't feel sick this time around. Just sickened.

As soon as they boarded the *Harmonia*, the new ship that was taking them back to school, Homer went into hiding—partly to get away from Theo, but mostly just to get away. He found himself a secluded haven, amidst stacks of wooden crates on the *Harmonia's* main deck. At first, he wanted to crawl *inside* one of the crates—he felt that low—but he couldn't fit. So he just wedged himself in between two of them and gazed absently at the setting sun.

Slumped amongst the boxes, Homer could see crewmembers stroll by, but they couldn't see him. This wasn't anything new to Homer, of course; he spent his whole life getting overlooked. But at this moment, he didn't *mind* being ignored; given his wallowing, self-pitying mood, he preferred it.

Not far from where he was sitting, Homer could see Mac standing alone at the railing, vacantly tapping his new flute—the aulos—against the wood. Pretty soon, Andie joined him. She leaned her back up against the rail, so she was facing the interior of the ship as he was looking out to sea.

"I think I have a test in Olympian History today," she said with a sigh. If Mac said anything in response, Homer couldn't hear it. "So…" she continued, looking at the flute in his hand, "what are you going to do with that?"

Homer watched Mac as he lifted the instrument, the object that had sparked the entire weekend adventure. "This," Mac said, and then, with a simple flick of his wrist, he tossed the flute overboard, into the sun-dappled water. Homer didn't even react; he just watched it travel in a high arc, to fall into the swirling sea, lost forever.

****

Homer could read the signs.

It was dawn, just a few hours after the narrow escape from Basileus and Blasios. They had just turned onto the Marsyas River when he heard the distant rumble of thunder. Soon after that, he could see the storm clouds gathering, seemingly from out of nowhere, readying their ambush. And not long after that, he felt the pelting rain combined with the gusting wind and the churning currents underneath. Homer knew all these signs pointed to one thing: someone didn't want them messing with the aulos. And Homer, for one, could not have been more thrilled.

All five had taken shifts sleeping throughout the remaining hours of nightfall, but there was no sleeping now; Theo needed everyone's help to navigate the raft through the frothing, unpredictable river. Mostly everyone, that is: *someone* needed to act as a guide, to figure out where they were going. So, while Theo, Mac, Andie, and Calliope paddled madly away, Homer sat in the back, gripping a railing with one hand and clutching his tattered, soggy map with the other.

By all rights, Homer should have been throwing up three weeks' worth of meals. After all, he'd gotten sick on the *Æton*, and that was the smoothest sailing anyone could ask for. But this time, even as the rapids tossed the raft every which way, even when the raging currents nearly capsized them, even when they came within inches of smashing into two giant boulders, Homer never felt the slightest bit seasick or nervous. Only exhilarated. He knew they were getting close — *very* close.

Only when he saw Mac almost get swept overboard did Homer have even a moment of legitimate panic. Mac had been paddling ferociously when suddenly a wave spiked out of the foam, tearing off the railing on the left side and nearly knocking Mac over in the process. If not for Theo, who shot out his arm to grab Mac's tunic, Mac would have surely ended up in the crushing rapids.

"I lost my oar!" Mac yelled.

"Never mind! Just try to get some of this water out!" Theo yelled, kicking a wooden bucket over to him. Meanwhile, Homer kept scanning the riverbank, searching, searching—until finally, he saw it.

"There! There it is!" Homer yelled, waving the map and pointing frantically to a distant spot on the riverbank. As they lurched closer, they all saw it: a wooden dock, jutting out from two piles of stones— black stones on one side, white and silver stones on the other. And at the top of the dock, on the shore, loomed a giant grey tree, with an upside-down V blazed into its massive trunk. Just as Homer's map depicted.

Theo, Andie, and Calliope tried to maneuver the raft to the dock, but the current didn't allow them to do it delicately; they ended up smashing right into the dock, ripping a chunk out of the raft's bow. "Well, that's not so bad..." Theo said sarcastically, as they hauled themselves onto the dock.

Soon, Mac, Theo, Andie, and Calliope were trying to secure what was left of the raft to the dock, none of them speaking but all of them—even Theo—thinking the same thing: *How are we going to get home now?* Homer, however, was on to more immediate concerns; he bounded up the dock to the giant tree. With his finger, he traced the V-shape blaze—an ancient symbol, no doubt, of the double flute—as he waited impatiently for the others to join him.

"OK, so now what?" he heard Andie ask. Homer looked down at the map in his hands, then at the tree, and then at the single, twisting path behind it.

"Now...we walk," Homer answered confidently, even though, at that point, he was going on pure speculation. His map didn't really say what to do *after* finding the dock. Or maybe it *had* said it at one point, but Homer's copy was missing the lower right-hand corner. That didn't concern him, though. Really, where else could they go but that one path? And besides, even if the corner *did* contain some information, how important could it really be?

They ventured into the woods, the tall trees providing a canopy that at least kept out *some* of the rain. Mac led the way, walking with what Homer wanted to call a purpose but was really probably a desire to get this over with. Not far behind him trooped Theo and Calliope, and then Andie, bow at her side. Homer lagged behind them all; he tried to keep pace, but the pain in his foot—aggravated by the dampness and the tumultuous ride on the raft—made it impossible.

Even from his position way in the back, Homer could hear Calliope and Theo bicker. "I can't believe you didn't remember my play…" she groused to her brother.

"In my defense, I don't even think I *saw* that play," Theo offered.

"You *absolutely* did. You sat in the *front row*! And afterwards, you came up to me and raved about how 'epic' the show was!"

"Are you sure? Maybe I was away or something…"

"You *saw* it…as did Mac, even though he *claimed* he didn't remember any of it."

Mac looked back over his shrugging shoulder. "I guess it came back to me."

"You know, I don't know what's worse," mused Calliope, turning to Andie. "This one here, gushing about the show he probably slept through, or the *supposedly* aloof, uninterested one who then magically recites the entire script practically word for word."

"For the record," Theo interjected, "I think the second option is worse."

"Enough! Enough!" Homer boomed, stopping the other four in their tracks. "Need I remind you what we're dealing with here? This isn't War Games, OK? This isn't some relay race put on by a bunch of morons! We're about to retrieve an ancient artifact, handcrafted by a goddess. This is a *serious* endeavor, demanding a *serious* mind. So, if you can all be quiet for once, I need to have a private conversation with Mac, about *serious* matters!"

His impassioned speech having had the desired effect of shutting everyone up, Homer then grabbed Mac by the arm and led him a few steps away.

"So…" Homer began, in an almost hushed voice, "how are you feeling?"

"How am I *feeling*? Well, let's see," Mac reflected. "I'm waterlogged. I almost drowned. I'm working on about two hours' sleep. And I have no idea where I am or how we're going to get out of here. So, yeah…been better, thanks."

"Ahhh...but you're still *excited*, right?" Homer asked. Mac shot him a look of disbelief and started trudging onward.

"I've got something for you," Homer called, hurrying up to Mac's side. He reached into his tunic, pulled out a dagger, and handed it to Mac.

"What's this?" Mac asked.

"The knife Basileus was using — the one he was going to use to slit my throat. He dropped it while they were scrambling with Calliope's medallion. I picked it up. No big deal," Homer downplayed, although he *was* pretty pleased with himself. "I thought you might need it."

"Why?"

"Haven't you been listening? The aulos was created by *Athena*. It's been hidden for a century. You think it'll be just lying there for the taking?"

Homer could tell by the incredulous look on Mac's face that he did, in fact, think the flute would be just lying there for the taking. "What will I have to do?" Mac asked.

"Well," Homer began, as another crash of thunder shook the trees, "you'll probably have to engage in a battle of some kind. Some physical encounter that requires you to best someone with feats of strength and cunning. Like you did with Melpagon."

"Why does everyone keep forgetting I *lost* that fight?" Sighing, Mac took the dagger, put it in the belt of his tunic, and again started walking away.

"Wait, wait, wait..." Homer said, limping up to him. "You know, Athena is the original owner of the aulos. We'd like for her to look favorably on us. So, would you like to say a prayer?"

Mac didn't respond, just marched on in apparent disgust. "Guess not," Homer mumbled, as Calliope, Theo, and Andie also strode on by.

As Homer resumed his spot at the back, the five ventured along the lone path into a part of the woods so thick with trees virtually no light or rain could penetrate them. Finally, their path took them directly to a clearing littered with rocks and boulders. The pelting rain had nearly subsided; now a mixture of fog and rising mist thickened the air so all they could make out in front of them were two circles of fire, like two glowing eyes, penetrating through the haze. They inched forward until another shape emerged: a large, pockmarked cave, with two banks of fire that flanked a wide abyss of a mouth. Homer couldn't have asked for anything better.

"Get down!" Homer commanded eagerly. Everyone immediately took cover behind the closest rock, except for Homer, who crawled, through the mud, right next to Mac.

"This is it," Homer announced to the group in a loud whisper. "It has to be!"

"OK," Mac said, peeking over the rock at the cave, "so what do we do now?"

"Now, you declare your presence to the guardian of the flute," Homer explained.

"The what?"

Sometimes Homer couldn't believe how much hand-holding Mac required. "The guardian of the flute. You need to say something like, *This is Telemachus of Ithaca, ordering you to hand over the flute of Marsyas, or I will have to use force.*'" (Homer adopted a dramatic voice as he fed Mac his line.)

"OK, I'm definitely not saying that," Mac whispered.

"You have to!" Homer insisted. "Now get up there!" With that, he pushed Mac out from behind the rock. Mac looked back with a glare and then took three tentative steps forward. Staring into the cave's yawning, misty maw, he declared his presence.

"Uh…hello?"

Homer hung his head in shame.

Mac cleared his throat and tried again. "Uh…hey, in there…anybody home?"

Popping his head up from behind his rock, Homer yelled out, in an affected voice so loud it actually echoed in the dense forest: "Kalakloptas! I am Telemachus of Ithaca! Hand over the flute of Marsyas!" And then, as quickly as he had shot up, Homer ducked back down.

An irritated Mac glanced back for a moment before returning his attention to the mouth of the cave; from where he sat, Homer could see Mac's fingers tightening around the hilt of his dagger, in anticipation of whatever might emerge from the gaping doorway. Suddenly, behind him, Homer heard a sound: Andie had stood up and, within seconds, moved herself next to Mac, her bow raised. And then, he saw Theo move next to Mac as well, on his other side, holding his walking stick in front of him like a club. Calliope didn't come forward, but Homer could see she was holding a large rock in each hand. Homer, of course, remained crouched behind the rock, no weapons anywhere. But *mentally*, he was ready for anything.

They waited, staring at the mouth of the cave—until finally, a voice croaked out from its bowels.

"Hang on a second!"

For a few confused moments, no one moved or spoke. Finally, Theo asked, "'Wait…did I *really* just hear 'Hang on a second'?"

"Sssshhhh!" Homer shushed. Inside, though, Homer couldn't deny his own doubts. *Hang on a second?* Not exactly the menacing response he had expected. Still, he tried to have faith they would face something dangerous and life-threatening soon enough.

The voice croaked again: "OK, come on in!"

Mac looked back at Homer before walking slowly toward the cave. The rest of the gang slowly filed one by one behind him, with Homer assuming his usual spot at the end.

Once inside the cave, Homer got a little more optimistic. He found himself in a twisty hallway so dank and dark, he could hardly see Calliope, only a few steps ahead of him. Finally, when he turned another corner and saw light up ahead, he knew, just *knew*, they had reached it: the secret lair of Kalakloptas. Overtaken by a zealous energy that invigorated his aching foot, Homer pushed his way past Calliope, Andie, Theo, even Mac. Without a trace of fear, he barged headstrong into the fire-drenched chamber.

He had to blink a few times, as his eyes adjusted to the well-lit room, illuminated by a large, cozy fire pit to his right, which bathed everything in the room—including everyone's confused faces—in an orange glow. Stunned into silence, Homer scanned the entire chamber: in the center of the room sat a small wooden table, laden with food of all kinds, including a roast lamb, cheese, and vegetables;

on the far side hung a gigantic red curtain that covered the entire wall. The other three walls, meanwhile, were lined completely with oversized, fluffy, multicolored pillows, decorated with all sorts of tassels and fringe. And on one of these pillows lounged a man—a large, swarthy man, gnawing on a leg of lamb, his bloated, uncovered belly jiggling with each hearty swallow.

"Sorry about that..." the man apologized. "I was indecent!" He smiled, and as he did so, his blotchy cheeks puffed up his face, making his beady eyes even beadier.

"We're looking for Kalakloptas," Homer demanded.

"Well, you found him," he said, resting his leg of lamb down on the cushion and then using his greasy hand to flatten out his wisps of hair. "So, who's looking for an aulos?"

And with the same greasy hand, he yanked on the cord next to him, opening the curtain that covered the far wall. As the curtain inched open, so did Theo's mouth. "Oh...no..." he said, bemused. "Don't even tell me..."

Homer didn't know what he expected to see behind the curtain, but he still held on to a shred of hope that whatever he saw could somehow redeem this quest. Maybe they'd find a riddle, carved into the wall—some puzzle they'd have to solve to prove themselves worthy. Or maybe they'd see the armor once worn by the brave warriors who had crossed Kalakloptas in the past. He didn't know what he'd find, but he certainly didn't expect to see a double flute, just sitting there on a shelf, for anyone to take. But that's exactly what he saw.

Except he didn't see just *one* flute. He saw hundreds.

Stacks and stacks of double flutes, on a series of crude wooden shelves. "Go ahead, take a closer look," urged Kalakloptas, as he dragged out four huge baskets, also filled to capacity with identical flutes.

As Theo, Calliope, and Andie started rummaging through the stacks of flutes, Homer glanced back at Mac, who hadn't moved since they entered the room; instead, he just shook his head, his expression cycling through various shades of dismay, anger, and even amusement.

"Hey, can we try one?" Theo asked.

"Sure, but you try it, you buy it," Kalakloptas gulped, returning to his leg of lamb. Theo experimented with a few notes on the aulos before launching into a tune that vaguely resembled their school fight song. Homer marched right over to Kalakloptas, who had oozed back down into his pillow. "I don't think you understand," Homer said, trying to sound diplomatic. "We came a long way, all the way from Pieridian Academy in Iarmithia—"

"No kidding?" Kalakloptas marveled, raising his eyebrows in such a way that the divots in his forehead narrowed. "That *is* far. Hey, do you think you could sign my guest book?"

He started to lumber up from the pillows, but Homer stopped him. "No, no, no. We need the *real* aulos. My friend, Telemachus, has to bring it back to our school…"

"The '*real* aulos'?" Kalakloptas laughed, a great big guffaw of a laugh. "Little man, if I had the *real* aulos of Marsyas, you really think I'd be here selling cheap knock-offs?" His laughing turned into wheezing and then gasping as he evidently started choking on a piece of lamb. Homer stood there, aghast and horrified, as the man started pounding on his own chest. When he finally regained his composure, he retreated to salesman mode. "Actually, they're not cheap at all," he assured Homer, pushing himself off the pillow and plodding over to the shelves. "Very sturdy, and as far as replicas go, they're amazing. Very realistic. Check out the detail. And all of them handcrafted."

"You make all of these?" Calliope asked.

"A lot of them. Some of them, I have shipped in," he said, grabbing an aulos in his stubby, greasy fingers. "And the sound! Listen to this." He played a few notes, trying to harmonize with Theo, and then handed it to Homer.

"How much?" Theo asked.

"Seven obols each," Kalakloptas reported. "So what d'ya say? You like?"

"Well, I gotta be honest. The product's great, price is right. But the *location*, dude… it's the *worst*. Look at this place: you're in the middle of freakin' nowhere here. You gotta travel this crazy river. You don't even have a *sign* anywhere. Who could ever find this place?"

"I know," Kalakloptas nodded sheepishly. "I guess I liked the idea of being close to the actual spot where Marsyas challenged Apollo…but, yeah, it's a bit off the beaten path."

"A 'bit off'? Try *way off*, dude. *Way off* the beaten path. You can't even *see* the beaten path from here. How are you gonna attract customers?"

Kalakloptas wiped his fingers on the curtain and then waddled over to the table in the middle of the room. "Well, I made up these advertisements to send around to some of the bigger city-states," he explained, picking up a stack of papers from the table. "Maybe you kids could take some back to your school?"

Homer rushed over and grabbed one of the flyers out of the man's hands. He looked at it quickly and then pulled out the soaked, crumpled map that he had received from his scroll buddy Demetrius. When he held them next to each other, he could see it plainly: they were identical.

Or *nearly* identical. The bottom right hand corner of Kalakloptas's flyer included some information about sales and prices—information that would have been on Homer's map, had that corner not been torn off.

Homer just stood there—stunned, immobile—the dual maps in his two frozen hands. He didn't turn to anyone, but he could hear, over Theo's attempt at music, Calliope and Andie start giggling. Then he felt Mac looking over his shoulder.

"You're missing a corner there," Mac observed.

"Yeah…" Homer whispered.

"Pretty important corner, I'd say, as far as corners go." Then Mac grabbed the map from Homer's hands, crumpled it up, and tossed it in Homer's face.

"So," Kalakloptas announced, "who's interested in an aulos?"

"You kidding?" Theo smiled, slamming his satchel of coins onto the wooden table. "We'll take five!"

Theo exuberantly passed out the flutes while Kalakloptas slowly counted out the obols into a clay pot on his table. After they had completed their transaction, Kalakloptas asked, "Anything else?"

"Maybe," Theo said slowly, as if trying to decide whether to voice an idea that had started to bubble. "Say, you're a businessman. Do you happen to have any sea-worthy vessels we could rent?"

"Sea-worthy vessels?" Kalakloptas repeated, with a smile.

"Yeah. See, we gotta get back up the river soon—like, an hour ago—and I don't think our raft can make it in its current un-sea-worthy state. So, I was wondering, in addition to selling these dandy replicas, if you were also in the business of renting rafts to weary travelers?"

"Can't say that I am," Kalakloptas said, clearly charmed by Theo. "But maybe I can do you one better. Let me show you something."

Soon, Homer and the gang found themselves out behind the cave, in the late morning air. They were all standing at a low stone wall encircling a large pond—except for Kalakloptas, who stood waist-deep in the water, as two large black forms swam in circles around him.

"What do you think?" Kalakloptas asked.

"That depends," Mac answered. "What are they?"

"They're my serphints," Kalakloptas replied, dangling a fish from his hand. Suddenly, one of the creatures—giant, shiny black, and eel-like—splashed out, took the fish from his hand, and fell back into the water.

"Your servants?" Andie asked.

"Not servants, serphints!" Kalakloptas said, not turning his attention away from the pond, his eyes following the eels as they swam around him. "A cross between a dolphin and a serpent. Hence the name: serphints. Here, let me introduce you. That one over there is Castor," he said, motioning to the creature that had glided to the far side of the pond.

Then he put one of the fish in his mouth and clamped the back fin with his teeth. "And this is Polly," Kalakloptas said, with the fish dangling from his mouth. Suddenly, the creature shot out of the water to take the fish gently from her master's mouth. At that moment, Kalakloptas grabbed his pet with both hands, right where her ears would be, and turned her in the direction of his spectators. Sure enough, the animal's face did look exactly like a cross between a dolphin and a snake. Her eyes definitely had a serpentine quality, while its curved snout and smile were more dolphin-like. Her body, though, almost entirely resembled a snake's, except for a dorsal fin and two small fins on her tail.

"I've never heard of a…a serphint before," Andie remarked.

"Well, I guess you wouldn't," Kalakloptas said. "After all, they're not real. Or, they're real…just not natural."

"What are you talking about?" Mac asked.

"OK, so about a year ago, I met this guy. He knew a doctor of some kind, a medicine man. I forget his name—X-something. Anyway, this guy came up with a technique of mating different kinds of creatures."

Calliope cringed. "Why would he do *that*?"

"Why do mad scientists do anything? But I saw opportunity! See, dolphins have a great sense of direction. So the idea was that sailors could use one of these guys if they ever got lost at sea. Just hook 'em up to a smaller boat, and let that boat lead the bigger boat to safety."

"Well, OK…but why not just use *dolphins*, then?" Calliope asked, still grossed out. "Why mess around with the natural order of things?"

Kalakloptas thought about it for a moment. "You can't exactly transport a dolphin around on a boat. But you can transport a serphint, because it can live on land. See?" He pointed to the other side of the pond, where five or six smaller versions of Polly and Castor were slithering around on a large rock.

"What are those—babies?" Theo squealed. "Little guys? How cute!" He looked over to Calliope, who still seemed very bothered by the unnatural ghoulishness of it all.

Mac also seemed less than impressed. "That's great…but who cares? I mean, why are you showing us this?"

Kalakloptas crinkled his forehead. "Uh, because your friend said you need a lift. And these guys are my lift. They can take me up the river in half the time it used to."

"What, are we all supposed to jump on their backs or something?" Mac asked.

"Or you could just do what I do and attach them to my sea-worthy vessel over there," he said, motioning to a wooden chariot-like contraption over on the other side of the pond, not far from the baby serphints.

"Nice, Kal!" Theo beamed.

"Just give me some time to hitch 'em up," Kalakloptas said. "Anyone want to help?"

Soon after, Mac, Andie, and Calliope were helping to harness the two serphints to the chariot. Meanwhile, a despondent and crestfallen Homer sat on the side of the pond, staring at his fake aulos. He just wanted this labor to be over.

Theo, on the other hand, couldn't have been more delighted with the way everything had turned out; in fact, he wanted one more keepsake of the experience. "Say, Kal," he said, "I have to ask: any of those little guys over there for sale?"

Kalakloptas looked across the pond to the baby serphints sliding in and out of the water. "Why? You interested?" He obviously knew he had Theo hooked.

"Theo, no!" Calliope said emphatically. "That's ridiculous. What are you going to do, keep it in your dorm room?"

"They can live on land," Kalakloptas reminded her. "Only need a little bit of water."

"What about when it gets as big as these two?" Calliope asked.

"Eh, I'll give it to Dad," Theo shrugged. "Maybe he could use it for something. My way of paying him back for ruining his raft." He turned back to Kalakloptas. "Let's do this. Name your price."

And so, when Theo plopped down into the back row of the chariot, in between Homer and Mac, he was carrying an aulos in one hand and a new baby serphint, dark and shiny and about the size and width of his forearm, in the other. "What do you think?" he asked everyone. "I'm going to call him Typhon!"

"Typhon?" Homer snapped. "Don't you know anything? Typhon was the most ferocious monster of all time, feared even by the gods!"

"Exactly," Theo grinned, shoving the slimy creature in Homer's face. "Epic name for my epic pet."

"Everyone ready?" Kalakloptas asked, as he gripped the reins.

"Onward!" Theo shouted, as he put the aulos in his mouth and whistled right into Homer's ear.

****

The return voyage on the Marsyas River differed in every possible way from the original one. There were no bandits to outwit, no rapids to overcome. Nobody even had to paddle this time; instead, the passengers just sat in the chariot as Polly and Castor, the two fantastical, majestic serphints, pulled them smoothly along. Homer had expected a much bumpier ride, but Kalakloptas, situated up front between Calliope and Andie, had obviously done this many times, and he had no trouble navigating through the rockier parts of the wide river. Homer didn't even get too wet, as the serphints barely kicked up any splash while skimming across the surface; if anything, Homer felt a refreshing spray in his face as they sped along.

To top it all off, the ride home took less than half the time as the ride there. In fact, they arrived at the mouth of the Marsyas River well before the *Harmonia*, the ship that Theo had arranged to pick them up for the journey back to school.

In short, it should have been the ride of Homer's life. But he didn't enjoy any of it.

First of all, for the entire ride, Theo played some stupid song on his stupid fake aulos; by the end, Homer had a splitting headache. But truthfully his pride ached more. He felt so humiliated, for dragging everyone out there for nothing. He was so down and distracted that by the time they met up with the *Harmonia* later that afternoon, Homer didn't even say goodbye to Kalakloptas and his serphints. Instead, he just dashed onboard and went into hiding. He just had to get away — from Theo, from his music, from *everything*.

Homer had known humiliation before. In fact, in his life, he hadn't really known much else. But not like this: this humiliation actually *hurt*, as if his pride had been assaulted so profoundly, he physically ached.

But even as he sat there on the deck of the *Harmonia*, hidden amongst those crates, he didn't just feel bad for himself; he felt bad for Mac, for letting him down. Not that Mac knew this, of course; Homer had never let him in, after all—never told him about his *real* master plan, for which the aulos was essential. Without the flute, what would he do?

"Still sea-sick?"

Calliope's voice jolted Homer out of his moping. When he looked up, her face shined so brightly in the setting sunlight, he almost had to shade his eyes.

"Sea-sick, sure…That's it…" Homer muttered. "So why don't you just throw me overboard and end this misery?"

Calliope smiled. "Hey," she said, as she rearranged some of the crates so she could slide down on the deck next to Homer. "You had some faulty information. It could have happened to anyone."

"I just…I thought this was going to be the real thing. I wanted to give Mac something. And all he got was a fake flute that he ended up throwing away."

"Well, if you think about it," Calliope suggested, "the mission *was* successful. Mac *did* get the flute."

"Theo had to *buy* it for him!" Homer reminded her. "There's nothing *heroic* about that. There was no obstacle. There was no peril. It wasn't…it wasn't the real thing." And he wasn't talking about the flute; he was talking about the whole adventure. He just couldn't put into words why he was so disappointed. As it turned out, he didn't have to.

"I know," Calliope answered. And Homer sensed that she really did.

An easy silence fell between them, as they listened to the sound of laughter coming from Mac and Andie, standing at the railing. After a while, Calliope spoke again: "Remember when we were trading stories about the Marsyas River? And I said how sometimes, something good can come out of something bad?"

"Yeah?" Homer mumbled.

"Well, I believe something good *did* come out of this whole adventure. Look over there," Calliope said, motioning to Mac and Andie. "Friends again."

"Whoopee," Homer mumbled, doing his best grumpiest-kid-in-the-world imitation.

"Well, I know *I* got something out of this," Calliope stated.

Homer turned to her. "What?"

Calliope smiled. "Something to cheer you up with?" From under her robe, she produced her own double flute, which she promptly brought to her lips. She started to play the Pieridian fight song.

"Stop!" Homer groaned, covering his ears. But he was smiling, too, and despite his best efforts, he couldn't stop a tiny laugh from escaping.

Even though the *Harmonia* sailed through the night, the ship got back to Port Florios later than Theo had expected. When everyone disembarked, Homer could hear bells in the distance, indicating that classes had just started. Never one to skip class, Calliope told Mac and Homer if they all hoofed it back up to campus, they would only be a little late for their Orations class.

"Which means Mac will be able to deliver his speech," Homer reminded him. "The speech I'm sure he didn't even remotely prepare."

"Don't worry. I'm sort of a fly-by-the-seat-of-my-tunic kind of guy…" Mac shrugged.

Calliope suggested he recite the Dynamene story. Homer sent Mac and Calliope on ahead, while he limped his way to campus. By the time Homer got to the classroom, Mac was already at the front of the room, giving his speech.

As Homer snuck to his seat, a few of the phrases Mac was saying began filtering into Homer's ears: "thrown it to earth…over-confident… challenge to a musical duel…two-headed aulos…god of music himself, Apollo."

Then Homer realized: Mac wasn't telling the Dynamene story. He was telling the story of Marsyas. *Homer's* story.

As Mac spoke, he glanced at Homer for just a moment and grinned. Homer grinned back, thinking that maybe he had given Mac more than a fake flute after all.

CHAPTER FOURTEEN
Test of the Slobbering Boar

After they got back from their adventure on the Marsyas River, everything pretty much went back to normal—on the surface, at least.

Calliope went back to the Drama Club and its latest production. Homer went back to his war figurines. Andie went back to…whatever she did when she wasn't with everyone else. And Theo went back to his endless rounds of parties, sporting events, and other social functions.

As for Mac, he still *avoided* all parties, sporting events, and other social functions. He still slept in the back of class. And he was still in the process of getting kicked out of school.

And yet, the several weeks that passed since the Marsyas trip did see two significant changes in Mac's life: one, he was now sharing a room with a foul-smelling serphint (which Theo kept in a crate at the foot of his bed); and two, for the first time in his life, Mac actually had…well, *friends*.

This unexpected development started the night the *Harmonia* returned them to Port Florios. Calliope proposed they all get together, to "debrief" about their experience. So that night, all five of them met at a student hang-out called the Grape Vine; they ate cheesy bread and fig cookies, harassed Homer about his map, and, to the surprise of probably everyone in attendance, enjoyed themselves.

"This *was* fun," Theo said, as they left the Vine. "We'll have to do this again some time."

"No, that won't work," Calliope announced firmly. "You don't just 'do' things again, 'some time.' You *choose* it. You *choose* to be friends with people. You *make* time to be with them. So let's make the time right now: next week — same time, same place?"

Honestly, Mac didn't see it happening. He knew *he* would go, because he had nothing else to do. And he knew Homer would go, because he had even less to do than Mac. Theo and Calliope — well, Calliope put it all together, and she could probably guilt her brother into going. The only wild card was Andie. Why would she come?

But when she showed up at the Grape Vine the next week, and the week after that, Mac remembered why: to hang out with her precious Theo. But Mac was strangely okay with it; at least he had an excuse to see her. And in a way, he couldn't blame Andie for liking Theo; he was so damn charming. And funny. Whenever they gathered at the Grape Vine, Theo entertained everyone with an endless stream of jokes that just flowed effortlessly out of him:

"What's invisible and smells like baby gods? Chronos's farts."

"Homer, you're a person of rare intelligence — that is, it's rare when you show any."

"Andie, who's the most handsome guy at school, and why am I?"

How could Mac resent a guy like that?

And so, their nights at the Grape Vine soon became a sort of tradition, a ritual; for that one night each week, the five of them came together, to laugh and mock and eat and forget every stupid, annoying thing that was happening in their lives. For that one night a week, Mac's world — a world with a missing father, a hundred nasty suitors, and nine humorless administrators just waiting for him to screw up — was actually not altogether unbearable. Because for that one night a week, Mac was actually *part* of something.

But only for that one night. For the rest of the week, everyone was pretty well immersed in his or her own stuff. Mac saw Calliope in class, but that was about it. And even though he *lived* with Theo, he really didn't see him that often. (Being the most popular mortal alive kept Theo pretty busy, after all.) Really, the only one Mac saw on a regular basis was Homer. And, surprisingly, Mac didn't *mind* this.

Initially, their relationship was all business: Homer would stop by Mac's room to talk about some madcap new labor, usually something involving the retrieval of an artifact from some distant and dangerous location. ("So, there's this girdle worn by a queen named Tyro. Only problem: it's rumored to be inside an active volcano...") When Mac would shoot down the idea, he and Homer would just end up talking.

Eventually, inevitably, they started sharing stories: Homer would talk about his bad foot, or some guy he had a crush on but would never work up the courage to talk to, or the pressure he felt from his parents, who didn't have a lot of money and could barely afford to send him to Pieridian; and Mac would let a few things slip, too, about his mom or his life in Ithaca—about everything, except his father. Homer would plead with Mac to tell him something— *anything*—about his idol, but Mac always steered the conversation elsewhere.

After a while, Mac was so used to hanging out with Homer that when he didn't come by his room, Mac actually went searching for him—usually finding him in the Logonis Library. One day, Mac entered the library's main reading room and saw Homer sitting at a table, his head buried in a scroll rolled out in front of him. He was reading so intently, Mac's "hello" legitimately caused him to jump.

"Uh...hey," a frazzled Homer responded, as he tried, not-so-subtly, to cover his reading materials with his hands.

"Whatcha reading there?" Mac asked suspiciously.

"This?" Homer squirmed as he folded the scroll in half. "This...is nothing. For class."

"Ah," Mac said, as he started to get his tablet from his satchel. Then, with the suddenness of a striking viper, he lunged across the table and grabbed the scroll with both hands. Homer valiantly tried to hold on, but a very loud *"Shushhh!"* from the librarian—a long-faced old crank named Lyncreas—distracted him just long enough for Mac to yank the scroll from his grasp.

As he spread out the parchment, Mac immediately understood why Homer was trying to hide it from him: on the far right, accompanying two columns of text, was a sketch of a hideous, bull-faced creature, snorting smoke and carrying a giant axe. Classic representation of the Minotaur.

"This is for class, eh?" Mac whispered. "Which one? 'Things That Are Fake 101'?"

Homer rolled his eyes. "Fine. It's personal. I was looking up stuff on Andie's dad, which led me to other theories people have about the Minotaur. For example, there's a guy who has come up with seven different possible locations for the second labyrinth. Another guy wore into battle what he claimed to be the head of the Minotaur—you know, as a sort of helmet. And this guy," Homer reached across and pointed at a name on the parchment, "Xenotareus. He believed that drinking the blood of the Minotaur would make a person immortal."

Mac didn't say anything, just let his eyes drift over the Minotaur sketch—from the long horns to the nose-ring down to the cloven hooves. Finally, with impressive patience, he began, "Homer..."

But Homer finished his sentence. "You want me to stop pursuing this Minotaur stuff. To focus instead on some realistic and attainable goals that will help you stay in school. Fair enough." Homer grandly rolled up the scroll, as if to show he was putting this Minotaur obsession to rest once and for all. "Since we're on the subject," Homer continued. "I have been mulling over a new labor for you."

"Where do we have to go for this one?" Mac asked. "Halfway up Zeus's butt?"

"How about across campus? You take Intro to Warfare, right? With Rhixion? And has he done the lesson yet with his pet boar?"

"Is that the stupid thing where Rhixion dares you to take off the collar from around the boar's neck? And no one can ever do it, so Rhixion can act all superior, and say—"

"That's it!" Homer interrupted, eliciting another *"Shushhh!"* from Lyncreas the librarian.

Mac shot an exasperated glance across the room as he leaned forward. "What?" he whispered.

"That's your next labor!" Homer beamed. "Removing the collar from Rhixion's boar!"

Mac didn't get it—or didn't want to. "Did you hear what I just said? No kid has ever done it."

"Which is why it'll be so awesome when *you* do it!"

"How could that possibly help me with Gurgus?"

"It's not for Gurgus," Homer said. "It's for you. If I learned anything from our last labor, it's that you severely lack self-confidence, which is a critical ingredient for any hero."

"No self-confidence?" Mac asked in disbelief. "Are you forgetting how I stood up to Basileus and Blasios? You're telling me that didn't take confidence?"

"Yeah, that was OK," Homer shrugged. "But that was born from *indignation*. You were mad when they didn't think you were Odysseus's son. That's not exactly the same thing as confidence."

"Oh, I see," Mac shot back. "So the next time someone has a *knife to your throat*, I'll make sure my motives are pure enough before *I save your life!*"

"Enough!" an at-the-end-of-his-rope Lyncreas shouted, "Out! Out! Out!" The exiled pair sheepishly trudged out of the reading room, not speaking again until they were midway down the library steps. "I don't get it, anyway," Mac said. "I spent a ton of time in the stables back home. What's the big deal about taking a collar off a boar?"

"You haven't met Rhixion's boar yet?" Homer asked.

"No. I think he's doing the lesson next week."

Homer smirked. "Then you'll see next week."

****

The boar was named Solobeus, but all the Pieridian students called him "Slobber." An apt nickname, since the creature's face was a dripping, sopping mess of drool and matted-down spittle. He had other less-than-flattering features: wild orange eyes; a tangle of four tusks that jutted way, way out of both sides of its pink snout; a strip of tall black fur that looked like a row of spikes running down his spine; and a nasty demeanor. But those qualities had nothing on the slobbering, which pushed him from merely foul to completely revolting.

Slobber belonged to a teacher named Rhixion, a former warrior who taught several combat training courses at Pieridian. Students flocked to his classes, partly because of the material (Rhixion actually trained his students in sword-fighting, spear-throwing, and hand-to-hand combat), but mostly because of *him*. He was just *cool*. With his slicked-back blond hair, a snake-like scar running down the left side of his face, and thick, muscular arms, he cut an imposing figure — though he was actually the gentlest, most chilled-out person on campus.

Mac liked Rhixion and the class, Introduction to Warfare. They didn't just sit in a room and listen to a teacher drone on and on; they actually got to do stuff. Rhixion offered one of his hands-on lessons to the class one overcast morning, when he assembled all of his students in a section of campus unofficially known as The Pen — basically one giant wooden cage with stables attached to it. The Pen housed all sorts of animals — horses, cattle, pigs, an occasional peacock — but Rhixion directed his students to a particular stable, its bars drenched with spray and drool; inside, raged his pet boar: the repulsive, squealing Slobber.

"Many years ago, I was on a ship heading to Troy," Rhixion addressed the semicircle of students, "when my fellow warriors threw me overboard. Hey, I deserved it. I was impossible to deal with back then. And when I was floating on the water, clinging desperately to a single piece of timber, praying for survival, I felt the spirit of Poseidon come upon me. The god saved me. He whipped up a breeze that brought me to a deserted island, populated with many fabulous and dangerous creatures, but none more so than this one right here."

He gestured behind him to Slobber, roared in response. "We had many encounters, Solobeus and I, during which he got the better of me." (As he spoke, Rhixion pointed to scars on his leg and on his massive shoulder.) "And in the process, I began to understand something: I could never overcome this beast, because I didn't *believe* that I could. When it looked into my eyes, it saw only fear, self-doubt. And I realized I would never win that way.

"One morning, carrying no weapon other than the conviction that I would win, I zeroed in on the beast...and stared him down. Ever since that day, he has understood who his master is."

With that, Rhixion calmly turned to face Slobber, directly on the other side of the cage. Rhixion squatted down and stared right into the creature's orange eyes. Silence fell over the crowd, as Mac watched his teacher reach his hand between the cage's openings and let it hover in between the two sets of gnarled, intertwined tusks. Finally, he tapped three fingers to his thumb, one at a time—first his index, then the third finger, then the middle one, which he snapped.

One, two, three. Snap. Then Slobber dropped to the ground, as if asleep.

Rhixion stood up and faced the class. "Unless you first win with these," he said, pointing to his eyes, "you'll never win with these." He held up his fists.

As the obviously impressed students started murmuring, Rhixion reached into a sack at his feet and took out a gray braided collar, on which hung various tokens: arrowheads, green jewels, even teeth. He reached inside the stable, tied the rope around the dazed creature's neck, and began rubbing it behind the ear. Slowly, Slobber opened his eyes.

"I want a volunteer to try to get this collar off Solobeus's neck," Rhixion explained. "But you can't just reach in, unless you want to lose a hand. You have to do what I just did: stare him down. Then, when he's sufficiently stunned, you can retrieve the collar. Who wants to try?"

Naturally, Theo jumped at the chance. "Oh, right here!" he announced, striding up to the stable. Rhixion grinned, put his hand on Theo's shoulder, and pushed him into a squat.

"Remember: confidence," Rhixion instructed softly as Theo looked into eyes of a revived Slobber.

"You ugly thing," Theo said. "I think you need a hug!" In response, Slobber roared and snorted a spray of drool in Theo's face.

"You'll never overcome a foe with jokes, Theseus," Rhixion instructed. "Who's next?"

"I think Mac wants to try," Theo offered, as he wiped Slobber's slobber off his face. Mac shot him a frigid glance, but it was too late. "Telemachus?" Rhixion asked. "Care to step up?"

Resigned, Mac stepped forward. When he got to the stable door, Rhixion reached out and covered Mac's eyes with his thick hand. "Confidence," Rhixion reminded him, as he gently guided Mac into a crouch. "Conviction. Believe that you can beat him and then make *him* believe it." He lifted his hand, giving Mac his first up-close look at Slobber.

Face to face, the animal seemed smaller and less imposing—not even five feet long and maybe only three feet high at the shoulders (although the strip of black spikes running down his spine made him seem taller). On the other hand, he was much, much grosser up close. And soggier: from his pink snout to his curled black lips to his ivory tusks—everything was just *dripping*.

Mac took a deep breath and then looked into Slobber's wet, fiery eyes. Not knowing exactly what he was supposed to do, Mac tried to picture in his mind the creature lying down, falling to the ground as he did under Rhixion's control. Slobber met Mac's gaze, and the animal tilted his head, confused. For one brief moment, Mac thought he'd won. As he kept his eyes locked on Slobber's, Mac slowly lifted his hand to grab the collar…

Then it all fell apart. Slobber roared, so suddenly and ferociously that it knocked Mac to the ground, and then let loose from his nostrils a foul spray that coated Mac's entire face.

****

"I don't even get the point of the whole thing," Mac complained, as he stood on a chair, trying to hang up a new tapestry, an illustration of Tithonus turning into a cricket. "I mean, this is supposed to be a class on war fighting. So, if Greece ever gets attacked by an army of pissed-off boars, we'll all know what to do?"

"It's not about the boar," said Asirites from across the office, his cane on his lap. "It's about leadership, about bending another's will to your own. Need I remind you you're the prince of Ithaca? And someday those people back there are going to expect you to rule them? Unless, of course, you get kicked out of school. Then they won't want anything to do with you." Asirites paused and smiled. "Oh, look at what I just did. We weren't talking about it, and now we are talking about it…"

"Yeah, well-played…" Mac adjusted the tapestry slightly. "Of course, maybe if someone would just *tell* me how to avoid getting kicked out, that wouldn't be an issue."

"Now, where's the fun in that?"

"How did I know you'd say something like that?" He got down from his chair. "So, what do you think?" Mac asked ironically, gesturing to the tapestry.

"Looks great," Asirites remarked as he stood up. "So, how about some dinner? I hear they're serving roasted quail tonight at the Faculty Dining Hall."

"Actually...I have plans. I'm...meeting people for dinner." In response to his advisor's raised eyebrow, Mac continued. "You know that kid Homer? He's weird, but I asked him for advice after you dropped this whole 'be your father's son' thing on me. We've been sort of...hanging out. My roommate Theo's going to be there, and his sister Calliope..."

"I know Calliope," Asirites said. "She's one of my students. Anyone else?"

"Just this...one other girl," Mac said dismissively, but not sure why.

"So let's see here," Asirites mused. "Exchanging advice, hanging out, sharing meals...I don't want to alarm you, but I think you may have actually made a few friends."

Mac returned the smile. "Don't tell anyone, OK?"

After Mac left the office, he spent his walk across campus thinking about what Asirites had said, about becoming king of Ithaca someday. Of course, he already knew this was an eventuality, but he avoided dwelling on it. Nothing about taking charge appealed to him. Even ideal leaders would disappoint at least half of their citizens—and Mac knew he was far from ideal. He could hardly stand disappointing his mom; let alone an entire kingdom.

Of course, this assumed the citizens of Ithaca even *wanted* Mac as king. Everyone already knew him as a screw-up. And if he got kicked out of school...

By the time Mac walked through the doors of the Grape Vine, he remembered why he avoided thinking about his future; it messed with his head too much. Luckily, the inviting atmosphere of the place — the cool stone walls covered in dried grapevines; the smell of spiced, smoky meats in the air; the mellow sounds created by the student lyre-and-pipe band over in the corner — lifted his spirits. And spotting Homer, Theo, Calliope, and Andie all sitting together at a table in the corner picked him up even more.

"Sorry I'm late," Mac greeted them, as he plopped down in the empty chair between Theo and Homer. "I was just talking to my advisor."

"Ah, the mysterious Ascertes," Theo said.

"Ah-SEER-a-tees," Calliope corrected him. "Emphasis on the '*seer*.' And I'm not sure I'd call him mysterious."

"I would," Andie insisted as she took a big gulp of grape juice. "Here he got Mac into this mess, and now he refuses to give him any advice on how to get out of it." She nodded in solidarity at Mac. "What else would you call that, if not mysterious?"

"Maybe, 'interested in creativity and self-discovery'?" Calliope offered.

"We don't need any advice, from Asirites or anyone," Homer assured Mac. "I have a lot — a *lot* — of ideas. We're going to do some amazing things, believe me."

"We can do them after dinner, though, right?" Mac asked, picking up the menu from the table. "Because I'm kind of hungry."

The night at the Grape Vine ended up being just what he needed, mostly because of where he ended up sitting — right next to Andie. They talked all night: Mac told her about how Typhon the serphint was stinking up the room. Andie then told a story about how she used to wear her hair long, until one day it became impossibly tangled in some brambles when she was chasing a rabbit, and her dad had to cut it. Mac was starting to feel that same connection he felt that day on the *Æton*.

Then he made the fatal mistake: he walked away. Just for a few seconds, to the counter to get some juice. But when he came back, Theo had whisked Andie away to play darts.

From where he was seated, Mac could tell Theo was instructing Andie on proper dart-throwing techniques. At one point, he took her arm, demonstrating how to bend it when throwing — and she let him do it. Finally, Theo threw his dart...right into the wall; Andie, of course, followed with a bulls-eye.

Mac knew Theo had no clue how to throw a dart. And he suspected Andie knew as well. But Theo didn't care; he just *acted* as if he knew. The confidence Rhixion was talking about earlier that day — Theo was overflowing with it.

"I'm going to ask you something," Homer said, jolting Mac back to reality. He had been so consumed with watching Theo and Andie, he had forgotten for a moment Homer and Calliope were also at the table. "This may seem to come totally out of nowhere," Homer continued, "but it feeds into a larger observation which I'll get to later."

"Can't wait," Mac sighed.

"When we got off the Marsyas River, and I asked you if you wanted to pray to Athena, you laughed. Why?"

"I don't know. Guess I've never been a 'pray-to-the-gods' kind of guy."

"You do *believe* in the gods, right?" When Mac shrugged in reply, Homer's jaw dropped.

"This is going to become a thing, isn't it?" Mac groaned.

"You just confirmed something," Homer said. "You don't believe."

"I don't believe in what?"

"In anything," Homer said, matter-of-factly. "In the gods. In me, in my ability to keep you in school. But worst of all, you don't believe in yourself. So it doesn't matter if I come up with the absolute greatest labor, the best way for you to show off your heroism, because you don't believe you could actually *do it*. You don't believe in *anything*."

Homer didn't say any of this in an accusatory way. He was simply reporting what he understood as a fact. And Mac didn't dispute him; he just looked across the room at Theo and Andie, when suddenly the scene melted away before him. He was no longer in the Grape Vine but back in Ithaca, as a nine-year-old kid watching helplessly as other ultra-confident flirters, a hundred of them, tried to impress his mother. Only these flirters weren't like

Theo. They weren't innocent, likeable charmers; they were aggressive, dirty thugs. And scary ones, too—so scary that Mac never stood up to them. Never believed he could. Never came to his mother's aid, even that one night when she needed him the most…

Mac ripped himself from the memory and turned back to Calliope and Homer. "Feel like taking a walk?" he asked them.

****

"No way we could do this tomorrow?" Calliope asked, as she carefully handed Mac a torch through the wooden bars. "When you could at least see what you're stepping in?"

Homer and Calliope were standing outside the tall vertical bars that comprised the Pen; Mac, with the aid of a ladder, had just climbed his way inside. A big risk, for sure; students were strictly prohibited from entering the cage without supervision. If Rhixion spotted them, he would have reported them in an instant.

"This is not what I meant," Homer whispered from the other side of the bars. "I told you to get Slobber's collar. I didn't say do it at night, while he's *sleeping!*"

"Hey, you said to get the collar," Mac reminded him. "You didn't specify how."

"Just do it, then!" Calliope said nervously. "Rhixion could come by any minute."

With his torch and the full moon lighting the way, Mac crept through the mud to the row of stables. When he reached the stable from earlier in the day, he shone his torch through the door of the cage; asleep, in the far corner, was Slobber the boar.

He looked back at where Homer and Calliope were standing, but all he could see was the orange glow from their torches. He was on his own now. Taking a deep breath, he stuck his torch upright into the mud and climbed up and over the locked door. He dropped to the other side, both feet landing right into a big pile of what was definitely not mud. Ugh. He inched through the long, skinny stall until he stood right behind the creature; Mac couldn't see his face, but he could tell by the rising and falling of his spiky back that he was still sleeping. So far, so good.

Mac crouched down by the creature's neck and saw what he had come for: the collar. He moved his hands forward, slowly, ever so slowly. Finally, he reached the knot, the same one Rhixion tied that morning. Carefully, painstakingly, Mac started to untie it.

He only had to stop once, when a grunt from Slobber made him freeze. But then the beast shifted and fell back to sleep. Within seconds, Mac finished his work and delicately slid the collar out from under Slobber's heavy body.

There! Nothing to it, Mac thought, as he placed the collar in his satchel and made his way to the door. He did it. He believed he could do it, and he did it. Only…he didn't. Because just when he was thinking this…Slobber stirred.

Mac was climbing over the door when he heard the moan. He looked over his shoulder to see, glowing in the darkness, two wet and orange eyes. Slobber had been awakened. Rudely.

Mac threw both legs over the door, but before he could jump down, Slobber charged across the stall, ramming the door with such force that his tusks ripped right through. The door flew off its hinges, sending Mac hurtling through the air and into the mud and manure.

"Mac!" Calliope screamed from the other side of the cage. "Look out!"

Mac picked up his head to see a lunging Slobber taking up his entire field of vision. Just as the boar's massive tusks grazed his arm, Mac rolled out of the way, onto a ragged plank of wood from the broken door. Grabbing the board, Mac bolted up and smashed Slobber on top of his head. The boar staggered, momentarily stunned, as Mac took a few steps backward, waving his makeshift weapon in front of him.

The two circled each other, and then Mac took another swing. This time, however, Slobber was ready: he caught the wood in his tusks, wrested it out of Mac's hands, and with a violent thrashing of his head, tossed it out of the way. As a show of superiority, Slobber let out a loud, ugly squeal, punctuated by a typical shower of drool.

"Just get out of there!" he heard Homer yell. "Get back to the ladder!"

Mac took off, the rampaging Slobber right behind him. The boar could outpace him but couldn't turn as quickly; only a series of sharp turns on Mac's part prevented Slobber from overtaking him. Finally, Mac reached the ladder and started climbing. When Slobber lunged at him, Mac swung his legs to the side to avoid getting impaled by the giant tusks. Somehow, he kept climbing and almost reached the top when he felt himself teetering; Slobber had started ramming his head into the side of the thick ladder, causing it to topple. Mac thudded gracelessly into the muck below, the heavy ladder collapsing right on top of him.

Slobber marched confidently over to Mac, as if it knew what Mac himself realized: he couldn't go anywhere. The fallen ladder had pinned him to the ground. And so, with no other options, Mac did the only thing he could think of: he flung out his hand and, just as he tried to do earlier that morning, stared with squinted eyes right at the monster.

Only this time, Mac wasn't *just* staring into the eyes of this one boar. He was staring into the eyes of the suitors. All of them: Polybos, Leodes, Eurynomos, Antinoös...He heaped all of them, all those wretched men who mocked him and tormented him and stole his childhood, onto the boar's spiky back and tried to stare them all down. And he didn't stop with the suitors. Gurgus, Melpagon, Odysseus, even Zeus, even the specter of his own self-doubt—he threw all of them on that same spiky back. And he tried to stare them all down.

It worked. Remarkably, miraculously, *it worked*. Slobber turned, staggered backwards, and then flopped his heavy head into the mud.

"I did it!" Mac shouted. "You hear that, you disgusting sack of spit? I did it!"

"Uh, Mac?" he heard Homer say. Mac turned, as best he could with the ladder on him, and saw Homer and Calliope on the other side of the cage. He saw someone else, too, standing next to them: Rhixion. His left hand held a goblet. His right hand was outstretched, just as it had been that morning, when he had subdued his pet boar.

"Strangest thing," he said, as he lowered his right hand and produced a key from his belt. "I was having trouble sleeping. Usually, I have no trouble, but tonight I did." As he talked, he used the key to open the cage door. "So, I poured myself a drink and decided to go for a walk."

By this time, Rhixion was inside the cage and lifting the bulky ladder, allowing Mac to slide out. "Good thing, too," he continued. "If I hadn't come by when I did, ol' Solobeus would have carved you up but good. We could've sent you home in five different boats."

"Thanks," Mac muttered, in a way that made him seem ungrateful, but he was really too ashamed to say anything else. With his mud-covered head down, he started walking out.

He had almost made it out the door when Rhixion called to him. "Hold on," he said calmly. Mac turned to see his teacher kneeling on the ground, petting Slobber's back. Without looking Mac's way, he said simply, "I think you have something of mine."

Oh, right. Mac reached into his satchel and pulled out the collar.

Rhixion took a long sip of his drink. Then he stood up, took the collar out of Mac's hand, and held it up, studying the jewels and teeth as they glinted in the moonlight. "So a student on probation," he began, "who has to do something heroic, is found sneaking around at night, *stealing* from a teacher. What would Gurgus think about that?"

Mac didn't respond. What could he say? He knew he was cooked. But Homer spoke. "Please, sir. Don't report him. It's my fault. I said I wanted to see the collar up close. He was just trying to impress us."

Rhixion glanced curiously at Homer and Calliope. "So, you want to see this?" he asked them, as he walked over to the cage and held out the collar. "This was given to me by an old Pontian medicine man, who wore it as a belt. I had saved his life—he had been cornered by a band of three robbers—and he gave it to me to show his appreciation. He told me that these teeth," as he spoke, he pointed to eight cracked teeth dangling from the collar, "were *magical*. You know the story of how Jason, while trying to fetch the Golden Fleece, was forced to sow a set of dragon's teeth, which sprouted into full-grown warriors? Well, these teeth came from that very dragon...at least, that's what this man told me. Of course, how many people over the years have claimed they possessed teeth from this single dragon? It must have had a pretty big mouth, that dragon, to have produced that many teeth, wouldn't you say?"

Slobber started to moan slightly, so Rhixion went over to scratch him under the ears. Mac, confused, looked at Homer and Calliope as Rhixion took another swig from his goblet and kept talking. "Truth? I've never been that impressed with Jason. And I'm not even talking about his callous mistreatment of his wife Medea. They call Jason a hero for getting the Fleece. Really? A hero? For what? Storming into a kingdom and *demanding* the king hand the Fleece over to him? He obviously forgot the most important lesson of heroism."

Rhixion, still grasping his pet's collar, had stood up by this point and walked over to Mac. "You *do* know the most important lesson of heroism, don't you?" he asked. When Mac shook his head, Rhixion took his student's hand and draped the collar across his open palm.

"Sometimes, all it takes to be a hero," Rhixion instructed, closing Mac's fingers over his prize, "is to *ask nicely*."

Demetrius—

Just so you know: I forgive you. Yeah, you gave me a defective map, and you got me thinking I was embarking on a grand adventure, when it ended up being a trip to a really, really out-of-the-way souvenir shop. But hey, an honest mistake, right? And to show you there are no hard feelings, I wanted to ask you to help me on a project I know you'll like.

First, a little background: I know I told Mac we were going to ditch the whole Minotaur angle, but I wanted to create a sort of tutorial on Andie's dad and his esteemed research...in case Mac ever got curious.

So here it is: a miniature Minotaur tutorial...or a mini-Mino-tu-Taur-ial. (Ha!) So far, I only have three questions, but I was hoping you could help me come up with some more. (And I apologize in advance for the elementary nature of some of these, but this is meant for Mac, after all. He's pretty elementary.)

Question #1: Which of the following is NOT true about the Minotaur?

A. The "Minotaur" (a term derived from King Minos of Crete) actually has a proper name: Asterion.
B. The Minotaur was born after Dionysus made Queen Pasiphae fall in love with a white bull; this was Dionysus's revenge after King Minos refused to sacrifice the bull to him.
C. Pasiphae had a wooden cow-suit made, so she could have sexual relations with the white bull; the result of this woman-bull union was the Minotaur.
D. By the decree of King Minos, fourteen Athenian youths—seven males, seven females—were to be sacrificed to the Minotaur every nine years.

Answer: B—duh!. Poseidon cursed Pasiphae, not Dionysus. (I warned you some of these were easy.)

Question #2: The scholar Hieronymus gave a lecture at Argus University entitled, "Maze of Truth: In Pursuit of the Minotaur." In it, he says, "We're all Minotaurs—that's what makes us compelling. A hero who's all noble all the time is as uninteresting as a villain who's exclusively deplorable." To what is he referring?

A. The immortality of the Minotaur

B. The Minotaur's ferocious appetite
C. The hybrid nature of the Minotaur

Answer: C. In that same lecture, Hieronymus says, "We all have different aspects—even opposing aspects—to our personalities. And the fluky mystery is how often these opposing traits are complementary rather than conflicting." I like that. It gives me hope I can find my own "other side" someday.

Question #3: Which theorist believed that ingesting the Minotaur's blood could make one immortal?

A. Phaedysthenes
B. Herniboea
C. Xenotareus

Answer: C Xenotareus: I have to admit, this definitely intrigued me. Apparently, this Xenotareus guy studied Centaurs, which got him interested in hybrid species. He first tried to figure out ways to breed different animals together—which got him interested in other ways he could manipulate life, including extending it. Pretty ghastly, sure, but fascinating, too.

Anyway, this is just a start. If you can think of some other questions, send them along.

-Homer

CHAPTER FIFTEEN
Naming Melons

One hot afternoon, not long after he and Slobber were formally introduced, Mac was alone in his room, trying to squeeze in a nap. He knew he didn't have long before Theo, out cavorting at the beach, came crashing home, doing his best impersonation of a big old dog—dragging sand across the floor, spraying salt water everywhere, begging Mac to play some game with him.

He was just about asleep when he heard a knock at the door. He ignored it, as usual, and whipped the blanket over his head. But then he heard a familiar voice, coming from inside the room: "What, you're not going to invite me in?"

He pulled away the blanket and saw Andie, standing there next to his bed, her bow slung over one shoulder and an oversized sack over the other.

Mac sat up abruptly, surprised to see her. "Come on in," he said—a dumb thing to say, since she was already in the room. Andie plopped her bag on the floor and sat down on the edge of Theo's bed—an association that didn't exactly thrill him. "Theo's not here," he told her. "He's at the beach."

"Thanks for the update," she remarked as she looked around the room. When she spotted, near the window, the makeshift wooden pen that Theo had made for his serphint, she stood up. "Ah, I was wondering where he kept…what did he call it?"

"Typhon…" Mac shook his head at the overblown name as Andie reached into the small crate and pulled out the creature, which had grown a few inches in the weeks since the group came back from the Marsyas River.

"He just keeps it here in this box?" Andie asked, as she held the serphint in front of her.

"Well, Kalakloptas said it can live on land, and Theo gives it water, I guess," Mac explained, even though he didn't really bother himself with the details when it came to caring for Theo's pet.

Andie held the serphint's head in front of her, as if studying it. "It's just the weirdest thing…" she muttered, before uncoiling the animal from her hand and putting it into its pen. She sat back down on Theo's bed and, for a few awkward moments, Mac and Andie looked at each other without speaking. Finally, Andie broke the silence: "So…feel like taking a walk?"

If anyone else had asked, Mac would have said no; he always preferred sleeping to socializing. But this wasn't anyone else. So, a few minutes later, Mac found himself out of bed, embarking on a walk that would ultimately take them through the woods and onto some familiar shores: that same secluded beach where he'd first met Andie, on the afternoon of War Games.

"I thought you didn't want anyone trespassing on your 'private' beach," he reminded her as he gazed out at the crumbled pillars.

"I don't, but since you've already been here once, I figured, why not?" she conceded, dropping her large sack into the white sands. "Besides, I need some help with target practice."

"Wait…you want to use me as a target?"

Andie laughed, and Mac warmed at the sound. "I'm not going to shoot *at* you. I'm going to shoot *with* you."

"I'm nowhere near as good as you."

"Of course not. And you never will be," she said with a grin. "But you can come close." Bending down, she produced a small melon from her sack. Walking about fifty paces across the beach, she balanced the melon on top of a tall stone slab, just about eye level. When she returned, she took a deep breath and raised her bow.

Mac watched as she closed her eyes and stood perfectly still. He could see her lips moving slightly but couldn't hear what she was saying. Opening her eyes, Andie stared at the melon, her eyes alive with a ferocity Mac had never seen in them before. The bowstring snapped, and then, in an instant, the arrow pierced the fruit, which flew off the stone slab.

Mac let out a whistle as a satisfied smile split Andie's face. "Your turn," she said.

Mac had always considered himself reasonably competent with the bow and arrow—not masterful, but decent. Having her *watch* him, though, made him feel self-conscious. Her stare weighed on him—as he walked to the stone slab and back, as he locked his eye on the melon, and finally, as he sent his arrow three feet above his intended target.

He offered up a hangdog smile, but Andie got right down to business: "OK, two things," she said. "First, you have to commit. When you pull back that bowstring, you can't second-guess yourself. As soon as you hesitate, it's over."

"OK," Mac said. He didn't realize he *had* hesitated, but he took her word for it.

"Next," she continued, "you need to give yourself a target."

"I had a target," Mac corrected her. "I was aiming for the fruit, just like you did."

"Ah, but I wasn't shooting the fruit."

"What are you talking about?"

"You have to give it a name," she said simply.

Andie placed another arrow in Mac's palm, closing his fingers around it and holding his hand between both of hers. He looked at her then quickly turned away, unnerved by her nearness. "Think of the person you hate most in the world," she continued. "Someone who stirs up to the surface every dark, blood-boiling feeling inside of you. Someone who makes—"

"Antinoös," Mac said suddenly, before he had a chance to take it back. At Andie's questioning gaze, Mac clarified, "He's…well, he's basically the ringleader of all the suitors."

"Nice. Now, look at the melon, and picture the creep's face right there. Really try to imagine that you're aiming for…what's his name? Antinoös?"

"Not this staring stuff again…" Mac grumbled, remembering his failure with Slobber.

"The melon's not going to spit on you," Andie insisted. "Let's go. Picture Antinoös." Mac felt silly at first, but he did what she told him to do: stare at the melon and picture the face of Antinoös. His slick, black hair…big, fleshy lips…eyes always fixed on his father's throne. As he positioned himself, Andie took a few steps back, stood quietly for a moment, and then said, "Now say his name, and let it fly."

Like she instructed him, he said the name out loud: "Antinoös." And in that moment, Mac let everything he felt for that man wash over him, a tidal wave of hatred, disgust, fear, and shame. In one swift motion he drew back the arrow and released it. A second later, the arrow cleaved the fruit in two.

Mac's breath left him in a whoosh. "Wow. That was incredible!"

Andie gave a sad little smile. "It helps if you have a lot of hatred inside of you." Then she turned and started walking toward the stone slab.

"I gotta try that again," Mac declared, catching up to her. "I have a lot of suitors to hit…Amphimedon, Eurymachus, Peisandros. We could be here a while."

Andie shrugged. "I've got time."

When they reached the slab, Andie and Mac crouched down to retrieve the arrows from the pile of broken melon. "So, what names do you use?" he asked, as he picked up a melon shard. "Melpagon? Gurgus? With all the jerks here, you must have plenty of good targets."

"I use the same name every time," she said, keeping her eyes on the ground.

"What name?" he asked, taking a big bite out of the now-exposed fruit.

She looked directly at him and said, "Minotaur."

Mac wasn't expecting that—not just what she said, but how she said it: so matter-of-factly, as if she just accepted this anguish as part of her life. He struggled with a reply, finally settling on distraction. "You think I could come back here with you sometime?" he asked, handing her a piece of shattered fruit. "Like I said, I've got a lot of melons to name."

Andie smiled, took the piece from him, and gave one of her patented shoulder shrugs. "Sure. But next time, bring your own bow. And your own melons."

And he did. A few days later, they met again for target practice, only this time, Mac supplied the fruit. And a few days after that, they met again. And a few days after that, until afternoon target practice became a regular routine. Each session, Mac would identify different suitors to skewer; in the process, he'd end up telling a story about each one, which invariably led to stories about his mom and then to stories about himself. But he never let things get *too* heavy; in fact, they spent a good chunk of their practices just goofing around — spitting seeds at each other or chasing each other down the beach or splashing around in the water.

Despite all this, Mac had trouble reading Andie. For one thing, she always wanted to keep their target practice sessions secret. Whenever the whole group met at the Grape Vine, she would never mention hanging out with him, and the few times Mac tried to say something, she abruptly changed the subject. At first, Mac couldn't help but feel insecure, worrying she was ashamed of being with him or something. Then he realized she didn't want to keep their activities secretive, just the place where they did them. "This is *our* beach, you know?" she said one day, when Mac suggested they invite Homer and Calliope along. "Let's not spoil it."

Happy to have something that belonged to just the two of them, he agreed.

Besides the beach, she kept other things under wraps, too. One afternoon, when Mac showed up at her dorm room a little bit early, he saw her standing on a chair and scratching at the wall with one of her arrowheads. When she noticed him, she seemed startled and hurriedly yanked on a huge curtain that covered the entire wall; clearly, she didn't want Mac to see what she was doing. He acted as if he didn't see anything, but he was definitely curious.

In many ways, she kept herself hidden under a curtain as well. Sure, she had opened up to him when they were on the *Æton* — about her father and his obsession with the Minotaur. But now that they were back on land, it seemed any additional questions on that subject would not be tolerated. Mac figured this out one day for certain after target practice; he was sitting by the shore on one of the large, flat rocks, watching Andie, crouched down a short distance away, as she drew in the wet sand with one of her arrows.

"What do you think?" she asked. Mac walked the few steps to get a closer look at her sketch—a surprisingly intricate picture of a large, round face, with crazy eyes and a huge tongue flopping out of an enormous mouth; piercing the circle was a single arrow, which went in one non-existent ear and out the other.

"Whoa, you got talent, kid," Mac remarked. "What is it?"

"One of your suitors, of course," Andie said, "getting shot in the head."

Mac admired her handiwork as Andie put on some finishing touches. "Think you could ever do it?" she finally asked, not looking up from the sand.

"What? Draw something like that?"

"No," she sort of laughed. "Kill the suitors. Think you could ever do it, for real?"

Mac sat back down on the rock and dug his feet in the mud. "I don't know. I mean, I hate 'em, but…taking a life…it's a pretty big deal, you know? Besides, there's a lot of them, and only one of me. Might not turn out so well." He looked over at her as she continued to draw with her arrow. "How about you? Do you think you could ever really kill the Minotaur?"

"Oh, yeah," she said, without hesitation.

"Well, do you think you'd ever get the chance? Do you think it's still alive?" Andie didn't say anything, just looked around the beach. "And even if it is, do you have any idea where to find it? Did your dad give you any indication where it might be?"

"Aren't you full of questions today?" she said, her way of acknowledging those questions while also making it clear she had no intentions of answering them. Then she stood up. "You hungry? I'm hungry. Let's get back."

Mac took the hint and never broached the subject again. He didn't want to push her to the point where she stopped wanting to hang out with him. Who cared if she didn't share her life story with him, anyway? He just liked being with her. And besides, while she seemed eternally closed-lipped about her dad, she did share other things with him: how her uncle was paying for her to go to school at Pieridian; how this same uncle was forbidding her to get a tattoo of the sun-chariot on her shoulder, even though she *really* wanted one; how she rarely ate in the dining hall because they put cumin in *everything*. One day, she spent their whole target practice complaining about her roommate, but the next day, admitted that she wasn't that bad. She just didn't know her, Andie said—and then admitted she really didn't know *anyone* at school very well. "Well, not before this year," she said, with a slight smile, which Mac returned.

Except for Homer, Mac had never had this kind of connection—being let into someone else's life, little by little, and letting that person into his. But he knew it felt good. In fact, the times spent alone with Andie had become the best parts of his week.

One day stood out as particularly glorious. Andie convinced Mac to blow off his morning classes so they could get target practice done early. After she helped Mac shoot that day's suitors (Polybus and Demoptolemus), they spent the rest of the time relaxing: some swimming, some clam-digging, but mostly just lounging on the shore. Not even talking much, not feeling the need to. Later, they both went back to their rooms, to get ready for a night out at the Grape Vine. Mac couldn't believe his luck: two opportunities to see Andie in one day. And even though he had spent most of the day with her, he couldn't wait to see her again,

He was breezing across campus, heading for the Grape Vine, when he heard The Voice—that soul-crushing, sniveling, voice he knew all too well.

"Telemachus."

He had a way of saying someone's name using the same tone a person would use upon realizing he had just stepped in manure. "Hello, Headmaster Gurgus," Mac said softly, trying to muster up the appropriate deference and humility. He didn't look Gurgus in his fat face but kept his eyes on the ground, where Mac saw, at the end of a long leash, the dog Iota—but not the frantic, yipping dog the student body had come to know and loathe, but a mute and immobile Iota, utterly frozen in fear, staring up at Mac with two gigantic, bulging eyes.

"Where are you off to in such a hurry?" Gurgus asked sneeringly.

"Library, perhaps?"

Mac smiled slightly, to acknowledge he got this oh-so-funny joke. "No," Mac answered. "I'm meeting friends for dinner." Mac still had his eyes on Iota, who had now crept behind his master's rotund leg.

"Ah, *friends*, eh?" Gurgus marveled. "Well, hopefully, these new 'friends' will help you see how profoundly you've been *wasting* your potential. And if these 'friends' can show you the value of education and hard work, if they can help drag you out of this pit of delinquency in which you've insisted on residing, then perhaps you could make something out of yourself."

Mac stopped listening at "wasting." He got too distracted by Iota, still staring up at him from behind Gurgus's ample leg. Mac knew something peculiar was going on with the dog, but he didn't know what, How could he? How could he have known that seeing that boy from the Disciplinary Chambers had flung the poor creature into the throes of a terrible flashback? That her tiny mind was reliving the memories of that terrible morning and those birds— those squawking, flapping, *crapping* birds?

Mac didn't know any of that. He only knew what he saw: Iota, its frozen eyes open wide, squatting over Gurgus's foot.

Gurgus, so immersed in his lecture, didn't even notice at first. But as he felt something warm and wet running over his foot, he looked down. *Then* he freaked out.

"Mother of Pan!" Gurgus shrieked at the sight and sensation of his own dog peeing on him. He did an awkward little dance, trying to pull his foot out of the way, before getting down on his knees to comfort the petrified beast.

While still on the ground, he glared up at Mac, his eyes ablaze with rage. "This is your fault! *Your* fault! She was a wonderful dog, never caused anyone an ounce of grief, and then you...you *traumatized* her!"

Mac didn't even try to defend himself; he just stood there, dumbfounded. Even when Gurgus picked himself up and shook a big, fat finger in his face, Mac didn't flinch. "I should have kicked you out years ago!" he blasted, cradling Iota in his non-pointing hand. "But no! Like an idiot, I always let Asirites talk me into giving you another chance. But no more! Next time, there will be no compromise, no compassion. Because you do not deserve it! You do not deserve my compassion, you don't deserve me, and you do not deserve *this school*!"

With that, Headmaster Gurgus turned abruptly and waddled away, whispering consoling words into his pet's ear. Mac, meanwhile, didn't move, just remained standing there as the full implications of what had happened started to sink in. Three realizations came to his mind: that he really freaked out that dog; that Gurgus really hated him; and that he didn't have a prayer of staying at school.

When Mac showed up at the Grape Vine, decidedly less excited than he had been when he started his walk across campus, he saw a line snaking out the door. He remembered that a student band was playing that night. The sight of the long line almost made him turn around. On the other hand, he knew Andie was already inside; if anyone could improve his mood, it would be her.

By the time Mac made his way into the Grape Vine's congested foyer, he found himself pressed up against a wooden post littered with announcements and advertisements, for clubs, tutors, and school activities. With nothing else to do, he glanced at some of the items on the post: an advertisement for the band, Cerberus Sal and the Four Heads; a big poster for the upcoming Harvest Dance; and—to Mac's surprise—one of Kalakloptas's flyers. Mac smiled, immediately knowing Theo had put the flyer there.

As the line lurched forward, releasing him into the darkened confines of the Grape Vine, a familiar sound caused Mac to look across the room. He saw Theo himself with the band, blasting away on his aulos. Mac shook his head as he crumpled the flyer in his hand, all the while marveling at Theo's magic, his ability to *command* a room. He made it look so easy.

Mac squeezed his way through the crowd until he finally spotted Andie, waving from a table in the torch-lit corner, where the rest of the gang was sitting. The sight of Andie calling him over brightened his spirits—until he realized Theo was coming right behind him. Mac was left wondering whose attention she was she trying to get—

his or Theo's.

"So, what's the word, my brother?" bellowed Theo, slapping Mac on the shoulders as they both arrived at the round, scarred table.

"The word..." Mac sighed, plopping on the bench next to Homer, "the word is *screwed*." He proceeded to tell everyone about his unfortunate encounter with Gurgus and Iota. Theo, Andie, and Calliope laughed at first, but they soon agreed the incident didn't exactly help Mac's case. Homer, however, seemed undeterred.

"It'll be fine," Homer assured him, rolling up the parchment he had in front of him. "Trust me. We just have to remember what Asirites said."

"Asirites talks in code!" Mac grumbled. "We don't *know* what he said."

"Yes, we do. We absolutely know," corrected Homer. "He wants you to prove you're a hero. And I really think this next labor will do just that. I just have to put a few more pieces in place. Of course, I wouldn't have to come up with *another* plan if a certain someone went along with the first plan." Homer stared pointedly at Andie as he spoke. "Maybe if we knew a little more information...say, the location of something?"

The group fell silent as Andie glared across the table at Homer. She didn't say anything. She didn't have to. Her eyes said it all: *Back off.*

"Wait! Wait! I've got it!" Theo exclaimed, breaking the tension by jumping off the bench and thumping Mac hard on the back. "Oh, this is epic! *Epic!*"

"What's the matter with you?" Mac winced.

"Oh, *I'm* fine...but Nikolas broke both his ankles yesterday!" he announced.

"Who?" Andie asked him.

"Nikolas," Theo explained. "You didn't hear about how he jumped from his bunk pretending to be Icarus? Doesn't matter. The bottom line is he can't even walk, the idiot. He had to go home for the rest of the term." Theo beamed and thumped Mac again. "So you know what that means?"

"Not even a little," answered Mac.

"It means Gia doesn't have a date for the Harvest Dance."

"Who's Gia?" Homer asked.

Theo sighed. "Don't you guys follow *anything* that goes on at school? Gia was going with Niko to the dance. But now he's out of commission."

"So, she doesn't go to the dance," Homer shrugged. "Big deal."

"As a matter of fact, it *is* a big deal," Theo insisted. "Gia's the head of the dance committee. She spent weeks planning for this. And now she can't even *go*? She's crushed."

"Why doesn't she just go with someone else?" Calliope asked.

"You don't think she's tried? I was just talking to her earlier," Theo says, motioning to another table with his thumb. "Everybody already has their dates all set."

"I don't have a date," Calliope countered.

"School dances are a silly waste of time," Homer huffed.

"I don't *do* school dances," said Andie.

Theo literally threw his hands up in exasperation. "You guys are ridiculously lame! And frankly, you're *all* in dire need of my help, but I gotta concentrate on my boy Mac, here."

"No, you really don't," Mac said, knowing and dreading where Theo was heading.

"Dude! You don't even know what I'm going to say."

"I'm *not* asking this girl to the dance."

"Why not?" Theo looked personally affronted.

"Because…uh…I sorta know her already."

"You do? Then you know she's nice, pretty, *and* desperate. Perfect combination, right?"

"Theo, it's not going to work. She hates me."

Theo paused for a moment as realization dawned. "You hooked up with her and then blew her off, didn't you?"

Shrinking into his seat a little, Mac came clean. "She came to see me the day of the disciplinary hearing. I couldn't remember her name and told her to get lost. Yeah, Theo, she definitely hates me."

"All the more reason you should ask her," Calliope piped in. "To make up for how you treated her."

"And how does any of this help him from getting expelled?" a pouty Homer interjected.

"Isn't it obvious?" Theo asked. "Mac's gotta prove he's a hero, right? And what do all heroes have in common? They're gallant," Theo smiled.

"You've got to be kidding me!" Homer snorted. "You actually think *that's* what Mac's quest is all about? To be nice to a *girl*? You think that's going to keep him here at school?"

"You know what, little-man? Change of the guard here. We tried it your way and look where it got us," Theo said as he produced his trusty aulos and droned out a long, atonal whistle.

"Can this joke just die, please?" Homer moaned.

"I'm just saying," Theo declared, "we're going to try it *my* way for once."

"No, we're not," Mac said.

"But *why*, dude?"

"I'm not going to take someone else's *girlfriend* to a dance," Mac insisted, as he tried to tramp down memories of his mom's suitors.

"They're not a couple, Gia and Niko," Theo said. "They were just going as friends.

So why won't you ask her?"

"Because *I* don't do dances, either," Mac told him. "If you feel so bad for this girl, why don't *you* ask her to the dance?"

"Dude, don't you know me at all? I've had my date for weeks. I'm going with Iris." Theo's face broke out into a devilish grin. "Very cool. Very pretty."

Mac couldn't help but glance over at Andie, to check out her reaction to Theo's gushing over this other girl. But Andie offered nothing, just kept her head down in her menu—which meant she didn't hear what he said, she was *pretending* she didn't hear what he said, or she just didn't *care* what he said. As usual, Mac had a hard time reading her.

And figuring out Theo wasn't any easier; if he liked Andie, he had a funny way of showing it, considering how often he talked about other girls in front of her. Then again, maybe he had some master plan cooking, to appear elusive and thus more desirable. To Mac, it seemed stupid, but who was he to judge?

Meanwhile, Theo was still trying to sell Mac on the dance: "Mac, listen to me, you obviously liked Gia enough the first time. She's nice. Almost to a fault, actually. I'm sure she'll say yes if you ask her, even after the way you blew her off. She's *that* desperate."

"I haven't talked to her since that day. I'm not going to just walk up to her now and ask her to the dance," Mac asserted.

"Fair point. Let me ask her for you." Before Mac could mount another objection, Theo had leaped from the bench and bounded across the room to a table jammed with seven girls.

"Great," Mac groaned. "Just great."

"You know, he may be on to something," Calliope postulated. "You're helping out a girl in trouble, right? I mean, yeah…it's just a dance; she's not chained to a rock or anything. But it's still heroic in a way. Besides, it wouldn't kill you to get *involved* in something, right?"

Mac let her theory sink in as he looked over at Homer. "Personally, I don't think it will help your issues with Gurgus," he said, unspooling his parchment. "But it can't hurt, I guess."

Finally, Mac turned to the last person at the table, the only one who hadn't yet weighed in, and the only one whose response would determine his decision. If he thought he had any chance with Andie, he wouldn't go to the dance with anyone else.

Did he expect her to object ferociously to the idea of him and Gia going to a dance together? Did he honestly think she'd use this very public moment to declare her feelings for him? He certainly would have welcomed either scenario, but deep down, he knew they were both ridiculous and impossible. Instead, Andie did what Mac knew she'd do: she casually looked up from the menu she'd been silently studying ever since Theo mentioned his date and said simply, "I think you should go with her. I mean, why not?"

He saw it coming, but it still hurt. If his heart were a melon, her words would have splintered it.

Dejected, but putting on a brave face, Mac looked across the Grape Vine at Theo, on one knee next to Gia, pointing in Mac's direction. Working his magic, obviously.

"Right," Mac said unenthusiastically. "Why not?"

CHAPTER SIXTEEN
Scenes from a Dance

Mac's mom always insisted he take at least one formal outfit to school—for school functions, she said, or in case someone died. Mac never really saw the point: he shunned social functions, after all, and since he hadn't made any friends, why would he need to dress up for anyone's funeral? But he eventually caved and brought the one outfit with him, just like she'd asked. When it came to his mom, he always caved.

And so, for the first time in two-and-a-half years, Mac pulled his dark green chiton out from a pile in the corner as he prepared to do the unthinkable: show his face at a school dance.

Even the act of getting ready—of dressing up, of fixing his hair, of actually *caring* how he looked—felt foreign to him. He had never done anything like that, not once during his whole time at Pieridian. He hadn't used a mirror in so long, he hardly recognized his own face.

In fact, Mac couldn't even find his mirror. Not surprisingly, his roommate had several readily available. Ah, Theo—the fool who got him into this mess, with his beyond-absurd notion that going to a dance would somehow reveal heroism. Mac wanted to be angry at him. But then, as he stood alone in his room, holding Theo's bronze mirror at different arm-lengths, he remembered the conversation he'd had with Theo, right before he dashed out to some pre-dance party.

"Hey, think about it this way," he was saying as he slicked back his hair. "You know what all heroes have in common? They're good with the *ladies*."

"Whatever you say," Mac mumbled.

"Listen, I know I put you up to this, and you're dealing with all this other crap right now, so this is probably the last thing you want to do. But I just want you to have a good time. OK?"

Mac knew he meant it: he really *did* want Mac to have fun—to go to a dance, to dress in nice clothes, to do something *normal*. But he also knew that "having fun" was something he just couldn't do, not completely—not when he saw, staring back at him from the mirror, the sad, unavoidable truth: that he was wearing his green chiton for the first and last time. Gurgus would never let him stay. His days as a Pieridian student were winding down. By the time the next school function came around, he'd be gone.

He had to make this one night count.

"Done admiring yourself?" said a familiar voice from the open doorway. Mac turned to see a virtually unrecognizable Homer—neatly combed hair, immaculately clean and wrinkle-free chiton, wide grin spreading across his face as he gently held a small bouquet of flowers.

"So," Homer announced with surprising self-assurance. "Ready to do this?" Mac put down the mirror and sighed. Yeah, he was ready.

****

Calliope sat on her bed putting the finishing touches on her hair, an elaborate series of looped braids pulled together with a glittering dragonfly clasp, a Drama Club good luck charm that she wore for every opening night performance. Thinking about the evening to come, she mused that school dances were a lot like theater. Lavish costumes, decorative scenery, music, and merriment. And lots of people pretending about one thing or another. Pretending they haven't been drinking when they walk past a chaperone. Pretending they don't like someone they do. Pretending they're not heartbroken when they see the person they like dancing with someone else, when all they want to do is break down and cry.

Calliope felt lucky she didn't have to pretend tonight. Maybe it stung a little that no one asked her to the dance. But the disappointment was eased by the knowledge that she'd be going with a good friend. She was going to have fun…no pretending.

Her thoughts drifted back to an afternoon earlier that week, when Mac had crossed the quad to find her, clearly on a mission.

"So, this Harvest Dance," Mac began awkwardly. "I know you said you weren't going, but…I was wondering what your stance is on asking someone to go?"

"My stance? Wait, I'm confused," she answered. "Did something happen to your date?"

"Me? No, no, no. I'm still going with Gia," he responded with zero enthusiasm. "I was thinking about Homer. I'd…well…I'd kind of like him to be there. He pretends that school dances are beneath him, but you and I both know that if Hercules himself came down from Mount Olympus to ask him, Homer would collapse with joy."

"Yeah, I get it," Calliope said with a sigh. "The boys at Pieridian aren't exactly lining up to go out with him, are they?"

"He's better than all of them," Mac answered with a frown.

"I agree," she answered, smiling at Mac's fierce loyalty to his new friend.

"So I'm thinking maybe you could convince him to be *your* date. Then I'd have two friendly faces around."

"Three. You're forgetting Theo."

"No way am I forgetting Theo. He got me into this mess. So whattya say?" Mac flashed a grin. "Will you ask him? Don't leave me alone out there."

True to her word, Calliope stopped by Homer's room just a few hours later. He'd been sitting on the floor, polishing his hero figurines, which he quickly shoved under a blanket upon seeing her. When she asked him to the dance, explaining that they'd be doing it to support Mac, he immediately said yes. He was a good friend. And Calliope liked that about him.

A knock on the door brought her back to the present. She took one last deep breath, quickly looked at herself in the mirror, and then walked purposefully to the door. Showtime.

****

Andie, an arrow clenched between her teeth, took a few steps back to take it all in.

If the administrators knew what she was up to, they'd be outraged. Students were prohibited from etching *anything* into the stone walls of their rooms, even their names. And here she was creating an elaborate mural that stretched across an *entire* wall? She'd get slammed for sure once they found out. But she didn't care. She had a vision.

For almost seven weeks, even before War Games, she had been slaving away on this mural. It had started simply enough: using one of her iron-tipped arrowheads, she carved a small labyrinth into the wall next to her bed. Over time, she enlarged the labyrinth, making longer and more intricate pathways. And then, within the corridors, she started inserting different characters: Arachne, moments after Athena turns her into a spider; a sleeping Argus, right before Hermes chops his head off; Actaeon, in the midst of being transformed into a stag. Her illustrations were all deliberately deformed and more than a little frightening—they literally chased Andie's roommate out of the room at night—but none could compare to the ghastly, incomplete figure in the middle of the maze.

With its gigantic head, oversized eyes, and fangs as big as its horns, Andie's version of the Minotaur was already a masterpiece, a thing of distorted, monstrous beauty. And she hadn't even started on the body. That's what tonight was for: while everyone else was at the dance, she planned on using this uninterrupted time to work on her creation. She was looking forward to it.

Except for her annoying roommate, Andie didn't let anyone see what she was doing on her wall; in fact, when she wasn't working on it, she hung a tapestry over it. As far as she was concerned, the mural was for her and no one else. She *needed* it, especially with the way gossip ran rampant at this school. These days, it seemed like everyone knew about her missing dad. Some looked at her with pity, while others asked about him with ghoulish fascination. Just a week ago, a random boy in her Constellations class asked if her father had killed himself. She wasn't sure what hurt more: being asked the question, or not knowing the answer.

From outside her window, Andie could hear laughter and the excited chattering of students heading over to the dance. She thought about her four friends and wondered how they were faring, especially Mac. Just picturing a guilty Mac trying to make conversation with an air-headed Gia made her smile. What could they possibly talk about? She actually felt sorry for him. Maybe she should take a break from her work and leave a note for him in his room, asking him to come find her after the dance. If the night was a bust, he might need a friend to talk to.

****

"Uh…the decorations look…nice."

"What?" Gia shouted, to be heard over the music.

"You were in charge of the decorations, right?" Mac asked, as he looked around the atrium, decked out with plants and tapestries and torches. "I was just saying they look nice. Very…harvest-y."

Even as the words left his mouth, Mac knew they were lame, but he had to say *something*. For the past hour, he had been hovering on the outskirts of Gia and her gaggle of friends, as they shot him mocking glares. Every time he tried to say something to Gia, she either pointedly ignored him or spit out a sarcastic "Whatever." He was beginning to think there was more to her agreeing to be his date than simple desperation. She was pissed and out for revenge, fueled by her loyal but kind of mean friends.

Eventually, he'd found himself so removed from the group, he was standing against the wall, wedged between two potted plants—essentially becoming part of the decorations himself. When a new song began, three of Gia's friends, squealing louder than the music, appeared at her side and pulled her away.

No, she didn't ask him to join in the dancing, but Mac didn't begrudge her. He kept remembering what Calliope said that night at the Grape Vine, about making it up to Gia for the way he treated her. She had every right to be mad. She was a nice girl who liked him. True, he didn't seek her out that night she came to his room, but he certainly didn't refuse her company, although he had no intention of taking it any further. And if he wasn't such a miserable loner, instead of ignoring her for months, he might've tried to get to know her a little. Maybe it was too late to make amends. Maybe all he could do was stick with her tonight and endure her hurt and anger.

He still felt a little awkward, though, standing there against the wall, especially after the band played two more songs and Gia still hadn't returned. Realizing he needed to do more than check out the scenery, Mac left the protective cover of the potted plants and paced around the perimeter of the room. He spotted Homer and Calliope, sitting at one of the tables, just the two of them, leaning in close and laughing. He started to walk over, but something made him stop dead in his tracks. Theo had just arrived. And he wasn't alone.

****

About an hour into the dance, Homer started to accept it: he belonged here. He was at a school dance with a date just like everyone else. Sure, it wasn't exactly the romantic date of his dreams, but he was here with an easy-to-talk-to friend who was spending all her time with him, talking about her life, her history, her favorite things. She could have easily joined her Drama Club friends on the dance floor; but she was sticking with him; and more surprisingly, she actually seemed to be *enjoying* herself. He let himself relax a bit. And then he noticed her foot, tapping in time with the music.

"You can go and dance if you want to," he told her bravely, sliding his own bad foot under his chair. "I'll get us something to drink."

He didn't want her to go, of course; he was having such a good time — talking with Calliope, sharing funny and embarrassing stories with her — and he hoped she felt the same way.

Calliope smiled. "Let's both get something. I'll tell you about the time Theo accidentally burned down my mom's asphodel garden." Homer smiled back.

****

Theo stood for a minute in the entranceway, assessing the scene like a general surveying a battlefield. Still early yet, he determined: plenty of folks still mingling, snacking on flatbread and olives, not dancing. Looked like he arrived in the nick of time.

It was touch and go there for a while. Who would have predicted that he'd show up at the door of his date Iris, only to find her making out with her ex-boyfriend (who apparently wasn't "ex" anymore)? Apparently, this guy begged her to come back to him, and after a long conversation, they reconciled. Iris told Theo she'd still go to the dance with him, but Theo waved her off. He claimed he wasn't mad—was genuinely happy, in fact, for the reunited sweethearts...until it dawned on him that their reconciliation left him dateless. He had no intention of showing up to the dance alone. But how could he find a date at this stage of the game? Everyone was at the dance already.

Then he remembered: not quite *everyone*.

As the atrium roared in recognition of the next song, Theo knew he had to get out there on the dance floor. "So, what do you say?" Theo yelled into Andie's ear. "Wanna dance?"

Andie leveled him with a disbelieving stare. "You're kidding, right?"

"Suit yourself, sunshine," Theo said, as he charged into the middle of things, taking it upon himself, as always, to get the party started.

****

Was it possible for someone to be *addicted* to fun? That's what Andie was wondering as she watched her "date" Theo literally hurl himself into the middle of a crowd.

When Theo showed up at her door earlier that night, all her instincts were telling her to send him on his way. She should have listened. But he could be charming, that Theo.

"Come on, we'll all hang out!" he pleaded. "What else are you doing? It'll be fun."

Yeah, fun. Standing in the atrium's doorway, completely alone, dressed down in her tan and wrinkled peplos while all the other girls were dressed up in their fancy gowns — *loads* of fun.

She was about to walk back out the door, but figured she should at least try to find her friends. She took a few steps to her right but had to make a quick detour when she saw Melpagon, along with his henchman Kerrtennikos, glaring at her. That's when she saw Mac, alone on the edge of the dance floor, staring at her, a bewildered look on his face. She gave him a big smile and a wave, and started to make her way over to him. But when she saw Gia walk over and lean into him, she stopped. Maybe she underestimated Mac. He seemed to be doing just fine. Embarrassed, but not sure why, she darted off to find Calliope and Homer.

****

At first, Mac couldn't even process what Gia had said. He was still reeling at the sight of Theo showing up at the dance with Andie. What happened to his real date? Did he ditch her to go with Andie? Just thinking about the two of them together distracted him so much it took a little bit of time to register that his own date just told him she was leaving.

"What?" he finally asked her. "Where are you going?"

"To the beach. A bunch of us wanted to head down for a little while."

"The beach?" Mac repeated. "But…didn't this just start? Weren't you, like, in charge of this whole thing?"

"We might be back," Gia snapped.

"Do you…do you want me to go with you?"

"No," she answered as two of her friends swarmed her, tugging on her arm. "Galene and Sofia will walk me home later," Gia informed Mac. "So, don't worry about it."

"No problem," Mac said, trying to sound upbeat. "I'll see you later, I guess."

As he watched her walk away, Gia broke away from her friends and ran back to Mac. "Listen," she whispered, her words coming out in a rush. "Thanks for doing this. I know I wasn't the friendliest date tonight. I'm sorry."

"You have nothing to apologize for," Mac answered. "I'm really sorry for...for before."

With a wistful sigh and a slight hesitation, Gia joined her friends, leaving Mac alone but feeling strangely better somehow.

****

"Can I apologize on behalf of my brother?" Calliope said to Andie, as they watched Theo flail around on the dance floor, one of the wall hangings now tied around his neck like a cape.

"What's to be sorry about?" Andie half-smiled, as she picked up her goblet, realized it was empty, and then let it clunk back down on the table. "He's the life of the party, right?"

"But not a very good date."

"Calliope, he asked me to a dance a half-hour *after* it started. We're *way* past 'good date' at this point."

Calliope sniffed out a chuckle, not really sure what to say. She felt bad for Andie, of course, but thinking about the contrast between their two dates—hers wouldn't leave her side, Andie's ditched her after two seconds—made her appreciate Homer even more.

After a few silent minutes of watching Theo slam-dance, Homer announced, "I think I'm going to see how Mac's doing. Does anyone want anything while I'm up?"

"No, I'm good," Calliope said, smiling.

As they watched Homer limp away from the table, Andie commented, "The shrimp's actually kind of sweet. Who knew, right?"

They turned their attention back to the swaying crowd, Theo's head bouncing over all of them. "It's weird," Andie said. "I used to have a big crush on your brother. That whole 'larger-than-life' thing he has going on—it was pretty appealing." She paused as she watched Theo jump up on the stage and dance spastically with the members of the band. "Until I realized what a goof he is," she sighed with a slight laugh.

As she listened, it occurred to Calliope she'd never really had any deep conversations with Andie before. In truth, despite all the time they'd spent together as a group, Andie always seemed a little unapproachable to her, as if she wanted to keep Calliope at a safe distance. It made her want to try and reach out…to ask about the topic that probably occupied most of Andie's thoughts, even though she'd never admit it.

"Why don't you ever talk to us about your dad?" she asked hesitantly.

Andie stiffened but didn't run away. Progress. "What's to say? I have zero information about what happened to him."

"Don't lose hope that he's still alive," Calliope offered as she reached out and squeezed Andie's hand. "I know that doesn't sound like much, but sometimes hope is the best we can do."

"How is that better?" Andie asked with a catch in her voice. "If he's alive, it means he abandoned me. Either way, I'm still alone."

Calliope paused for a long moment, treading carefully before speaking from the heart. "The way I see it, for the moment he's gone. But you're not alone. You have us. And you won't be alone when you find out for sure."

Andie responded with a deep sigh and a watery smile. "Thanks. That means…a lot."

Sensing she had pushed this as far as Andie was willing to go, Calliope lightened the mood. "You're right about Theo, you know," she said. "But he's not malicious. Just clueless."

"No, I know that. Hey, he needed a date. Someone—*anyone*—to walk in with. Once he did that, he didn't need me anymore. I get it."

"And you're not upset by that?" Calliope asked.

Andie responded with a grin. "No…but *you* might be, since I plan on clinging to you and Homer all night."

Calliope smiled back and grasped her hand again in a show of solidarity.

****

Homer finally found Mac hiding out in one of the small courtyards surrounding the atrium. "Where's Golly-Gia?" he asked.

Mac sank down onto a nearby stone bench and said with a sigh,

"Gone."

"Gone? Wow. And look at that: she lasted—what?—almost a whole hour. Usually, people are repelled by you in under fifteen minutes, so that's gotta be a record for you."

Mac smirked absently as he looked out at the full moon. "Yeah...a record. She was actually repulsed by me long before we got here."

"Oh, please," Homer waved his hand dismissively as he parked himself next to Mac on the bench. "Like going to a dance was going to keep you here at the school. Never listen to Theo. The whole idea was stupid. Besides," he said, leaning in close, "I have a new labor."

"Can't wait," Mac grumbled.

"Have you ever been to Soricon's Corner?" Homer asked. "Just past the falls?"

"No..."

"Really? You've been here two-and-a-half years, and you've never been to Soricon's Corner? Man, you really are a loner, aren't you? Whatever. There's this main street, right, with all these shops and taverns? Well, *off* that street, way down this alley, there's this rundown apothecary shop."

"Apothecary?" Mac repeated. "Like medicines?"

"Yes, like medicines, but more exotic than that. I'm talking potions. Elixirs. Somehow the lady who runs the place—this wrinkly old crone named Abibathia—can get her hands on all sorts of crazy stuff—*including* a bottle of water taken from the very pond where Narcissus drowned himself."

"Stop right there," Mac interrupted. "Where did you get this information? And please don't say your 'scroll buddy.'"

"Last time was an honest mistake," Homer insisted. "This time, he's right. I *know* it!"

"Just kill me now," Mac mumbled, burying his head in his hands.

"Listen to me," Homer continued. "The water from this pond is supposedly the purest water in the world. No fish ever lived in it, no leaf ever touched it. Plus, the pond is guarded by wood nymphs, so there are only like twelve bottles of this water in all of Greece. And this Abibathia lady has one of them. Can you believe our luck?"

"I don't even know what you're talking about."

"What am I—? I'm talking about your next mission!" Homer said in exasperation. "To get the water from her."

"Why?"

"Why?" Homer repeated, stalling for a few seconds. "Because this water, see, has mystical powers. Narcissus, remember, was this very handsome guy, and he drowned in this water. So now whoever drinks it will look youthful and physically appealing as well." Homer put on a big smile, hoping Mac bought the story. He felt bad about misleading him, but he couldn't tell him the *real* reason he needed that water. He'd only go blab to Andie, and that would blow the whole thing. He had to wait it out.

"I don't get it," Mac mumbled. "You think if I were more handsome, they'd let me stay here? That's even stupider than going to a dance..."

"No, no, no. The water's not for *you*," Homer corrected him. "You're plenty handsome. Think about it: we get this water, this mystical, beautifying water, and you give it, as a gift, to someone who could probably use a little touching-up. Maybe, say, a certain disgusting headmaster?"

Mac stood up, taking all this in. "Bribery?" he finally said. "You want me to *bribe* Gurgus? That doesn't seem like your style."

"It's not a bribe," Homer assured him. "Consider it a show of good will—you know, as proof that you're trying to change your delinquent ways. Plus, it's not *just* the water. The mission is more important than the end result."

"'Mission'?" Mac asked. "We're buying a bottle of water. Where's the mission in that?"

"Well, two things," Homer said. "First of all, not 'we'; it's you. I can't go with you."

"Why not?"

"Well...I can't exactly...I'm not allowed back there anymore."

"You got banned from an apothecary?" Mac said with a laugh. "Why does that not surprise me? Nice to know I'm not the only one you drive crazy. What'd you do this time?"

"Doesn't matter," Homer said, brushing off the topic. "Second thing: you can't just buy it. What's adventurous about that? Even if she wanted to sell it to you, which I'm sure she wouldn't. You have to *get* it from her."

"Get it from her?" Mac echoed. "And how do you propose I do that?"

"Again, I'm more of the 'big picture' guy. Some things you have to figure out on your own," Homer said, standing up. "Anyway, I should get back to Calliope. You coming?"

"In a minute," Mac sighed, more to the moon than to Homer.

"You should join us," Homer urged. "Andie's here. She came with Theo."

"You don't say…" Mac muttered.

Homer turned and made his way to the doorway. When he got there, he heard Mac ask, "Why'd you go see her, anyway?"

"What?" Homer asked, even though he had a pretty good idea what Mac meant.

"That apothecary lady. Why'd you go see her?"

Homer stood in the doorway, with his back to his friend. After a long pause, he said simply, "For my foot." Then he limped inside.

****

Even Theo needed to take a break once in a while.

Drenched in sweat from head to toe, still wearing the tapestry around his neck, he stumbled over to the concessions table. Picking up a goblet of water, he drank about half of it, and then poured the rest over his head. As the water dripped in his eyes, he completed another survey of the atrium, noticing the crowd had thinned out. Where did everyone go? Was something else going on?

All the way across the room, Theo spotted Mac, alone, no girls in sight. Damn. He was about to go over to him, when his friend Maceo intercepted him. "Hey, we're all going down to the beach. You in?"

Of course, he was in. "Yeah," he said, glancing over again at Mac. "I'll meet you down there. Just have to check in with some people."

****

From where Mac was standing, he could see her — sitting there, along with Homer and Calliope. He wanted to go over, take those fifty or so short steps across the room to her table. But somehow he couldn't. Couldn't make his feet move.

He knew it made no sense. They were friends, after all. They hung out all the time. Why was tonight any different? But it *was* different, and he knew it, and that difference left him frozen in his tracks, just watching — until, that is, he heard this voice behind him, saying, "You don't have a chance in Hades, you know." Mac looked over his shoulder, to see Melpagon standing there, arms crossed.

"What are you talking about?" Mac said.

Melpagon snorted an accusation that stung Mac worse than any punishment he dished out at War Games. "I see you looking at her. And you might as well forget it. Because a girl like that will never, *ever* be interested in someone like you. And you know why? Because you're a weak, gutless loser, with no friends and no life and no hope of getting either."

The insults didn't faze Mac. But realizing someone else noticed him staring at Andie — *that* humiliated him, enough to want to punch Melpagon's smug face. Mac knew that getting into a fistfight at a dance could seal his fate as far as Gurgus was concerned. But at this point, he honestly didn't care.

As he clenched his fist and moved towards Melpagon, Mac felt a hand on his shoulder. "What's up, gents!" exclaimed Theo. "How you doin', Mel?"

"Theo," Melpagon acknowledged, not even trying to hide his scorn.

"Hey, I gotta speak to my boy Mac, if that's OK," Theo said, leading Mac away by the arm. Once they were a few steps away, Theo asked, "Is he getting in your face?"

"Him? No, he's…just an idiot…"

"So, where's Gia?" Theo asked, looking around.

"At the beach," Mac admitted.

"Perfect. That's where I'm going right now. Wanna come with?"

He had to ask. "Is Andie going?"

"Andie?" Theo said, looking around. "How would I know?"

"Didn't you two walk in together?"

"Oh, yeah, but not as a thing. My date fell through," Theo explained. "I haven't talked to Andie all night…which sounds kind of horrible, now that I say that out loud. Crap. Well…at this point, I'm better off avoiding her. Anyway, what d'ya say? Should we beach it?"

"Uh…you know what? Thanks for the invitation, but I think I'll pack it in," Mac declined, stealing glances at Andie as he spoke. "Don't want to overdo the socializing."

Theo continued to badger him about leaving, but Mac somehow fended him off. After Theo finally left, it struck Mac that this might be his chance. Here, he had spent most of the night feeling miserable about Theo and Andie showing up together—only to find that they weren't actually "together." Now, Theo was gone, and Andie…was right across the dance floor.

As he thought all this, Mac tried not to stare at her, but he honestly couldn't help it; he couldn't take his eyes off her. She hadn't even dressed up, and she was still the prettiest girl in the room.

****

"You told him we were back here, right?" Andie asked Homer.

"Well, not exactly 'back here,'" Homer said. "He knows we're in here somewhere."

Andie folded her hands on the table and looked at Homer and Calliope. It was clear they were having a great time. They were making every effort to include her, but an evening of shared jokes and mutual bonding left Andie feeling envious and a little bit lonely.

"I think I'll see what he's up to," she announced abruptly as she stood up.

****

Mac took a deep breath and reminded himself he could handle this. He'd stood face-to-face with Melpagon at War Games; he had outsmarted Basileus and Blasios; he had even marched straight into the cave of Kalakloptas, having no idea what lay inside. He could handle *this*.

And as he made that impossible trek across the room, he kept repeating to himself those five simple words: *Would you like to dance?* Nothing to it, right? Just walk up and ask her. She wouldn't think it was weird, would she? *Would you like to dance?* He could handle this.

But then he saw her, walking towards *him*, and any sense of what he could "handle" went right out the window.

"Hey, stranger," she greeted him. "I was looking for you."

For a few moments, they both just stood there; meanwhile, all around them, couples started drifting toward the dance floor as the band started playing the last slow song of the night. "This night wasn't what you expected, huh?" Andie finally asked.

"I didn't have any expectations," Mac replied. "I've never been to one of these before."

"Me neither," Andie said, glancing at the couples slow-dancing around them. "I'm not even sure what I'm supposed to do."

Mac looked down at the floor, trying to summon his nerve, and then before he even knew it, the words came tumbling out of his mouth: "Well, we could dance, I guess."

"OK," Andie said—a simple answer that nonetheless paralyzed Mac. He had been so focused on just the *asking*, he hadn't quite worked out what to do if she said yes. He quickly looked around, trying to assess other couples' techniques, and then took that one tentative step forward. He put both his arms around her lower back—hesitantly at first, gracelessly. But when he felt her wrap her arms around his shoulders, it all suddenly seemed like the easiest, most natural thing in the world.

****

The time Homer had been dreading the entire evening had finally come: last song of the night. Soon, the dance would end, the band would pack up its instruments, everyone would file out of the atrium, and Calliope wouldn't have danced once. Homer was consumed with guilt.

"If you want to dance, that's OK with me," Homer said to her, for about the fifth time.

"Homer, it's a *slow* song," Calliope reminded him. "I'd look a little funny dancing by myself. Don't worry. I'm fine."

Homer once again hid his foot under the chair as he stammered out an explanation. "It's—it's not that I don't want to. It's just—"

"I know," she said sweetly, before looking back out at the crowd. A few moments of fidgety silence took over before Calliope spoke again: "Does it hurt?"

"Not really," Homer lied. "I've lived with it all my life, so I've learned to—"

"Homer...don't." She didn't say anything else. She didn't have to. Homer knew what she meant: *Don't do this. Don't act all invincible. Not for me.*

"Yeah, it does," Homer said quietly. "Not all the time. And not when I'm standing or sitting, like this, or lying down. But when I have to run to class or get somewhere fast...Yeah, it hurts. But that's only part of it."

"What's the other part?"

"It's embarrassing," Homer admitted. "Limping around all the time, losing my balance, stumbling all over myself...That—that hurts, too."

Homer looked at the floor, at the walls—anywhere but right at her—so at first he didn't notice her standing up and walking over to him. When he looked up, she was holding her hand out. "You trust me, don't you?" she asked.

Homer nodded but said nothing. And neither did she; instead, she led him silently by the hand to the edge of the dance floor. She placed her arms around his neck and rested her head on his shoulder. Then Homer—slowly, awkwardly—put his arms on her waist, right above her hips. And then...they just stood. For the rest of the song, their bodies swayed to the music, while their feet remained firmly planted on the dance floor.

****

"What's a 'Telemachus,' anyway?"

"What?" Mac asked.

"The name, 'Telemachus,'" Andie clarified. "I never met anyone with that name before. I was just wondering what it meant."

"According to my mom, it means 'distant fighter,'" he explained. When Andie responded with a look of bewilderment, he just sighed, "Yeah, I don't get it, either." Then he didn't say anything for a little bit; he had trouble concentrating with her so close to him. "How about you?" he finally asked. "Did your folks name you after the real Andromeda?"

"Oh, the 'real' Andromeda, huh?" teased Andie, as she swatted the back of his shoulder, easing closer to him. "What, I'm not real enough for you?"

"No, you're all right," Mac answered, knowing this was the understatement of the year.

"My mom wanted something simple, like Nell or Rhea. But my dad really pushed for Andromeda. He just loved the poetry of it," she explained, leaning in as she spoke, her mouth just inches from his ear. "And the story too, of course. I remember, as a kid, re-enacting the story of her rescue; my dad would put me on top of this big rock near our house, and he'd say the sea monster was coming, making all these scary noises. Then, at the last minute, he'd swoop me up in his arms and save me."

Mac chuckled softly. "I didn't think you needed *anyone* to save you."

Andie looked at Mac with a small, sad smile, and then she rested her head against his shoulder.

Mac closed his eyes as everything inside of him screamed for him to go for it, to go ahead and kiss her. It's not like he hadn't kissed anyone before. Why would this be any different? He lowered his head, so his cheek rested in her hair. At that point, it would have taken nothing to whisper her name, to make that journey from her ear to her mouth.

But he just couldn't do it.

Throughout his time at Pieridian, Mac had only been with a few girls. He didn't seek them out; he didn't have to. Maybe they were attracted to his looks, or his brooding charm, or his royal pedigree. Whatever the case, when they made themselves available to him, Mac went along with it, happy to lose himself for one night and forget his troubled past. He wasn't proud of it, but the girls themselves didn't matter to him, beyond offering a temporary balm to his loneliness.

But tonight…tonight, was different, and it all came down to one simple fact: this one particular girl *mattered*.

And when he realized that, black doubts descended on him, like a swarm of hoopoe birds: What if she doesn't feel the same way? Or what if she *does*…what happens next? What if he messes it up, like he'd always done?

All this was swirling through Mac's head as he heard the band play its final notes. The song ended. The dance was over. Mac stopped, leaned back, and looked at the girl in his arms. She stared back with wide eyes, parted lips. Then she dropped her arms to her sides. That was his one and only moment—the moment to which everything had been building, a moment that stretched beyond endurance. And he let it slip away.

****

Theo hadn't been at the beach party five minutes before he hustled back to school. It had nothing to do with the party or the people there; he just couldn't ignore the nagging guilt over leaving Andie like that. By the time he got back to the atrium, he saw Mac and Andie filing out the main door onto the patio.

"Hey, remember that lame guy, Theo?" he asked. "You know, the guy who invited a girl to a dance at the last minute then ditched her?"

"I think I'm familiar with him, yeah," Andie deadpanned.

"Well, he's hoping he could make it up to her by walking her home," Theo said.

"Tell him it's fine," she smirked.

"No, come on. I'm feeling bad. Let me walk you home," Theo pleaded. "Tell you what: you don't even have to say anything to me.

I'll just walk *near* you."

"Really, it's fine. Mac said he'd do it," she informed him.

"Mac? He didn't even want to go in the first place. He can't wait for this night to end," Theo said, winking at Mac. "Let me do it. If you don't, I'll feel like a weasel."

"Well, I guess we wouldn't want that, would we?" she said, looking over at Mac.

Theo knew she couldn't resist. He gave Mac a friendly pat on the shoulder and then hooked Andie's arm, leading her away.

****

A half hour after he watched Theo whisk Andie out of his sight, Mac found himself sitting on the steps of Homer's dorm, still dressed in his green chiton, the one he had sworn, just a few hours before, he'd never wear again.

Earlier in the night, when he was looking at himself in Theo's mirror, he'd told himself to make this night count. He hadn't. Granted, most of the night was lame, so what did it matter? But then came that one moment that *did* matter, the only moment in the whole miserable night that could have redeemed all these miserable years at Pieridian. And he let it pass him by. He had to get that moment back. But he needed more time.

Right then and there, on the steps of Homer's dorm, while he replayed in his mind Andie's wistful "oh-well" look as Theo swept her away, Mac made a pact with himself: he *would* wear that stupid, uncomfortable chiton again. Somehow, he would find a way to stay at school.

Soon, he saw Homer bouncing toward him, his face beaming so brightly he practically illuminated the night sky. When Homer reached the steps, Mac asked him about his night and listened intently. When Homer was done, Mac ran through the events of *his* evening, including the last dance with Andie and the kiss that wasn't. Then he started telling Homer a bunch of other Andie-related stuff: their visits to the beach, the life-talk they had on the Æton. And all that sharing must have stirred something up inside of

Mac, because then he started revealing a bunch of other stuff—stuff he hadn't told Homer before—about Ithaca and the suitors and his mom.

The two of them talked for hours, right there on the steps. Finally, Mac just sort of shook his head and said, "OK, we have to focus: that thing you told me earlier, about the apothecary? Have you told anyone else? Calliope? Theo? Anyone?"

"No. No one else."

"OK, take me through it again."

Demetrius—

Do you think it's weird that Mac and I never hang out in my room...only his? Logically, it doesn't make sense: my dorm is more centrally located on campus; we wouldn't have to worry about disturbing my roommate, since I don't have one (and that was by choice...in that no one chose to live with me); and finally, my room lacks that signature "teenage-boys-mixed-with-disgusting-serphint" smell that permeates everything in Mac's room.

At first, I thought Mac worried I was interested in him romantically and was staying away from my room intentionally. But honestly, Demetrius, I don't like him that way. (Well... maybe I would if he liked boys, too, but he doesn't, so it's a moot point.) He's a good friend, and I don't think I've ever given him reason to think otherwise.

This may sounds weird, but you know what I think might be the reason we're always in his room? Mac never wants to be too far from his bed. Truly, he seems to crave sleep more than any person I've ever met. For a while, I thought he was just pretending to be asleep, to get rid of me, but now I know that's not the case.

Still, it stings a little. Especially when I know there's a certain someone who can always get Mac out of bed. Don't get me wrong, I'm happy that he and Andie are getting along, but if I'm being honest, my favorite times are when it's just him and me together. (I know how that sounds, so I repeat: I do NOT like him that way!) Even when Mac's fast asleep in his bed, it's nice to have company. Occasionally, to pass the time, I tend to Typhon the serphint, feed him or let him roam around Mac's room. (I wish you could see how cool this thing is, Demetrius! A snake-dolphin hybrid. A two-in-one freak of nature, confined in a place it doesn't want to be. Does that not sound exactly like another fantastical creature?)

Speaking of which...Remember, on that Minotaur quiz I sent you, I name-dropped a guy named Xenotareus? The guy really into hybrids, who had this idea that drinking the Minotaur's blood would make you immortal? Well, I was feeding Typhon the other day, and it occurred to me: serphints are hybrids...Could this Xenorateus have something to do with them? So I went to the library and went through scroll after scroll, trying to find another mention of this guy. Finally, I stumbled upon a document that mentioned a "Xenotareus."

It was a speech—more of a rant, really— given by someone named Creuseus, about the dangers of learning too much and how humans need to know our place and all that. As an example, he talked about this guy who went to study a village of centaurs and ended up wiping them out. But the speech glossed over that part: Creuseus seemed more appalled about how this crazy centaur-killer apparently discovered a way of breeding different life-forms, "defying the will of the mighty Olympians by combining spiders and fireflies, stags and dragons, snakes and dolphins." It was only a passing reference, but I figured this had to be the same guy with the Minotaur obsession.

Anyway, if you have any information on this Xenotareus guy, I'd appreciate it. I feel I'm on to something—I just don't know what.

-Homer

CHAPTER SEVENTEEN
Abibathia

Honestly? Theo had trouble not taking it personally. Hearing about the new labor from *Andie*? What, was Mac trying to keep him out of the loop or something? And why? Because of the dance? That was a *week* ago. Move on, dude.

But when Theo saw Mac sitting at the fountain in front of Calchas Hall—exactly where Andie said he'd be—he decided to set all hurt feelings aside and put on his game face. "All right, brother!" he exclaimed as he approached. "Let's do this thing!"

Mac looked up and asked suspiciously, "Let's do...what thing?"

"You know, the *thing*. The mission, or labor, or whatever."

Mac's eyes narrowed. "How do *you* know about the thing?"

"Ah, fair question!" Theo said, with an arch of his eyebrow. "How *would* I know about it, since *you* didn't tell me? Instead, I had to hear the scoop from Andie, when she ran into me today, all stressed out, and asked me to pass along a message that—"

Mac, all mumbles, finished his sentence: "She's not coming..."

"Nope. Rather, she's serving the first of five detentions, the result of skipping too many classes, because she's been hanging out with *you*," Theo smiled. "Apparently, you're not supposed to do that. Did you know this?"

Mac didn't seem to be listening. He sat there on the side of the fountain, not responding, just shaking his head. "But, hey," Theo continued, plopping down next to him and slapping him sportingly on the back. "It's just Andie, right? Who needs her? Where's everyone else?"

"There is no 'everyone else,'" Mac shot back. "It's just...Forget it." Then he stood up and stalked away.

"*I'm* here," Theo reminded him. "You're telling me the two of us can't handle this?"

"Not in the mood," Mac waved him off. "Maybe next week, OK?"

"Next week, right," Theo said, as he stood up. "Of course, who knows what might come up then, right? Maybe someone else will be out of commission—had some bad feta, say. So maybe the week after that? Or the one after that? Or after that? Until one day, you wake up and find yourself in the Disciplinary Chamber saying, 'Oh, hello, Headmaster Gurgus. You mean today's the day I have to show you what I've got? Today's the day I have to convince you not to kick me out? Gee, I thought I had until *next week*!'"

By the time he finished, Theo was standing right in front of Mac. The two roommates just stared at each other, until Mac huffed out a "Fine!" and stormed down the road that led off campus.

For the first leg of the journey, Mac didn't say anything beyond that "Fine!"—just trudged, head down, through the countryside. Several times, Theo tried to make conversation with him ("So, where are we going, anyway?"), but Mac never bit. Eventually, Theo got sick of the whole brooding act and purposely slowed down, allowing Mac to get a few steps ahead. Man, was he glad he'd tagged along for *this* trip.

About halfway to Soricon's Corner, Theo spotted the path that led to the top of Kataraktos Falls. "Hold up, will you?" he called out as he veered off the main road, gesturing for Mac to follow. The small path ended at a wide outcropping of rock, shiny and slick with water that flowed over the rocks into wildly cascading froth twenty-five feet below. Theo had taken in this view plenty of times before, but he never got tired of it. The crashing of the waters beneath him, the smell of the damp, misty air, the calm and crystal waters of the pool below—the whole scene never ceased to invigorate him. Mac, on the other hand, didn't seem even remotely impressed. Instead, he just stood there, sighing resentfully, acting oblivious to the glorious view surrounding him.

With a sigh of his own, Theo turned back to the falls, wondering if everyone else was right. Ever since the beginning of the year, when the administration first paired them together as roommates, people around school had asked Theo, "How can you stand to live with that guy?" But Theo, ever the diplomat, would always stick up for him. "He's not that bad," he'd say, "once you get to know him." And sometimes he actually meant it: for the most part, they got along better than Theo had expected. But other times, like this moment right here, he couldn't wait for the semester to end, when the administration would lift its sentence and let him live with someone else, someone not so damn allergic to fun.

Gazing down at the rushing waters beneath him, Theo decided he wasn't going to let Mac's grumpiness spoil his entertainment. "How're we doing on time?" he asked, loud enough to be heard over the cascade.

"What?" asked Mac.

"How about a swim?" Theo requested as he slipped off his sandals.

"A swim?" Mac repeated, in disbelief.

"Don't tell me you've never jumped off Kataraktos Falls. Oh, dude, it's a blast," Theo howled, as he pulled his tunic shirt over his head and inched closer to the edge of the rocky landing. "Come on. I've done this a zillion times. Nothing to worry about."

Mac didn't take the bait. "Weren't you just lecturing me about not wasting time?"

"One quick jump, and we climb back up," Theo pleaded. "Come on. You need this. It might loosen you up a little."

"You know, I'm getting tired of you telling me to 'loosen up.' I'm 'loosened' plenty. Why do you think I'm in this mess? If anything, I'm *too* loose!" Mac said. "So, tell you what: I'm gonna get this stupid thing over with. And you—you do whatever you want. Want to hang out, get 'loose', act like a six-year-old? Great. I'll see you on the way back."

Theo, still standing at the edge of the falls, shouted out to Mac as he starting walking back to the main road. "Why, exactly, are you so pissed at me?"

Mac stopped and turned around. "I'm not pissed at you."

"Oh, OK. So this is your kindly, pleasant side I've heard tell about?" Theo said, stomping back towards the main road. "Look, I'll say it again: sorry about your date. If I had known she was out to punish you, I would never—"

"What are you talking about?" Mac interrupted. "What date?"

"Your date for the Harvest Dance. Gia?"

"Are you insane?" Mac interrupted again. "This isn't about my date!"

"Then what is—"

"It's about *your* date!"

"*My* date? What does that even—?" Then it hit him. "You like her! You like *Andie*! *That's* why you didn't tell anyone else about today. You wanted to be alone with her!"

"Keep it down, will you?" Mac said, looking around nervously.

"Who's gonna hear us? Don't be embarrassed. You like her—that's great!"

"Yeah, great," Mac muttered, as he folded his hands and looked blankly back towards the falls. "Except it's kinda hard to *do* anything about it since she's obviously still hung up on *you*."

"Me? Are you kidding?" Theo pulled his tunic back over his head as he continued. "Dude, with Zeus as my witness, I swear I had no idea."

"Well, now that it's out there..." Mac said finally. "I have to ask you something. I don't even know how to...Is there any way you could not, you know, do your *thing* with her?"

"My 'thing'?" Theo repeated. "I have no idea what that means..."

"Oh, yes you do. Could you not *flirt* with her, or pursue her, or do whatever you do that makes you so damn irresistible!"

"So, back off, in other words?" he considered. "Well...I don't know. She *is* kinda cute." In truth, Theo never had any intention of "pursuing" Andie; he was just having a little fun with Mac. But then he took a hard look at Mac and quickly deemed him too fragile to torture.

"Dude, I'm totally messing with you," he smiled. "No problem. I'm not really that into her, to be honest."

"OK...well, thanks, then," Mac said slowly, giving a look that conveyed more surprise than gratitude—the same expression he'd worn that morning when Theo agreed to hook him up with his father's boat. Mac, it seemed, just didn't get the concept of good deeds.

Once they started walking again, Theo pounced on this exciting new topic. "OK, so you've admitted you like her. Good start," Theo counseled. "Now how about her? You think she likes you back? Are you getting any vibes?"

"I don't know about 'vibes,'" Mac shrugged as he kicked a stone on the road. "I mean, we hang out together a lot."

"Hang out?" Theo exploded. "Dude, that's the *worst* thing you can do." Clearly, Mac needed some *major* help when it came to girls.

"What are you talking about?" Mac said indignantly. "We're friends."

"Exactly! *Friends!* That's the problem! See, you want to be *more* than friends. But keep 'hanging out,' you'll find yourself marooned on Friendship Reef forever, and then what? You gotta do more. You gotta take this game to the next level!"

"You think I haven't tried? Just last week at the dance, we *almost* kissed. I mean, we were *this* close!" Mac related, making the "this close" sign with his thumb and index finger.

"So what happened?"

Mac lowered his head. "I...chickened out. I just couldn't do it. That's never happened to me before. Is that weird?"

"For normal guys, yes, that would be weird. For you...it makes total sense."

"Why?"

"Because you're falling for Andie. That's why you froze." He smiled, proud of his diagnosis. "The other girls you've been with meant nothing to you."

"I wouldn't say they meant *nothing*," Mac answered defensively. "Besides, you're with girls all the time. How does that make us any different?"

"Because I actually care about the girls when I'm with them. For however long it lasts, I'm totally invested. Like soulmate-level invested. I'm a hopeless romantic. You're just hopeless."

"You did *not* just say soulmate to me."

"What? You've never had a soulmate? You've never been in love?"

"I think it's pretty obvious that I haven't, as evidenced by this entire conversation!"

"Well, let's try to analyze that," Theo said, enjoying his new role of relationship counselor. "What was your first experience with a girl?"

"She was the daughter of one of the cowherds back in Ithaca," Mac answered reluctantly. "One day I kissed her in the back of the stables. Well…OK, I guess she kissed me. And things just sort of took off from there…"

"Stables? Is that cool or kinda foul? I mean, the smell in there…"

"It wasn't ideal," Mac admitted, pushing his fingers into his eyes as if attempting to force the memory back into his mental cellar.

"Nice!" Theo laughed. "I can see why you have issues. Maybe you need to take Andie to the campus stables."

Mac gave Theo a shove. "Let's move on."

And they did. First, Mac related to Theo everything Homer had told him about this particular mission, which led to a discussion of Homer and all his idiosyncrasies, which eventually led to Theo's animated reenactment of the event that started all of this, the hoopoe bird prank. Just remembering the look on Gurgus's face as the birds flapped all around him sent Theo over the edge; at several points, he was laughing so hard, no sound came out. Naturally, Mac cracked up, too—not at the story as much as Theo's retelling of it. They both laughed so hard they could hardly stay standing. And before they knew it, they stumbled into their destination: Soricon's Corner.

Even though the sun had started to set, the crowded main street still buzzed with activity. Everywhere the boys looked, they saw vendors, jugglers, musicians, even fire twirlers. Theo wanted to stop at every attraction, but Mac was eventually able to maneuver him down a dark, deserted alleyway. Following Homer's directions exactly, they arrived at a decrepit wooden door into which were carved two swans facing each other, necks intertwined.

"Should we knock?" Theo asked.

Mac held up his hand. "Wait. Before we do anything, don't you think we should come up with a plan or something?"

"A plan? I thought we're buying a jug of water."

"We can't just buy it," Mac explained. "Homer says we have to secure it somehow, in a heroic way…or something."

"Oh, *screw* that!" Theo said as he knocked on the door. "We're *buying* it. And on the way back, we'll concoct some story of our amazing bravery." He knocked again, harder this time, causing the door to creak open slightly. The roommates waited for someone to come to the door; when no one did, Theo shrugged his shoulders and walked inside, Mac right behind him.

They found themselves in a small, gray room cluttered with clay jugs—short jugs, tall jugs, jugs with two handles, jugs with skinny necks. Open jugs on a table. Broken jugs on the floor. Shelves upon shelves, from floor to ceiling, of jugs. With so many to choose, Theo figured they'd be out in no time.

"Hello?" Mac called out to the empty room. No response.

"Anybody home?" Theo shouted, as he picked a jug off the shelf and brought it up to his nose. Just one whiff was enough to make him gag.

Then, from behind, they heard the voice: "No touching, babykins. Just with your eyes."

The voice was deep and raspy, almost mannish. But when the two boys turned, they saw instead an older woman, dressed in a low-cut, raggedy red peplos. She was a tiny thing, barely taller than the bar she was leaning against, and so skinny that the bones in her wrinkly face and chest seemed to jut out like rocks in a cliff wall. She had dark, sunken eyes, blood-red lips, and frizzy, dark brown hair that reached only slightly below her ears. Her left arm, sleeveless and skeletal, cradled a one-handled jug, while her right arm rested on the bar—an obviously affected pose, which also (it seemed to Theo) served the purpose of keeping her steady.

"Uh, sorry," Mac said stupidly. "We're looking for someone named Abibathia."

"Let me get her for you," the woman said. "Abby!" she hollered. When no one responded, she giggled and called out again, this time more sing-song-ily: "Ab-*beeee!*"

When no one answered again, Mac smiled nervously. "Let me guess: *you're* Abibathia."

"Smart *and* good-looking!" the woman said, stumbling a few

steps forward. "A rarity!"

"Indeed. Well…perhaps you can help us," Theo spoke up, putting on his formal, all-business voice. "We're hoping to purchase some special water, supposedly taken from the river where Narcissus drowned. Do you happen to have this item?"

"Do I *happen* to?" Abibathia repeated thrillingly, flashing a gap-toothed smile. "Do I happen to? Well, that all depends," she mused, as she took a swig from her jug. "Why do you *happen* to want it?"

"Is that important?" Mac asked.

"Oh, no. Not ordin-inarily, no," Abibathia slurred, as she staggered over to them, letting the jug in her left hand dangle by her side like a dead cat. "But this is different. Short supply, big demand. After all, you know what they say about this water? It brings it all back, baby — your youth, your prettiness, your *vigor!*" She sang those last few words, causing Theo to cough as the smell of her booze-drenched breath invaded his nostrils.

"That's a lovely singing voice you have," Theo remarked, glancing at Mac.

"Oh, I'm a Siren, all right," the old lady tried to purr seductively.

"Yeah, so…the water?" Mac interjected, trying to steer the conversation back to the business at hand.

"Oh, you two don't need any magic water," Abibathia grinned. "Believe me, you two don't need help with any restoration. You're doing just *fine.*"

"Awww, that's sweet…" Theo winked. "Just the same, though…"

The woman took another swig from her jug and asked, "So, what are your names?"

"Our names?" Theo said, shooting a glance at Mac. "Certainly. My name is Basileus, and this is my friend, Blasios."

Abibathia narrowed her eyes at the boys. "What kind of names are those?"

"Just…names," Theo smiled. "Normal names."

Abibathia said nothing, just looked right at Theo's face, as if studying it. "Basileus…" she finally declared. Then she turned the same penetrating stare onto Mac: "Blasios." Finally, starting with Mac, she reached out with a bony finger and daintily touched the tip of each boy's nose as she christened them with pet names. "Blazzy…and Silly…"

"OK, then," Theo said, staring down at the finger lingering on his nose. "As it turns out, we're in a bit of a rush, so if you don't mind procuring the item, we'll be on our way."

Abibathia grinned devilishly at them. "You'll have to come in the back."

"The back?" Mac asked.

"Something this special, I keep in the back room," she smiled, wobbling backwards as she spoke until she bumped into the counter. She stopped to steady herself, then slowly, carefully, made her way around the obstacle and toward a small, dark doorway on the other side.

"Come on," she beckoned with a crooked finger. "I won't bite…*much!*" Then she let out a hoarse giggle before she disappeared.

Theo and Mac stood for a moment, silent and immobile, until Mac finally whispered, "Well, it's official. We're gonna die."

"Chill out, Blazzy," Theo advised. "I think we can take her."

"Why do I have to be Blasios?" Mac muttered as he followed Theo through the doorway, down the three steps, and into the backroom—a smaller, grayer, and even more cluttered version of the main room. Across the way, Theo immediately spotted the bony, wrinkled bare feet of Abibathia, who was high on a ladder, shuffling jugs around on the top shelf.

"You can come closer," she invited, looking down at them from over her shoulder. "But remember, no peeking!"

Theo looked in mock revulsion at Mac and puffed out his cheeks, pantomiming he was throwing up in his mouth. Meanwhile, Abibathia narrated her actions from above: "It's somewhere up here. I—ah! Here we go!" She produced a small, stout, two-handled jug and shook it. "Hmmm. Not much left. I didn't think I—*whoa!*"

It all happened so fast: one second, Theo saw her on the ladder; the next, she was slumped in Mac's arms, with Mac sort of embracing her awkwardly from behind.

"My hero!" Abibathia gushed. Then she looked down at the jug, which she was still gripping in her right hand, just inches from the stone floor. "Didn't lose a drop!" she exclaimed as she lurched forward and picked a high stool off the floor and emphatically stood it upright. "Let's say we celebrate!"

"Uh, Abibathia?" Mac began, as he watched her take two small cups from the shelf behind her and thump them on the stool.

"*Abby*, baby," she corrected him, spilling the precious water all over the makeshift table while filling the two cups.

"OK, Abby," Mac said. "If it's all the same to you, we'll just take it to go."

She looked up at Mac, tilting her head sideways. "You're cute, you know that, Silly?"

"Actually, *I'm* Silly," Theo couldn't help but remind her.

She kept talking to Mac, ignoring Theo's comment. "You remind me of my second husband. Cute, *so* cute…but always so serious. So by-the-book. Never wanted poor Abby to have any fun." Her mouth slowly curled downwards as she dipped deeper into her recollections. "They were all like that."

"All?" Theo asked.

"Oh, I was married five times, babykins," she cackled. "Five times. And every single one tried to bring me down. Tame me. Don't let that happen to you, boys," she counseled, shaking her finger at them. "Don't let anyone tie you down. Not stallions like you. You're born to run free!" She held up the water jug in her right hand. "To freedom!" she toasted.

When Theo and Mac didn't move, and instead just stared at the two cups on the stool, she said, "Come on. Drink up. It's very good."

"You've…*had* some?" Theo asked, trying hard to keep his face straight.

"As a chaser, baby," she explained. "It's real smooth." As a demonstration, she brought the water jug to her lips and took a big swig, letting some of the precious elixir drip out of the side of her mouth. When she was done, she closed her eyes, licked her lips and sighed, "Smooth!"

Meanwhile, Mac shot a tense look at Theo, and even though no words passed between them, Theo knew what he was thinking:

judging from the sound of the water sloshing around in that jug, there was maybe only one more cup left.

When Abibathia opened her eyes, she looked alert, as if a thought just occurred to her. "Hey, that question you asked, if I've ever had any of this before…" she said accusingly to Theo. "What does that mean? I don't look young enough for you? You don't think it's working?"

"Well, that depends," Theo deadpanned. "Have you had *a lot*?"

"I'm sure it works fine," Mac said. "And you're a great advertisement, believe me. We're sold. So, how much do we owe you?"

"Owe?" Abibathia repeated, widening her eyes. "Oh-oh-oh. What do you owe? Who's to say? Enchanted water, after all," she reminded them, shaking the jug to drive home the point. "Can you really put a price on something like this?"

"You could try," Mac said meekly.

"I tell you what," she proposed, her gap-toothed smile widening. "Because I like you, you don't have to pay me anything. I don't even want your money."

"You don't?" Mac said suspiciously.

"Nope," Abibathia smirked. "Instead, how 'bout you two just give ol' Abby a kiss?"

Mac didn't even pretend to think over her offer before he stammered, "You sure you don't want our money instead?"

She didn't say anything at first, just offered the two young men a look of tragic recognition. "I get it. I do," she finally said. "And because I get it, I'm gonna tell you something important, and I want you to listen: Don't get old, boys. That doesn't mean anything now, because you're young and beautiful and stupid. But some day, some day, it will, and when it does, you'll say, 'Why didn't I give that nice old drunk lady a kiss?' Because I wasn't always like this, you know. I was a dancer. I was *something*. And the men…I tell ya, the men…" She trailed off, and Theo watched as her eyes fixed on the jug in her right hand.

"I never let 'em get to me," she continued, more to herself than to her audience. "Never let 'em tame me, tie me down. Because I didn't *need* anyone. And now..." She didn't finish her thought, just absently waved her left hand at the room. "Don't get old, boys," she said again, closing her eyes. "You think you're something, but tomorrow...it's all, all *gone*."

And then, with her eyes still closed, she raised the water jug to her mouth, to drink down the final gulp.

Theo never moved; he didn't have time. Instead, he could only watch as Mac jumped forward and—in a single, deft motion—put his hand over the top of the jug as he pushed it in Theo's direction. And in that same instant, he substituted the jug's mouth with his own, planting a giant kiss right on Abibathia's lips.

Theo pried the jug out of the sufficiently distracted Abibathia's fingers. Mac, seeing out of the corner of his eye that the jug was secured, pulled his face back. Abibathia, dazed, stumbled back into the ladder behind her. For a moment, everyone and everything froze. Then Abibathia's face transformed.

Apparently, it took just one smooch from Mac to do what an entire bottle of magic water couldn't: restore Abby's youthful vigor. Her eyes lit up. Her wrinkled lips broke into a wide, hungry grin. And she got a little bit frisky.

"Whoo-eee!" she squealed. "Let's have some more of that!" She lunged forward at Mac, who fell backwards, knocking over the stool behind him. Theo looked on with horror at the two of them on the floor, with the salivating Abibathia grabbing Mac's leg.

"Theo!" Mac yelled, as he tried to wriggle himself away. "Let's go!" Mac freed himself from her bony grip and then bolted toward the door, with Theo—jug still in hand—in hot pursuit. The two were almost out the door when they heard an inhuman screech followed by a crash, as something hit the frame over their heads. With fragments of stone raining down on him, Theo turned to see a wild-eyed Abibathia—on her knees and armed with a cup in each hand. The scorned woman launched another cup at their feet as the boys fled out the door.

Mac bounded up the three steps and vaulted over the counter blocking his way. Right behind, Theo tossed the jug over to him and started to leap over the counter himself; halfway through the jump, he felt something slam against his left shoulder blade. He crumbled clumsily to the floor as a second jug shattered next to him.

Theo felt Mac yank him up by the arm. When he got to his feet, he saw a seething Abibathia, emerging from behind the counter, screaming barely decipherable threats as she hurled jugs as quickly as she could grab them from the shelves. She may have had terrible aim, but her throws had some ferocious velocity; most of the jugs missed the boys but ended up smashing into the other containers lining the shelves around the room.

"Come back here!" she demanded, as she fired jug after jug at her prey. "Come back here, you crooks!"

Now, Theo wasn't always the most upstanding citizen ever, but he didn't like being called a crook—especially since Mac *did* give her the kiss she'd asked for. Still, as they stumbled to the doorway, dodging the projectiles and fragments of exploding jugs, Theo reached into his pouch and grabbed as many coins as he could. "Sorry about the mess!" he shouted, tossing coins on the floor as Mac pulled him out the door.

They could still hear the old lady's screeching as they ran as fast as they could into the new night—down the dark alley, past the jugglers, through the crowds. Finally, they ducked into the alcove of a tavern, far from Abibathia's shop. Hunched over and panting, Theo managed to ask, "Still got the goods, Blazzy?"

Mac, leaning up against the doorframe, held up the jug by one of its handles. "Mission accomplished," he wheezed.

"On both counts," Theo said, cryptically.

"What do you mean?"

"Based on that hot make-out session back there," he smiled, "maybe you found your soulmate after all?"

They both laughed—a hearty, good-buddy laugh that carried them out of town, past the falls, and all the way back to school.

PART THREE

Demetrius—

This scroll will have to be short, because we're leaving for Delphi in a little while. I'm not sure I can find the words to describe how excited I am to see the Oracle. (Ah, I probably don't need the words...you'd be feeling exactly the same way.)

The "Master Plan" is a go. I have everything we need, just as we laid out. I know this is going to work. Mac's going to do it and the Disciplinary Committee will rule in his favor.

But you know, Demetrius, this is about so much more than just staying in school. It's about...it's about being counted. It's about that row of statues in Clio Hall, of all the heroes who have gone before us. Who have walked the same halls we walk, taken the same classes, eaten in the same lousy dining hall. Menelaus, Agamemnon, Achilles, Odysseus...they're all there, along that wall. Mac should be there, too, someday. That's what this is about: being counted, among the greats.

I'm just lucky to be going along for the ride.

-Homer

CHAPTER EIGHTEEN
On the Road to Delphi

So, you're going to Delphi?"

"How do you know that?"

"I know things…"

As he took a seat, Mac looked at his advisor, wondering how he could have possibly determined that bit of information. Then it occurred to him.

"Calliope told you."

"Yeah," Asirites said, sitting down behind his desk. "But tell me again: You're going to the theater at Delphi? With the Drama Club?"

He was mostly right. Mac, Homer, Theo, and Andie *were* tagging along on Calliope's field trip, with Grimbar's permission, but not just to see the theater at Delphi. Instead, Calliope had an idea: to sneak away and see Delphi's famous Oracle.

Of course, when she mentioned this to the gang one night at the Grape Vine, Homer literally jumped up and down in his seat with sheer giddiness. "Oh, yes! Yesyesyes! Every hero needs to see an oracle! This is perfect!" Mac, on the other hand, needed some convincing. For one thing, Grimbar apparently had stressed they were just visiting the theater and specifically identified the oracle as off-limits. Mac didn't want to risk getting into any trouble, not with his hearing coming up in just a few weeks.

Besides, the whole notion of glimpsing into the future always gave Mac the creeps—thanks, mostly, to his mom. She didn't believe in learning about one's destiny, even though many, people—Mac included—had encouraged her over the years to go visit the Delphic Oracle, so she could get some information about her husband. But she would always give her standard answers. "This life does not belong to us," she'd say. Or: "The gods reveal things when we need to know them, not before."

Mac first heard this lecture when he was seven years old. A festival was being held at the palace, to honor Leto the Titan. As part of the festivities, someone hired a soothsayer. Although Mac couldn't remember his name, he could still picture him clearly: this charismatic man, with a dark, neatly-trimmed beard and a scarlet-red robe, standing on a tiny stage surrounded by a throng of people, all waving their hands at him, trying to get his attention. The man would then pick someone from the group, clutch her hand, and then answer whatever question she had about her future.

The whole scene captivated the young Mac, who made up his mind to speak to the soothsayer. After all, he seemed to have all the answers, and Mac had a very important question: "When is my dad coming home?" But before he could worm his way up front, Mac felt someone grab his arm; the next thing he knew, his mom was dragging him out of the crowd. As Mac screamed his opposition, a stern Penelope took him behind a stone column and told him that under no circumstances was he ever to talk to someone like that again.

As Mac kept whining, she calmly told him a story, one which he heard many times since then. "When I was a little girl, I went to a wedding, which was supposed to take place outdoors. As the big day approached, the bride became nervous about the weather and consulted a soothsayer, who closed her eyes and said, 'I see your wedding guests...soaking wet.' And so, at the last minute, the bride moved the entire wedding indoors, into a room much too small for all the guests. The tight quarters—combined with the extreme summer heat—resulted in some very hot guests; some were literally dripping with sweat, while others poured jugs of water on their heads to keep from passing out. Meanwhile, outside...not a cloud in the sky." She paused, while Mac stopped pouting and took it all in. "You can't avoid your future, Mac. No sense racing toward it."

As he got older, Mac began to doubt the story actually happened, but it made an impact on him nonetheless. Now, almost nine years later, Mac felt he would be betraying his mother by going to the Oracle. On the other hand, Homer seemed absolutely convinced this was the right course of action, and so Mac felt he just had to trust him.

Still, when Asirites asked him about the field trip, he didn't want to go into too much detail; after all, going to the Oracle meant breaking Grimbar's only rule, and Mac didn't want to implicate Asirites in case they got caught. "Well, I've never been on a field trip before," Mac told him, sidestepping the whole Oracle detail all together. "Plus, I thought it wouldn't hurt for the committee to see me taking an interest in school activities."

Asirites nodded in agreement. "Very true. And how are things going on that front?"

"Fine…I think…" Mac said. "I told you about how Homer has been helping me out. So, hopefully, I'll have some good stuff to show the committee." He didn't mention his secret weapon: the final few sips of water from the Narcissus pond, which Homer was now hoarding in his room until the day of the disciplinary hearing. In truth, Mac doubted bribing Gurgus would help, but he went along with it anyway. Even though Homer had made a few blunders along the way, Mac still trusted him completely. "I guess we'll just have to wait and see what happens," Mac concluded.

"I guess," Asirites agreed. "Of course, you could always ask the Oracle, I suppose."

"What?"

"I'm just saying," Asirites said, as he leaned back and started casually twirling his cane in the air, "if you're going to be in Delphi anyway, maybe you could ask the Oracle about the outcome of the disciplinary hearing."

Mac didn't know what to make of that comment. It almost seemed as if Asirites knew he and his friends planned on sneaking off. "Uh, we're just going to the theater," he explained slowly. "No Oracle for us."

"Of course," Asirites said. "Kind of a shame, don't you think? I mean, to be right there, so close to the actual Oracle…"

Mac fidgeted in his seat. "I'm not sure I want to know too much about my future, to be honest," Mac told him, trying to deflect the conversation away from the field trip. "I mean, I suppose seeing the future, or whatever, probably has some perks..."

"Probably," Asirites mused.

"But only if you have a *good* future. If my future's bad...well, I'd rather not know."

"Yeah, you're right," Asirites nodded. "Still, what do you think you'd ask? If you ever did get the chance to have an audience with the Oracle? What's the one thing you'd ask?"

Mac had actually been mulling over that very question for a week, ever since Calliope proposed the idea of going on the field trip. He had so many uncertainties in his life. How could he possibly choose just one question to ask? Would he want to know about whether he'd get kicked out of school? Would he ask about his mom, and if she'd ever marry one of the suitors? Or about Andie, about whether they had a chance? Maybe he should ask if Homer would come up with an idea to keep him in school that didn't involve risking his life.

But in the end, he knew that he wanted, he *needed* to know the answer to only one question, the same question he had when he was seven.

When is my dad coming home?

Mac could have admitted this to Asirites, but for some reason he decided to take refuge in a joke. "Well, it's obvious, isn't it?" he said, half-smiling. "I'd have to ask the Oracle who's going to top my prank at next year's Opening Ceremonies?"

"That *is* a mystery," Asirites smiled back.

****

When Mac left Asirites's office, he found Homer waiting on a bench outside, his face buried in a scroll.

"What are you doing here? Stalking me?" Mac said with a grin.

"You told me this is where you'd be," Homer explained, as he stood up. "What did Asirites want? You didn't tell him about your plan to see the Oracle, did you?"

"Take it easy. I'm not a complete idiot."

"I know, but guidance counselors have a way of getting people to talk. Mine once got me to admit I slept all night in the hallway because I was afraid of a bee in my room."

"I didn't say anything, don't worry," Mac said.

"I just want everything to go smoothly," Homer answered. "You've got a lot happening all at once. Mid-Terms, then the big disciplinary hearing…"

"Yeah," Mac said absently. He paused, before broaching a concern that had been on his mind. "I just hope you know what you're doing. Going on these labors, fetching these lame trinkets…Is this what the Disciplinary Committee even wants?"

Homer, who usually resorted to defensiveness whenever Mac questioned him about the labors, instead responded in a calm voice. "The committee wants you to do something heroic. And we've been doing that. We're on the right track. You have to trust me."

"OK." It occurred to Mac almost immediately how much doubt was betrayed in that "OK" — much more than he had intended. Doubt had been his standard emotion for so long, he almost responded that way out of habit. But he really *did* trust Homer, really did have faith that he knew what he was doing. Somehow, this strange, little hero-nerd had turned Mac around, from a doubter to a believer.

****

The next day, Mac was on a boat for the short trip to Delphi, smelling the salt air and listening to Calliope and her Drama Club friends sing an oddly cheery song about Hera's tormenting of Io. He was feeling upbeat and optimistic.

Until something happened — almost as soon as Mac's sandals hit the dock in Delphi — that changed all that.

Calliope, Theo, and Mac were among the first to disembark, with Homer and Andie lingering behind; Mac later learned Homer had misplaced the satchel he brought with him (containing "gifts for the Oracle" he explained), and Andie agreed to help him find it. As Mac stepped off the gangplank, he took in his surroundings.

The pier ran the entire expanse of the harbor and was lined with carts, scarred wooden tables and benches; behind each one stood peddlers, fish mongers and other street vendors, all desperate to sell their wares. The area around the harbor was bustling with activity and all kinds of people: villagers shopping for their families, politicians gathering crowds, travelers looking for lodging, entertainers weaving through the throngs, along with the usual sketchy characters typically found at city ports—drunks, scammers, and petty thieves. Tempted by the delicious smell of sesame honey fritters, Mac grabbed some coins out of the pouch tied to his belt, about to head over to the baker's table.

He would never really remember what caused him to look up, to glance across the wide pier. But what he saw froze him in place. Calliope was standing by a peddler's stall holding a red silk scarf. A large, swarthy man came up behind her. He had leathery skin; dark, curly hair; a bushy beard; and shadowy eyes, virtually hidden under the serpent of his lone eyebrow. He was wearing a dirty, sleeveless tunic, open down the front, to show off his hairy chest and arms. He was carrying a bottle of something. He took a swig and then smiled lewdly at Calliope.

From where he stood at the bottom of the gangplank, Mac could see Calliope smile back nervously at the man before subtly stepping away from him and turning her attention back to the scarves. He didn't take the hint as he edged closer to her, trapping her against the table with his thick body.

Mac's gaze darted to the peddler, a tiny white-haired woman, gesturing to the man to go away. Ignoring her protests, the swarthy man moved even closer and placed a big, hairy arm, the one holding his bottle, around Calliope. With his other hand, he grabbed the scarf she was clinging to and used it to pull her right up against him. Sucking a shaky breath through a clenched jaw, Mac watched Calliope squirm as she tried to break away from the man's grasp. She stumbled backwards, and as she did, the scarf ripped in two.

Calliope's attacker yanked her back up against him. Acting on instinct and adrenaline, the frightened girl stomped on his foot with her sandal. With a bellow of rage, he smashed his bottle to the ground and grabbed both of her wrists.

Calliope was in real trouble. Mac knew at his core that this man was going to hurt her. His brain shouted at him to get over there...but his feet remained rooted to the spot where he stood at the edge of the gangplank, paralyzed with shock and the overwhelming presence of a distant memory. It was Homer's voice that finally broke through his trance.

"Mac! Do something!"

Mac quickly looked back toward the boat, to see Homer at the railing, waving his arms and pointing desperately to the scene that unfolded before him. Frantically turning back to Calliope, Mac began to run over to her. Too late. Seemingly from out of nowhere, two large hands appeared on the swarthy man's chest.

"Get lost," warned Theo, appearing at his sister's side. As he spoke, he gave a mighty shove, launching the thug toward the center of the pier.

A small crowd began to gather with a few shoppers shouting for help. The man with the hairy arms made a move towards Theo but stopped, obviously deciding the whole thing wasn't worth it. He sauntered away defiantly. Calliope picked up the torn scarf and returned it to the peddler with an apologetic look as Theo whisked her away.

By the time Mac made his way over to the stall, the white-haired peddler was calling out to no one in particular, "Someone's gotta pay for this scarf!" Realizing all other parties had fled the scene, Mac handed her a few coins as she babbled on about "thugs" and "miscreants" scaring away her customers. At that moment, Homer appeared right next to him, silently glaring at him with a look of disgusted disappointment.

Luckily, Andie intervened, sparing Mac from having to justify his slow reaction. "All right, here you go," she said, slapping Homer's satchel across his chest. "Hold on to it this time." Homer, his grim eyes still fixed on Mac, clutched the satchel and stomped off.

"What's up with him?" Andie asked.

"Ah, this guy was harassing Calliope," Mac mumbled.

"Is she OK?" Andie asked, immediately scanning the pier. "Did you see what happened?"

"I was too far away," Mac said, perhaps a little too quickly. "It's fine. Theo helped out."

When they reached the end of the pier, they overheard Calliope lecturing her brother. "You know, I was handling it," she informed him, but her voice shook a little, suggesting she was more scared than she let on.

"You should be able to go shopping without being manhandled by some piece of dock trash. I'm your big brother. It's my job to protect you."

"We're the *same age!*" Calliope reminded him.

Just then, a whistle cracked the air. They looked up to see Grimbar, playing his role as the frazzled Drama Club advisor, standing on a bench and flailing his arms in an attempt to get everyone's attention. Apparently oblivious to the whole confrontation between Calliope and the man, Grimbar started with yet another speech about how they represented the school and needed to be on their best behavior. "And remember," he said again. "We're just going to see the *theater*! No sneaking off to go to the Oracle!"

Grimbar led the students to the two decrepit wagons that were going to take them to the theater and divided them into two groups: Theo, Homer, and Mac ended up in one cart, and Andie and Calliope in the other. Before he boarded his wagon, Mac went over to Calliope. "Are you OK?" he asked.

"Oh, yeah," she shrugged. "Just a little flustered, that's all."

"I'm sorry I didn't get over there sooner," he said, before quickly adding, "I didn't see what was happening....I mean, by the time I saw, Theo was already—"

"It's fine," she said with a shaky smile, as students brushed past her. "Really. Don't worry about it."

Mac climbed onto the wagon and automatically took a seat beside Homer, feeling worse than before he had apologized. He hated the fact that his apology sounded suspiciously like an excuse. He hated that Calliope, the one that needed the comforting, ended up comforting *him*. But most of all, he hated that he had lied to her. Because no matter what he may have claimed—to Andie on the pier and to Calliope now—he knew in his heart he *did* see what happened. And he didn't do anything about it.

Mac and Homer didn't speak at all. In fact, for the first part of the trip, Homer didn't even look in Mac's direction; he just stared blankly at the terrain going by, his arms folded across his chest, his mouth frozen into a thin, motionless line. Mac, meanwhile, spent the whole bumpy ride fidgeting under the weight of the uncomfortable silence, seriously pondering jumping out and walking the rest of the way.

Finally, Homer started in on him. "I just don't get it," he said, quietly enough so no one else on the wagon could hear. "Why did you just *stand* there?"

"I got over there," Mac responded weakly.

"*After*. After I screamed at you. What were you doing?"

"I didn't even see what was going on," Mac lied.

"You did. You absolutely did. I saw you, watching her, standing there like an idiot, like you had been turned to stone or something."

Mac's empty gaze drifted over to Theo, the man of action and Calliope's true rescuer, who was now chatting with some girl at the far end of the wagon. "I...I don't know what to tell you," Mac sighed. "I guess I didn't react fast enough..."

"Not fast enough?" Homer echoed, his voice getting louder the angrier he got. "How about not at all? What have we been doing the past two months? Here I am, trying to teach you how to be a hero. You think a hero would stand there and watch as some brute attacked a poor girl? If you can't handle something like this, how are you going to face the Minotaur?"

As soon as he said that last part, Homer swung his head away, suddenly done talking. But Mac needed some clarification. "What did you just say?"

"Nothing."

"What do you mean, how am I going to 'face the Minotaur'?"

"Don't try to change the subject," Homer deflected, turning back to face Mac. "We were talking about—"

"*You* said Minotaur," Mac reminded him. "And *I* want to know what that means. Especially since you said we were done with the whole Minotaur thing."

"I never actually said that. Andie did. And that was before she really got to know you."

Mac's eyes narrowed as he asked simply, "What are you doing?"

Homer paused before he continued in a low, emotionless voice, "She's close. I'm telling you, she's very close to spilling the beans about where the Minotaur is. And when she does— "

"Spill the beans? Have you *met* Andie? She doesn't *spill* anything she doesn't want to spill!"

"*Shhhhh!* Quiet!" Homer insisted, even though Calliope and Andie were riding on the other wagon. "OK, fine. But just *in case* she ever did, I wanted to have a few things in place."

"What things? What are you talking about?"

Homer leaned in closer. "I've done research, OK? I know what I'm talking about. The Minotaur is tough. You can't just waltz up and hit it over the head. You have to stun it first. And, according to my sources, one of the only things that can stun the Minotaur is the high-pitched sound generated from the aulos."

The mention of the aulos got the mental wheels turning for Mac, who looked right at Homer with growing suspicion. "Even then, it's only down for a few seconds," Homer continued, still talking in a low voice. "So when it's dazed, you have to shoot it with an arrow, the tip of which has been dipped in some special waters—the purest water there is, not harmful to humans but *deadly* to a demonic creature like the Minotaur."

"And this water? It wouldn't be from the pond of Narcissus, would it? Because that would just be *ridiculously* coincidental."

Homer ignored the sarcasm. "Granted, we don't have the real aulos, but I thought—"

"And the collar from Slobber's neck?"

"Arrowheads. The dragon's teeth from the collar would be used as arrowheads."

"So, let me get this straight," Mac said slowly, not really worried about anyone else hearing him. "For three months now, I've been running all over the place, risking my life—never really understanding why, but doing it anyway, because I *trusted* you...and the whole time you were *lying* to me?"

"I didn't lie," Homer justified sheepishly. "I *wanted* to tell you the real reason. But I knew if I did, you'd run off and tell Andie, and then she'd shut down for sure. So I was just biding my time until she felt comfortable enough—"

"She will never feel 'comfortable enough'! Don't you get it? She will never, *ever* tell you, me, or anyone else anything about the stupid Minotaur. So stop involving her, stop manipulating her, and stay out of her business!"

"Oh, so I'm manipulating her, is that it?" Homer shot back, relocating his anger from earlier in the conversation. "Well, it's interesting to me that you're so quick to jump to the defense of your *girlfriend*, yet when Calliope needed your help, you did nothing."

"She's not my girlfriend! And what happened back at the dock was a *mistake*," Mac hissed. "An accident! How does that compare to you purposefully *lying* to me for months?"

"Don't call me a liar!" Homer said fiercely. "Especially since everything single thing I've done has been for *you*! So maybe instead of accusing me of things, you should try showing a little more gratitude for a change!"

"Oh, please! This isn't about me! This is about *you*. About you finding someone to *live* through. Someone who'll jump through all your hoops, while you sit there on the sidelines moaning about your useless, crippled foot!" Stunned by the force and ugliness of his own words, Mac jumped up, trying not to see the shock and hurt in Homer's eyes. "You know what? Find another puppet. I'm through with it."

When Grimbar called to Mac to sit down, he stormed to the front of the wagon, glaring coldly at the Drama Club girls near him. They immediately shifted around to accommodate him, but Mac didn't thank them; he just plopped down and kept his eyes on the floor, not saying anything. Once, Theo reached across the way and slapped his knee to get his attention, but Mac only responded with an icy stare. Theo got the message.

CHAPTER NINETEEN
The Oracle

It was…everything.

From the bustling crowd, to the columned temples dotting the winding road, to the shining hills of Mount Parnassus towering majestically in the distance, Delphi was everything Homer imagined it would be. And thanks to his horrible fight with Mac, he couldn't enjoy any of it.

Hey, you're the one who's mad at him, Homer kept reminding himself. But two feelings overpowered his anger: the guilt over lying about the missions, and the fear that Mac might never forgive him for it. The fear weighed on him more than the guilt; Mac was the closest thing he ever had to a best friend. What if they never got past this? What would Homer do then?

By that point, the students had disembarked from the wagons and were being led, on foot, through the city to the theater. The road—what their guide called "The Sacred Way"—was packed with pilgrims and shops and tiny temples. Unfortunately, it was also snaky and all uphill—bad news for Homer, whose foot never fared well with inclines. Not long into the walk, he found himself limping at the back of the pack, all alone, until Calliope and Andie noticed him and held back as well. As for the other two, Theo had thrown himself into the middle of the crowd, becoming everyone's new best friend, while Mac stalked off by himself, twisting his face into the coldest, most uninviting scowl imaginable.

"Man, Theo's on fire today," Andie marveled, watching three drama girls just about collapse in overly uproarious laughter at something Theo said.

Yeah," replied an unimpressed Calliope. "Can't say the same for Mac, though. What's up with him? He just seems so…distant."

"He has a lot on his mind," Homer mumbled.

"You think?" Andie asked, her voice tinged with sarcasm. "In three weeks, he could be gone. Expelled. Even if he does everything *right*, Gurgus might still kick him out. I think he's earned the right to be distant once in a while, don't you?"

"Well," Calliope ventured after a pause, "you *could* help him out, you know."

Andie looked at her, "What does that mean?"

"I'm just saying," Calliope began, obviously choosing her words carefully. "If a friend of mine was in trouble, and I had some information that would help, then I'd tell him."

Andie sneered. "Oh, you would? Well, I guess you're a better friend than I am." With that, she stormed off.

Homer felt bad for Calliope; no one ever got angry at her, and she obviously didn't know how to process it. For a while, the two walked in complete silence, until they caught up with the rest of the group, which had stopped at one of the many small temples lining the street, listening to the guide's prepared speech. The buildings were called treasuries, he explained, and they were used by pilgrims on their way to the Oracle. "Now, of course, we won't be going to the Oracle today," the guide reminded them, "but if we were, you would stop at one of these treasuries and place an offering to the Sun God."

As the guide launched into a lecture about Doric columns, Homer drifted over to one of the treasuries on his left and peered into the marble boxes out front, filled with gifts to Apollo: silver and jewels and golden chalices. Knowing he couldn't put it off any longer, he slowly removed the bag from his shoulder. Then he hesitated, reached inside, and pulled out a handful of heroes: Ajax, Diomedes, Paris. He closed his eyes, not sure if he could actually bring himself to part with them, when he heard Calliope's sweet voice behind him.

"It's for a good cause," she whispered.

"Yeah..." Homer sighed, putting the figurines back in the bag, which he then placed delicately into one of the boxes. He said a quick prayer, for Mac, before limping as quickly as he could back to the group.

For what seemed like an eternity, the group walked and walked up the twisting path. Finally, just when Homer thought he couldn't take another step, he looked up to see a massive stone structure surrounded on all sides by a series of columns. "And this is the Temple of Apollo," the guide informed them. "Even though we won't be going inside, I'd like to talk briefly about the kinds of things you might find here." He rattled off some of the sacred items stored within—the tomb of Dionysos, for example, and the Omphalos, the famous stone that marked the center of the world—but seemed to be avoiding the good stuff.

"How come we can't see the Oracle?" Theo interrupted him.

The guide gave a ready smile, one that suggested he had been asked this question many, many times before. "Well, for one thing, the Temple is a sacred site, and in order to maintain its sanctity, the administrators have asked us not to take groups through its halls," he explained. "In addition, the Oracle is not a tourist attraction or a novelty act; it's not like talking to a soothsayer at a fair. Instead, seeing the Oracle requires a great deal of preparation, a serious mind. And it can be scary; many pilgrims leave this temple disappointed at best and horrified at worst by what the Oracle has to tell them." He paused and then clapped his hands together. "So, if you can follow me, our next stop is the Delphi theater, just a little bit up the road."

Homer groaned at the prospect of more walking, but it turned out the guide spoke the truth; the theater was actually in view of the Temple. In a matter of minutes, the students found themselves within the massive, open-air, five-thousand-seat structure. While Grimbar frantically waved his hands around and corralled the students into their benches, Homer dutifully sat in between Calliope and Andie, a few seats away from Theo; to no one's surprise, Mac sat off by himself.

As Homer watched Grimbar count the heads of all the students, a thought occurred to him. "By the way," he said softly to Calliope, "how exactly are we going to sneak out of here?"

"Just wait until the play starts," Calliope answered. "You'll see."

Before long, a man in a costume made up of a hundred small eyes strutted out to center stage to begin the play, called *The Imprisonment of Io*. Within a few minutes, in the middle of a monologue debating the severity of different prisons ("of chains, of circumstance, of destiny," intoned the hundred-eyed Argus), Homer felt Calliope tap his shoulder.

"OK," she whispered, "let's go."

When he looked over to see Grimbar, sitting way down front, far away from the students, leaning intently forward in his seat, Homer understood: for the duration of the play, Grimbar wasn't going to be doing a lot of chaperoning. He'd come for the show.

While Calliope quickly got the attention of Theo and Andie, Homer shout-whispered to Mac (incurring a few angry *shushes* from the crowd). Mac finally looked over, rolling his eyes in exasperation, before stomping over — going out of his way, it seemed, to be as loud and *un*-sneaky as possible. Homer shook his head disgustedly, wondering when exactly this behavior would end.

"All right, then," Calliope announced, when all five gathered by the main entrance to the theater. "Let's do this."

"I might hang back," Theo announced. "This *destiny* thing…it's not really my gig, you know? Besides, you'll need someone to run interference in case Grimbar notices you're gone."

"What will you say?" Andie asked.

"Ah, I'll come up with something. Maybe Homer was crying, after he got scared by the eye-monster. Something like that." Then he turned to Mac and asked, "Unless you really *want* me to go."

"I'm fine," Mac muttered, as he trudged down the road toward the temple. Homer gritted his teeth and followed after him, hoping the Oracle didn't turn visitors away for excessive moodiness.

As the four teens journeyed back to the temple, Homer used the time to make the final calculations for the visit. "Andie, keep your eyes open for a stray goat," he said.

"A goat?" Andie repeated.

"Didn't the guide say something about sacrificing a goat before seeing the Oracle?"

"We won't be doing that," growled Mac, still a few steps ahead of everyone else.

"Just out of curiosity, how do we get in?" Andie asked, as the temple came into view. "Just walk through the front door?"

"Probably not. In all likelihood, a guard will be stationed at the entrance," Homer warned, before breaking into a coy smile. "Luckily, I know a special password."

"Of course you do," Andie said drolly.

"What is it?" Calliope asked.

"It's a word that has special significance to Apollo," Homer began, his eyes walking up one of the temple's mighty columns, "because it refers to his son, Asclepius, a physician so skilled in the healing arts that he could actually bring people back to life. Now, as you can imagine, this didn't exactly thrill Hades, his business being death and all, so he asked his brother Zeus to help him. Zeus ended up striking Asclepius down with a thunderbolt, but then he felt bad about it. So he put Asclepius among the stars, in a constellation known as...Ophiuchus."

"That's the password?" Calliope asked. "Ophi—what is it??"

"Oh-fee-YOO-cus," Homer annunciated. "We say that, and we can stroll right on in."

"And you know this how?" Mac asked, still with his back to Homer. "And if you say scroll buddies...."

"This time Demetrius knows what he's talking about," Homer insisted.

Mac didn't respond or even turn around, just shook his head and walked up the ramp to the main entrance. The rest followed Mac into the vestibule, a surprisingly compact area filled with laurel and incense. Across the way loomed the immense doorway into the main temple. And in front of the doorway, as Homer had anticipated, stood a guardian.

"I'll handle this," Homer confidently told the others as he marched up to the guard, a rotund old man in a green robe and a matching green headdress. As his friends looked on, Homer stood in front of the marble counter and announced, "We've come to see the Oracle."

When the guardian didn't respond, Homer said again, slowly, "Um...the Oracle."

The guardian finally acknowledged the loiterer with a dismissive glare. "The wise reflections of the Oracle are for kings and generals — not for children on idle or foolish errands. So, if you please, kindly move along."

Homer paused and, leaning in, whispered knowingly, "Ophiuchus!" When the guardian stared at him blankly, Homer repeated, "Ophiuchus!"

Again, the guardian remained stone-faced before turning away. A thwarted Homer sulked away, head down. Once again, Demetrius had given him faulty intelligence; there was no password. They wouldn't be going to the Oracle after all; they couldn't even get through the first line of defense.

Then Andie stepped up.

"Excuse me, sir," Andie said to the guardian, in an affected, dramatic voice, "but with all due respect, I don't think you know whom you are addressing. This young man here is Telemachus, Prince of Ithaca, son of the great Odysseus, and he comes before you in his most desperate hour. As you may know, his father, the war hero, has been gone for sixteen years, and in his absence, his home has been overrun with vultures and parasites, who have taken everything from his father but his good name. Young Telemachus has endured much in those sixteen years, and he has done so patiently, and with great dignity. But now he wants guidance. Today he seeks audience with the great Oracle, not as a prince, but as a *son*, looking for answers about his father. Please do not deny him his small request."

Homer couldn't believe what he was hearing; he didn't know Andie had it in her. Neither, apparently, did Mac, who tried to stay in character but whose eyes betrayed his bewilderment. The guardian, however, seemed stoic, unmoved. Finally, though, he looked at Mac and, showing no expression on his doughy face, waved him forward. "The adyton is at the end of the aisle," he said to Mac.

Homer watched as Mac walked around the marble counter. Then he stopped, turned to the guardian, and asked, "Can my attendants come as well?" The guardian frowned, clearly not thrilled, but ultimately waved the rest of them on.

"Where did *that* come from?" Mac whispered to Andie, as she sidled up next to him.

"I have no idea, but it was pretty cool, huh?" Andie said simply as they walked—four across, the boys flanking the girls—through the massive doorway and into the cavernous, high-arched room.

Down the long, wide aisle, they took small, hesitant steps, humbled by the grandeur and immensity of their surroundings. Everywhere they looked, they felt the eyes of Apollo weighing on them: from the enormous busts perched on marble columns; from the statues of the Sun-God playing the lyre or standing atop balls of fire; from the mural stretching across the entire ceiling, depicting Apollo in various scenarios—pursuing Daphne, or enlisting the aid of the satyrs, or fighting some fanciful beast with five eyes and five legs. And then there was the green laurel, accentuating not only the artwork but the entire interior: laurel topiaries lurking in the alcoves; laurel garland strung around the towering columns; laurel wreaths adorning the ends of the stone benches that ran down both sides of the center aisle.

The scent of laurel and incense—combined with the faint, hypnotic chanting which filled the room—made Homer feel almost light-headed, and he found himself leaning on Calliope for support. But Calliope, so entranced by the setting, didn't even notice him. Instead, an awed smile consumed her entire face—a smile which Homer tried to copy, but deep down, he felt a distinct sense of doom, as if they were willingly marching straight into the mouth of Hades. And the other pilgrims in attendance didn't exactly put him at ease: some were face down in front of statues, laurel leaves clutched in their hands; some were wandering down the aisle, faces buried in their hands; one woman was collapsed in a heap in the middle of the aisle, wailing and hurling curses at the gods. All in all, not ringing endorsements for what lay in store.

After the painfully slow trek, the four reached the arched double-doors at the end of the aisle. Green alabaster, into which was carved various animals—wolves, ravens, snakes, even swans—outlined the doors, and on each side stood two female singers, decked out in long white robes and matching white headscarves. Finally, to the right of the door stood a thin, bald priest, also dressed in white, his eyes closed in deep meditation.

As the four stood there in silence, waiting their turn, Homer realized he was shaking. He shoved his hands to his sides, to hide them, and then became aware of another sensation: he looked down at his left hand and noticed Calliope's in it.

Finally, in a high-pitched and decidedly creepy voice, the priest opened his eyes and addressed them: "Have you prepared yourselves to enter the sacred adyton of the Oracle?"

Only Calliope and Andie answered, "Yes."

"You may proceed," he responded. "One at a time, please."

Homer glanced over at Mac, who seemed frozen, immobile. For a few awkward moments, no one moved or spoke—until Calliope announced, with a sparkle in her eye, "I'll go." Without another word, she let go of Homer's hand and strode confidently up to the priest, who instructed her to wipe her feet on the green mat in front of the door. As the singers pulled open the double doors, she turned around, smiled quickly at Homer, and stepped through.

Homer couldn't believe she'd done it—mostly because he knew *he* couldn't do it himself. Not because he harbored any philosophical objections about knowing your destiny or altering your future or anything like that; he was just too damn *scared*. But after watching Calliope, he had second thoughts. After all, when would he have this opportunity again?

As he weighed his options, he overheard Mac talking quietly to Andie. "So, are you gonna do this too?" he asked.

"Yeah," she said, nodding her head in steely confidence.

"Any idea what you'll ask?"

Just then, the two singers opened the double doors to release Calliope, who carried a rolled-up slip of parchment in her hands and an unreadable ex-pression on her face. As she rejoined the group, Andie peered right into the doors. "Yeah, I do," she said, answering Mac's question. Then she stepped forward, wiped her feet on the green carpet, and disappeared into the darkness behind the doorway.

Homer looked over at Calliope, who reclaimed her place by his side. But she didn't look over at him—just gazed straight ahead, stoically, expressionlessly. She didn't seem sad, but she wasn't exactly bubbling over with jubilation either.

"That didn't take long," Homer whispered to her.

"Nope," she said simply.

"So…want to tell me what happened?" he asked.

She finally turned her face and smiled, "Can't," she whispered, holding up the rolled-up parchment. "It's a secret."

In what seemed like no time at all, the doors re-opened, and out walked Andie, whose face—like Calliope's—gave no indication as to what had happened inside. Next up: Mac. Or so Homer thought. But when he looked over, Mac only responded with a slight shake of his head.

Homer didn't know how to interpret Mac's hesitation. Did his headshake mean "No" or "Not yet"? Was he still angry? Chickening out? Just trying to put this off as long as possible? Homer had no idea. Nor did he know why he found himself, a few moments later, wiping his own feet on that green mat and taking a deep breath as the singers opened the double doors. Maybe he wanted to buy Mac more time. Maybe he wanted to look tough in front of his friends. Or maybe, he just *really* wanted to see what was on the other side.

The doors closed behind him, and he stepped into a wall of haze. Squinting through the soupy vapors, he tried to get a sense of the room: it was *smaller* than he had imagined, not much bigger than one of his classrooms, and made even smaller by the stream—more like a moat, really—that cut through it. On the other side of the water, Homer could barely make out a large, cone-shaped stone, covered with a net: the Omphalos, Homer assumed, the stone that marked Delphi as the world's center. Next to the stone, Homer saw the hazy shape of a person dressed in a long, white alb, swaying back and forth and singing a soft, indecipherable chant. Even though he couldn't make out this person's features, Homer knew immediately this was who he came to see: the Pythia, the official mouthpiece for Apollo's Oracle.

A low voice filled the room: "Step forward," it said, "and pose your question to Apollo's priestess." Homer peered through the steamy mist to find a tall, bearded man standing only a few feet away from him, on his side of the moat that separated the room. Careful not to fall in the water, Homer took two timid steps forward. Then he froze.

For years, ever since he first learned about the Oracle, Homer thought about what he would ask him. At school, in almost every grade, teachers would use as a writing prompt some variation of the question, "What would you ask the Oracle, and why?"—and he never had trouble thinking of one. But now, here he was, standing before the actual Pythia...and he couldn't muster up a single question. Finally, after an agonizingly protracted pause, he thought of one—a strange question for a teenager, perhaps, but really, the only question to which he ever wanted to know the answer.

"After I die, will anyone remember me?"

Upon hearing the question, the Pythia eased her way down from what Homer could now see was a high tripod. As she floated toward the moat, her long, white robe flowing all around her, Homer got a better look at her face. She was an older woman, but not as old as he anticipated; he expected a grandmother, but this woman was more like a pretty, middle-aged aunt. In her graying hair, she wore a crown of laurels and chaplets of beads; in her hands, she held a sprig of laurel and a small stone dish.

Homer watched as the woman, still shrouded in mist, bent down to the moat, and with the small dish, scooped up water from the stream. She stopped singing as she gazed intently into the small pool in her hands. Then, after a few moments of study, she looked up and closed her eyes. And then she started shaking. And then chanting, but much louder than she had before—almost screaming, in fact, but in words Homer couldn't begin to understand. And then, just as suddenly as it began, the frenzied chanting stopped, and she retreated into the obscuring mist.

"Is it over?" Homer wondered. Then he looked over at the bearded priest next to him, who was feverishly writing on a ragged piece of parchment, and he understood this man's purpose: to translate the Pythia's wild chanting.

When the priest finished writing, he rolled up the parchment and handed it to Homer. "The Oracle has spoken to you and you alone," he intoned. "Share these words with no one."

Homer took the sacred scroll and walked back toward the doors. But before rejoining the others, he opened up the parchment, his fingers shaking the whole time, and held it up to a nearby torch so he could read the Oracle's prophecy.

****

Soon, Homer was back on the other side of the green alabaster doorway, not speaking a word to anyone, just taking in the easy chanting of the white-robed singers.

Only moments before, he had watched his friend Mac traipse into the adyton. He saw the resigned look in his eyes, but he couldn't figure out the reason for it. After all, he was Prince Telemachus of Ithaca. What did he have to be worried about? Did he really think this Oracle would give him anything less than a glowing prophecy?

All the hurt and anger he felt from earlier in the day started melting away as Homer began imagining what great things the Pythia could be saying about Mac at that very moment, just on the other side of that door. He pictured in his mind Mac peeling open the parchment and reading about the destiny Fate had woven for him. "You will slay the Minotaur," the parchment would say. "But more importantly, you will become King of Ithaca. A peaceful Ithaca, one that has been long washed clean of parasites and vultures. You will be respected by your people, for whom you will have profound compassion. Because, like them, you too have struggled, have made mistakes, and have learned to ask for help."

Homer smiled to himself, imagining that someday, years from now, Pieridian would erect a statue in the main foyer, of a tall, self-assured man with a signature crooked grin. Underneath, a placard would read: "Telemachus, Compassionate King of Ithaca, Slayer of the Minotaur." And all of the young students walking by would look at that statue with reverence and deep admiration. None of them would know the real truth, about how close he came to getting kicked out, about how often he screwed up along the way.

As Homer was imagining all of this, the doors suddenly opened and out flew Mac, eyes blazing. "Great idea, Calliope!" he hissed, flinging to the stone floor his crumpled-up piece of parchment as he bolted down the aisle.

For a moment, no one knew what to do. Then Homer reached down to pick up the parchment. As Calliope and Andie leaned in, Homer opened up the Oracle's message for everyone to see.

The page was blank.

Nothing.

CHAPTER TWENTY
Revelations

As soon as she saw the blank parchment, Andie took off.

Sprinting down the aisle, she managed to shut out of her mind the cryptic message she had just received from the Oracle. There would be time to figure that out later. For now, all she could picture was the devastated look on Mac's face before he ran out of there. Suddenly, catching up to him—helping him—became the most important thing in the world to her.

He had quite a jump on her, and Andie knew calling out to him wouldn't exactly endear her to the other pilgrims. So she sprinted down the aisle as fast as she could, but by the time she got to the temple's front doorway, she couldn't find him anywhere. She looked around frantically, finally catching a glimpse of him fleeing into the woods.

As Andie crashed through the brush, pictures flooded her mind. Mac laughing as he tried to balance a melon on top of his head. Winking at her after he bested Basileus and Blasios. Staring into her eyes after they fell from the wooden horse at War Games. Without her knowing it, without her even seeking it, Mac had become a fixture in her life. When did that happen? At what point did he become so important to her?

While she searched through the woods, in her mind she looked back on her life over the past three months. And she realized something extraordinary: she'd let him in. For a year, she'd built a wall around herself—to keep herself in, to keep everyone else out. She lost herself behind that wall, buried herself so deep inside, she knew no one would ever bother to find her. But somehow, bit-by-bit over these past few months, she'd let it crumble away. And standing right on the other side of that wall—was Mac.

She followed him into a clearing, only to find he had vanished. She fixed her eyes on a giant weeping willow tree across the way, the biggest and widest tree she had ever seen. In fact, it looked more like a hut than a tree, with massive green branches that swept down so low, they touched the ground on all sides. Testing a hunch, Andie ran to the tree, parted the branches, and ducked inside.

The shady interior of the tree resembled the nighttime sky: just about pitch black, save for the specks of light stabbing through the tiny openings in the thick curtain of sheltering leaves. She called out Mac's name—no response. Soon, though, her eyes adjusted, and she spotted him, sitting on the other side of the broad tree trunk, gazing off into nothingness. Without a word, she sat down next to him. Together, they silently stared out at the expanse of shimmering "stars" all around them.

"Did she chant something?" Mac finally asked, keeping his eyes straight ahead. "That lady, the Pythia, or whatever. Did she chant something weird as she looked into her little bowl?"

"Yeah," Andie said softly.

"And then you got a message? Something written on the parchment about your future?"

"Yeah," she admitted carefully. She didn't want to rile him up any more.

He leaned back, rested the back of his head on the trunk, and looked up at the firmament of branches overhead. "I...I don't get it..." he stammered, almost huffing out a laugh, although his eyes seemed on the verge of tears. "What happened? I got *nothing*. No message. No guidance. Nothing about my father, about my future. You mean to tell me the great Oracle of Delphi, has *nothing* at all to say to me?"

They were sitting right next to each other, so close their shoulders were touching, but Andie felt as if she were still chasing him. Try as she might, she just couldn't reach him. She remembered what the name Telemachus meant: "distant fighter," he had said. It didn't make sense to her before, but now, under that tree, the term absolutely fit.

It was the night of the Harvest Dance that he had shared with her that tidbit about his name: the night they danced, the night she thought he might kiss her. It didn't occur to her until this very moment just how much she wished he had.

"There must be some reason," she tried to reassure him.

"A 'reason,' right…" Mac scoffed. "How about I'm a loser? How's that for a reason?"

"Don't say that."

"Why not? You, Homer, Calliope—everyone got a message but me. If that's not proof enough I'm a loser—"

"Don't *say* that!" Andie said again, her voice rising with conviction. "You're a good person. And a good friend."

"Tell that to Calliope," Mac snorted, as he got up and walked over to the drooping branches of the tree.

"Calliope? What does she have to do with—?"

"You weren't there," he reminded her. As he spoke, he pulled back one of the leaves, releasing a shard of fractured light into the darkness. "On the pier, with that thug. You didn't see what happened. *I* did. And I didn't do a damn thing."

"From what I heard, you didn't need to 'do' anything," Andie said. "Theo had it covered."

"What if Theo wasn't there? What would have happened to her? She would have been hurt by those guys. Just like…" Then his voice cracked, and he stopped talking, occupying himself instead with tearing leaves off the wall of branches.

"Just like what?" Andie pressed.

Mac didn't turn to look at her. "Let's just say," he said quietly, "this isn't the first time I let something like this happen."

"What does that mean?"

"It means…" he started, but then, as if realizing he'd already said too much, he shook his head slowly. "Nothing. It means nothing," he shrugged, making a fist, crushing the leaves inside.

"Mac," she said softly, breaking the thick silence as she stood up and moved toward him. "We're friends. Whatever it is, you can tell me."

With the barest hint of a sad smile, Mac finally met Andie's eyes. "You won't want to be my friend if I tell you this."

Andie gently took his hand, the one balled up in a fist. He was shaking. He turned to her and slowly uncoiled his fist; as their palms touched, she felt the sensation of crinkled leaves and the icy coldness of his skin. "Try me," she said.

With a shuddering breath, Mac looked at Andie again, but she could somehow tell he wasn't really seeing *her*, but instead was peering into some remote, haunting memory. Closing his eyes, Mac began to speak, haltingly at first, his voice very low, but gaining in strength and desperation as his story gushed forth like a raging river.

As a child, Mac rarely slept through the night — mostly because they never slept through the night. Two or three times during the course of an evening, he would be awakened by some hideous sound coming from somewhere in the palace — shouts, drunken laughter, occasionally a crash of something valuable hitting the wall or floor. Usually, he'd fall back to sleep within a few minutes. But not this night.

A loud, violent sound shoots him out of bed. In the fog of sleep, he first mistakes the sound for the barking of a wild dog, but he soon recognizes it as laughter. Not a light-hearted laugh, though; this is sinister, cruel, mocking. He listens for a while, thinking he hears another voice — a woman's voice, he determines — which is soon swallowed up by a cacophony of roars and jeers.

He glances out his window; the summertime moon sits high in the dark violet sky. Shaking off the last remnants of sleep, Mac climbs out of bed and silently pads on bare feet — out his bedroom door, down the open corridor, to the fancy balustrade overlooking the courtyard. Down below, everything is dark, the torches having been snuffed out much earlier, a fire smoldering in the giant hearth providing the only light. And gathered in a semi-circle around the blaze, still gorging on food and wine, are some suitors, maybe ten or twelve of them — including Antinoös.

In the entire world, Mac fears nobody more than Antinoös. For as long as he can remember, all nine years of his life, Mac has been tormented by this man: taunted, teased, shoved, hit, and threatened with worse should he ever rat him out to his mother. Even from way up on the darkened balustrade, Mac ducks down — a conditioned response to the sight of him.

Usually, some servants were saddled with the job of attending to the suitors until they passed out. But on this night, even the servants have gone to bed, leaving only one other person to deal with this rowdy band: a woman armed with a jug of wine in one hand and some sort of cloth—some mending, perhaps, or a scarf—in the other. Although she's facing away from Mac, he recognizes her plainly. What is his mother doing down there? Is she drinking with them? Why? Isn't she supposed to hate them as much as he does?

From his vantage point behind the balustrade, Mac can't make out what they're saying. But he can see everything: his mother, reaching her hands out in a calming gesture; then Antinoös, standing up, grabbing the wine jug she held, trapping her small hand underneath his meaty fist; bringing the jug up to his mouth, pulling her arm along with it; taking a long, generous swallow. As she yanks the wine jug away for the second time, Mac notices his mother's arm is shaking. She's afraid, he realizes. She wants them to stop drinking; Mac can understand why. Drinking makes them mean...and angry.

Up in the shadows, Mac is shaking too, gripping on to the railing, watching helplessly as Antinoös, bolstered by the drunken cheers from his comrades, grabs at his mother's wrist, squeezing tightly to force her to release the jug. Letting out a low sound of pain, she won't let go, and Mac can see her straining to get the jug, and her arm, free. Antinoös changes tactics and grabs at her other hand. She struggles to avoid his grasp and the scarf she holds rips in two, falling to the ground and becoming tangled underneath their feet.

Undaunted, Antinoös stands up, an angry bark spewing from his twisted mouth. He pushes toward her, forcing her to back up, into the shadows, out of the view of her son, as her pursuer moves right in front of her.

Mac can no longer see her. But he hears the sounds—the loud crash as the wine jug hits the floor, his mother's shriek followed by Antinoös's bellow of rage. Then he sees nothing but the walls of the corridor flying past, as he flees—frantically, recklessly—to his bedroom. The echoes of the angry roar still echoing in his ears, he slams his door and hides under his bed until morning.

He doesn't go back to sleep.

Mac and Andie were no longer holding hands. At some point during his confession, Mac had pulled away and turned back toward the wall of branches, to hide his face. Andie respected the distance he put between them—appreciated it, even, because it gave her time to process what she had just been told. Finally, she whispered, in a voice devoid of judgment, "Did you ever talk to her about it?"

"What could I say?" Mac asked. "She never said a word about it. So neither did I."

"Never? You never said anything to her?" She saw him shake his head, and it occurred to her he had probably never told *anyone* about this before right now. "So you don't *know* what really happened?"

"She didn't come out of her room for two days after that night. It's pretty obvious what happened," Mac said with a contemptible laugh. "My mother needed me, and I completely failed her. What kind of person would do that? Would just run away and leave his mother at the mercy of a monster?"

"Mac, you were just a kid. Only nine years old. You can't blame yourself—"

"Why not?" Mac interrupted, turning back to level her with a devastating glare. "Who am I supposed to blame, then?"

Andie paused, knowing she couldn't say anything to make it better, though she desperately wanted to try. "OK, fine. So your mom was hurt, and it sucks, and you want to blame yourself. But you were a kid then, and even if you weren't, it's in the past. All that matters is what you do *now*." She softened her voice a bit. "You're making it up to her, Mac. Everything you've been doing—the labors, trying to stay in school…I'm sure she's proud of that."

"Oh, sure," Mac laughed bitterly. "I'm sure she'd be beaming with pride to find out her son's a coward *and* a liar."

"What does that mean, 'liar'?"

He finally turned to face her. "I'd love to believe I've been going through all of this to make it up to her. To prove that I won't fail her again, that I'm not a complete screw-up. But the truth is, I'm not even sure that's the only reason I've been fighting to stay in school." He closed his eyes and winced. "Andie, what if I'm afraid to go back home? What if I just don't want to face them?"

As Andie stared at the embattled young man in front of her, lost in a maze of pain and regret, her own demons flooded her mind. She thought about her father and the obsession that destroyed him and could do the same to her if she let it.

"You'll have to face them someday," she said, quite possibly to herself just as much as Mac. "Whether it's two weeks, or two years, or twenty years, you can't run from them forever."

"Gee, thanks," he muttered. "What a comfort."

"What I mean is, you have to go forward, into the future, even if you don't know what that looks like. Screw the Oracle. Come up with *your own* plan. Make your move. Finish school. Prove you are your father's son. Then go home…and kick some suitor-ass. Hey, I'll bring my bow and be right there with you, if you want me."

Mac looked at her, and his eyes told her that she'd won: she brought him back from the brink. When she returned his gaze, he somehow seemed different to her. Stronger, taller, as if sharing his story relieved him—for the moment—of the terrible weight he'd been carrying on his shoulders for years.

"You're not in this alone, Mac," she reminded him. "Maybe you haven't noticed, but in the past few months, you've gained quite a devoted following. Heck, Homer and I are almost ready to fight each other over who gets the distinction of being your best friend."

"I'm pretty sure you could take him," Mac said with a reluctant smile.

Andie waggled her eyebrows. "I don't know…he can be pretty scrappy."

Mac laughed, his face splitting into a wide grin, as he wrapped Andie in a fierce hug. She realized how right it felt. How she always wanted to feel like this.

They held each other for a long while, in silence, until she heard him whisper in her ear, "I'm still a liar, you know."

"Why?"

He leaned back and fixed his gaze on her. "Because I didn't tell you about the other reason I'm fighting so hard to stay in school." Before she could say anything, Mac's mouth covered hers. Her heart raced as she pressed herself closer to him and kissed him back. He held her tightly, as he gently kissed the corner of her mouth and the line of her jaw. His lips were so warm, she shivered when he pulled away.

They held each other's eyes until Andie broke the silence. "We should go," she said.

"Oh…OK…" mumbled a clearly embarrassed Mac, as he brought his hands back down to his sides. "I guess they're probably waiting for us."

"No, that's not what I meant," she said, grabbing one of his hands and holding it tightly. "I mean we should go and finish this, once and for all."

"Finish what?"

"I've got an idea for your last labor," she told him. "And this one's a sure bet."

Mac took a step back and looked at her suspiciously. "What are you talking about?"

Andie balled her free hand into a fist. "Any interest in going to see a Minotaur?" she smiled.

Mac looked even more confused, "Are you saying —?"

"It's time, Mac," she declared. "I'm ready." And she was. She wanted to do this — for her dad, for herself. But more than that: for Mac.

For a moment, Mac just studied her. "So you mean Homer was right?" he asked. "You know where the Minotaur is?"

"Yep. And so do you."

CHAPTER TWENTY-ONE
Into the Labyrinth

Mac knew exactly *where* he was. Just not why she took them there.

Neither did Homer. "I don't get it," he said, as he emerged from the trees. "Why are we stopping here?" But Andie didn't answer, or even turn around; she just kept marching forward, silently, into the middle of the ruins.

In almost every way, this scene looked thoroughly familiar to Mac. With her bow in her right hand and her large bag flung over her left shoulder, Andie looked exactly the same as she did any other day the two of them journeyed out to this spot, to shoot melons, to swim, just to hang out. But when he moved up next to her, amidst the crumbling towers, she seemed like a stranger to him. Her eyes made it that way — icy, determined, fixed on the cliff to their right. Mac had no idea what was going on inside her head, but he knew one thing for sure: the time for shooting melons was over.

"Andie!" shouted an exasperated Homer, as he limped up behind her. "I said why —"

"We're here," she responded, in a quiet, measured voice, still staring at the cliffs.

"You said you were taking us to a labyrinth," Homer insisted. "Where's the —?"

"You're standing on it," she cut him off.

Homer looked down incredulously at the white sands under his feet. "What?"

"Come on," Andie ordered, as she started walking diagonally through the ruins, toward the cliff to the right. The other four followed, not at all sure what she meant or what she had planned. But Mac was the most confused of all: over the past few months, he and Andie had logged in many, many hours at this beach — "their" beach. His and Andie's. Was there something about this place he didn't know? Or, more accurately: Was there something she hadn't told him?

"All this was supposed to be a castle," Andie began. "Years ago, this wealthy Athenian banker named Apsophon had it built, as a graduation gift for his only son Tycho, who was a student here at Pieridian. But he never finished building it."

"Why?" Mac asked.

"Because when his son was seventeen," Andie said, "his name got picked."

"Picked?" Calliope repeated, helping Homer negotiate the rocks. "Picked for what?"

By this point, Andie had reached the bottom of the cliff wall, only instead of hiking up, she started walking down, into a narrow crevice at the base of the cliff. "For years, Athens and Crete were involved in a feud," Andie explained, as she gracefully maneuvered through the jagged rocks. "Very one-sided feud, actually: Athens routinely got its butt kicked. Finally, the two kings worked out a truce: Crete would leave Athens alone, but in return, every nine years, Athens would have to send over fourteen youths—seven boys, seven girls—to be sacrificed to the Minotaur. All Athenian kids had to throw in their names. They randomly chose fourteen; this kid was one of them."

"Well, *that* sucks," Theo muttered.

Cold shadows, cast by the rock walls on both sides, started to overtake them as they made their way down the sloping, uneven path, which led them to the right, back toward the woods. Andie continued: "The father, Apsophon, was devastated, of course, by his son's death, and bent on revenge. But he didn't want the Minotaur dead; he wanted to see it *suffer*. So, when he hears that the king's son Theseus had volunteered to go over to Crete and slay the Minotaur, Apsophon meets with this Theseus guy and proposes a deal."

"I knew it!" bleated Homer, from way in the back. "The Minotaur's not dead! Theseus never killed it!"

Andie arched her neck and shot him a silencing glare. "*Apparently* not. But he nearly did; legend has it he incapacitated it just enough so

Apsophon could have it secretly transported to a custom-made prison—a new labyrinth, built underneath what would have been his dead son's castle. Which, if I'm right..." she said, as she stopped at her destination, a partially obscured rock wall, made of lighter-colored stones than the rest of the cliff, "...is behind this."

"So you're saying on the other side of this wall is a labyrinth containing a murderous, flesh-eating monster?" Theo clarified. "That's what you're saying?"

"Maybe," Andie answered, as she dropped the pack from her shoulders, dumping out onto the ground two hammers and a small pickaxe.

"But if the Minotaur were in there," Calliope wondered, "wouldn't it be dead by now?"

"It was granted immortality," Homer quickly explained, as he pushed his way forward and put his hand on the wall. "It can be killed, but it can't die of old age."

"What's it been doing all this time?" Calliope wondered, with more than a trace of sympathy in her voice, as she looked at the rock wall before her.

"Getting tortured," Andie said matter-of-factly, as she picked up the two hammers. "At least at first. That's why Apsophon had it brought here, after all—to get some payback for the death of his son. As for the rest of the time: Who knows?"

"So it's not just a murderous, flesh-eating monster," Theo mused, "but a murderous, flesh-eating monster that's pissed off after being tortured and incarcerated for, like, a hundred years? All right, sounds good. Let's do this."

Andie, all business, tossed one of the hammers to Theo. Then she flipped the other one to Mac, who was still processing everything she had said to them. "Just for the record...you've known about this labyrinth for a while, right?" Mac asked.

"Yeah..." Andie affirmed, reaching down to grab the pickaxe.

"You probably found some documents or something your dad left behind, right?"

"Right."

"And you never thought to mention this to me before, even

though we've come here *every week*, for the past *two months*?"

"Guess it never came up…" Andie answered humorlessly, as she swung her pickaxe into the wall.

They all got to work: Andie, Theo, and Mac smashing away at the wall; Calliope building a fire and preparing the torches; Homer fiddling with some arrows. No one made any jokes or even spoke to each other, which suited Mac fine; he had too much on his mind to make small talk. After all, if what Andie said were true, about the Minotaur being trapped behind this wall for the past century, wouldn't it pounce at any opportunity to get out?

Just as Mac was considering that possibility, something did pounce at him — not any monstrous creature, but the wall itself. He had been standing on a rock and swinging his hammer, vigorously, into the top of the wall — too vigorously, as it turned out; a large chunk of the wall came loose and avalanched down on him. As Mac fell backwards, one of the rock-chunks landed on his right ankle.

"Mac!" Theo shouted, leaping over to him in a flash. "You OK, dude?" he asked, as he picked up the rock pinning his ankle

"I'm fine," Mac winced as he slowly got up and returned to work. But the distinct limp he had as he tried to walk around suggested otherwise.

"Hmmmmm…" Theo grimaced. "Not a good omen…"

Andie glared at him. "Oh, so you believe in omens now?"

Theo shrugged. "Just saying…"

"Sit there," Andie said to Mac. "We'll finish the rest."

Not wanting to appear weak, but needing a moment to let the worst of the throbbing pain subside, Mac limped his way over to Homer, who was sitting on a stone. "You gonna be OK?" he asked, scooting over so Mac could sit next to him.

Mac nodded but grimaced. "Is this what your foot feels like all the time?"

"No, no…maybe a little."

Mac reached down and rubbed his ankle in silence. Finally, he said, "Hey, before we go in there, I wanted to say…what I said to you on the way to Delphi? I was upset. It wasn't…I mean, I'm really sorry…I didn't mean it, OK?"

"I know," Homer answered. "I'm sorry, too, for not telling you—"

"Let's forget it. We're good, right?" Mac leaned back and stretched out his leg.

Homer nodded, pausing for a moment before getting down to business. "So, do you have your aulos?"

"My aulos? Are you kidding? I threw that overboard, remember?"

"Well, you're gonna need it to stun the Minotaur. Here, take mine."

Mac, stupefied, looked at the aulos and then at Homer. "But this isn't real," he reminded him. "This is a souvenir."

"Well, the *Minotaur* doesn't know that!" Homer shot back, patronizing as always. "Next: I prepared the arrows you're going to need. I took teeth from the boar's collar and converted them into arrowheads. Remember, Rhixion said these teeth were from the same dragon that Jason used to grow those soldiers…"

"Actually, he didn't say that at all," Mac corrected him. "He said he doubted that story was even true."

Homer ignored Mac's comment and kept going. "Then I dipped as many arrows as I could into the water taken from the pond of Narcissus. If my information is true, an arrow dipped in this water should be enough to kill the Minotaur."

When he finished speaking, Homer handed Mac the prepared arrows—his only defense against the raging, supposedly immortal Minotaur.

"Three?" Mac asked, staring at the fang-tipped arrows in his hand. "That's it?"

"You didn't exactly leave me with a lot of water to work with…" Homer said meekly.

"Three," Mac repeated.

Homer tried to smile. "It only takes one…right?"

"Just the same," Mac said, as he gingerly pulled his right leg onto the rock, revealing a leather strap tied to his calf. "I thought I'd bring along some back-up." Tucked into the strap was a dagger.

"Ahhh!" Homer said, wide-eyed. "The dagger I wrestled away from Basileus!"

"Right," Mac nodded. "That one." Then, hearing a pronounced grunt, he looked up to see Theo heave a giant rock to the ground. "Done!" he announced, clapping his hands.

Mac limped off the slab and joined Theo, Andie, and Calliope at the hole, just big enough for someone to fit through. They peered into the darkness, a chilly draft hitting their faces. As Mac tried to look around the walls and the ceiling, he heard something—a small, scratching sound. They all backed up, as specks of light—maybe a dozen of them—emerged from the darkness and trickled out of the hole they had made, crawling their way across the cliff wall at lightning speed.

"What was that?" Calliope asked, definitely spooked.

"I don't know…" Theo said, watching as the light-specks skittered away. "I think…I think they were spiders, or something."

Mac glanced over at Andie before turning to the cliff wall, onto which four glittery bugs had attached themselves. He leaned closer; if they were spiders, they were like none he had ever seen before. Each one was quite large, maybe the size of a walnut; each head had two antennae; and the back third of each was a round ball that seemed to glow, eerily so.

What's more: they *bit*—a fact Mac determined when one of them jumped from the rock wall and suctioned itself onto his shoulder. "Ow!" Mac yelped, feeling the pinch. Immediately, Andie plucked off the glowing bug, threw it on the ground, and stomped on it.

As Mac grabbed his shoulder, Andie bent down and investigated the squashed carcass at her feet. "Yeah…a spider," she concluded.

"A spider…crossed with a firefly, then crossed again with a piranha," Mac winced, moving his shoulder so he could see the welt that had started to purple there.

Calliope grimaced. "It's so…bizarre…"

"*That's* bizarre?" Theo asked. "We've just uncovered an underground labyrinth, supposedly the home of a man-beast-hybrid spawned from a queen who mated with a bull. And a *bug* is bizarre?" Mac picked up his three arrows and sheepishly limped back over to the opening in the wall, knowing Theo was right: if he couldn't handle a few bugs, how could he handle any other potentially scary stuff they may encounter?

"How are we going to find our way around in there?" asked Calliope, once again peering into the dark hole.

"Well, we can start with this," Andie said, reaching into her pack and pulling out a handful of twine. "I gathered up as much as I could find."

"Ah, the twine gambit! How original," Theo said. "But I got a better idea…"

He picked up his own pack, which he had set on the ground next to the cliff wall. He untied the top, lifted it upside-down and shook it—releasing his pet, Typhon the serphint.

"What are you doing?" Mac said, as he watched Theo try to grab the slithering creature off the ground. "You think that thing has a Minotaur-tracking system or something?"

"Yeah, that's *exactly* what I think," Theo sneered, as he picked the serphint up by the neck. "No, dummy. Don't you remember what Kal said? Serphints were made for navigation. He's not going to help us find anything in there. He's going to help us *get out* once we do…"

Andie shoved the twine back into her bag. "Fine," she said tersely. "We'll go with the stupid snake. Now, let's go."

Silently, they began making their final preparations. As Calliope handed out torches from the fire she had started, she realized someone was missing. "You ready?" she called back to Homer, who was still sitting on the rock.

"Actually," Homer said, his eyes falling to the ground. "I was thinking I should sit this one out…"

Theo looked incredulous. "Are you kidding me? You've been yapping about this Minotaur for months, and now, you're getting cold feet?"

"My feet are a fine temperature, thank you," Homer shot back. "It's just that one of them…doesn't work all that well." He paused, clearly embarrassed, and then said softly, "I'm not chickening out. If the Minotaur's in there, I want to see it. You have no idea how much. But I don't want to slow you down."

Theo grinned at Mac, an *Aww, isn't he cute?* kind of grin. "As much as I love pity-parties," Theo said, walking over to Homer, "all warriors are required to march in the front lines. That includes you." He extended his hand in a gesture of helping Homer up off the slab. Homer stared at his hand for a long moment until, finally, Theo grabbed his arm and gave it a gentle tug. "This is your mission too, buddy."

"You're wrong, Theo," Mac said. "This is my mission. I shouldn't be asking any of you to go in there with me. Who knows what we'll find? I won't let you risk your lives." He looked back at the entrance to the labyrinth. "I'm going in alone."

As Mac stood firm in his determination to do this on his own, his friends continued their preparations without a word—Homer lighting his torch, Theo putting a leash around Typhon the serphint, Andie and Calliope strapping on their packs.

"Oh, did you say something?" Andie finally asked Mac, before she turned and made her way to the entrance. Mac shrugged his shoulders and smiled.

When the five of them gathered at the opening in the wall, Mac paused, expecting Andie to go first; after all, she was the one who had brought them to this point. But she just stood there, unmoving. And so, with a torch in one hand and a bow in the other, Mac took that first step into the unknown.

He almost didn't do it, *couldn't* do it; the fear he'd be torn to shreds the moment he stepped through all but paralyzed him. Once he had both feet inside, though, he relaxed a little; he was still alive, for the moment. While the others made their way inside, Mac took in his immediate surroundings: they were in a narrow corridor carved out of stone, except for the floor, which felt damp and squishy. Mac had anticipated a vast, cavernous space, big enough to accommodate something like the Minotaur, but this felt tight, claustrophobic; the corridor could maybe fit two people across, and the ceiling hung just a few inches above his head. He saw no windows of any kind, no sources of air or illumination. Andie told them the labyrinth was underground, but Mac didn't appreciate what that meant until he looked down the dark, sloping corridor stretching out before him…into nothingness.

With Mac in the lead, the group made their way down the long, sloped corridor. As they kept descending, Mac could feel his anxiety rise. When he felt something slimy slither by his leg, he jumped; even after he realized it was just Typhon the serphint, sliding out in front of them in the ankle-deep water, he needed a little time to calm himself down.

They finally made it to their first decision, the moment where the path forked. They didn't know what to do; they had no way of determining which was the "correct" path to take, so when Typhon took the left fork, they just followed. That path, of course, led them to another fork, at which point they once again arbitrarily followed the way set by the serphint. After doing this several more times, Mac realized they needed a better system.

"We have no idea how big this place is," he told the group when they reached the next fork. "At this rate, getting around here could take a long time. Days, maybe."

"Days?" Theo repeated. "Dude, I have a history exam coming up."

"Let's split into two groups. We'll cover more ground that way." Mac pointed his torch in the direction of his roommate. "Theo, you got your flute with you?"

"Naturally."

"OK," Mac paused, tried to collect his thoughts. "Each group takes an aulos. If you get into trouble, blow into it to alert the rest of us. Maybe there's enough of an echo down here that we can hear each other."

"OK, but…what if a group actually runs into the Minotaur?" Theo asked.

"Just start blowing that flute like crazy," Mac explained. "Homer says the sound of the flute may stun it. Then again, it may not. Who knows? Either way, just run. Get out of there. Once we all join back up, we'll face it together."

"So what are the teams?" Calliope asked.

"The two of us," Andie declared immediately, motioning to Mac and herself, "and the three of you." Mac looked over at Andie and nodded.

"Remember, Mac's the only one who can kill the Minotaur," Homer reminded everyone. "So, if you see it, don't engage it."

"Got it…no engaging…" Calliope said nervously.

Theo, Calliope, and Homer decided to take the left path, simply because that's where Typhon started to go, so Andie and Mac took the right one. Before he left, Mac turned back and saw Homer, standing in the middle of the dark hall, staring at him. Mac realized the two of them were sharing the same fear: that they might not ever see each other again.

Mac took a few steps toward his friend and looked at him for a long, lingering moment. Then, without a word or a hug or even a handshake, they hurried back to their respective groups.

CHAPTER TWENTY-TWO
Descent

He went with his gut. And just hoped that it was working.

Other parts of him may not have been faring too well: he was still hobbling from when the rocks fell on his ankle, and his right shoulder, the one which got stung by that spider-firefly thing, had also started to throb. But Mac hoped that his gut—his sense of intuition that told him which way to go whenever he and Andie came to a fork—was working more effectively.

Of course, how would he know? Every dark, musty, twisting corridor in that place looked and smelled exactly the same as every other dark, musty, twisting corridor that came before it. And so, the two of them had no choice but to wander aimlessly through the halls, not knowing where to go next and, even with the aid of a torch, not able to see more than four feet in front of them.

The only thing Mac knew for sure: they were going down. With each step, they were going deeper and deeper underground. Most times, the floor sloped gradually; at times, though, the decline was steep and sudden. Once, the two took a corner and then immediately felt themselves slipping down a slimy wet slide, into a channel of stagnant, knee-deep water. When they got out, their feet and shins were covered with leeches. Barely holding back a scream, Andie threw her torch to Mac as she ripped off the bloodsuckers; then she held both torches while Mac did the same.

After the leech incident, the two didn't talk much, which suited Mac just fine. It gave him time to think, to recall everything that had happened over the past few days. His non-answer from the Oracle. His confession to Andie. Her acceptance of him after he told her. And, of course, the kiss.

That kiss…Just the thought of it almost made him forget where he was. He had never before felt such an overpowering flood of emotion. Never before experienced such a feeling—that everything bad in the world had fallen away, and that everything good in the world was suddenly summed up in one person, who just so happened to be in his arms, kissing him back. He couldn't name that feeling, exactly. But he had a hunch.

They kept meandering through the corridors, past endless stretches of damp, rocky walls, when they found something different: a worn wooden door, which opened with the slightest push of Mac's hand. After exchanging uneasy glances, Mac and Andie pointed their torches into the darkness and walked inside. Almost immediately, Mac bumped into something hard; the light from his torch revealed it to be a low, stone table, covered with a greasy ash, into which was stuck fragments of ripped parchment. Mac picked up some of the torn slips and tried to read them by torchlight, but he could only make out a few smudged words: "man-bull," "extraction," and "proceeding as planned."

****

"OK, I'll say it: this place scares the bezeuses out of me," Theo admitted, as he followed his pet serphint through the dark, damp corridors.

"Well, that's quite the about-face," remarked Homer, walking on Theo's left, "considering what you were saying to me outside."

"Yeah, key word: *outside*," Theo said, his usual swagger suddenly gone. "It's a different story in here, where any time we take a turn, we have no idea what kind of horrible, disgusting agent of freak-me-out ghastliness could jump out at us. Which reminds me," he said to Calliope, who was shining her torch at a single glowing spider darting along the maze's walls, "why are you way over there? Come stand closer to me."

"Uh, I can take care of myself, thanks," Calliope said. "I took Intro to Warfare just like you…except unlike you, I actually paid attention."

"Oh, and I'm sure skinny, little you will be able to protect us from any twelve-foot tall flesh-feaster that comes our—"

He didn't get to finish. At that moment, as he followed Typhon around a corner, a shadowy figure lurched out from the wall and smashed the side of Theo's head. Momentarily dazed, Theo wobbled backwards, dropping his torch in the process (but managing to hold on to Typhon's leash). Fortunately, Calliope sprang into action, shoving Theo's attacker to the wall and then driving her elbow into his gut, bringing him down.

Theo and Homer stared in disbelief at Calliope, who said, "I told you I paid attention in Warfare." Then they looked down at their mystery adversary, who was lying in a puddle, groaning, putting up no resistance. Homer's torchlight illuminated the attacker: a man, with wisps of white hair and an equally patchy beard. His face was pale, gaunt, emaciated; his light blue eyes, in their sunken sockets, quivered wildly. In his bony right hand, he was barely grasping the stick that he had used to strike Theo. He was wearing a long, ash-gray robe, ending in tatters at his gnarled and blackened bare feet.

Theo knelt down and addressed his prone attacker. "Unless you want my sister to continue kicking your ass," he said, "I suggest you start talking."

****

"Check this out," Andie called.

Mac had been shining his torchlight into the chamber's dark corners. He had determined that the room—more of a cave, really—was small, and made smaller by so much clutter; all around were stone slabs, littered with toppled jars and cracked clay pots. And inside several of these pots: dead and dried-up leeches.

Sidestepping the junk scattered across the floor, Mac made his way to Andie. She was standing next to a long, low table, on which were placed what looked to Mac like all sorts of misshapen golden blobs. They seemed as if they might ooze right off the table, but when Mac moved closer, he could see the blobs were actually solid, almost stone-like, as well as translucent. And trapped inside each one was an assortment of dead creatures—spiders, wasps, even small snakes.

"It's amber," Andie said, anticipating Mac's question. "It comes from trees. Sticky stuff that hardens into lumps. You can use it to preserve things." She paused and then responded to Mac's suspicious look: "I don't *always* sleep through class!"

Waving the torchlight over the amber blobs, Mac tried to see what other kinds of things were frozen inside. The more he looked, the more disgusted he became: he saw not only small creatures trapped inside the amber, but parts of larger creatures. Horns. Hooves. Even eyeballs.

Sufficiently grossed out, Mac turned back to Andie, who was investigating another wall, covered with strange etchings. First, he saw numbers—long stretches of them, in no discernible pattern, intelligible only to their creator. Next to them: shapes—images of fire; squiggles; an army of diamonds, each of which contained a small circle. And in the center of all of these random etchings: the outline of a bull's head.

"What in Hades went on in here?" Mac asked

"Don't know," Andie said, her voice shaking. "Nothing good."

****

"That serphint…" the man rasped, pointing a bony finger at Typhon, "where did you get it?"

Homer, Theo, and Calliope were standing over the stranger, who was now sitting against the wall, his legs unable to support him. Theo looked protectively at Typhon. "Why do you care?" he asked.

"Because he created it," Homer announced. "Well, maybe not Typhon here. But he probably created its mom and dad."

"What are you—?" Theo began.

"If my hunch is right, allow me to introduce Xenotareus," Homer announced, stunned that all his research had paid off. "A medicine-man who figured out how to breed different life forms. Then he moved on to another challenge: achieving immortality…by drinking the blood of the Minotaur." Homer looked the gaunt man square in his wild eyes. "I'm right, aren't I?"

"I don't know how you know any of that, but you have to leave!" the stranger wheezed. "I found this place. It's mine. You can't keep me from finishing my experiments."

"Experiments? On the Minotaur, you mean?" Homer pressed. "Did you find it?"

"Enough! No more questions! Do as I say, and leave!" The stranger pushed his way up the wall and tried to hustle away, but he was so weakened, he only made it a few steps before he collapsed.

Calliope eased over and crouched down next to him. "We're not trying to hurt you," she said calmly. When she put his hand on the man's back to comfort him, she could feel his individual bones through his thin robe. "We're not trying to take anything from you. If you let us, we may even be able to help you."

The man looked up at her and spoke with genuine concern in his voice. "This labyrinth is no place for children. Go. I'm not going to ask you again."

Calliope glanced back at her brother and Homer. "Well, we have two other friends in here—one of whom knows a lot about the Minotaur. Can you help us locate them?"

The man Homer called Xenotareus said nothing, just shifted his wild eyes from Calliope, to the two boys, then back to Calliope. He tried to stand, swatting away Calliope when she offered to help. When he finally made it to his feet, he said, "This way."

He led them—slowly, methodically—through many forking corridors, his knowledge of the place clearly evident. He hunched forward as he walked; every few steps, he had to reach for the walls to steady himself. He didn't speak or volunteer any information about himself, so Homer kept firing off questions: "How did you find this place?" He didn't get a response, so he tried another question. "How long have you been down here?"

"Not long enough," Xenotareus said.

"And how long do you plan on staying here?"

"Until I'm done."

"Ah, evasiveness..." Theo muttered. "Always a way to win people over."

"And what about these glowing spiders here?" Homer asked, as he waved his torch in the direction of one of the tiny lights on the wall. "Is that your handiwork as well?"

"My creations, yes. Spiders, mated with fireflies…" Xenotareus muttered.

"OK, but why? What's their purpose? What are they for?" Homer asked.

"They're tools," he responded.

"Tools for what?"

"For extracting the blood."

Once again, Homer pressed him. "The blood of the Minotaur? You're saying it's here? And you're experimenting with its blood?"

"And you use these spiders to suck its blood out so you can test it?" Calliope shuddered.

"Your sympathy is unfounded, young lady," Xenotareus frowned. "As is your judgment of me. The Minotaur is ungodly. My aim is pure." He pushed at a door, which opened up to a large room lit with several torches. Xenotareus hunched in, and the rest hesitantly followed.

Homer took in his surroundings. In the middle of the room was a table, littered with scrolls and pots; out from one of the jars crawled a huge glowing spider. To Homer's left, covering the entire wall, hung a giant cloth tapestry that looked like a map. Across the room, three stone steps climbed to a large wooden door. And filling the room was a low humming.

"What is that sound?" Calliope cringed. But their guide didn't answer, just slowly made his way across the room.

"Guys…check this out," said Homer, who had been studying the giant tapestry covered in dark swirling markings. "This must be the map of the labyrinth. I just can't figure out what anything is…" Theo and Calliope watched Homer's finger as it traced a black mark in the shape of a bull's head.

"Hey, Xenotareus," Homer called out. "Is this supposed to represent the Minotaur?" When he didn't get a response, he asked again, "Xenotareus, is this marking here —?"

"I'm sorry," they heard Xenotareus say. They turned to see him across the room, standing on the top step of the small staircase. He stood beside the wooden door, his bony hand on a lever, his quivering eyes on the verge of tears. "You should have left when I asked."

He pushed down on the lever. The door flung open, releasing into the room a blinding flash of light. When he could finally focus, Homer realized what was happening: Xenotareus had unleashed an army of glowing spiders—thousands upon thousands of them—into the room.

"Everyone!" Theo shouted. "On the table!" Still gripping onto Typhon's leash, he tore the giant map off the wall with both hands. As the spiders started coating the floor, Calliope jumped on to the table and helped pull up Homer. Then Theo, with Typhon in one hand and the tapestry in the other, joined them.

With the mass of fire-spiders illuminating the entire space as they blanketed the floor and walls, Theo could clearly see Xenotareus, looking confused as he teetered on the top step across the room. Then Theo flung the giant map over their heads, covering the table and everyone on it.

The map didn't protect the teenagers completely; quite a few spiders scurried up from the floor, onto the table, into their hair and across their backs. But ultimately, the covering proved to be an effective shield; as Homer, Theo, and Calliope crouched under the tapestry, they could feel thousands of spider-legs crawling on the other side. They covered their ears, to block out the near-deafening humming. But another sound rose even higher: screaming.

They never saw for themselves exactly what happened to Xenotareus, never saw how the fire-spiders had crawled up his skeletal legs, causing him to lose his balance and topple to the floor. They could only hear his screams, as thousands of glowing spiders immediately swarmed over their master. They didn't witness the two or three times his face emerged from the swarm, gasping for air, as if he were drowning in pool of light, before he finally sunk underneath.

While under the map, Homer, Theo, and Calliope didn't see the thousands of fire-spiders move as if one, out the door. But when the humming subsided, Theo guessed the worst was over and peeked his head out. A few straggling spiders remained, but the majority of them were gone.

As was Xenotareus. He had been swept away.

Theo breathed a sigh of relief. But then a horrific thought filled his mind: those spiders were now on the loose in the labyrinth.

"Mac," he whispered.

****

As Mac scanned the markings on the wall before him, images from another wall came flooding back into his mind: those from the mural he once saw, fleetingly but distinctly, in Andie's room. He had stopped by unexpectedly and caught her throwing a curtain over her wall, trying to cover something up; when he asked her about it, she evaded him, saying it was "personal." He'd let it go, never telling her what he'd seen: a quick but clear glimpse of a giant, bull-headed monster.

Thinking about her secret mural reminded Mac just how long Andie had been waiting for this moment. Still, something didn't add up. "Andie…" he hazarded. "If you knew…"

"Don't," Andie interrupted him, as she turned away from the hieroglyphics and started walking towards the door. "Just…don't."

"Don't what?" Mac asked, following her as she left the room.

"I know what you're gonna ask me," Andie said, storming down the dark corridor, not turning around. "If I knew this place existed, why didn't I do something about it before? Why did I take so long to come inside and see for myself?"

She was right; that was *exactly* what he was going to ask. "It doesn't make sense," Mac continued, doing his best to keep up with her, despite his limp. "If people think your dad is crazy, shouldn't the very *existence* of this place prove them wrong? Shouldn't this be enough to restore his reputation?"

"No!" she exclaimed, finally whipping around to face him. "It's not enough. Unless we find the Minotaur, all this will *never* be enough!" Then she stopped, leaned up against the dank, sweaty wall, and tried to collect herself. Mac stared at her, not saying a word, just listening to the sound of the dripping water that filled the corridor, until she spoke again, with a quiet, trembling voice. "Do you know how often I've thought about this? About busting down that wall, walking around down here? Not even to kill it. Just to *see* it, just to see if it were *real*—this horrible, *horrible* creature that destroyed my father's life. Do you know how many times I walked up to that wall, pickaxe in my hand? But I could never do it. I'd *want* to do it. I'd have that stupid pickaxe over my head, and I'd start to swing it. And then...I'd just stop. And I'd cry my eyes out, just asking myself, 'Why? Why can't I just do it?'"

Mac had never seen this Andie before—wrecked, and defenseless. She was always a labyrinth herself—a beautiful, impossible puzzle. But somehow, seeing this pillar of a girl break down in front of him made him want to reach her all the more. "Because you were scared," he said, taking her hand in his.

"Scared? No..." she sniffed. "I was terrified. Even now, I'm not sure what frightens me more: finding the Minotaur and maybe even my dad's *corpse* down here...or finding nothing at all. Because if there's nothing in here, that just means everyone was right: that my father was crazy. That his life was a joke. That he abandoned me...for nothing."

Mac moved in to face her. Taking both her hands in his, he looked right into her eyes. "Maybe your dad *was* crazy. Maybe he wasn't. That doesn't change how he felt about you. It doesn't mean he—"

Then he stopped, in response to a startled look that flared up in her eyes, as if all her senses became heightened in an instant. "What?" Mac asked her.

"Do you hear something?" she whispered, leaning forward and narrowing her eyes.

It happened in the span of a few seconds. First, he heard it: the sound of skittering coming from behind, getting louder. Then he saw it: a huge mass of blinking lights, coating the floor and walls of the corridor, racing towards them. Finally, as Andie's shouts of "Run!" reached his ears, he identified it: an army of those glowing, walnut-sized spiders.

Mac started running, as fast as he could on his hurt ankle, right behind Andie, through the dark, twisting corridors. As the sound of thousands of clicking legs filled the hall, Mac glanced back; the skittering spider army was practically right underneath his feet. The next thing he knew, he felt himself tripping, into a shallow pool of water; he bolted back up immediately, but the fall had extinguished his torch.

"Mac!" He heard Andie yell, but he couldn't see her; the glittering from the spiders lit up the area right behind him, but anything else in the distance was still enveloped in darkness. So, when he looked forward, he could only make out the orange blur of Andie's torch. He tried to keep up with her, but the constant turns, coupled with his injured ankle, made that almost impossible.

As the walls, now covered with spider-light, seemed to press down on him, Mac flew around another corner and suddenly he found himself on the ground again—this time, on his back. Plunged into a complete and immediate darkness, he felt himself careening down a steep, watery slope. He tried to grab onto something—anything—to stop himself, but the rocks beneath him were too slick. He kept sliding, sliding into a black void.

Seconds later, he plunged into a deep pool of warm, murky water. Fully submerged, he opened his eyes, but it didn't make any difference. All around him: dark as the grave. He started to swim, toward what he thought was the surface, but was it? How could he tell? Disorientation led to panic. Then he felt something slippery move past his leg…

He flailed around and finally saw what seemed to be a light over his head. Having no other option, he swam frantically in that direction. Kicking wildly. Lungs burning. Just when he thought he would burst, he broke through to open air.

"Mac!" screamed Andie, torch in hand, standing on a stone ledge. As soon as she saw Mac's head blast out of the dark pool, she dropped her torch on the ground, shot out her arm, and grabbed Mac by his tunic. "Hold on!" she yelled, as she tried to drag him to safety. Still taking deep, desperate breaths, Mac clutched her arm with both hands. With Andie's help, he pulled himself halfway onto the ledge.

Then he felt something coil around his calf, yanking him back into the water. He tried to grip one of the rocks that jutted out from the floor of the ledge, but whatever was pulling on him—something snake-like—was too strong. As he struggled desperately to keep his grip, he heard a splash: Andie had jumped into the water, wielding an arrow, which she jammed into the snake-creature's side. Immediately, whatever it was released Mac's leg.

Andie and Mac quickly made it to the ledge and pulled themselves up. Mac lay on his side, taking jagged breaths as he gazed into the pool. "What was that thing?"

"I don't know," Andie said, waving her torch into the pool. Kneeling down to get a closer look, she saw several scaly, serpentine forms skim across the surface of the dark water. "They look like...like deformed serphints or something..."

Mac crawled backwards and sat with his back against the wall, sinking his head into his hands. "Are you all right?" Andie asked.

"I—I fell..." Mac panted. "I slipped, and I couldn't stop, and then I landed in the water, and I couldn't find my way out..."

Andie crouched down next to him, putting her free arm on his shoulder. "It's OK," she consoled him. "But next time...take the stairs." With a weak smile, she pointed her torch in the direction of the stairs behind her.

He huffed out a chuckle as he tried to calm down. "What happened to those crazy spiders?" he asked.

"I don't know," Andie said. "I just turned one way. They went another." She stopped and looked over his shoulder. "Do you still have your bow?" she asked. Mac reached around his back and felt for the bow with his fingers. He pulled it out, but either the clumsy ride down the slide or the fall into the water cracked it, rendering it unusable.

"Well, I have mine," she tried to reassure him. "What about the arrows?"

Mac whipped his quiver from around his neck and peered inside. He knew it would be empty. It was.

Mac fell to his knees and started peering into the water. He knew he wouldn't find anything; even if any of those three arrows were in the water, they'd probably be at the bottom of the pool by now.

"Let it go," Andie insisted. "I have my own arrows."

"No!" Mac yelled. "Homer said we needed *those* arrows!"

Andie shook her head, not sure she understood, as she waved her torch across the rocky ledge, trying to locate any of the arrows. Amazingly, some good luck came their way. "I got one!" Andie yelled, picking up a tooth-capped arrow, teetering on the edge of the hole in the wall, the one which had spit out Mac after his ride down the slope. They kept searching for the other two arrows, but this was the only one they could find.

One arrow. Against the Minotaur.

"We're not going to get out of here," Mac said, "are we?" Andie didn't respond. She just stood there, silent, motionless, clutching the one arrow, their one shot, in her fist.

Mac looked into Andie's eyes and his heart filled. He realized, in that moment, he needed to tell her how he felt. This might be his last chance. "Andie," he started to say, but then her eyes lit up again, with that same distracted, hyper-alert look he saw on her face just before the fire-spiders pounced on them.

"Do you hear that?" she asked. He listened closely; over the sound of sloshing water, he could hear something off in the distance. Heavy breathing. Moaning. Snorting.

"Maybe it's the others?" he offered.

"It's not the others," Andie said, stone-faced.

They walked along the ledge to a doorway on the other side. Following the howls, they negotiated their way through another blackened passageway, turning down one corridor, then another. With each turn, the wailing increased in volume and intensity. They took one more turn. And then, in the middle of a barely lit cave, they saw it.

CHAPTER TWENTY-THREE
Facing the Beast

Two cloven feet, large enough to support its twelve-foot frame. Two powerful, sculpted legs, as thick as its two massive arms. Ten sharp, bloodied claws, capping ten long fingers. The chest of a Colossus. An enormous, hideous head, with two horns, two glowing eyes, and a long snout that ended in flaring nostrils and a slavering mouth, crammed with jagged fangs.

The Minotaur from legend. The Minotaur Homer was so desperate to find. The Minotaur on Andie's wall. And there it was, seven feet in front of them.

All this time, Mac had never truly believed they'd find it, never was deep down convinced it actually existed outside of legends and stories. Homer, after all, was the believer, Mac the cynic. But here it was before them, in all its heaving, snorting hideousness, looking much like the way Mac had envisioned it: with a bull's head and hooves, a man's arms and chest. At first, the creature was hunched over, so Mac couldn't get a clear sense of its size. But when it threw its arms up and let out an anguished roar, Mac could tell it was *big* — maybe not the Titan-sized monster depicted in legend, but at least three heads taller than Mac, and twice as broad.

This Minotaur, however, differed from every other version in one significant way: this Minotaur *glowed*. Its entire body from its heavy head to its frayed tail — was dotted with specks of light.

Spiders. Hundreds of those big, mutant spiders, glittering in the dark lair. Darting across its body. Attaching themselves to the monster's thick, sinuous muscles. Sucking blood, the smell and taste of which would attract even more insects. In fact, so covered with these spiders was this Minotaur, it virtually shimmered — as if it were wearing some kind of glowing cloak.

Looking at the bloodied, glittering creature, Mac began to understand the meaning behind the etchings on the chamber wall — the bull's head, flanked by the diamonds. "Are they...are those things sucking out its blood?" he asked. Andie didn't answer, but she didn't need to: they both could tell that was precisely what was happening. What's more: the tormenting of these spiders — combined with the years and years of solitary confinement — seemed to have driven the man-beast crazy. As Mac and Andie watched unnoticed, the Minotaur conducted itself like an insane, diseased animal: alternately pacing, shaking, slamming its horned head against the stone wall, all the while roaring and wailing at the top of its lungs. As he listened to the howls, Mac was reminded of the anguished echoes of the dying ram on the *Æton*.

Mac took out his aulos and started blowing — vigorously at first, and then weakly, before stopping altogether. Obviously the aulos wasn't going to work, and blowing on it would only alert this manic, crazed beast to their presence. As he let the aulos fall to the ground, Andie handed him her bow, already loaded with the lone arrow she had saved in the other room.

Mac hesitated. "We said we'd wait for the others..."

"We're not waiting!" she snapped through clenched teeth, her words echoing off the damp stone walls. "Just do it!"

Mac clenched his swollen shoulder, trying to bring back some feeling into his arm. On his injured foot, he limped forward a few steps, so the beast was not even five feet in front of him. He had shattered melons farther away than this.

Still, the Minotaur did not notice him.

Mac took a deep breath and surveyed his surroundings. Thanks to the spiders, which covered the Minotaur like barnacles on a ship's hull, Mac could see blood splattered on the walls, probably from the times the crazed beast had thrown itself against them. Drilled into the bloodied wall were several iron circles, from which hung broken chains.

Suddenly, the Minotaur stopped pacing, stopped moving all together. It buried its pained head in its clawed hands and started moaning. Mac knew he had to strike. He pulled the bow back and, without even consciously willing it, a prayer swelled up within him. To Athena. *Please, help me not die.* Then he took aim, right in the center of the Minotaur's skull.

And in that instant, the beast sprang to life.

Before Mac could react, the monster lurched forward, slamming Mac to the ground, knocking the bow and unreleased arrow out of his hands. Roaring horrifically, it pinned Mac to the ground with its massive hands. With wide eyes, Mac looked up to see giant, broken fangs mere inches from his face.

Just then, Andie jumped on the Minotaur's back and attempted to choke the beast with a length of twine, the very twine she was going to use to navigate through the labyrinth. With a wheezing roar, the beast reared its head violently, shaking off dozens of spiders and then Andie herself in the process. Seizing the opportunity, Mac kicked both of his feet into the creature's broad chest, sending it flying backward; when it slammed into the rocky ground, hundreds of specks of light skittered off in all directions.

Mac scrambled to grab his bow, only to find the lone arrow gone. "Where's the arrow?" he cried out to a disoriented Andie, who had hit her head during the fall. "Get the arrow!" Trying desperately to sidestep the fleeing spiders that darted across the floor, he turned back toward his frenzied foe, just in time to see it lunging at him once again.

With many, but not all, of the glittering bugs gone, the cave had darkened considerably. So when the Minotaur swung its spider-encrusted arm, Mac could barely make out anything but a blur of light streaking through the air. Mac managed to dodge the attack and instead, the beast's fist hit the rock wall with such force that Mac could have sworn he heard the sound of shattering bones. While the creature wailed, Mac tried to reach for the dagger strapped to his calf, but that left him open to an attack from the Minotaur's good hand; as claws slashed through the back of his tunic and into his left shoulder, Mac fell to the ground, grunting in pain. Once again, his bow flew from his hand before he hit the floor.

"Mac!" Andie yelled from across the lair. Mac whirled around to see the partially illuminated Minotaur, on all fours, bearing down on him. Unable to stand, pain radiating through his body from his wounds, Mac started inching backwards, until he felt his shoulders hit the wall; he could go no further.

"Mac!" Andie yelled again as she charged toward him. Only this time, the beast was ready: it shot out its left hind leg, slamming its hoof into her stomach and sending her backwards. She started to get up, but then fell back in a heap. Screaming out her name, Mac tried to go to her, but the Minotaur blocked his way. Anticipating triumph, the monster stood up and let out a mighty roar.

Looking past the monster to the shadowed body of Andie, still knocked out on the floor, Mac reached down to his calf and whipped out his dagger. Then he leaped forward, driving his shoulder into the mutant's midsection, and sunk the blade into its side.

Had time, fate, and millions of relentless spider bites make the Minotaur weaker? Or did Mac call upon reserves of strength he didn't know he had? No matter: Mac was able to go toe-to-hoof with the monster, meeting his mad attacker blow for blow. Locked in endless combat, aware of only each other, boy battled beast. Again and again, they exchanged brutal attacks, wrestling, warring, struggling for the upper hand. Finally, after breaking away from one particularly bone-crunching grip, Mac rolled away from the Minotaur, got to his feet, and stomped on the beast's broken hand. Listening to its roars of pain, Mac turned and bolted toward Andie, still on the ground, clutching her stomach.

"Andie!" he yelled out, when suddenly he felt his right leg yanked out from under him. The Minotaur, with its one good hand, had grabbed Mac's damaged ankle. Howling in pain, Mac tried to pull away, but the Minotaur leaped on his back, flattening Mac facedown on the floor of the cave.

Mac tried to reach out toward his bow, on the ground just beyond his fingertips. But he couldn't move; the Minotaur had him pinned to the ground. Letting out a wild roar, the beast prepared to sink its giant fangs into the back of Mac's skull.

The roar changed to a horrifying, pained cry; a recovered Andie had shoved her lit torch into the Minotaur's eye. As the creature reared back in pain, Mac retrieved his dagger, embedded in the Minotaur's side. Desperately, he thrust his weapon deep into the beast's heart. The double blow of fire and steel sent the Minotaur reeling back even further. Scrambling free, Mac quickly picked up his bow.

"Behind you!" Mac heard Andie yell. He turned only slightly while Andie tossed the arrow, the one Homer had dipped in the Narcissus water, through the air.

Meanwhile, the Minotaur—wounded and weakened, but not defeated—readied to strike again. It pulled itself up from the floor, stumbled toward its enemy, and slowly raised its arm.

The young warrior was standing there, bow in hand, string pulled all the way back. With cold, confident eyes, he stared down the shaft of the arrow, right into his prey, into its scarred, cloudy eyes, into its tortured soul.

Believe that you can beat him, his teacher Rhixion had told him. *Then make* him *believe it.* And in that moment, Mac believed.

Unable to tear itself away from Mac's stare, the creature seemed to wage an internal battle with itself, struggling to move toward Mac but weakened and weighed down by the extent of its injuries. Mac maintained his position—focused and unmoving.

He had it. All Mac had to do was release that arrow, and the Minotaur—the vicious, legendary, immortal Minotaur—would be dead. By Mac's hand. He would be the hero. All it would take was this one arrow. Just like Homer had said.

But Mac didn't release it.

Something stayed his hand, as he recognized this as a turning point. Something that would change him forever.

Was he ready?

"You need to do this, Mac," Andie said, reading the exact thoughts in his head. "You *need* this."

He knew what she meant: if he wanted to stay in school, he needed to kill the Minotaur. He *needed* to do this. For his mom. For his dad. Even for Homer, who had poured everything into these missions. How could Mac let him down? How could he let them *all* down?

But most of all, he needed to do this for Andie. If he got kicked out of school, what would happen between them? He would move back to Ithaca, she would stay at Pieridian. She'd keep on trying to find out what happened to her dad, but she'd do it on her own. Her life would move on, without him in it.

He made up his mind: he would slay the Minotaur.

To prove himself a hero. To rid the world of some evil. To show he was his father's son and to make things up to his mother. But mostly to stay in the life of this incredible girl.

Mac stepped forward, his arrow trained at the beast's head. But as he drew back the bowstring, he heard something, a barely stifled sob, behind him. He turned to see Andie, her hands in tight fists, shaking. Her eyes were welling up, and as he watched a single tear trace its way down her cheek, Mac recalled something she'd once said to him, months before, on their beach.

Always give it a name. The first time Andie took him out to shoot melons, she gave him two bits of advice: never second-guess yourself, and always give your target a name. Over the next few months, they shot more than a hundred melons together, and she named every single one of them the same exact thing: *Minotaur.* Every time she prepared to shoot, she would whisper that name, the name of her pain, the name of the atrocious phantom that had consumed — probably ended — her father's life. And every time her arrow exploded a melon to bits, she envisioned the Minotaur's skull doing the same.

For months, Andie had been practicing, preparing for this moment. Slaying the Minotaur — be it for revenge, for spite, for justice — was *her* mission. How could he take that away from her?

He needed this. But she needed it more.

Mac lowered his weapon and turned around. "This is your kill," he said, as he handed the bow and arrow to her, "not mine."

"Mac," Andie whispered, backing away from him. "No…"

Mac didn't say anything, just nodded. They looked into each other's eyes, and even though no more words passed between them, he knew she understood: surrendering the bow to her meant risking his future, *their* future; and yet, in his mind, if he denied her this moment, they would have no future.

She swallowed hard, took the bow from his hands, and stepped forward.

Mac expected it to be over in a split second. After all, he had watched her in action; she had perfected her craft to the point where she could aim and shoot almost simultaneously. In a split second, she could release the arrow and put this horror to rest.

Only this time, she did something he hadn't seen her do before: she broke one of her own rules. She hesitated.

"Get up!" she shouted at the weakened creature, whose immortal blood was slowly draining from its gruesome body. When it didn't respond, she said again, louder: "Get up!"

Mac saw the point of the arrow shake before she let her arms, holding both arrow and bow, fall to her sides. He met her eyes and could hardly stand to see the pain etched there.

"It needs to suffer," she whispered, defiantly.

"Andie..."

"No!" she screamed, refusing to pull her tear-filled eyes away from her enemy. "Killing it's too easy. It should *suffer*, the way it made everyone suffer!"

"It *has* suffered," Mac said simply, as he limped towards her. Realizing that Andie was too emotional at that moment to make this decision, Mac reached out for the bow, to finish the job. But just as his fingers touched her arm, Andie leaped forward. In one fluid motion, she loaded the arrow, raised the bow, and pulled back the string; the arrow went streaking through the air, finding its home in the exact center of the Minotaur's gray, fleshy forehead. The creature's head jerked back and then dropped unceremoniously to the floor.

For a long minute, they both just stared at the trail of black blood dripping down past the creature's open but lifeless eye. Neither one of them said a word. Finally, Homer's distant shouts broke the silence: "Mac! Andie! Where are you?"

"In here!" Andie called out, still staring at the carcass. Finally, she turned around, her face a blank mask, and closed the distance between her and Mac. She pulled his head down and pressed her face close to his. Mac could feel her push her bow into his chest.

"Congratulations," she whispered into his ear, taking his hand and placing it on the handle of the bow. "You just killed the Minotaur."

She stepped back, just as Homer, Calliope, and Theo, closely followed by Typhon, stormed in. "He did it!" she announced breathlessly, pointing to the beast. "He killed it!"

Mac looked over at Andie and then down at the bow, which he was still clutching in front of him. "Wait..." he started to say, quietly, but a fierce look from Andie silenced him.

The three newcomers, meanwhile, didn't even seem to notice this mini-drama; instead, they focused all their attention on the dead Minotaur before them. Theo let out an amazed "Whoa!" as he crouched down for a closer look. Calliope, horrified and fascinated at the same time, held back and stared at the monster from a distance. Homer held back and stared too, only not at the beast. Instead, he was looking at Mac, with eyes that were positively glowing, brighter than an army of those spiders, with pride and admiration.

Demetrius...

WE DID IT!!!

After all these years of sitting on the sidelines, I was part of a real hero's labor.

Mac killed the Minotaur! He shot it with his arrow. Andie told us all about it on the way out of the labyrinth—how he fought with the Minotaur, stared it down, how he shot it with his bow. I saw the beast with my own eyes! (Granted it was dead by the time I got there, but still!) Now Mac joins the league of beast-slaying heroes—Bellorophon, Perseus, even Heracles.

It was quite an adventure and I can't wait to tell you all about it. The weird thing is, Mac is insisting we tell no one. (By the way, can you burn this scroll as soon as you read it? I promised Mac I would keep my mouth shut.) After the deed was done, we left in a hurry—mostly to escape these killer spiders, which I'll tell you all about later. When we got out, Mac made us cover up the opening to the labyrinth with stones, so no one could find it. I just don't get it...why wouldn't he want to shout this from Mt. Olympus? He's a hero!

Oh—and Demetrius, I was right! I saw Xenotareus down there—not a nice guy, it turns out. He was behind the spiders and probably other stuff I'm still trying to piece together. I know this all sounds confusing, but I'm too excited to write clearly. When I see you in person, I'll tell you all about it.

Speaking of which, I wrote to my parents about coming to see you over the break. They said yes!

-Homer

CHAPTER TWENTY-FOUR
His Mother's Son

Mac sat on a bench next to a door, in a long hallway filled with benches and doors.

He didn't anticipate sitting there alone for long. Any time now, he figured, Asirites would tap his way down the hall. He'd sit next to Mac, sigh some comment—"Well, here we are again"—and ask about his game plan for the Disciplinary Committee. And Mac would have nothing to say.

Mac knew all he needed to save himself was that horn, the one Theo had indelicately pried off the Minotaur's head five days before. That simple token was all the proof the committee would require, the material confirmation of his heroism. But Mac didn't bring it. He didn't bring Theo either, or anyone else who could attest to what he had done or at least tried to do over the past three months. In fact, he told all his friends to stay away. He couldn't bear for them to witness his humiliation.

And as a result, he planned on walking into that cavernous room behind the door with nothing—no witnesses, no physical evidence, no tales of heroic deeds. And the committee would have no choice but to kick him out.

He would disappoint Asirites. But then, he had disappointed everybody.

Mac wished there could have been another way. After all, just five days before, he was everybody's hero. Theo, Calliope, Homer—Mac was their man. For the entire trek back to Pieridian, they couldn't stop gushing about how he had defeated the Minotaur. They wanted to hear the story, again and again. Finally, when they got to Pieridian's main gate, Mac made them swear they wouldn't utter a word of it to anyone—at least, until after the disciplinary hearing.

"Are you crazy?" Theo bellowed. "This is *so* epic! I'm telling *everyone*—after, of course, I tell my bit of heroism, saving us from those crazy spiders. But then I'll get right back to talking about *you*. You'll be, like, the most popular guy in school when I'm done!"

"Did you hear what I said?" Mac insisted, more forcefully than he intended. "Don't tell anyone!"

"But why?" Theo pressed. "Give us a reason." Mac glanced over at Andie and then walked off, without answering Theo's question.

Nevertheless, Theo, Homer, and Calliope did as ordered; they didn't say a word to anyone. Still, keeping his mouth shut just about killed Homer, so Mac gave him the Minotaur's horn as a consolation prize—one that Homer hungrily accepted.

The five days leading up to the hearing left Mac anxious and exhausted as he slowly recovered from his injuries. He could barely focus on his mid-year exams. And on top of that, he had to listen to Homer drill him over and over again about what to say and not say at the hearing. Homer left nothing to chance; he even got Calliope to trim Mac's hair, believing a neater look would score points with the committee. Mac could handle studying; he could even handle Homer. But the constant pressure to be "on," to muster up fabricated cheer whenever he was around Theo or Calliope or Homer—*that* wore him out more than anything. Several times, he tried reaching out to Andie, the only other person who knew the truth, who could understand, but she seemed weird, too. Distant.

And so, for five days, Mac treated the campus as his own private labyrinth, through which he wandered aimlessly, on edge, biting back his rising feelings of guilt—for lying to his friends—and paranoia—that someone would blow the lie wide open. He couldn't sleep; towards the end, he could barely even stand to talk to anyone. And that was after *five days*. How, he kept asking himself, could he possibly keep this up for the rest of his life?

This was Mac's emotional state as he trudged through the rain over to the Grape Vine on the eve of the big showdown with the Disciplinary Committee. Theo had suggested a dinner for the five of them, to celebrate Mac's imminent victory. Mac reluctantly agreed to go—what else could he do?—but mentally, he just wasn't there. In fact, when Theo stood up to offer a toast, Mac only vaguely noticed.

"To my roommate," Theo began, raising his wooden mug filled with watered-down mead, "for his successful completion of his final labor, thus securing his spot at the school—good news for him, not so good for the rest of us, who now have to put up with him for a while longer. But hey—congrats!" As they laughed at Theo's teasing remarks, everyone clinked mugs—everyone, that is, but Mac.

"You don't know that," he said, gripping his mug with two hands.

"I don't know what?" Theo said, after taking a big swallow.

"You don't know they're gonna let me stay," Mac said. "Why would they? What have I really done that's so great?"

"What have you *done*?" Homer echoed, incredulously.

"Are you kidding me?" Theo asked. "When you walk into that room tomorrow, with that story and that horn…The look on Gurgus's face alone will be worth the price of admission."

"You still don't seem to appreciate the magnitude of this," Homer said. "Killing the—"

"Hey! Hey!" Mac shushed him, looking around nervously. "What did I tell you?"

Homer rolled his eyes. "OK. That *thing that you did*…it's huge! As far as heroism goes, nothing can top that. You proved that you're your father's son…and then some. You more than lived up to your end of the deal. They *have* to let you stay. They have no choice."

"Unless," Mac said slowly, gazing vacantly into his mug, "they have a problem with that *'thing I did'*…"

"Problem?" Homer said. "What kind of problem could they possibly have?"

Mac looked across the table at Andie. She'd been avoiding eye contact with him the entire evening, but now she was staring right at him, her expression a mixture of warning and desperation. But he couldn't stop now.

"That I didn't actually do it?" he said quietly.

"What does that mean?" Homer pressed.

"I didn't do it," Mac said again, lowering his head. "I didn't kill it."

"But it was *dead*," Theo reminded him. "I saw it. The arrow right in the middle—"

"I didn't shoot it," Mac interrupted. "Andie did."

Homer whipped around to Andie. "Is this true?" At first, she didn't respond, just sat there, as if turned to stone. When she finally nodded, Homer whipped back to Mac, his face flush with terrible disappointment. "You…you didn't kill it?" he asked.

"What difference does it make?" Andie asserted. "He could've shot it. He was going to. But he didn't. He backed off. He let me do it. Who cares?"

"'Backed off'? *Backed off?*" Homer repeated, disgust boiling over. "You needed to do *one* thing. The one thing we've been talking about for months. And at the last second, you 'back off'? This is your *future* we're talking about here. How can you 'back off'?"

Mac didn't respond. Didn't yell, didn't fire back some retort. Instead, he just kept staring into his drink, as a brainstorming Calliope tried to make the best of the things. "OK. Let's think. What else can you tell the committee? What other things have you done?"

"Oh, gee, let's see here," Mac offered. "I went to a dance. I bought a cheap flute from a fat guy in a cave. Oh, and I kissed an old lady. Wonder how many hero points I'll score for that?" He paused and looked around the table at all of them before continuing. "Let's face it: I *lost*. At everything. War Games, Oracle, Minotaur— all *failures*. Colossal flops!"

"Hey, I worked hard on those flops!" Theo said. "We all did. We killed ourselves for you, dude. Almost literally. And if you go in there tomorrow, all 'it's a flop, it's a flop,' and don't even try to defend yourself…I don't know, dude, it's kind of insulting."

"Well, I don't know what you want me to say."

"I want you to say that you killed the Minotaur," Theo said, with a chilling, uncharacteristic seriousness. "I want you to go into that hearing tomorrow and say exactly that. That you played their game, you killed the Minotaur, and that you're sticking around."

"So, just say I did it? That simple?" Mac said, lazily tossing up his hands. "Does everyone else feel that way?" He scanned the table again, stopping on Andie. He needed to find something in her, some reassurance in her eyes. But she looked down at the table, denying him.

"I don't know if lying is ever the answer," he heard Calliope say, "but like Homer said, this is your future we're talking about."

"Yeah, I know," Mac muttered, pushing back his chair. "Which is why I can't do it."

"Mac…" Homer started.

"Look, just let me go, OK?" he said, not just to Homer but to the whole table. "I know what you've done, what you're still doing, and I appreciate it, all of it…but it's over." He stood up and then added, "Do me a favor, will ya? If you were thinking about showing up at the hearing tomorrow…don't. Students aren't allowed. There'll be nothing to see, anyway."

With that, he turned and walked out, into the stormy night. The rain had really picked up, and he got drenched almost immediately, but he didn't run; he just didn't have any energy left. Andie caught up to him in no time.

"I thought we had a deal!" he heard her yell out to him.

"I don't remember agreeing to any 'deal'," Mac said, not turning around. "I remember you shoving a bow in my hands so I could take credit for something I didn't actually do."

"Credit? Who cares about credit?" Andie said, now right behind him. "Don't be a martyr, Mac. Just lie to them. For crying out loud, you trained a flock of birds to take a crap on them. Now you can't tell them this one simple lie?"

"'Simple lie'?" he scoffed. "OK…"

"Mac, think about what you're doing here…"

"I have," he said as he stopped and turned around. "For five days, I've thought and thought and thought about it, all the way to the end, and here's what I came up with: I walk into that room tomorrow and say I killed the Minotaur. You think a story like that is going to stay quiet? You think news isn't going to get out? And I'm not just talking about school. I mean everywhere. 'Telemachus, the Slayer of the Minotaur'—that's what people will call me. That's who I'm going to be, for the rest of my life. And I'm not. I'm not that guy, Andie."

He started to walk away, but Andie grabbed his hand. "Mac, don't do this," she pleaded, finally looking right into his eyes.

For an impossibly long moment, they stood there, holding hands in silence, getting soaked by the rain but not caring. Mac knew this moment was his to forfeit but he also knew, if he told this lie, she would never look at him the same way again. She could try, but deep down, she would always know him for what he was: a fraud. She would know that better than anyone. Try as she might, she could never again see him as a hero.

"You know," Mac finally said, "when Asirites first said that thing about 'being my father's son,' I had no idea what he meant. I still don't, really. I've never known my father. He's just a name to me. A legend. I know as much about Odysseus as you do. But let me ask you this: do you think he would live his whole life letting people believe he did something great, something heroic, that he didn't actually do?"

Andie didn't say anything, just stood there. But Mac could see the answer on her face.

"Me neither," Mac said, then let go of her hand and walked off, leaving her standing there. This time, she didn't follow him.

****

He knew then—just as he knew now, sitting on that bench, reliving the events from the night before in his mind—that walking away from her meant that he was saying goodbye. Forever. Oh, they'd see each other once in a while; maybe he could come to visit, if the administrators let him. But how long could that last? How could they keep up a long-distance relationship from Ithaca? But then again, even if he stayed, even if he went along with the ruse, they were doomed; deep down, she could never respect him for the lie.

No, Mac tried to reassure himself while slumped over on the bench waiting to be summoned by the Disciplinary Committee, he had done the right thing. This thing between he and Andie, whatever it was—they needed to end it. Clean break, before he got in too deep. Then he realized he was kidding himself. *Before* he got in too deep? How could his feelings for her get any *deeper*?

"You cut your hair."

Lost in his maze of thought, he didn't even hear her coming down the hall. But when he looked up and saw his mom standing in front of him, he was immediately filled with relief. He didn't know for sure if she was coming, and just seeing her put him at ease, if only for a moment.

Mac smiled, tiredly. "Yeah. A friend suggested the clean-cut look might help influence the Disciplinary Committee."

"Think it'll work?" she asked.

"Probably not," he sighed, his initial sense of relief draining away, replaced with the guilt and shame he always carried whenever his mother was around. "I think this is it for me, Mom. They're going to kick me out. They're going to ask me for some proof, some reason they should let me stay…and I don't have anything for them."

Penelope sat down next to her son on the bench, so close that their shoulders were just about touching. The nearness surprised Mac—unnerved him a little. He didn't look over at her, just stared straight ahead at the tapestries adorning the wall across from him. "I tried, Mom," he said weakly. "I really did. But…it just never came together. I'm sorry."

"No, *I'm* sorry," Penelope insisted, shaking her head slowly. "I did this. I didn't do what I was supposed to do as your mother. When your dad left, you needed someone strong, a role model. Instead, you got a bunch of thugs, who came into your home and took over…and me, who just sat back and let them do it. And I know I could have done something about it. You have no idea how many times over the years I said to myself, 'Just *marry* one of them! Just pick one, and the rest of them will leave.' Why didn't I just do it?"

"Why?" Mac repeated disbelievingly, finally looking over at her. "Because they're horrible!"

"Yeah, but at least there'd just be *one* horrible man in the castle. We could probably take *one* of them down, right?"

Penelope offered a soft smile, which Mac returned. He liked the idea of teaming up with his mom. But then the reality of the situation flooded back to him: whether there were a hundred or one, Mac knew he could never protect his mom from the suitors. He couldn't stand up to them; he'd proven that to himself. He had failed her, even though she didn't know it, and never would. A long time ago, he'd sworn to himself he would never tell her his secret.

So when the words started spilling out of his mouth, he couldn't really say why he was letting them. Maybe he remembered the support he got from Andie that day under the tree, when he told her the truth about what he saw that night. Maybe he felt bolstered by his mother's slim yet strong shoulder pressing up against his own. Maybe he was just tired of feeling so damn guilty all the time.

"Mom...I know what happened that night..."

"What night?"

"I know what Antinoös did to you..." he began. And then the confession poured out. He told her everything: how he watched from the balustrade, how he saw Antinoös grab her, how he ran away. All of it. He couldn't bring himself to look at her as he spoke to her, but he owned up to it all. He finally wanted to take responsibility for everything he had...or hadn't...done.

Penelope took it all in, staring at her son as he stared at the wall, until she finally whispered, "You were there that night?"

Mac closed his eyes and sighed, "Yeah."

"And you never said...All these years, you never said anything to me?"

"I'm sorry, Mom," he whispered, lowering his head and staring at his hands. "I'm...just really sorry."

He kept looking down, readying himself for the disappointment, the *disgust* she'd feel. He felt her shift on the bench, so that her shoulder was no longer pressed up against his own. Then he felt her arms wrap around him.

"Oh, Mac, why didn't you say something?" she asked him, tiny tears trickling down her face. "Why didn't you ask me about this, years ago? I could have told you."

Mac leaned back, trying hard to choke back tears, though a few disobedient ones squeezed out. "Told me what?"

"That I'm not as helpless as you think. Apparently, you didn't see everything that happened that night between me and Antinoös. Yes, he was rough and I had some bruises the next day. But I got away before he could really hurt me."

"But...how?"

"My knee, slamming into the place where men are...most vulnerable," she said delicately, with a slight smile. "It sent him right to the ground. He was so drunk, he couldn't even get up. Just wallowed on the floor. Before the other suitors could get any ideas, I ran to my room."

"But you didn't come out for two days," Mac stammered. "I thought it was because—"

"I was hiding, yes, but I wasn't hurt," she assured him, brushing away the stray tears on her son's cheek, just like she used to do when he was little. "I felt it was best to give Antinoös some time to cool off. But nothing else happened that night. OK? Nothing else happened."

Mac nodded, and the tears arrived in earnest. Not tears of grief or sadness, but of intense release, as the burden of this long-kept secret finally slipped away. He cried longer and harder than he had in years, his sobs muffled into his mom's shoulder, as she pulled him in close. For a long time, they just held each other in silence.

"I wish your dad could see you now," she finally said.

"Yeah, I'm sure he'd be really impressed," he sniffled, breaking away from her embrace and wiping his eyes in embarrassment. "Seeing me here, an emotional mess, on the verge of getting expelled from school..."

"No, I mean, I wish he could see you *now*, as a young man," she smiled. "He loved you so much. Did you know he tried to get out of going to war because of you?" Mac shook his head no; when he was growing up, his mother never shared much about his father. He used to begrudge her for it, but now he understood, perhaps for the first time, that Odysseus was her husband, as much as he was his father, and his absence hurt her as much as it did him.

Penelope sighed as she began her story. "When my cousin Helen married Menelaus, your father pledged to help them if they needed anything. Well, years later, when Helen ran off with Paris and Menelaus assembled an army to get her back, he called on his friend

Odysseus to make good on his promise. Your father was stuck. He had given Menelaus his word, but that was before he had a family. You were only three months old; he didn't want to leave you."

"So, what did he do?" asked Mac, swiping at some lingering tears with the back of his hand.

"He pretended he was crazy," she smiled, overtaken by the memory. "When they came to recruit him, he went outside and hooked up an ox and a donkey to his plough—you know, so the lines would be out of whack— and then started sowing the fields with salt, so nothing could grow there. It would have worked, too, but this guy Palamedes wanted to test just how crazy he was. He grabbed you out of my arms and stuck you in the dirt in front of the plough. Luckily, your father saw you and veered off at the last second. He saved your life but blew his cover; everyone saw he was absolutely sane."

"Dad pretended he was *crazy*? He wasn't worried this would make him look like a coward?"

"Oh, sure. But he didn't care. He's the strongest, bravest, greatest man I've ever known. And I'm not just saying that because I'm his wife. Everyone thinks that. Everyone. He has the respect of all. But none of that mattered if he couldn't be with his family."

Family—not a word Mac often associated with his father. To Mac, nothing about him said "family"; he was the consummate warrior, who ran off to the Trojan War without a thought for anyone he left behind. And all these years, Mac had resented him because of it—resented him so much he never even considered that his father may have gone to war under duress, that he may not have had a choice, that he may have wanted to *stay home*. Then he considered something else: if his father didn't want to leave in the first place, then maybe he wasn't staying away by choice. Maybe, this whole time, he's been trying to find his way home. Only now, after hearing his mom's story, could Mac open himself up to the possibility that his dad may have actually loved him—and might love him still.

When Mac looked over at his mom, he noticed *she* was now staring at the wall; the reminiscing, it seemed, weakened her, to the point that she appeared small and far away, even though she was sitting right next to him. "I'm coming home, Mom," he reassured her, resting his hand on hers. "Either today, if they kick me out, or after I finish school...but either way, I'm coming home."

They smiled at each other, until a familiar voice shattered the moment with a booming "Telemachus!" Mac looked past his mom to see Gurgus looming in the doorway.

"Let's go!" the headmaster said gruffly. But when he looked over and noticed Penelope sitting on the bench as well, his tone changed. "Oh, good morning, Your Highness" he said graciously, acting as if he didn't plan on kicking her son out of school. "I didn't know you were here." Then he turned to Mac and said, with phony civility, "Telemachus, we'd like to begin."

"Shouldn't we wait for Asirites?" Mac asked.

"We'd like to start now," Gurgus said emphatically as he shut the door.

Mac sighed as he stood up. "I guess you should wait out here," he said to Penelope.

"No, I'm coming with you," she told him, rising to face him.

"Thanks, but...I think I should do this on my own,"

"You will. I'll sit in the back, if you want. But I'm your mother and I'm going with you." She reached over and straightened out his tunic. "I'm done waiting outside."

Mac turned to the door. He took a deep breath, hoping to Zeus the committee wouldn't be able to tell he'd been crying. With his mother standing by his side, he pushed open the door and was immediately greeted by an eruption of yipping.

CHAPTER TWENTY-FIVE
A Hero Speaks

The last time Iota the dog had seen Mac, she was so traumatized, she'd urinated all over her owner's leg. But that was weeks ago: now, apparently, the creature had reverted to the same wretched, yipping mutt she had always been, only now with an appetite for vengeance. As soon as she spotted Mac at the top of the center aisle, the tiny hound flew into a frenzy, filling the cavernous chamber with a burst of yips and snarls and growls so deafening even Gurgus acknowledged the dog had to be removed if they had any hope of getting down to business.

From the back of the room, Mac did his best to appear unshaken, both by the barking and his mom's departure from his side. True to her word, Penelope quickly took a seat in the back. Then Mac began his long, solitary journey down the center aisle, his eyes darting around the chamber as he walked. Nothing much had changed since his last visit to this room, at the beginning of the school year. Same white marble columns, reaching up to the same ornately carved ceiling. Same ghastly statue of a blindfolded Themis, holding the scales of justice, in the back corner. Same nine administrators, in the same red robes, sitting in the same tiered thrones up front. The only thing different from last time: no Asirites to do the talking for him.

Mac sat in the first row on the right and glanced up at Gurgus, glaring at him from his throne at the center of the marble platform. On either side of Gurgus sat two more robed judges; behind them, on the second tier, sat the remaining four. Mac looked down, disgusted by the exaggerated pageantry of the whole thing. Then again, the committee was getting ready to expel the prince of Ithaca;

they couldn't appear as if they were taking it too lightly.

The man sitting to the left of Gurgus, a thin, bearded administrator named Krentor, formally began the hearing. "Good morning. We have gathered today, as you know, to discuss the expulsion of Telemachus from Pieridian Academy," he announced, in an absurdly thunderous voice, as if he were addressing an audience of thousands and not just Mac and Penelope. "Telemachus, you have been charged with destroying Garthymedes Field, making a mockery of the prestigious Opening Ceremonies, and destroying the school mascot." Gurgus then cleared his throat, prompting Krentor to add, almost reluctantly, "And causing psychological trauma to the headmaster's dog. Serious charges, all worthy of expulsion. However, out of deference to your father, the great Odysseus, this committee decided to give you one final chance, to prove to us, to your fellow classmates, to yourself, that you are truly your father's son, and not the lost, directionless child you have, time after time, appeared to be. And so, we ask you: What, if anything, has changed in these past three months? What have you done to prove to us that you deserve to be a Pieridian student?"

Mac paused, hoping if he stalled long enough Asirites would magically materialize in the seat next to him. When that didn't happen, he glanced at his mother, way in the back. She smiled gently at him, sending him her strength from across the chamber. Bolstered by this, Mac slowly stood and stepped up to the podium.

"You know, the last time I was in this room, all I wanted was to get out," he began. "Not just out of this room, but out of this *school*. I sat in that chair, right there, hoping you'd give me the boot. You didn't. You gave me an ultimatum instead: prove I'm my father's son. And after three months, I think I've finally figured out what you meant by that: you want *him*. My father. You said you wanted me to be my father's son, but I think what you really want is for me to be *him*."

He stopped, lowering his head. "And I can't do that. I can't be him. And that's not me being spiteful. I get what you want, and why you want it. After all, my dad is a great man. A war veteran. A hero. But he's also a *man*, and I'm not...not yet. I'm still figuring things out. I'm still making mistakes, just like my father probably did when he was my age. And that doesn't mean I'm lost, just still…" He smiled to himself, recalling something Homer had said to him in the woods, the very first day they met. "Still in the process of finding,"

"You ask me if I've changed," he continued. "I don't really know how to answer that. I think I have, but I can't prove it. There's no document, no artifact, no mark on my body I can point to and say, 'Here! Look at this! I've changed!' All I have is my word. I want to stay. I didn't before, but I do now. I want to stay here. That's all I've got."

He returned to his seat, head down. When he looked up, he saw something he didn't anticipate: Krentor actually seemed interested. "Now, when you say you want to stay here," the administrator began, "does that mean you now understand the code of behavior that we—?"

"Excuse me!" Gurgus blurted out. "I'm sorry, sir, but I have to cut you off. It's obvious to me the boy didn't take any of this seriously. If he had, he would have brought something substantial to show us, instead of this lame appeal to our sense of mercy. He has clearly learned nothing at all from this experience, and so I recommend we end this charade and move to an immediate vote on the boy's expulsion."

With that, Gurgus shot out of his seat; the other administrators dutifully followed. Mac watched helplessly as they all began to shuffle out of the chamber, until a voice from the back stopped them in their tracks.

"Oh, don't go just yet, gentlemen. You'll miss the best part."

Mac knew the voice, of course, so he wasn't completely surprised when he turned to see Asirites in the doorway. But the fact that he wasn't there alone—that came as a *huge* surprise.

"I see you've started without me," Asirites was saying. "An oversight, I'm sure. In any case, if it's all the same to you, we have a few statements we'd like to add to the record."

What were they doing here? Mac had no idea. But there they were, in the entranceway, all crowded around Asirites—Homer and Andie to his left, Theo and Calliope to his right—and all with serious, determined looks on their faces. Even Theo wasn't cracking a smile.

"This is a closed session, Asirites," a still-standing Gurgus said curtly from the platform. "Students are not allowed in here. You know that."

"My guests, sir," Asirites said confidently, as the group proceeded as one down the aisle: "Character witnesses, to speak on behalf of Telemachus—that is, if his fate has not already been predetermined."

Gurgus's eyes drifted to Penelope, still in the back of the chamber. "I'm not sure I like what you're implying, Asirites," he responded slowly, trying to sound diplomatic. "We gave Telemachus ample opportunity to plead his case."

"Oh, 'ample,'…of course," Asirites said, just as diplomatically, as the group reached the front of the room. Mac leaned forward, to see Andie, but she just kept on looking straight ahead. "And yet," Asirites continued, "I wonder if Mac had all the necessary information to mount an adequate defense."

"Asirites," Gurgus scowled, "what are you—?"

Asirites cut him off. "Which is why I'd like to submit for the record and for the benefit of everyone here—the committee, Mac, Queen Penelope—the transcript of a speech given by a distinguished graduate. It's a commencement speech, delivered on Garthymedes Field roughly sixteen years ago—before even *your* time, Headmaster Gurgus," he added, smiling slyly.

By this point, Mac's friends had taken their seats on the other side of the aisle. The nine administrators sat back down as well—an outward sign that indicated to Mac they had effectively surrendered control of the hearing to Asirites. "Now, over my thirty-one-year career at Pieridian," the blind counselor continued, "I've had the pleasure of hearing many excellent speeches, by many accomplished orators, but this one was particularly memorable. For this speaker, you see, was one of my former students—one of my favorites, in fact. Not because he was always the best student, or even the most mature. To be honest, sometimes he drove me absolutely crazy. But there was a magnificence in him, a greatness, that drew you in, made you want to follow him to the end of the world.

"When he graduated, I expected great things—we all did. And when he returned to campus, years later, I sat him down in my office and told him how proud I was of him—for becoming King of Ithaca, for being promoted to general for the upcoming war in Troy. But he waved it all off. Instead, he kept steering our conversation back to the only accomplishment that seemed to matter to him: becoming a father."

Asirites turned in Mac's direction and seemed to be looking right at him, right *into* him, in that unnerving, almost mystical way he had. "I'm speaking, of course, about the legendary Odysseus—whose words I would like to share with you today," Asirites informed the audience. "Now, since reading is not my strong suit, I asked one of my students, Calliope, to assist me. Calliope, if you please..."

With her typical grace, Calliope rose from her chair and stepped toward the podium. In her hand, she held a scroll, which she unrolled delicately and placed on the podium. She paused for a moment, keeping her eyes down at the words in front of her. Finally, with her steady, captivating voice, she started to read:

"This speech almost didn't happen. In fact, I almost didn't even make it here today, due to a pair of, shall we say, significant distractions. You see, three months ago, my wife and I had a son—our first. He fills me with unspeakable joy and, at the same time, near-unbearable sorrow—for I know I will have to leave him soon, due to my other distraction: my imminent deployment to join the conflict in Troy.

"And because I fear I will be gone for a long, long time, I had decided not to make the trip here today, so I could spend as much time with my family as possible. And yet, I had made a commitment to be here, and what example would I be setting for my son if I didn't honor that?

"So here I am, to talk to you about...well, about what, exactly? For some time, I didn't know. My muse, it seemed, had utterly departed—or perhaps I was too preoccupied with my other concerns to listen to her. Finally, upon the advice of your administration, I decided upon a somewhat trite though not completely uninspired speech about the pillars of leadership: ambition, perseverance, courage, and resourcefulness. That's the speech I had

composed four days ago when I left Ithaca.

"Before I continue, a confession: I am not particularly good with maps. Rather, I probably could be, if I ever bothered to read them, instead of insisting I can find the way on my own. Often I do, but occasionally, I get lost.

"Last week saw one of those occasions. I was traveling from Ithaca, and I navigated my crew squarely onto the shores of an island nobody recognized. As it turns out, I wasn't that far off – we were on Avalka, just off the coast from here; not realizing this, however, I sought the advice of a young fisherman who happened to be on the shore.

"This kind stranger, who introduced himself as Koutsainos, gave us proper directions and even helped replenish our supplies. I thanked him, and after I introduced myself, he asked if I were the same King Odysseus who would be leading a battalion in Troy. When I confirmed I was the very same, his eyes lit up like the sun. He had always dreamed of being a warrior, he said, but when he was a young boy, his leg had been crushed by an ox; the bones eventually healed, but not properly, and as a result, he walked with a limp for the rest of his days.

"As he finished his story, this hobbled fisherman looked at me and said despairingly, 'You have the opportunity to be a hero. That's something I can never do.'

"I assured him he was wrong, that heroism is not confined to those who can take up arms, that even small acts of kindness – the help he was providing at that moment, for example – were heroic. And as we spoke, I recognized something: our meeting was not, in fact, a chance encounter. Indeed, this young man and I were fated to meet, at this exact moment in time – if only to usher back my long-dormant muse.

"So if you don't mind, I will not be sharing with you my thoughts on ambition, perseverance, courage, and resourcefulness. Instead, I want to talk about four other qualities that, in my mind, comprise a true hero. The kind of hero found not just on a Trojan battlefield but anywhere – on a random shoreline, or a graduation field. Indeed, the kind of hero I would like my own son to be someday.

"And so, from this distracted king, four hastily-composed scraps of advice on the nature of true heroism. In no particular order:

"First: Be loyal. Our gods do not want us to be alone in this cold, complex world. Open yourselves to friendships, to people whom you can trust and upon whom you can depend. Don't stop searching until you find those friends, and then be that kind of friend in return.

"Second: Be a believer, not a doubter. Have faith in the goodness of the world and the worthiness of all who populate it. Believe that every single person you meet has something to teach if you just pay attention and let them in. So pay attention, and not just to what is, but what could be. Envision the potential in others; be their muse; help them do that which they could only dream of doing.

"Third: Decide who you want to be, and then be that person. Define yourself; don't let yourself be defined by what others might think. Life will throw enough problems at you without you surrendering to the opinions of others.

"Finally: carve out room for joy in your life. Negotiate the balance between work and play. Laugh. Dream. Scheme a little. At least once a day, do something completely irrational and impractical. And then laugh some more.

"I'd like to thank the administration for inviting me to speak here today; And I want to thank the graduates for listening. We actually have a great deal in common, all of us: just like me, you are on the brink – of a new journey, of a grand and glorious adventure. And so, I say to you now, one adventurer to another: Go. Push off, into the treacherous, unknown sounds. Stand at the edge, and with wide eyes and outstretched arms, take in the entire world rolling out before you. But even as you journey ever onward, please remember this last bit of advice: never travel so far that you can't find your way back home."

Mac had never heard his father speak before. True, the voice was Calliope's, but the words came from his father. In that moment, those words meant everything to him; if he could have, he would've plucked them out of the air and held them in his hands forever.

Mac watched Calliope sit back down next to her brother, who clapped loudly before wrapping her in a tight hug. Andie, sitting next to Theo, punched his forearm and shot him a stern, disapproving look. But then she glanced over at Mac and grinned. He returned her smile before looking to the back of the chamber, where his mother was sitting. Even though she was seated far away from him, the glistening on her cheeks revealed she had been crying.

A contemplative silence overtook the chamber. Finally, Mac heard a sound he had come to know so well: the *step-drag, step-drag* of a damaged gait. He watched as Homer awkwardly made his way to the front of the room, positioning himself not at the podium but squarely in front of the committee.

Homer looked back and caught the eye of Calliope, who offered a supportive smile. Then he addressed the panel, in that same affected, booming voice he'd used for his first Orations speech, the one that inspired Mac to seek him out in the first place:

"Gentlemen of the Disciplinary Committee, allow me to introduce myself. My name is Homer, and for the past three months, I have been serving as Telemachus's chief advisor for all things hero-related. While serving in this capacity, I sent Telemachus on a series of dangerous missions, in an attempt to prove to you, to me, to himself that he could be mentioned in the same breath as Perseus or Agamemnon or, yes, even Odysseus. And so, after working with him tirelessly for these past three months, I can report with confidence that I...am a complete idiot."

He paused, then continued in a quieter, humbler tone. "I didn't mean to be. I honestly thought I was giving Mac good advice. All my life, I equated heroism with fighting in battle or undertaking labors or defeating bad guys. But now I see it takes a lot more to be a great man." He paused, looking over at Calliope, then added. "Or a great woman."

Mac stole a glance back at his mother, who had raised him, all by herself. His gaze then fell upon Andie, who was willing to sacrifice her chance to avenge her father, all for him and his future. Both of them, in their own ways, had given up so much for Mac...and showed him a kind of strength and courage he could only hope to have.

"And so," Homer continued, pacing in front of the assembled judges, "speaking not as Mac's 'chief advisor' but as his friend, I can promise you this: the true hero Odysseus talks about in his speech...that's Mac. All the qualities his father describes, he has. He's funny. He's loyal. He knows who he wants to be: a man of principle and honor, who won't lie or cheat or take the easy way out to win, even when everyone around him is telling him to do just that. And he listened to me. Even though everything I told him was wrong, he still listened to me. Had *faith* in me, something no one had ever done before."

Homer stopped, as if unsure whether to continue. "You know," he finally said, with a shake in his voice. "I've been at this school for two and a half years. For most of that time, I've had zero friends. Mac was the first person here to notice me, to give me a chance. He's the first real friend I've ever had. I'd do anything for him, and I know he'd do the same for me."

Mac watched as Homer fidgeted, the face of showy confidence he had put on for his opening remarks having completely fallen off, to make way for something more vulnerable and genuine. "Maybe none of this matters," he said to the committee. "Maybe you've already made up your minds. But when you deliberate, remember this: Mac really did what you asked him to do. He is his father's son. But to me, he's…more."

With that, Homer began limping slowly back down the aisle. As Gurgus announced to the room that the committee would be taking a recess to discuss this matter, Homer paused for a moment next to Mac. They just locked eyes and smiled—a brief, slight smile, but one full of gratitude and mutual affection, the kind that only true friends can share.

CHAPTER TWENTY-SIX
Destinations and Artifacts

Packing took a while, longer than Mac anticipated. He hadn't accounted for nostalgia; he didn't realize he'd have to. He had never attached *significance* to anything before. But now, everything he picked up to put in one of his trunks—the second-place medal he won at War Games, the jug from Abibathia's shop, even the green chiton he wore at that disastrous dance—seemed encrusted in memory.

From his shelf, he took the map from Kalakloptas's cave and packed it away. Then he picked up another document from that same shelf: the scroll on which was written his father's speech. He carefully laid it in his chest, making sure it wouldn't get damaged on the trip home. He *definitely* couldn't let anything happen to that.

Asirites had given Mac the scroll the day after the hearing, when Mac dropped by his office, armed with two pomegranates. As soon as he walked in, Asirites handed him the scroll—a "welcome back" gift, he first called it, even though that didn't sound right, seeing as he didn't go anywhere. "Maybe more of a 'staying put' gift, right?" he suggested.

For a while, the two sat in Asirites's office, eating pomegranate seeds and talking—about the hearing, about Mac's plans for the intercession, about Andie. Finally, Mac just had to ask: "So, I'm not mad or anything, because everything worked out, but I have to know. Why didn't you tell me?"

"About what?"

"Uh, about this?" he said, holding up the scroll in his hands. "The speech my dad gave? That may have been useful to know about *beforehand*, don't you think? And I swear, if you say I needed to find out for myself, I'll hit you with your own cane."

He said all this good-naturedly, and Asirites replied in kind. "OK, I won't say it, but you have to admit, if that *were* my reason, it's not an altogether bad one. Think about it...perhaps that could explain why the Oracle didn't give you a prophecy."

Mac silently considered the validity of his reasoning for a moment as he plucked out some pomegranate seeds. He put one to his mouth, then paused and looked up. "Wait...did I ever tell you about what happened with the Oracle?"

"I think you may have *mentioned*—"

"No, I'm sure I *never* told you anything about that," Mac insisted. Then, more seriously: "How did you know?"

Asirites smiled. "I know things."

Mac was thinking about that conversation, still bewildered by Asirites's uncanny intuitiveness, when he heard a knock on his open door. "You said to meet here, right?" Calliope asked from the doorway.

"Hey, come on in," Mac said cheerily. "You're the first one here."

"Why are we eating so early, anyway?" Calliope asked as she sidestepped the clothes, Typhon's leash, and assorted junk strewn across the floor.

"I have a surprise planned for afterwards," Mac answered with a mischievous smile.

"Ooh...I love surprises," she gushed. "Speaking of which, did my brother tell you where we're going for break?"

"Oh, yeah," Mac said. "Matala, right?"

She nodded excitedly. "Our dad just sent word yesterday. We're leaving tomorrow morning. Our family went a couple years ago, and it was a blast—beaches, dancing, shopping, and a big open theater. I can't wait. How about you? Are you still going to Ithaca?"

"Yep," Mac nodded, as he shoved two tunics into a trunk. "It's been over a year. Thought I should go back for a bit—sort of on my own terms, you know?"

"Well, I'm going to miss you," Calliope said as she sat on the edge of her brother's bed, a mess of rumpled blankets and unpacked clothes. "I mean it. I know you're not much for sincere expressions of emotion or anything, but…I'm really glad I got to know you this year. You're a great friend."

"You realize I'm only going away for a *month*, right?" Mac smirked, wondering where her outpouring was coming from. "I'm not actually getting kicked out. You got that, right?"

"I got it," Calliope smiled. "In fact, I was thinking: since you're going to be around next semester, maybe you'd want to try out for one of Grimbar's plays?"

"A play?"

"Why not? You were pretty good on the raft, right?" she reminded him, leaning back on the bed. "I think you could really —" Suddenly she squealed and jumped forward, as if startled by something. She flung back the pile of blankets to uncover Theo.

"Not so loud," he mumbled, burying his face in his pillow.

"You're unbelievable!" Calliope remarked, shaking her head in disgust at the state of the bed. "Look at this…this *squalor*! How do you *live* like this?"

"Don't know, *Mom*. Guess I'm just squalid," he yawned, kicking off the rest of the covers. "Hey, what's the deal with the super-thorough packing job, dude?" Theo asked Mac, resting his head on his arm. "They let you leave stuff in the room, you know."

"Well…" Mac muttered. "Who knows if I'll be in this room when we come back?"

His comment woke Theo up in a hurry. "Not in the room?" he repeated. "What are you talking about?"

"You know the deal," Mac shrugged. "We were only supposed to live together for this one semester. Who knows where they'll put me next?"

"So, what's this? You don't want to be roomies anymore?" Theo asked, a look of betrayal dawning on his face.

"Of course, I do." He really did, too. On the other hand, he knew the administration had *forced* Theo to live with him. A guy like Theo had tons of people he'd probably rather live with, if he had a choice. "I just don't know if it's up to me, that's all."

Theo maintained the serious face as he got out of bed and walked over to Mac. "Nice try, pal," he said sternly before he suddenly threw his arms around Mac in a massive, Theo-style bear hug, the same kind of suffocating hug he had given him at the conclusion of the hearing. "Think you can get rid of me that easy?" he bellowed, shaking Mac back and forth. "I took care of it! Weeks ago, when we got back from Soricon's Corner. I went to Housing and said, 'Hey, I don't know what's going on with him, but if he's here next semester, I want him!' So, it's all set!"

Mac started to say thanks when he was swept up in another Theo hug. He actually felt himself being lifted off the ground when he heard someone say, "Take it easy, Theo. I don't want you to break him."

As Theo plopped him down, Mac looked over at Andie standing in the doorway, somehow appearing even more beautiful than she did when he'd left her room only an hour earlier. And she wasn't even trying: she was wearing the same casual peplos she wore the night of the dance, the night Mac *almost* kissed her, but more importantly, the night Mac admitted to himself he was crazy about her.

Mac knew everyone had figured out the deal between him and Andie; still, they tried to play it cool when around other people. So, the four of them just talked in Mac's room for a few minutes, waiting for Homer to arrive. Finally, Mac told the other three to head to the Grape Vine; he'd fetch Homer himself. He needed to give him something, anyway.

As Calliope and Theo exited the room, Andie held back. "So," she began, maneuvering right in front of Mac, "when am I going to find out where you're taking us after dinner?"

"As soon as everyone else does," Mac grinned.

"I knew you'd say that," she muttered. "Fine. See you in a bit." Then she leaned forward and gave him a quick kiss before she left the room

During the walk to Homer's room, Mac savored that kiss, marveling again and again at his good fortune: he actually got to *be* with this amazing, beautiful girl. Hang out with her, all the time. Talk with her late into the night. Kiss her…a lot. So much had changed between them in the four short days since the hearing. They had already been good friends, but now that all the stresses of the past three months had been lifted away, they were looking at each other differently. And they both seemed to like what they saw.

But it was more than their circumstances that had changed; Andie, it seemed to Mac, had changed, too. She was still beautiful, still fiercely independent and reckless. But her anger, always lurking right underneath the surface, was gone. She didn't even want to shoot melons anymore. Mac had asked her, two days after the hearing, if she wanted to go shoot a few, but she declined. She didn't give a reason, but Mac thought he understood: she just couldn't tap into that reservoir of hate any longer.

The next day, Mac showed up at her door with a bucket of wet clay. When she asked him what it was for, he just smiled and yanked down the tapestry from her wall, revealing the grotesque etching of the Minotaur underneath. "I thought this wall could use a touch-up," he said, as he dipped his hand into the clay and started spreading it across the stone surface. For a few moments, Andie stood there watching him, not moving, not speaking. Then she nodded and sunk her hand deep into the bucket of clay.

A comfortable silence fell over them as they covered up the mural. Eventually, Mac worked up the courage to ask her a question.

"Are you going to tell anyone about the Minotaur? That it really did exist and you're the one who killed it?"

"Do you think I should?"

"Well…it would clear your dad's name. Isn't that what you want?"

"What I want is something I can't have."

Mac took her hand and squeezed it, knowing exactly what she hoped for…the return of her father.

"Honestly," she said after a long pause, "I don't know if I'm ready to tell anyone just yet. Maybe it's enough that I know. I guess I need some time to figure it out."

"Speaking of time…" he began, facing the wall, trying to sound casual. "Since you're not doing anything for break, do you think you might want to spend some time in Ithaca?"

"Well, that depends," she said, likewise concentrating on the wall.

"Are you asking because you want to be with me, or because you want me to beat up the suitors for you?"

"No, I want you there," he smiled, turning to face her. "Of course, it wouldn't hurt to let the suitors see that the girl I'm in love with is totally fierce..."

He couldn't believe he said it. He lowered his gaze, worried that he'd blown it, that he'd scared her off by telling her so soon. And when she didn't respond, he knew it for sure.

Andie dropped her lump of clay to the floor. "I love you, too," she whispered, taking his sticky, messy hands in hers. "And you're right, I *am* totally fierce." She leaned forward, and they kissed for a long, long time.

Mac was still thinking of all the spots in Ithaca he could show Andie when he reached Homer's open door. He peeked in to see Homer darting around the room, grabbing items from the shelves and shoving them into the small trunk on his bed. Before Mac had a chance to say anything, Homer noticed him. "Am I late? Sorry, sorry. I was packing. Lost track of time."

"No worries," Mac assured him as he walked inside. He glanced at his trunk, half-filled with tiny scrolls. "Why are you taking all these?"

"Didn't I tell you? I'm going to visit Demetrius over break."

"Ah, the infamous scroll-buddy..." he remembered. Mac couldn't resist. "Is he going to send you a map?"

"Funny," Homer said, closing the lid to his trunk. "Should we go?"

"Yeah. First, I want to give you something." Mac unhooked from his belt a small pouch he'd brought along with him from his room. He handed it to Homer, who looked quizzically at Mac as he reached inside. He pulled his hand out to reveal three small figurines, of Menelaus, Diomedes, and Odysseus.

"Replacements," Mac explained, "for the ones you gave as an offering at Delphi."

Homer stared at Mac in disbelief and then studied the pieces. "Where'd you get these?"

"Calliope knew a kid in the Drama Club who's a collector," Mac explained. "Apparently, there are even bigger nerds here than you, if you can believe it."

"Shocking…" Homer said, as he kept investigating the pieces. "Well, this was very generous," he finally said, giving Mac a hug before walking over to his shelf. "Especially since everything I told you to do was *wrong!*"

"Eh, you were off on a few details," Mac shrugged. "Who cares? It got the job done."

"I guess," Homer murmured, keeping his back to Mac as he slowly put the figurines on the shelf. "Mac, there's something I've been meaning to tell you," he said carefully. "But I don't really know how to say it…"

His sudden seriousness unnerved Mac. "What is it?" he asked.

"Remember the day after Opening Ceremonies?" Homer began, still facing his shelf of figurines. "Gurgus assembled the whole school, said he had an anonymous tip about the person behind the hoopoe bird attack?"

"Yeah, I'm pretty sure I won't be forgetting that day any time soon," Mac smirked.

Homer took a deep breath. "Well, I'm the anonymous tipper," he admitted. "I told him."

"You…you told him it was me?"

"I came back to campus a couple days early," he explained, his head dropped in shame. "One morning, I got up early and went out to the hill leading down to Garthymedes Field—to work on a scroll, actually. And I saw you down there, feeding the birds. I didn't really think much of it, until…well, you know. So then I put two and two together, and…"

"You told him," Mac said again, as he nodded in vague admiration. "Wow. I didn't know you had it in you."

"Mac, I'm really, really sorry," Homer said, finally looking up at him with fear and shame in his eyes.

"Don't worry about it," Mac shrugged. "It all worked out for the best, right?"

"But I tried to ruin your life."

"Oh, come on. You didn't *ruin* it. You *saved* it!" Mac told him. "Think about it: if you hadn't snitched on me, you and I never would have met. Which means I never would have gone on any of your crazy missions. Which means I never would have gotten to know Andie, or Calliope, or even Theo, probably. It all starts with you. You made all that happen."

Homer didn't say anything at first, just smiled as he considered Mac's words. "Gee, when you put it that way," he finally said, "I guess I *am* pretty awesome."

Mac rolled his eyes. "You ready?" he asked.

Within a few minutes, the two were walking over to the Grape Vine to meet the rest of the group. "Hey, since you snitched on me and all," Mac grinned, "maybe you could pay me back by telling me something?"

"Sure," Homer said. "What do you want to know?"

"What was your message? In Delphi. What did the Oracle say to you?"

Homer squinted as he looked up at the sky. "To tell the truth, I'm not sure I get it completely. But the message said, '*You will achieve immortality not in body but in words.*'"

"Huh," Mac considered. "What does that even mean?"

"Calliope thinks it means I should write down some of my stories," Homer explained. "She's trying to inspire me."

"Well, what do you think? Are you going to do it?"

"I don't know," Homer shrugged, kicking a stone from his path. "I mean, I could write them down, sure, but...would anyone ever want to read them?"

"Are you kidding? Your stories are great. You should totally do it. It would be..." Then he grinned, recalling one of Theo's favorite words. "It would be *epic*."

Homer bobbed his head, weighing the possibilities. "OK, maybe I will. Thanks." He paused and then asked, "So, what's this big surprise you've got planned for us, anyway?"

"I've got one last labor for everybody," Mac said cryptically.

"*You* have a labor, for *us*? What is it?"

"You'll see," he said with a mischievous grin.

Homer pestered him a few more times before finally giving up. The two friends continued walking in companionable silence, their shadows from the late afternoon sun leading the way.

Epilogue

He had to remind himself that he could do this.

After all, he said to himself, *you almost beat Melpagon in War Games. You outsmarted Basileus and Blasios. You even stared down the Minotaur! Compared to those things, this is nothing!*

But as Mac stood on the edge of the chasm and took his first good, hard look at the raging waters of Kataraktos Falls, churning far below him, he had second thoughts.

The drop was *steep,* much steeper than he remembered.

An impatient voice from the frothy waters below echoed through the canyon. "What's going on, you coward?" shouted Theo, who had jumped in the moment they got there. "You brought us all here! Now you're chickening out? Come on! It's great! Trust me!"

Swallowing hard, Mac glanced back toward Homer, Calliope, and Andie, all sitting nearby on the rocks, looking expectantly at him.

"You know, maybe this wasn't such a good idea, after all," he said.

Andie sighed as she stood up, walked over to Mac, and took his hand. "Let's go, hero-boy," she smiled. Mac looked at her and smiled back. He really *could* do this.

"On three," Andie announced. "One!"

As she counted, Mac and Andie looked at the churning waters below them...

"Two!"

...and then at each other, their eyes locked as tightly as their fingers.

"*Three!*"

And then they leaped, into the froth, holding hands all the way down.

ABOUT THE AUTHORS

For many years Mark, a high school English teacher, and Sheri, a freelance writer and blogger, wrote independently. No matter the writing project—newspaper articles, retreat talks, college recommendation letters, fanfiction, blog posts on spirituality or 80s pop songs—they tended to work alone. Separate rooms, separate computers. But raising their twin sons helped them discover an important truth: All Good Things Come in Twos. Mark and Sheri teamed up to write their debut novel, *Labors of an Epic Punk*. (And yes: even this bio is a collaborative effort!)